MURDER
IN
MADTOWN

DAVE HEISE and STEVE HEAPS

DEDICATION

To Mary and Sam, who made this project possible.

ACKNOWLEDGMENTS

This book is based on an original idea by Steve Heaps.

All characters and events portrayed in this novel are entirely fictional. Any resemblance of characters to any real persons, living or dead, is coincidental and unintentional. We have on occasion borrowed some names or portions of names of real people known by us personally for use with some of the fictional characters. This was done as a salute to these people and in a shameless attempt to get them to buy this book. The personalities, descriptions, and actions of the fictional characters in no way depict the people for whom they were named.

Thank you to the Chocolate Shoppe Ice Cream Company for granting us permission to use the store name in the book and related materials.

Thanks to Jason Kritz for the cover design and art.

And, thanks to our friends and family members who proofread early drafts and offered constructive criticism.

We'd also like to acknowledge the occasional lines of dialog quoted from classic films such as *Casablanca* and *To Have and Have Not*. They continue to be an inspiration.

Sincerely, The Authors

CHAPTER ONE

The metal doors at the side of the Memorial Union burst open and a slim figure in a black sequined jumpsuit bounded out with a mob close behind him. The Great Stephano grabbed a three-foot drum-major's baton from a waiting band member, flourished it above his head, and then spun around and pumped the baton as he high-stepped up the block. On the downbeat thirty members of the University of Wisconsin Marching Band, waiting in the street, began a spirited medley of beer commercial songs and followed. People poured out of the Union; some marched with the band, others ran up the sidewalk, and the bulk puffed along behind the band up the steep, tight curves of Observatory Drive. Past the red-turreted Science Hall and the Helen C. White Library, past a clump of trees sheltering the historical marker of Blackhawk's retreat, they skirted the side of Bascom Hall and swarmed over the hillcrest and down to the Social Science building. There, a small crowd of students too cheap to fork over the forty bucks for tickets to Stephano's show had already gathered near the Carillon Tower.

The Tower stood eighty-five feet high, on a hillside terrace in front of the sixties-era Social Science building. A wall of metal scaffolding surrounded the tower to its peak, and the stage lights mounted on it blazed down on the camel-colored sandstone block structure. Black curtains lined the scaffolding, screening the sides, and the tower could be seen only through a gap in the front. The band took up residence against the doors of the Social Sciences building and began to play the march theme from the *Wizard of Oz*. Stephano's road crew herded the

1

crowd down the hill and across the street, a hundred feet from the perimeter of the scaffolding.

Stephano took his position on the terrace in front of the Carillon and a roadie handed him a wireless microphone. He combed his thinning blond hair back with one hand and waited as the last of the crowd arrived. Another lame show in another lame town; he mused, then on to the next one. This life was getting old. Just a few more minutes, then back to the hotel and maybe that young red-haired cocktail waitress would be there again – Darlene? No, Diane. That was it. She liked his sleight-of-hand tricks, simple deceptions with coins and bar napkins. And she hadn't noticed his facelift scars, or at least was kind enough not to mention them last night in his room or in the morning when the light was better and the haze of liquor had lifted.

"Ladies and gentlemen," Stephano began, but no one heard. The band played on. He dispatched a roadie to silence the band, then rapped his microphone on the stone terrace until he heard a bleat of feedback and began again.

"Ladies and gentlemen, or shall I just say 'people,' let me just say again that I am honored to have been part of the start of your Homecoming festivities. *Most* of you have already been witness to the most amazing feats of magic ever brought before the residents of the glorious State of Wisconsin."

The crowd erupted in cheers, the band launched into the UW fight song. Stephano hung his head. This is going to take fuckin' forever at this rate, he thought, and I've really gotta take a leak. He waved at the roadies again, and they finally brought the band under control.

"You've seen an exceptional demonstration of magic so far. Feats of extra-sensory perception, levitation, and the movement of objects using only the power of my mind. I've escaped from the Cabinet of Fire. Later on I'll escape from this town . . . I've made people disappear and reappear from locked cages before your very eyes. And, I've made forty bucks disappear from your pockets this evening. Now you're going to witness something even more amazing. With the help of this tower, erected in 1935, I'm going to make a UW erection completely disappear and re-appear in less than thirty seconds!" Raucous laughs, boos, and cheers came from the crowd. "What? Oh, I'm sorry – the UW women tell me that they've been doing this trick for years." More laughs, boos, and cheers. Two band choruses of "If You Wanna Be A Badger" later, he resumed.

"Let's get started, shall we? Let me introduce Mr. Dan Daman, associate professor of music here at the UW, and also the chief Carillon artist." A softening, dark-haired man in his thirties in a blue blazer with a sweater underneath stepped forward, waved briefly, and stepped back again. He looked more like an insurance company manager than a musician. "Dan's going to be locked in the Carillon and play for his own disappearance. Dan, what are we going to hear tonight?"

Daman stepped forward and Stephano thrust the microphone toward his mouth. "Uh, a delightful piece, *Nocturne*, by-"

"Great, Dan, nobody really cares. You can step back now." The crowd laughed. "Also, please meet Mr. David Helms, a private detective hired by the Student Union at my invitation to try to deduce how this trick is performed. He'll get a first-hand look at things too – he'll be locked in the Carillon with Dan. Lucky guy." Helms, a roundish senior citizen in a cargo-pocketed camouflage jacket with an untamed gray beard and a bemused expression on his weathered face stepped forward and tipped his baseball cap. "If he figures it out he'll get a bonus of five grand. If he doesn't – well, there's always that Santa gig coming up at the mall. Mr. Helms, have you anything to say?"

Helms addressed the microphone but as he began to speak Stephano thumbed the switch off and looked intently at Helms and nodded at him as he spoke. When Helms finished, Stephano thumbed the switch on again. "Yes, wasn't that fascinating, folks? Thanks, Mr. Helms, for your amazing insights." The crowd laughed again. "Now, gentlemen, if you please." With a sweep of his arm Stephano ushered the two men to the wooden six-panel door of the Carillon. They stepped inside and Stephano pulled the door closed. He placed a steel bar cross-wise against the doorframe, looped a large chain through the door handle and around the bar, then locked the ends of the chain with a padlock.

"We've got a mic on Mr. Daman so we can keep in touch. Dan, can you hear us?"

"I can, Stephano."

"Are you nervous?"

"Not really, I've played this quite freq-"

"Dan, I meant about disappearing with the Carillon. We've got a mic on Mr. Helms as well. Mr. Helms, are you ready?"

"Yes, indeed."

"Then, Dan, please begin what may be your last concert!"

Daman began playing. As the bells rang Stephano motioned to the band, which began an undercurrent of Stauss' *Also Sprach Zarathustra*. A black curtain rolled down from the top of the scaffolding, obscuring the front of the tower. When the curtain hit the ground Stephano strode around the base of the scaffolding, making a pretense of inspecting everything. Then he climbed to the top of a stepladder at the edge of the crowd, and waved his arms. The band fell silent; the Carillon played on.

"Now, ladies and gentlemen, I need your help. I need your concentration. I need to borrow your energy to help me summon the power to complete this magic. Band, give me a B-flat . . ." The band began to play and hold a B-flat. "Please, folks, now link your arms or hold the hands of your neighbor – hands, I said – and hum that B-flat with the band . . ." A white fog began to seep out from under the base of the curtain wall. "That's it . . . hum and concentrate, visualize this square empty . . . hum . . ." The crowd followed direction and hummed or sang along with the band. "I feel it, the power is growing . . . we're almost there . . ." Stephano hunched over at the top of the ladder, arms hanging limply. "More. *More!*" The band played louder, the Carillon continued to peal. "Come *on*, people, *give* it to me!" Then, summoning his best tent-revival impression, he began to quiver. "I feel it, I feel it!" With arms shaking he slowly straightened up, then began to raise his arms. He started making guttural sounds, nonsense syllables, eyes closed as the crowd noise grew louder. Then he shot his arms straight up toward the night sky.

"NOW!" he screamed. A tremendous explosion erupted from the top of the scaffolding, the band and Carillon stopped playing, the crowd was startled into silence, and the front section of the black curtain fell down from the scaffolding, revealing . . . nothing. The tower was gone. Blinding stage lights and scaffolding and a portion of the Social Science building were all that were to be seen in the currents of stage fog. A swell of applause and cheers rose from the crowd, and then the black curtain began to rise back up the scaffolding from the ground.

Then two loud retorts, like backfires, and an amplified scream silenced the crowd. A groan came over the PA system and echoed between the buildings, followed by a loud soggy slap like an open hand hitting freshly poured concrete.

"Stephano, what was that? This is Dan . . . hey, what's going on . . . Helms? Helms! Why doesn't he answer?" The sounds of someone running on stairs came over the PA.

The magician scrambled down the ladder. "This wasn't in the goddamned script," he cursed under his breath. Shit! And the soundman had forgotten to kill the mics. Stephano angrily made a throat-cutting gesture to one of the roadies in an attempt to get the microphones cut off, but it was too late.

"Helms? Help! Something's wrong with Helms! Stephano, holy Jesus, get in here, *get in here!*" The crowd fell silent and the top of the black curtain continued to climb up the scaffolding. "Ohmygod, ohmygod . . .he's. . ."

"Go! Go! Go!" Stephano yelled to the crew as the curtain completed its ascent. Then the bottom of the curtain began to rise quickly, and as the Carillon was revealed again from the bottom up Stephano ducked under the curtain and reached the door, followed by a pair of policemen and the road crew. He stripped off the padlock, chain and crossbar, and shoved the door open. There on the floor in front of him was Helms with Dan Daman kneeling beside him. A dark wet pool was growing on the stone floor.

"Ambulance," Stephano yelled, "call an ambulance!" He pushed Daman aside and felt Helms for breathing and a pulse. "CPR! I'll compress and count, you breathe!"

Daman stood up, shaking, and stared at his hands. He touched his fingers and felt the blood, warm and thick. "I-he's-I-"

Stephano and a cop worked CPR on Helms for a few minutes, and others found the wounds and pressed them but the blood kept coming, and then it stopped. They heard sirens, and the cop sat back and shook his head.

CHAPTER TWO

A rare near-calm that morning on Lake Superior had enabled Phil Bardo to paddle easily along the shore from the beach parking lot. He had headed away from shore to chase some loons; they led him about half a mile offshore before disappearing, leaving him alone save for the occasional gull. He ate an early lunch there, drifting in the offshore quiet, and watched the clouds build to the west. He was glad that he had taken the precaution to zip up the windows of his tent as it looked like rain might get to his campsite before he could. He stowed the lunch remnants and began to paddle at an angle back toward shore as the wind and waves kicked up.

The waves built higher. Phil saw that the storm was coming faster than he had expected. His kayak rode the troughs, climbed broadside up the wave faces then slid over the crests and back to the troughs. The skirt kept the water out, mostly, as he churned parallel to the shoreline.

On his first real vacation in three years, miles from any other human, cell phone turned off and shoved under the seat of his truck, surrounded by the natural beauty and order of life, Phil thought about work. The Chocolate Shoppe had consumed him for the past five years, first as a partner then as sole proprietor. His vacation wasn't even a paid one; the least he could ask for was a mental escape, but the daily rituals that he had perfected marched off against the clock in his head. Pick up the day's raised donuts from the Donut Factory. Check and log ice cream freezer temperatures. Make bagel dough. Preheat oven and fryers. Change menu board for specials-du-jour. Make bagels. Brew six thermal carafes of regular, flavored, and decaf coffees. Top off whole-bean bins for all the specialty brews. Fill napkin and lid dispensers. Touch up restrooms. Wake up computer, fax machine, and cash register. Count cash. Turn on neon sign. Unlock front door. Plaster on smile. Greet staff. Call missing staff. Post regulars' pre-orders for filling. Check fax, website, and answering machine for new orders. Make up cinnamon-raisin bagel with schmear, a large regular – black, and an almond biscotti for Uncle Dave. Watch Susanne raise the shades on La Boudoirderie on the other side of State Street. Wish Susanne drank coffee. Remove staff's death-metal tape from the sound system and replace it with Al Jarreau. Smile as staff feigns severe ear and stomach pains. Count customers. Clear tables. Harass cops at table six. Take a coffee back to the desk and pay bills. Write up orders for suppliers. Look at clock – almost mid-morning . . . and on it went.

A breaking wave caught Phil in the face as the troughs deepened. He spat out Lake Superior and peered into the distance, looking for the shore. He could catch a brief glimpse of it as the waves lifted him, then lost it as they passed underneath and dropped him four or five feet into the trough. His arms were tiring, but it was not a good time to stop and rest. I've got to re-think this solo vacation stuff, he thought. At least with a partner there'd be someone to find my body. He stole a moment to tighten the straps on his life vest and then resumed paddling.

Clouds blackened the sky. He didn't know if it was wind-driven spray or rain that he felt, stinging, but it didn't matter. A wave lifted him again, and his favorite white baseball cap with his travel pins on it disappeared into the wind. He turned his head and tried to catch a glimpse of it, but it was gone. Just great, Phil thought. Jack always said that you lose ninety percent of your body heat through your head, and he didn't have much insulation up there anymore. Just where did that percentage come from? Maybe he was full of crap with that one; his dad had occasionally shaded the truth to prove a point, but said it with such authority that he had rarely been questioned.

Phil's arms were burning, his hands were going numb, and his head was freezing. The waves build to nearly ten feet, and the shoreline was obscured by a gray gauze of fog and driven rain that came on quickly and surrounded him. He could see to the next wave-crest but the rest was a gray wall. Shivers began. Phil knew the end result of lowering body temperature, and now he regretted leaving his wetsuit in the truck. It had been so calm that morning that a wetsuit seemed overkill.

He decided to turn directly toward shore regardless of where he'd land. He timed his turn at a wave-crest, and the stern of the kayak dipped backwards down into the trough, buried momentarily, then rode up the face of the coming wave. He swung the double-ended paddle furiously to try to "catch" the wave and surf it but missed it and went up and over the crest backward as the wave passed beneath. More paddling, another miss, and then rest for a couple wave sets. This one – go! Phil caught the wave at an angle and shot toward the shore. He couldn't see it, just see the gray curtain of rain and fog in front of him. He heard wind, the roar and tumble of water, very faint church-bells – must be noon, getting close to shore.

The crossing wave came at an angle and knocked the bow of his kayak dead-on toward shore. The stern rode up the wave face, the bow went down and buried deep in the trough, and the wave broke. Phil had an instant to grab a breath as the kayak went vertical. The bow struck bottom, and Phil felt rather than heard the crack of splintering fiberglass as a ton of water twisted and pounded the boat. Then, he was swimming. He surfaced, gasped from the forty-degree water and frantically breast-stroked toward shore. His feet touched bottom and the next wave tossed him up on the rocks.

Phil crawled out of the wave zone and struggled to his feet. About 200 yards to his left he could just make out the end of the parking lot where he had left his truck. He still wore the kayak skirt around his waist but there was no kayak, not in the breaking waves and not on the shore. A quick self-check revealed no obvious broken bones or at least none he could feel through the numbness. He removed the kayak skirt and dropped it on the rocks, then took off his life vest. The keys he had safety-pinned to the vest were still there. He fumbled to free them and stumbled back to his truck, his feet aching from the cold water squishing in his running shoes.

Inside, he pulled an army blanket from under the driver's seat and wrapped himself in it, started the truck and turned the heater on full as the wind and rain beat on the windows. Fatigue overcame him, and he slept.

The storm passed. Phil woke, roasting, and turned off the heater. The numbness was gone but his muscles screamed at him with every movement. He stepped on his cell phone, which had come out from under the seat when he grabbed the army blanket. He stared at it. What the hell. He picked it up and turned it on, then dialed.

"ChocolateShoppeGretchenspeakinghowmayIhelpyoutodayourspecialsare-"

"Gretchen, slow down. It's me."

"Phil!ThankGodyoucalledwe'vebeentryingtocallyouforday sbutyourcellphonehasn'tbeenonandwe'vehadaterriblethinghapp enthatyouhavetohearaboutandyougottacomeback- "

He sighed. "Gretchen, slow down. Put Sam on."

Sam was Phil's longest-term employee, and could run the business almost as well as Phil could. It was tough to master how to spell or pronounce her real full name correctly, so everyone called her "Sam" and spelled that way at the store.

"Hey, sailor, you like a good time?"

"Not so much. What's going on? What's Gretch so worked up about?"

"Sorry," she said. "Things are actually going okay at the ChoSho. Business has been like usual, we ran out of croissants during the Farmer's Market yesterday 'cause you forgot to order extra for the weekend, but all in all it's been okay."

Phil noticed something odd in her voice; things weren't okay. "But, what?"

"Yeah, there's a 'but.' It's bad, Phil. I don't know how to tell you this. I'm so sorry – it's your Uncle Dave. He's dead."

"Oh, man. When? Was it a heart attack?" Dave was in his seventies, and Phil had prepared himself some time ago for this eventuality. Attacks ran in the family.

"Three days ago, Friday night. Phil, he was murdered."

"Murdered? Shit! Did they-"

"Yes, they got the guy."

"Who? Why? Why did he do it?"

"I don't know; he says he didn't."

"How? What was it?"

"He was shot twice."

"Jesus!"

"Phil, you really need to come back. Now."

"Yeah. I'm on my way."

Phil ended the call, pulled off the army blanket and drove out of the parking lot. The news made him sick, and his thoughts swamped him. Dave was his only remaining relative, his late mother's brother and a fixture at table three at the store. Granted, the PI business could get rough at times, but why would anyone want to kill him? He had been around so many years that everyone knew him and liked him; that made it difficult for him to get any meaningful PI or undercover work. Phil drove back to the campground, uprooted the tent and threw it and his gear into the back of the pickup, tied a tarp over it all, and took off.

Three hours later he reached Eau Claire and realized he remembered little of the drive. He had another three-and-a-half hours to go before he hit Madison. Time for a break and some food, some caffeine to get his head back into the game before he ran somebody off the road. There was an old diner called Cleveland's just outside of town, an aluminum relic from the fifties. He pulled off the road and came to a stop in a parking space next to the front door.

Phil climbed out of the cab and realized that his clothes were still wet. He untied a corner of the tarp covering the truck bed and rooted around until he found his duffel bag. He dug out a dirty pair of jeans and an old Chocolate Shoppe t-shirt that had seen too much duty, but they were dry. The tarp secured again, he got back into the cab. Halfway through his change he looked up and saw two kids watching and pointing at him from the diner window directly in front of his pickup. He stuck out his tongue and he saw them laugh. They disappeared, replaced by the faces of their frowning parents. Phil tried to look apologetic but they didn't appear to buy it. They left the window and moments later hustled out the front door. As their car drove off Phil hopped out of the truck and zipped up, then headed in.

Formica tables in vinyl-upholstered booths lined the walls. Swiveling chrome toadstool seats were bolted to the floor in front of the long counter. The waitresses wore sea-foam green uniforms, hair up, and perpetual grimaces. The grill was behind the wall and orders and the food were exchanged through a two-foot by three-foot service window. Through the window he saw the torso of a man in a stained white t-shirt moving about as he set plates on the window ledge. A freestanding sign with push-on plastic letters read 'Please _eat yourself' so Phil found a booth in the corner away from other customers.

A whorl of sea foam rushed up to him holding a pot of coffee. "Hi hon, my name is Marge and I'm your waitress. Can I help you?"

Phil nodded. "Do you have a pen I can use?"

"Sure hon, right after you order. Coffee?"

"Do you have any Earl Grey tea?"

"We got the best tea there is – Lipton's."

"Coffee's fine."

Marge plunked a sturdy cup and saucer down in front of Phil and poured the coffee. She looked to be in her sixties, and probably worked at the diner since high school.

"Marge, who's Cleveland?"

She looked puzzled. "Why, hon, Cleveland's a place."

"But the diner's name?"

She rolled her eyes and slapped a menu onto the table in front of Phil. "Our specials are meatloaf and mashed, fried chicken and mashed, or chicken-fried steak and gravy. And mashed. With a side of green beans and a roll. I'll give you a minute." She bustled off, polyester rustling.

Phil picked up the menu, and scanned it, wondering what it would be like to own the diner. Twenty-four hours a day, seven days a week. He bet the owner lived out back. Who the hell is he, and what kind of a life must he have? Shitty, he thought, but it beats being murdered.

Marge returned. "Now hon, what can I get you?"

"Bacon and cheese omelet, hash browns, and whole wheat toast. And a pen." She was off, leaving the pen behind.

Phil started a list on one of the napkins. Call staff meeting about scheduling. Find will. Find lawyer for estate. House. Detective business. Pay bills. Set up funeral. Homecoming promos. Increase staff for Homecoming. Increase staff for Halloween. Lots of things to do, and he'd have to rely on others to help out. If he could do just half-days at the store for a while he could get it done. Sam would help.

Marge returned and deposited his plate on top of his list. "Can I get you anything else?" she asked as she thumped a ketchup bottle down on his table.

"No, thanks." He set the pen aside and picked up a fork.

The food was actually good, and he ate quickly. Dave would have liked this place, Phil thought. Basic, honest, no frills. Lots of character, and cheap. If this were in Madison he would have come daily, would have known all the help and the regular customers by name. This booth – Dave would have chosen this booth, where he could watch everyone coming and going. Phil wished he had spent more time with Dave, but these last five years were crazy . . . and now it was too late.

Phil finished his food and found the bill tucked under an ashtray. He left a ten on the table.

He coaxed the pickup it to life, checked the fuel gauge and got back on the highway. As he drove he laid his list on the dashboard and fished his cell phone out of his pocket.

Maybe Sam's right, he thought, these things aren't such a bad idea after all. He hit the preprogrammed number for the store.

"Chocolate Shoppe, may I help you?"

"Gretch, it's me again. Yes, I know. No, there's nothing you can do right now. Yes, I'm heading home. Yes, it is terrible. Put Sam on, please." Gretchen had been very nervous during her interview six months ago, but she had an honest face and he had hired her on the spot. He thought that by now she would have been more relaxed, but that just wasn't in her genes.

"Hi, Phil."

"Sounds like you've settled her down quite a bit. She going to be okay?"

"Oh yeah. She tends to get a little excited."

"No kidding. Sam, a couple of quick things. Call a staff meeting for Wednesday morning after the first rush. Make sure we have enough croissants. Any of our cops in right now?"

"A couple. Shooting the breeze instead of doing their jobs."

"Is Carl there?"

"He's the fat, gray-haired one, right? Yeah, he's here."

"Sam, get him to the phone. And thanks. I'll be home in less than four hours."

Phil heard her set the receiver down, and he listened to background noises – milk frothing, beans grinding. Cash register ringing.

"Phil, you there?"

"Okay, Carl, what the hell happened?"

"Sorry about your uncle. He could be a pain in the ass sometimes but we all liked him. We got the guy, no doubt about it. He shot him in the Carillon on campus, was locked in with him. We can go over the rest in person when you get back."

"One more thing. What was the name of the law firm my uncle did PI work for?"

A hand muffled the receiver and there was some talking, unintelligible, in the background. "That would be the Jackson brothers, if we remember right. See me when you get back. We'll talk more then."

"Thanks, Carl. Put Sam back on, would you?"

The receiver clunked on the counter and in a moment Sam returned.

"What else? We're kinda in a mini-rush here."

"Sam, if Tom calls, tell him you don't know when I'll be back. And call Yellow Jersey. See if they can send over a kayak catalog and price list."

"Uh-oh, I don't like the sound of this. Just what did you do? You only had a couple days."

"I'll tell you when I get back, I promise. Bye."

Phil ended the call and set the phone on the seat. Tom wasn't going to be very happy about his kayak.

CHAPTER THREE

"It's really quite simple, Phil. I can read the whole thing to you if you like, but strain out all the legal boilerplate and what we have left is that you are his only living relative, and as such, his sole heir." Lars Jackson laid the will on his desk blotter, clasped his fingers behind his head and leaned back in his chair. The back of the headrest came within a few millimeters of sweeping the framed photos from the wall. Jackson in ski clothes in the Swiss Alps. Jackson with his wife and son. Jackson shaking hands with an ex-pro football player on the golf course. Jackson with two other Nordic-looking men. The family resemblance was clear – tall, almost gaunt, thin nose, sandy-colored hair, and high cheekbones. Undergraduate and law diplomas from the University of Wisconsin hung there, too, along with the membership certificate for the Bar Association. A team photo from a youth soccer league with the kids holding a 'Jackson, Jackson, and Jackson' sponsorship sign and a framed thank-you letter from the Governor completed the collage.

Phil nodded. "So, what are the next steps?"

"Jackson, Jackson, and Jackson are named to act as executors for the estate. We'll get the probate process started, we'll file death certificates with insurance companies, and so forth. It is going to be quite a while before I can tell you the size of the estate, the tax bite, and what you'll wind up with."

"Is there anything that I should be doing?"

"Yes, a couple of things. One, you can go to his house and deal with the mail. Pull out bills and bank statements and bring them to me so that we can pay them and discover where assets and liabilities are. We'll have to maintain the house until we've got the probate process pretty much nailed, then you can sell it if you want to. Two, you need to do the same for his detective agency; go and get the bills and statements and bring them over here. If he's got clients and cases in the works, it would be a good idea for you to call them and tell them to find a new PI. There won't be much value left in that business, since really the business was all him, his skills. So, after we've documented any stray assets and liabilities for the probate process you can decide what to do with it."

Lars dug in the bottom drawer of the old walnut desk and pulled out a plastic bag. "Here are his personal effects. Wallet, keys, pager, watch, notebook, and some papers and stuff he had in his pockets at the time. The police are done with them. You'll need the keys for the house and the office. Oh yeah, his car is down at the impound yard, you can pick it up there. Just get it before Friday or they'll start charging you for storage."

"What's the status on the case?"

"The police and the DA think it's an open and shut case, and they've stopped any further investigation. The carillon player did it, there's no way anybody else could have, as the door was locked and there were only the two of them in there. They haven't found the gun yet, but that won't be a problem in getting a conviction. The guy is in the city jail and he won't make bail. They set it high claiming he may be a threat to others and possibly a flight risk."

"Have they figured out a motive?"

Lars shook his head. "No, it just makes no sense. That's why they think he's a threat to others; a nut case that can kill somebody for no reason, right in front of hundreds of witnesses. They'd rather have him in jail than in a mental institution, though, so I expect the DA will make up a rational motive and try to make it stick."

"Thanks, Lars," Phil said, as he stood and grabbed the bag. "I guess I'd better get started." He shook hands with Jackson, and noticed that the man wore a high-school class ring on his right hand and a University of Wisconsin class ring on his left, but no wedding ring. The massive Rolex on his right wrist was too big for his shirt cuff to fit over.

Phil left the offices of Jackson, Jackson, and Jackson, went down the stairs and out onto the sidewalk. He stopped and looked up at the State Capitol Building. Sam would be working that catering job in the House conference room now, a mid-morning break in a training session for House interns. She had borrowed his truck for that, so he'd have to wait or hoof it back to the store. Or, maybe it was a good time to liberate Uncle Dave's car.

The impound lot was about a mile down East Washington Avenue, downhill all the way. A twenty-dollar "service charge" later Phil was behind the wheel. The car was nothing special; a twelve-year-old blue Buick sedan in decent condition, power-everything, with only seventy-six thousand miles. Phil mused that Dave hadn't gotten out much, or at least hadn't gone very far when he did. He turned left from East Washington onto Blair, then a right on Wilson Street. Nine blocks later he passed Bassett Street and came to a stop at the second house from the corner.

Uncle Dave's house was a tiny one-story two-bedroom bungalow with a patch of well-trimmed weeds for a front lawn. A narrow concrete driveway led along the side of the house to a detached single-car garage in the back, with two sagging barn-style doors that looked like they hadn't been opened in a decade. The black metal mailbox hanging on the white siding next to the front door was stuffed full, and Phil found more mail when he opened the screen door. He grabbed one of the newspapers from the front stoop, shook it out of its plastic bag, and stuffed all the mail into the bag. He tried a couple of keys on the front door and then he was inside.

Phil hadn't been in the house in years, but all was as he remembered. The hardwood floor, the worn oriental rugs in the living room, the spartan furniture. Dave hadn't changed anything since his wife died; it barely looked like he had lived there at all since then. Phil found two more small piles of mail, unopened, and added them to his bag. The tiny old gas stove in the corner of the kitchen put out heat and an odd burned gas odor from the pilot lights. The cat dishes on the floor were empty; Barney had died two years ago. A couple of coffee mugs lay in the sink. What was left in the refrigerator wouldn't pass for edible; Phil tossed it all into a grocery bag to haul out to the garbage can. In the front bedroom Phil found nothing, no furniture in the room, only some of Dave's winter clothes in the closet. The back bedroom held a made bed, a dresser, and a nightstand. A TV on the dresser, a Bose clock radio and a telephone on the nightstand were the only evidence of a modern existence. Phil went back to the kitchen, tucked the garbage under one arm and the bag of mail under the other and left through the front door. He went to the back of the house and dropped the garbage in the can. The back yard was small, covered by a single large maple tree dropping its leaves to the dirt below. He'd do the garage another time. Phil went back to the car and headed for Dave's office.

The Discreet Detective Agency was located on the second floor of an ancient red brick building a block off of State Street on Gilman. The ground floor held a Laundromat and a sandwich shop. The only access to the 2nd floor was by a painted wooden staircase that led up the side of the building in the alley. Phil parked in a gravel lot behind the building, and climbed the stairs. The Georgian-style wooden door was painted a rich green, with an Irish claddaugh knocker and a simple brass sign saying "Discreet Detective Agency, D. Helms, Prop." He let himself in with the key.

Phil had never been in his uncle's office. He was embarrassed to admit that, given its proximity to his Chocolate Shoppe. Dave appeared at the coffee shop every morning so there was never any need for Phil to go to the office, and Dave hadn't ever encouraged him to drop by. Phil found himself in a waiting room big enough for one wooden chair, one end table and two old copies of National Geographic. He had to close the outside door and nearly sit in the chair in order to be able to open the paneled inside door that led to the office itself. He found and flicked a light switch mounted on the wall next to the doorjamb.

The room was nearly full. With the exception of two narrow paths leading off in different directions the room was floor to ceiling and wall to wall piled with books, magazines, newspapers, and boxes of every imaginable size, shape, color, thickness, and age. Phil's first thought was of his Shoppe's fire-fighter customers and what they would say if they ever saw this archive. His second thought was of the grave danger that the Laundromat customers were in from the sheer weight on the second floor. He began to explore. The book-lined path to his right led him directly to a tiny bathroom with a toilet, sink, and mirror. There were no towels. He used the toilet and sink, then wiped his hands on his pants and returned to the office door. The second path began a maze through the stacks. He wandered, noting books on art history, war pictorials, law abstracts, poetry, science fiction, and Wisconsin yearbooks. He came upon an alcove against an outside wall containing a small desk, a computer, printer, a gooseneck lamp, and a wastebasket beneath a dirty window. Nothing in the wastebasket. That figures, Phil thought; Dave evidently threw nothing away in his entire life, and it was all right here. He wandered further, trying to head in what he assumed was the direction of the back corner of the office. A few more turns and twists, and a clearing appeared.

The clearing was in the rear far corner of the office, and its center contained a massive oak roll-top desk. Lining the walls between the windows were wooden, glass-fronted barrister cabinets stuffed with manila file folders. to one side of the desk was a well-used leather easy chair and a floor lamp, and to the other was a cot with one pillow and a couple of blankets folded at its foot. The desk was open. A bottle of twenty-two-year-old Ardbeg Scotch held down a handful of papers on the desktop, and a Chocolate Shoppe foam cup left a coffee ring on a copy of the *Wisconsin State Journal*. The pigeonholes were crammed with papers and envelopes.

Phil sat down behind the desk in the wooden swivel chair

and pulled open a drawer. It held dozens of black BIC pens. He closed the drawer, leaned back in the swivel chair, closed his eyes and wondered what in God's name he was going to do with the mess. He had a business to run, and no time for dealing with this. He opened his eyes and saw an old dial telephone on the floor under the desk. He tried to pull it up to the desk surface but the cord was too short. He got down on hands and knees and dialed.

"Chocolate Shoppe," Sam answered.

"Sam, it's me. How'd things go this morning?"

"No problem. Had them eating out of my hand, literally. Didn't even lose any fingers. I foresee a return engagement, probably next month."

"Good job. I guess I won't have you deported after all."

"Gee, thanks. My mama will be so pleased. Are you coming by?"

"Doesn't look too likely today, I've got a mess here. Unless you really need me."

"I'll tough it out today. But you've got opening tomorrow. Promise?"

"I promise. And thanks."

Phil hung up. He sat in the chair for a while. No inspiration came. There was no good place to begin, and he didn't know what he was beginning anyway. He flipped through a pile of papers and picked out a brochure. *Solar Heat Your Pool.* It went into the wastebasket. He decided to drop by the store after all, to get an cappuccino for an afternoon kick. He had missed lunch, and a croissant would be good.

Then he heard a noise, a muffled bang, from somewhere in the office. He got up, picked a path into the stacks and started in. A turn or two and he was back at the computer alcove, then a couple more turns. There on the floor was a hardcover book. He picked it up and read the title – *Poltergeist.* How appropriate. He put the book on the nearest stack. Then – bang. He walked to the next aisle and turned. Another book on the floor. This one was *Through the Looking-Glass.*

"Hello?" There was no response to his call. He listened,

holding his breath. Nothing. Book in hand, he moved silently to the next aisle, paused, then quickly turned the corner. There was no one, but another volume lay on the floor. *The Odyssey*. "Cute," he laughed. "Are you Cyclops, Circe, or Siren?" Still no response. He picked up the book and doubled-back along the path he came, hoping to out-flank the intruder. A turn, nothing, and then another turn. There was a book on the floor. *What A Long, Strange Trip*. A book about The Grateful Dead. "All right," he said, "I'm about out of patience with this-"

He stopped, as something hard jabbed against his spine.

"Who the *fuck* are you?" A woman's voice. "Tell me quick, and don't play games! I don't miss at this distance."

Siren, Phil decided. He'd been lured onto the rocks. "Please, take it easy, I'm Phil Bardo, my uncle was Dave Helms. He left this place to me." He felt her take the gun away from his back, and heard her back away.

"Hold it right there," she commanded. "I can still make a pretty nice hole in you. Put your hands on your head and walk back to the desk."

He put the books down and did as he was told. He found his way through the aisles back to the desk.

"Now," she said, "lean forward, hands on the desk. Spread your legs. Wider."

He did, and then he felt her press the gun barrel against his spine again. She kicked his feet to spread his legs wider. After a leisurely pat-down she pulled his wallet from his back pocket. A few seconds later she put it back and backed away.

"Okay, now turn around."

Phil straightened and turned to face his captor. She stood about six feet away, legs apart, shoulders squared, arms extended toward him supporting a gun pointed directly at his face. The gun commanded his complete attention; he couldn't look at anything else. It looked like one from the old police and detective shows – a snub-nose .38, Phil guessed. He felt beads of sweat collecting on his forehead, and the sound of his own breathing seemed loud in his ears.

"Sit," she ordered after a minute of silence, "on the floor.

Cross-legged. Sit on your hands."

He sat, and took a moment to really look at the woman for the first time. She was about five-foot-six, wavy brown hair pulled back in a stubby ponytail, lean angular face with high cheekbones, gray-green eyes behind round wire-rimmed glasses resting on a slightly crooked nose. A baggy REM sweatshirt hid her build. She wore jeans and was barefoot. No makeup, no distinguishing marks, lips drawn in a tight line. Maybe in her late 20's, Phil guessed.

She backed up to the leather chair and sat with her legs tucked under her, then laid the gun on the chair arm. She smiled. "Nice to meet you, Phil. Sorry about your uncle. He mentioned you a couple of times."

Phil's breath came out in a rush. He pulled his hands out from under him and rubbed his face. "Why didn't you just ask me who I was when I came in? Would have saved us both a lot of trouble, and me a couple years of my life."

She shrugged. "I had to make sure who I was dealing with. You passed the test."

"How about losing your gun? It makes me nervous."

"Sure. It's yours anyway, I guess. Used to belong to the Old Man. It's not loaded. Here." She tossed it to the floor in front of Phil.

Not even loaded? Now that's embarrassing, he thought. "Ok," he said, "so what test did I pass? How do you know that I'm really Phil Bardo? I could have a fake license – half the students do. Maybe I'll just jump up right now and strangle you. I sure feel like it."

She laughed. "Let me explain. There are a number of things that told me you are who you say you are rather than somebody else. I'll take it from the beginning. When I got here, you were already inside. I found the door unlocked, not jimmied, a good sign. I took off my shoes so I could sneak around and see what you were up to – I hate it in the TV shows where the people enter the warehouse to sneak around and they keep their shoes on and make all kinds of noise walking around – nothing like tipping off the bad guys! I saw you at the Old Man's desk, and you didn't act like somebody searching for something, you looked like somebody overwhelmed by the moment. The gun was in the desk, but you only opened one drawer, so you didn't find it. You made a phone call, something you probably wouldn't do if you weren't supposed to be here unless you were one really stupid crook. But, I still needed to know for sure, so I lured you out with the first book, and when you left the room I came in and snagged the gun. Then I led you around until I could get the drop on you."

"It really would have been a lot simpler just to ask."

"But not nearly as much fun. Plus, if you weren't you and I had just asked, I might be assuming room temperature right now. You may know coffee, but you don't know beans about this business. Yet. Anyway, the frisk was necessary and something I always wanted to do, so I did it. Your driver's license looked real and I didn't see any 'permit to carry' in your wallet, and I didn't see any badge either, so things were adding up in your favor. The acid test was the face-off. I gave you a full minute to study the gun up close. Anybody with experience would recognize that gun as a snub-nose .38 revolver, a five-shot cylinder, pretty inaccurate due to its short barrel, kick, and hard trigger pull. Plus, anybody with experience could see from your angle that of the five chambers, four are visible and empty. From your perspective, it would be reasonable to assume that the whole gun would be empty – why would I have loaded only the first chamber of the cylinder? But you didn't see that, and you clearly believed that the gun was loaded and I was ready to pull the trigger – otherwise you wouldn't have sat down so nicely." She flashed another smile.

"Have you ever considered using your considerable talents for good rather than for evil?"

"That *is* what I do."

"Just what is it that you do? And who the hell are you? And what do you have to do with my uncle?"

"For the past year I've worked for your uncle as his research assistant, part time. Helped him with case background, administrative stuff, some occasional fieldwork. That's my computer that you saw by the window."

"He never mentioned you."

"It's really handy to have somebody who can operate anonymously on a case. He couldn't do that anymore, 'cause everybody knew him. If he told anybody about me he'd blow my cover, so to speak."

"And you are . . ."

"Mary Haiger. Grad student in the criminal justice program. B.A. in Communication Arts – that's radio, TV, and film, with film concentration."

"And you live . . ."

"Where I like."

Phil got to his feet, walked to the desk and sat in the swivel chair. He didn't know how much of her story to believe, but he had no way to check any of it at the moment.

"Hey Phil, it's been fun, no hard feelings I hope. If you don't mind, I'll just collect my computer and be on my way. Your uncle owes me three hundred bucks for the last week. I'll stop by your Chocolate Shoppe in a couple days to pick it up." She stood up.

"Whoa, hang on a second. Let me think for a minute." If she's telling the truth, Phil thought, she might be the only person with any knowledge of cases in-progress, where Dave's accounting records are, and how to make sense of the clutter of the office. If he was going to wind this down and still run his regular business, he needed somebody for a few weeks to deal with this. If she walked away now, it was hopeless.

"Mary, I honestly don't know what to do about this business at the moment, but I do know that I could use your help. How about staying on here until I get it all figured out?"

She pursed her lips. "Well, maybe. The Old Man paid three hundred a week for about twenty hours. I actually did more like forty, but he never acknowledged that. Cash. No benefits, no social security. 'No traces,' he said. I want six hundred."

"How about this. Fifteen bucks an hour for however

many hours you work. You log your hours. I'll put you on payroll through the store; you do more than thirty hours a week and you'll get benefits like the other employees."

"Traces?"

"I don't care about traces." Indeed, he did. He wanted them, especially with her. He couldn't help but smile; she had spunk, a personality and smarts to match.

"Deal. What do you want me to do?"

Phil looked around. "You can start by finding any bills or bank statements that might be lying around. And I want to go over any open cases with you tomorrow to figure out how to shut 'em down."

"Ten-four, Chief." Mary grabbed two handfuls of ponytail and tugged to tighten it up, then she picked up a stack of papers from the desk and sat down again in the leather chair.

Phil watched her work for a minute – sorting, opening, and tossing papers. She filled her jeans well. He couldn't help but wonder what was under that sweatshirt. Christ, he thought, he had to be at least fifteen years older than she was, and now her employer. Isn't that always the case.

"And how can I get in touch with you?"

"Oh, don't worry, I'll be around," she said.

Phil picked his way to the door and left.

A lopsided smile passed quickly over Mary's face and then was gone, and she continued to work. A half-hour later, she stopped and went to the desk, dropped to her hands and knees and picked up the phone handset and dialed a number.

CHAPTER FOUR

Phil saw that the staff was starting to nod off. It was time to finish the meeting. " . . . and we will post the kids' artwork in our windows, as some of the other stores are, until Saturday after the Homecoming Game. What else – oh, whoever closes, please remember – get the last customers *out* of the store and lock the door before you start counting cash. And don't count the cash out where everybody on the sidewalk can see you; take it back to the office. Now, are there any questions? Jessi?"

"I think we have a problem with the oven. I don't think it's maintaining temperature right, and I'm havin' to throw out a lot more overdone stuff."

"Okay, I'll call Frank and get him to come out and look at it again. Aaron?"

"Ah, yeah, uh, are we going to get paid for this meeting?"

Phil hung his head down, clapped both hands to his scalp and grabbed what remained of his hair. Snickers erupted from the staff. "Aaron. Just like last time. And the time before that. Any time I call you in from your time off, whether it is for a staff meeting or whatever, I pay you for your time. Remember?" Aaron grinned and rattled his piercings.

"There's one more thing, folks. I've got a bunch of stuff to do to get my uncle's affairs in order, so I can't spend as much time here as I'd like. I need to rely on each of you to put in some extra hours, maybe double-up on shifts here and there." Groans. "Sam will coordinate the schedule. And thanks again, everybody, for the card and the flowers."

Most of the staff bolted for the door in an attempt to get back to campus for their next lectures. Some remained and

27

took up stations behind the counter. Phil walked to table three, Dave's table. It was wrapped in yellow 'Police Line – Do Not Cross' tape, a small memorial from the cops who were regulars at the store and old buddies of Dave's. Phil decided to leave the tape in place for a few more days.

"Hey, Phil." Dale Nivek, one of the beat cops, had a double espresso in one hand and a doughnut and napkin in the other. Phil pulled out a chair, and after an exaggerated brushing of crumbs from the seat motioned to Dale to sit. Phil took a seat next to him.

"Dale, you've got powdered sugar on your gun handle again. How's any bad guy going to respect you, looking like that?"

"I'm not worried. Besides, it makes for a better grip. How you doin'?"

"I don't think it has really sunk in yet. At this point I'm just mad. It doesn't make any sense to me why that guy would kill Dave."

"It doesn't have to make sense. A lot of what I see never does." Dale took a bite of doughnut and dusted the crumbs from his mustache. "But, at least we didn't have to look far to find the killer. What a dumb son-of-a-bitch."

"Were you on duty that night?"

"Yeah, actually I was on crowd control right there, saw the whole thing."

Phil leaned forward and put his elbows on the table. "Hey, tell me what you saw – I really haven't heard much about it other than what was in that *State Journal* story."

Dale sipped, then shook his head. "Can't. Case is still open. The guy was just arraigned on charges a couple days ago. No bail granted and no trial date set yet."

"Oh, c'mon. It's not like it'll make any difference. He's going to jail. Period."

Dale took another bite of doughnut and another sip of espresso. "I can only tell you what was obvious to everybody, and you've already read that in the paper. We got into the Carillon within a minute of hearing the shots. Dave was on the floor right inside the door. Daman was beside him. It was two shots, one to the chest, one to the neck. Severed aorta and jugular. Blood everywhere. I haven't heard what the coroner decided about the gun. We didn't find it. The slugs went right through him and mashed flat against the stone wall. Can't tell anything from them, but they looked pretty big. The only weird thing was that Daman was clean."

"Clean?"

"Clean. No spatter on his clothes. Shoot somebody that close-up, and you'd likely get some on you. He had blood on his hands, from touching him. But nothing on his clothes."

Phil thought about that for a minute. "Dale, how do you know it was close-up?"

"No choice. The floor space in the carillon is really cramped due to the staircase, can't get very far away."

"Are you saying that maybe you think he didn't do it?"

"I'm not saying anything like that. I just can't explain it, that's all." He finished the doughnut. "Sometimes when there's no other explanation, then what you're left with is what happened. Or, at least it's good enough. Well, gotta go and look busy." Dale rose to leave. "Be good, Phil."

"Thanks, Dale. See you tomorrow, maybe." Phil saluted as Dale turned and left, espresso cup in-hand.

There was still some time left of the morning. Phil got up and went back to the office next to the storeroom. He sat down at the desk in front of the Apple, dug through some piles of papers and prepared to update some of the accounting.

"Now, you don't want to go and double-enter all that stuff, do you?"

Phil jumped in his seat and turned around. "Jeez! Did you have to sneak up on me like that? Whistle or hum or something to let me know you're coming."

Sam stood there, hands on her hips. She was dressed in black, all five-foot-even of her – black jeans, black cotton blouse, belt, and shoes. Her straight black hair, jaw-length, had one braided bead extension hanging alongside her right ear. She had an ageless, flawless complexion and a round face; a fake scowl crinkled her Poly-Asian features.

"And just where, young lady, are your Badger colors today?"

She pointed at her lips. "Here, and thanks so much for noticing. I went out and bought this Big Red lipstick. Figured I could use it again at Halloween. You really don't need to do that data entry. I did it last night after closing."

"Humph. Yes, I know, I was just double-checking your work. Looks okay."

"Right. Actually, if you could look at this pile," she said as she picked up some papers and handed them to Phil, "some need your signature, and a bunch we need to talk about. We've got a few flavor and supplier problems that need your attention." She pulled a folding chair from behind the desk and planted it next to Phil.

They worked side by side for a couple of hours, and the pile dwindled. When Phil finally looked at his watch it was 1 p.m. "That's all I can do for now," Phil said, "I've got some appointments this afternoon for my uncle's estate."

"Good. I need the computer to work up new staffing schedules."

"Thanks, Sam, I'll owe you one. Or two. Or three, before we're back to normal."

"Don't worry, I intend to collect."

On his way out Phil nodded at the staff and yelled out a few greetings to regular customers, then he hit the sidewalk. After a stop at Mike's Subs he was on his way to his uncle's office. He didn't have reason to expect that he was being followed, and he didn't notice. The figure stayed about a block behind him, matching pace until he turned down the side street and climbed the stairs to the office door and went inside.

The lights were off. "Mary?" he called. No response; Phil was alone. He found his way back to her computer. It was on and displayed a screen-saver. He jiggled the mouse and the Windows password screen came up. That was good, he thought, he couldn't screw things up by prying.

He found his way back to his uncle's desk and sat in the

chair. There were a dozen envelopes on the desk that weren't there the previous day, rubber-banded together with a yellow Post-It stuck on top. It read "Phil – all I could find. I'll be in by 2. M." Electric bill, dry cleaners bill, VISA bill, and the rest junk mail. He tossed the junk into the wastebasket and the bills to the side. There was a bit more order to the loose papers; Mary must have sifted through them to find the bills. He decided to start with the drawers.

There were the black BIC pens again. Another drawer held a collection of drinking glasses and coffee mugs, no two alike. One of the mugs held paper clips, another a handful of change. A bottom drawer was half filled with new and partly used legal pads, the consumed pages missing. The middle drawer of the right pedestal held the gun and nothing else – Mary must have put it back, Phil noted, as he had left it on the floor yesterday. He picked it up. It felt heavy and cold. He pressed a catch and the cylinder flopped to one side. Sure enough, empty. He flicked his wrist and the cylinder snapped back into position (just like on TV, he thought), then he rested the heel of his right hand in the palm of his left and sighted down the barrel at the bare light bulb in the ceiling fixture. Clank! It did take quite a pull on the trigger. He put the gun back in the drawer. In the bottom drawer he found an old Nikon 35-millimeter camera with a large film magazine on it, a motor-drive unit, a collection of accessory lenses, and a number of fresh rolls of film of varying speeds. There was still film in the camera. There was also a small hand-held tape recorder in the drawer but no tape cartridge.

The search through the roll-top's cubbyholes proved more fruitful. He discovered a few checking account statements, some cancelled checks, and the checkbook and register for Dave's business account. The balance was $2,354.65, but there was one check missing that was not recorded in the register. He set these items aside with the bills. There were many handwritten notes on scraps of paper – Phil recognized his uncle's handwriting, all in that black BIC ink.

He heard the outside door of the office open and close,

and after a few moments Mary appeared in a red UW letter jacket with cream-colored leather sleeves.

"Hey, Chief!" she said as she planted herself in the leather easy chair and pulled her legs up underneath her. "Didja find my note?"

"Yes, thanks. Looks like you got a lot done after I left yesterday. Hope you didn't have to stay too late."

"Nah, it wasn't too bad," she said. "What's on the calendar for today?"

"First, let's talk about the accounting for this business. I haven't come across any records so far except the checkbook. Do you know where they might be?"

"I can't say where all the old records are," she said, "unless they're in folders in the cabinets behind you. I've never seen them. But for the year that I've been here all the accounting has been done on my computer. I gave the Old Man the usual stuff — income statement, balance sheet and so forth after the end of every month. I can run those off for you. But FYI, break-even would be a very good month. We've lost money most of the time, and Dave had to keep putting in cash to keep this going."

"What about receivables? Anybody owe him money right now?"

"The closed cases are all paid up. He's put in some hours on a few open cases, so in theory they owe him for those, but since he's not going to finish them I'd feel guilty sending out bills. He tracked his hours in the notebook that he carried. I couldn't find it around here."

"I've got it. What kind of cases did he have going?"

"There were two domestic cases that I know of; you know, wife suspects husband of cheating on her, or husband suspects wife of cheating on him, or husband suspects mistress of cheating on him. He had me help a little with surveillance on those. And, there was something he was getting into that he didn't explain to me; he asked me to research a few things, but I never saw any hours to bill or checks from a customer. Then that magic gig came along. It was supposed to be a quick and easy payoff, really just a few hours of fun and a little intellectual challenge trying to figure out the trick. He gets paid and a little free publicity whether he figures it out or not, and that magician gets more press and adds a little more suspense to the event." She sat back in the chair and folded her arms across her chest. "I'd really like to go ahead and bill that last one."

Phil nodded. "I agree. Bill them; they got more than they asked for out of that. As far as the domestic cases, if we don't have anything yet that proves cheating, then send the clients a letter of termination and tell them how many hours we're not going to bill them for. No, wait – better call the clients; letters can have consequences if the wrong person picks up the mail. If we do have some proof let's call the client in here and show 'em what we've got, then hit 'em up for payment." He paused. "You agree?"

She smiled. "You sounded just like your uncle there, for a minute. Yes. I'll pull the case files on those and you can decide if we have enough proof. To bill or not to bill, that is the question." Mary pulled a small spiral notebook out of her jacket pocket and made a few notes. "What's next?"

"I'd like to find out more about the magic case. Do you have a file for that?"

Mary got up and went to one of the barrister bookcases. She raised the glass door on the top row, pulled out a file, and handed it to Phil, and he spread its contents on the desk. There was a letter from the Student Association, introducing the magician's act as the kickoff of the Homecoming events and asking Dave if he'd be interested in the job of "debunking" the disappearing Carillon trick. He'd get an hourly rate plus a nice bonus if he could figure out how it was done by the end of Homecoming Week. There were a number of old stories about the Carillon Tower reproduced from microfilm, with the stamp of the Wisconsin Historical Society on them. Thirty-three color photographs showed the Carillon Tower from all sides and angles, close-ups and distant shots. An architect's drawing of the main floor of the Social Sciences Building also showed measurements of the terrace and the site of the Carillon. There were some computer-printed lists of books and articles about magic, apparent lookups from the UW library catalog. And, there were three receipts from McDermott's bookstore.

"That's all?" Phil asked. "Where are the books that he bought?"

"I've got them back at my place. I was reading them to try to get a clue on how the trick might be done. There's one more thing. Dave asked me to do a wire-frame 3-D rendering of the Carillon Tower and the terrace on my computer. It's done, but we didn't have a chance to use it."

"Do you know what he wanted to do with it?"

"No."

Phil shuffled everything back into the file folder. "There's still a couple days left before the Homecoming Game. It might be fun to figure this out and collect the bonus. That cash would come in handy as we wind down this business. And I've always wanted to know how these illusionists make these big buildings and things disappear. Want to give it a try?"

Mary shrugged. "Sure, why not. Might give us a clue to the bigger mystery too."

"What do you mean?"

"The murder, of course. You don't actually believe that Daman did it, do you?"

"Well, yes," Phil said, "there doesn't seem to be much reason to think otherwise."

Mary smacked her palm to her forehead and began to pace around the desk. "There's no motivation! Daman's some poor schmuck assistant prof, hoping to hang on long enough to get tenure. He spends his days teaching music theory and his nights listening to and grading student recitals."

"Sounds crazy to me."

"Boring, yes, but crazy? I doubt it. His being thrown together with your uncle in the Carillon was pure coincidence. Why in the world would he bring in a gun and kill your uncle when he would have nothing to gain from it, and he'd be sure to be arrested since he's locked in with him? Plus, no gun.

Anybody stupid enough or insane enough to kill under these circumstances wouldn't even think of hiding the gun."

"Hey, calm down," Phil said. "This isn't one of your film-noir detective dramas. I think you're making too many assumptions. Why do you care, anyway?"

She coasted to a stop and sat down, hard, in the leather chair. "Your uncle was very good to me over the last year. I want to see the guy who did this pay. And I hate to see an innocent get nailed for something he didn't do." She paused, and after a few deep breaths, continued. "And there's something else you should know. I was there when it happened. Dave had me taking some infrared photos outside during the trick . . . I . . . heard the shots."

"There's nothing you could have done to make it turn out any different."

"Shit. Aw, shit!" Mary covered her eyes with one hand. Phil saw her shoulders shake. He got up and stepped forward to reach out a hand to comfort her, but she waved him off with her free hand. "Just . . . just give me a minute," she said.

Phil backed off and sat down again, and gave her a minute. Then another. Her breathing came back to normal, and she took off her glasses and wiped her eyes with the back of her hand.

"Damn," she said, "I hate it when that happens."

"Aww," Phil said with a smile, "you're not so tough after all. What would you say if I told you that I heard from a reliable source that there was no 'spray'?"

"Huh?"

"Spray. Uh, splash. Spatter. No blood on Daman."

"Given the neck wound I'd say that's remarkable, if he's the killer. It's pretty tight inside that tower. I've been in there."

"Yeah. Take out your notepad." Phil gave her a chance to comply, then continued. "There's a few things that I'd like you to do. First, make those client contacts we talked about before. Then, track down any public info you can on that magician – past gigs, bio, etc. Do you have any contacts in the Student Union? I'd like to know how my uncle got that job."

"No, I really don't know anybody down there."

"Okay, I've got someone else I can ask to do that. Then I want you to go through this desk again and look for anything that might tip us off as to what was going on with that 'client-less' investigation that you mentioned. Show me exactly what research you did for him. Oh, and I'd like to see those infrared pictures."

"Got it," Mary said. "I haven't had the film developed yet, but I'll take it in today. It should be back tomorrow. Hand me the Nikon from the desk."

Phil retrieved the camera from the desk drawer and gave it to her. "And," he continued, "I want to sit with you and go over the wire frame computer model. And also the phone bill, VISA bill, and checkbook register. Might find something useful in those. There's a check missing – could you call the bank and find out if it has cleared, for how much, and to whom? We should get a call log from his pager company and the phone company; I'll get somebody else to do that. I'll read his notebook tonight and you can read it tomorrow. Will that keep you busy for a while?"

"Yes, maybe." She tilted her head and raised one eyebrow. "I might be making too many assumptions again, but I'm thinking that maybe you're taking up the case after all."

"We'll see. No, actually, hell yes! Why not." Phil pulled open a drawer and retrieved two glasses. He opened the bottle of Ardbeg that still sat on the desk and poured a splash into each glass. "I don't get many opportunities to try something completely different. This PI business is certainly that." He pushed a glass toward Mary with one hand, and raised the remaining glass in his other hand. "Here's to taking chances."

She took the glass and sipped. "Yuck. You actually drink this stuff? It tastes like gasoline."

Phil took a swallow. "Hmm. You're right. It's Scotch, sort-of, but certainly not Ardbeg. The Old Man taught me Scotch during family gatherings over the years." He put the glass down and laughed. "We're probably drinking a clue. Why would anybody put bad Scotch in an Ardbeg bottle? Now that's a real crime!"

"Then I guess I'd better get started." Mary rose to leave, then stopped, half-turned, and her voice dropped to a lower register. "*If you need me, just whistle. You know how to whistle, don't you . . .? You just put your lips together — and blow.*"

A charge ran down Phil's spine and lodged, glowing, somewhere south of his belt. Bacall was only nineteen when she said those lines to Bogart in *To Have and Have Not*. "Do you do that a lot?"

"What?"

"Talk like Bacall in an old Bogart movie."

"Only when I'm on a case, shweetheart." She turned and headed for her computer.

Phil pondered that for a moment as he watched her walk away, his eyes drawn to the movement of her hips. Then he picked a paper off of a pile and began to read.

CHAPTER FIVE

It felt good to get back into the normal routine, at least for the morning. Phil liked to do the open, in spite of having to get up at four a.m. And when he was running through his dough-making, baking, and other routines on autopilot he had the time to think without anyone interrupting.

But today the morning rush of customers frustrated Phil. He yearned for the commuter rush to drop off. He spun from the counter to the coffee machines to the bakery case and the cash register, with an occasional side trip to the tables to help clear. This was normally the fun time, working the regulars with jokes and insults, jostling with the rest of the crew in the narrow runway behind the counter. He watched the clock. Finally, nine o'clock came. The customers who needed to be on time for work had left over an hour ago, and those who could survive being late had packed up and left, too. The only ones remaining were students trying in vain to get their blood flowing and commuters who decided that they were better off not showing up at all for work than to show up this late. In another hour or so the next wave would be there for mid-morning break.

"Ellen," called Phil, "could you come here a sec'?" A tall, willow-thin blonde coed jammed an armload of paper cups, plates, plastic knives and bagel leftovers into one of the big trashcans, wiped her hands on her apron, and approached Phil.

"Yes, Phil?" she asked, leaning against the countertop.

"You're involved with the Student Association and the Student Union, right?"

"Yes . . ."

"Do you happen to know the people on the Homecoming Committee?"

She nodded. "I know a few."

"I'd like to ask you a favor. Would you mind talking with them and seeing if you can find out about the selection process for that magic stunt? I'd like to know how my uncle came to be picked as the celebrity de-bunker of that trick."

"Sure," she said. "I have classes with some of them tomorrow."

"Would you know where to find them today?"

"I think so."

"Why don't you go ahead and try to track them down right now? We've got enough staff to cover here. I'll pay you for your scheduled shift. If you find something, just call me on my cell. And we'll see you tomorrow right here as usual. Okay?"

She had her apron off in an instant and handed it to Phil. "I'm on it!" she said, and after she retrieved her backpack from the back room she was out the door.

Good, he thought, that was pretty easy. Time to try another one.

He followed Lauren's French braid until he caught up with her at the espresso machine. "Lauren, how'd you like to put those acting classes to work."

"Yeah, sure, Phil, what do you have in mind?" Her voice reminded him of honey. A nice fit with acting talent.

He handed her a slip of paper. "Here's the phone number of the pager company that my uncle used. I'd like you to call them later today, tell them that you work for Discreet Detective Agency. That was Dave's company. Tell them that you're in the accounting department, doing an audit of their bill, and you need call detail for the last three months before you can pay it. They can fax the info right here to our fax machine."

Lauren scowled. "What's this all about, anyway? Can I get in trouble with this?"

Phil laughed. "No, it's no big deal. I'm cleaning up his

bills, and I just need to do an audit of charges ASAP. I'd get them myself except that I really have no official tie to his business yet, and now with companies worried about privacy, it would be ages before they'd release anything to me if I asked them directly. And I'm such a rotten actor I'd never get them to believe my story over the phone. But you, you're good . . ."

Her features softened. "Okay, if you're sure it will be all right."

"Trust me, it'll be fine. And could you do the same for the phone company? A detailed list of calls, inbound and outbound, local and long distance for the past three months? Here's the number." Phil wrote the office number on another slip of paper and gave it to Lauren. "Thanks!" He turned and walked back to the office. Maybe I'm not such a bad actor after all, he thought. Or at least I'm learning to be a better liar. He dropped a pen and a pad of paper into a thin leather portfolio, slid a stack of envelopes in there as well, checked his watch, and headed for the door.

"Gretch," he called on his way past the counter, "I'm meeting with the lawyer. I'll be back in an hour."

Lars Jackson had left a voicemail on Phil's home machine the previous day asking for a brief meeting. Phil lengthened his stride and blew past the idling shoppers on the State Street sidewalk. The 'shopper shuffle' drove him crazy. He rounded the corner onto the Capitol Square. Nothing happening on the Square this weekday, no art fairs, no 'Cows on the Concourse,' no 'Taste of' going on. The weekend should see a lot more action. He bounded up the stairs to the offices of Jackson, Jackson, and Jackson. He was about five minutes late, but since Lars usually made him wait ten minutes anyway this was as good as being five minutes early. Someone had left a newspaper in the waiting room, and Phil scanned the front page. His breathing had just returned to normal when Lars stuck his head out around the corner and with a nod motioned Phil back to his office. They both sat down.

"Hey, Phil. Thanks for coming. Say, I didn't see anything in the paper about services or anything."

"It's a cremation. No service, just a wake at the Irish Pub when we get around to it. That's what he wanted."

Lars nodded. "Let me know when, will you? Good. Now, I know you're busy so I'll get right down to it. Did you find any bills, statements, and so on?"

Phil pulled the bundle of envelopes from his portfolio and laid them on the desk. "This is it so far, but I've got more to go through."

Lars picked them up and dropped them into a desk drawer. "Thanks. I'll look 'em over later. Just how much do you know about Dave's estate?"

"Next to nothing. His business is nearly broke. Why?"

"As executor, we are in custody of his will and some additional papers he left with us for safekeeping. Some of them had account numbers at 1st National. It's preliminary, but in very round figures he's got maybe $200k in the bank between business and personal accounts. Now remember, you're his only heir. After Uncle Sam gets his cut and the Governor gets his, and we pay off any outstanding debt, you should still wind up with something. That is, if your lawyer doesn't take the rest. That's a joke."

"Oh. Very funny."

"And, by the way, he paid off the mortgage on his house about three years ago. But here's the interesting part." Lars leaned forward. "There are a couple life annuity policies and a whole life policy here. The face values add up to over one million."

"Holy . . . I had no idea."

"Granted, you'll lose some to taxes, but still that's a nice chunk of change." Lars watched Phil's face for a minute and futzed with his pen, then continued. "Probate, that's the pain in the ass. That means we've got to go to court to prove the size and disposition of the estate. That costs some, too, but the worst of it is the delay. It will be months, if not a year before we get this wrapped up. Now, can I assume you'd like us to go ahead and handle this for you?"

Phil nodded. "Please."

"Okay, no problem, we'll work on it. We'll keep in touch and let you know what's going on from time to time. Otherwise, keep bringing the bills in here and we'll take care of them from the estate." Lars stood up. "That's it, unless you've got any questions."

Phil rose. "No, I guess not, or at least not until after I've left. I never expected this." He reached out and shook Lars' hand. "Thanks. This is going to take some time to sink in. See you later."

Phil stood out on the sidewalk in the sunlight. He spotted a vacant park bench at the edge of the Capitol lawn, and he crossed the street and sat. People filed by on the sidewalk, some stretching summer, coatless, and others in windbreakers and hats. He knew to them he was just another guy in jeans on a park bench, maybe on the way back from the unemployment office. Ha! If he could just keep the store at break-even eventually he'd be able to do some upgrades that'd really help business. He wished he had known; he couldn't thank Dave now.

He got up and walked back to State Street. A couple of blocks down on the left he entered State Street Liquors. There may be a few ways to honor him, Phil thought. Figure out the trick, solve the murder, and drink his Scotch. "Hey, Dominick. A bottle of the good stuff, please. Know what I mean?"

The counterman pulled a mass of keys from his pocket and unlocked a display case behind the cash register station. "I do," he said as he grabbed a bottle of Ardbeg. "Don't get much call for this, just Dave and you and a few others. Nice there are some folks that know quality. An acquired taste." He triple-bagged the bottle and rang it up.

As Phil pulled his credit card out of his wallet a thought struck him. An acquired taste. Somebody could have had a taste for that bottle on Dave's desk, and not just Dave. "Dom, how many regulars would you say buy this brand?"

"Oh, not including you and Dave, I get maybe six guys who come in for it. And I think that's because I'm the only store in town that has any stock of it." He finished with the credit card, handed it back to Phil and presented the slip for signature.

Six. Most people wouldn't drink Ardbeg after an initial taste, wouldn't appreciate what they had. Certainly wouldn't drain a bottle of it, unless they were experienced . . . Phil felt his face flush, and he closed his eyes and grabbed the counter with both hands. Six names. He needed those six names.

"Phil? You okay?"

After a moment Phil opened his eyes again. "Yeah, fine." He signed the charge slip. "I've been thinking. Maybe I'll open up a single-malt and cigar bar somewhere. If I do, I'll come to you if you can supply me."

"Oh, yes indeed," Dominick beamed. "You come right here, we'll make a deal for sure."

"Sounds good. I'd like to gauge interest first, maybe find some partners. Any chance you'd share the names of your regular Ardbeg buyers with me? I'd like to talk with them about the idea, as they'd be prime candidates as customers."

"Sure, sure." Dominick wrote on the back of a brown paper bag. "Here you go. Sorry, I don't have phone numbers."

"Dominick, you're a saint." Phil folded the bag and tucked it into his back pocket. Once outside and a few paces from the door he pulled the bag out of his pocket and read the names. One looked familiar, but he couldn't place it. The rest were completely unknown to him. He put the bag back in his pocket. Another opportunity for research.

Back at the store the cops were holding forth at their customary tables. When Phil walked in, they noticed the brown-bagged bottle.

"Woo-hoo! Here we go, here we go, our delivery has arrived. Right over here, son. Put it down *right here*. Six glasses, please."

"Sorry boys, you're on duty! Besides, I think some of you might be under-age. Otherwise, I'd be glad to." Phil hid the bottle behind his back and edged his way backward to the office.

After setting the bottle and his portfolio on the desk, he

re-entered the table area of the store. Dale was there again today. Phil called to him and motioned him to one side.

"Dale."

"Phil, buddy, what's happ'nin'."

"Anything new?"

"Phil, you know I'm not supposed to talk about this stuff."

"Yeah, yeah, come on. I need to hear something, and there's nothing showing up in the press. Anything else from the coroner?"

Dale looked down at the counter. "I wouldn't do this for anybody else, you know. I could be busted from the force for this. This is the *last time*." He stabbed at the counter with his finger at each word for emphasis. "The full report came in. The shots entered here," he deliberately turned his back to the rest of the cops and pointed discreetly to his chest, "and here." He pointed to a spot on his neck. "The shots traveled at a forty-five degree angle from entry to exit. The body will be signed out tomorrow to the funeral home."

"But-"

He continued. "Now that's the end of it. Don't ask me again. And I'd strongly recommend you leave this alone. It's over. The Mounties got their man. End of story. Case closed. Class dismissed. ¿Comprende?"

Phil spread his arms with palms turned up, smiled, and said "But of course. And how can I ever repay you? A double espresso, perhaps?"

"Forget it. Just don't ask me again." Dale went back to his table.

Phil made the rounds of the staff. Things were pretty normal. Frank had finally come and replaced the thermostat on the oven. It was the third time this year. He cleared a couple of tables and went back to the office.

He noticed the fax sheets on his desk; detailed lists of phone numbers that called his uncle's pager. Three months of them. And, there was a detailed list of calls made to and from the Discreet Detectives phone in the office. Lauren had been successful.

Lauren's face appeared at the doorjamb. "Hey Phil, real quick: is that what you wanted?"

"Yep, perfect. Thanks. Any trouble?"

She shook her head. "Nope, piece of cake." She disappeared.

There were no signs of Ellen's progress. His cell hadn't rung, and there were no messages waiting on the answering machine. Phil took the brown paper bag out of his pocket and looked at the names again. He turned to the Apple and launched the web browser. He linked to a search engine, selected 'people search,' keyed the first of the names into the search engine and limited the search with 'Madison' and 'Wisconsin,' then hit the 'enter' key. No hits on the first one. The second name had two name-and-address hits, one in Monona and the other in Shorewood Hills. He copied down the addresses and phone numbers. The third name – James Bradley – turned up some online news stories. He linked to them and discovered that Bradley was the sitting District Attorney. The next name hit only one address, on the southwest side. He noted that info on the bag. The fifth – nothing. The sixth turned up a reference to an import shop on State Street; a member of the State Street Merchants Association, Phil realized.

Then Phil keyed in 'Mary Haiger' and clicked on 'go.' Nothing. He had no way to reach her other than when she showed up at the Discreet Detectives office, as she hadn't yet turned in her employment paperwork. She remained essentially anonymous. He found his way to the university's site in hopes that there might be some sort of student directory. No such luck. A couple more clicks and he was at the pages for graduate programs. He typed 'criminal justice' into the search dialog box and clicked 'go.' Odd; there was no such Masters program. He tried again to be sure, but still no results. Must be a relatively new program, he decided. He was sure she had said "criminal justice."

He heard footsteps approaching, and he turned around in

time to greet Sam arriving for the noon-to-close shift. She stretched to hang her red leather jacket on a hook on the office wall.

"Greetings, Phil. How's it goin' today?"

"Good, good. Say, I've got a few new ideas for some product for Homecoming. I'd like you to try out some of them today." He handed her some loose pages of handwritten recipes.

She studied the papers, holding them in one hand while stuffing her shirttails down into her pants with the other. "Mmm. This one looks good. This one too. This one – eh, we'll give it a try, but I don't know . . ."

"Different subject. Take a look at these names. Any familiar to you?" He handed the paper bag to her.

"No, not really. Who are they?"

"Well," said Phil, "that's the question. I don't know but I'd like to find out. I'm thinking of a new business proposition – Scotch and cigar bar – and they might be good as investors or customers. Any ideas how I might find out about them?"

"Oh. Upper-crusty types. People with money. Or power. Or at least wannabes." She thought for a minute, tapping her foot on the floor. Phil put his foot on top of hers to make her stop. "Ah, sorry. Have you tried the Chamber of Commerce directory? Or maybe that Downtown Development whatever-it's-called-"

"Council. Downtown Development Council."

"Yeah. That's it." She put the bag down on the desk and swept her hair back from her face. "Hey, I saw a list of sponsors for the Homecoming Charity Ball in the paper this morning. These people are expected to shell out for these sorts of things. Hang on a sec." She trotted out of the office, and after a few moments reappeared with a newspaper. She spread the paper on the desk in front of Phil and flipped a few pages. "Here. The Ball is this Saturday evening, and here's the list of sponsors."

Phil ran his finger down the list. "I'll be damned. We've got most of 'em right here. Nice work, Sherlock."

"And I'd bet that they'd show up there, too, to take proper credit."

"Sam, I've got to go to this thing, find these guys and chat them up a bit. I don't suppose you, ah, uh . . ." He started again, and watched her face for reaction. "I mean, I need somebody to go with me. A business thing, not a date. Would you . . ." His voice trailed off.

She enjoyed his discomfort. "Oh, I suppose. But I don't have a *thing* to wear!" She held the back of her right wrist against her forehead and fluttered her left hand on her chest, heavy-breathing in exaggeration. "Whatever shall I do? I've only got a couple days to get ready, I must start *immediately*!"

Phil sighed. "Okay, Scarlett. I may live to regret this . . . but thanks." He checked the paper again. "Seven to midnight. Let's meet here at seven and then drive together to the ballroom."

"It's a date. Or a not-date, whatever. Don't forget my corsage," Sam laughed, and left the office with the new recipes.

Phil turned back to the computer and located the Homecoming web site. A few clicks and he'd ordered two tickets to the Ball on his credit card, will-call at the door. Then he placed a phone call to Tuxedo Junction and ordered his usual formal getup. A call to the florist came next. Should probably get the truck washed and vacuumed too, he thought. It really was decent of Sam to go along with this. It just might wind up being fun. And maybe, just maybe, he could make some sense out of the Ardbeg connection.

Noon already, time to change hats again. Phil scooped his lists, notes, newspaper and faxes into the portfolio and made his escape. He stopped at Ella's Deli to pick up a large pastrami on rye.

Mary was already in the offices of Discreet Detective when Phil arrived.

"You want half a pastrami?" he asked, and opened the bag at the roll-top desk.

"Sure!" She accepted the portion he offered and bit into it. "What, no chips?" she mumbled through the mouthful.

Phil dug into the white paper sack and produced a small bag of potato chips.

"Good. Hand 'em over. You were gonna hold out on me, weren't you."

"The thought had occurred to me."

"What else you hidin' in there?"

"Damn." He took the dill pickle out of the bag.

After they had eaten and shared the pickle and a napkin, Phil dumped the contents of his portfolio on the desk. They crowded the desktop, sitting shoulder to shoulder, and went over every item. The pager call lists. The Scotch drinkers. The Ball sponsors. The still-open question of how his uncle came to be tapped for the job. And, especially, the cop's information about bullet trajectory. Everything but his meeting with Jackson, his Ball plans and his web searches about the graduate programs. Phil detected a faint hint of perfume when Mary leaned close and brushed against his arm. A clean scent, and he tried to breathe it in deeply without her noticing. Was she sitting closer to him than she had to? Maybe. It felt good, regardless.

"And that's it, so far." Phil said. "Getting some interesting stuff, but nothing's tying together yet. Maybe you can find out some more about those names before Saturday?"

Mary nodded. "You have been busy. I'll take a crack at the names. Sam had a good idea about the Chamber of Commerce and Development Council – I'll check with them first. Sam's a smart guy."

"Sam's not a guy."

"Oh, really? My mistake. Anyway, between my reading and watching a few videos of magic shows from the video store last night, I think I have an idea of how these 'disappearing' tricks can be done. It's a matter of perspective and distraction." She set up a cup and then folded a couple of sheets of paper ninety degrees and stood them on edge around it. "Now, if I have another sheet of paper right here," she continued, "and I force you to watch from over here," she pushed Phil into a crouch to one side, "then I say the magic words and distract you with something." She nudged a book off of the desk to the floor with a bang. "Voila! I move *this* sheet of paper and the cup has vanished. See?"

"Yeah, sort of. So Dave must have asked you to build a wire-frame computer model-"

"So that we could work out the angles and test the theory," Mary finished for him.

Phil frowned. "But the Carillon is only part of the story. You need to lay in the location of the audience and the precise location and size of the screens or curtains or whatever. And maybe also the lighting direction and intensity."

"You're right. Unfortunately, I don't have that information. I'll have to make it all up, which compromises this whole effort."

"Maybe not. Those infrared shots – did you get them developed?"

"Duh. Of course, why didn't I think of that!" Mary ran back to her computer desk and returned with some photo-processing envelopes. "I haven't even looked at these yet." She pushed her sweatshirt sleeves up her arms and got down on the floor and started to lay the photos on the hardwood.

Phil got down on his hands and knees with her, and they spread out the photos and studied them. There were shots taken well before the crowds had arrived and from a number of angles. And there was a long series taken in rapid succession during the actual execution of the trick.

"These," she said pointing to the series, "I did with the motor drive. One shot every second, from the time Dave entered the Carillon to the moment they broke in after the shooting. Thought I was going to run out of film, but good thing I had the large magazine on."

"Excellent," Phil said, picking up shots from different angles. "This might actually work. We can measure distances between the tower and the curtains and scaffolds and the lights on the photos. We can convert those measurements based on known tower dimensions and lay these things into your computer model!" He set a stack aside and studied a few more on the floor. "How'd you get these angles, anyway? You can see almost to the ground. And you're not tall enough to see over that crowd."

"Magic. Actually I bribed a football player to let me sit on his shoulders."

"I'm sure it was a great hardship for him. Now these," Phil pointed, "seem to show no evidence of anybody getting near the tower. There's nobody in front of or behind the curtains during the sequence, at least from this angle. No phantom murderer coming or going. There's no help for Daman here. I wish we could see where Dave and Daman were in the tower."

"The stone's too thick, hides any body heat or muzzle flash. Let's chase that one later - we're running out of time to debunk the trick." She picked up the stack that Phil had set aside. "I'll go get started. Can you find a ruler or something to measure with? Get a couple and then we can both work at it." She got up and went to the computer.

Phil rifled the desk drawers again. He could hear a clatter of keys and mouse-clicks in the distance as he searched. Under the stack of paper pads in the desk he found an architect's rule. He quickly marked off six inches worth of sixteenths on a piece of paper with one of the black pens, and wheeled his desk chair through the maze to join Mary at the computer.

They measured and marked, estimated and argued, drew, dropped and dragged for hours. The wire-frame model grew scaffolding, curtains, and lights all in different drawing layers so that they could be removed and added individually. The software permitted rotation, zoom, and perspective adjustment; they worked to match what they saw on the screen to what was captured in the pictures. Phil ran out and picked up a pizza and a bottle of Cabernet, and they ate while they worked. It got late.

"I think I have the animation ready," Mary said. "Let's try it. Here we go." She clicked through a series, following the movements depicted in the photographs. "Curtain coming down, down, down, stop. A moment for bullshit magic words.

Then the explosion for distraction and a light flash to blind the audience. Then the curtain moves . . . to reveal . . . no, that's not it." She studied the photos again. "I've gotta cut back this object, and it's gotta move *that* way, not *this* way. What do you think?" She looked over at Phil. He had fallen asleep in his chair. She poured the last of the cabernet into her glass and drank it while she watched him. It was happening again, she knew, and it was at once both wonderful and terrible, and she was powerless to stop it. Her glass was empty, and she put it down. "Hey." She reached out, grabbed his knee and shook it.

"Huh?" Phil struggled to rouse. "Sorry. I was up early."

"I'm gonna be at this for a while. Why don't you go catch some Z's on the cot. I'll wake you up when I've got something."

"Okay." Phil got up and dragged himself back to the desk area. He turned out the overhead light, leaving the dim glow of the small desk lamp. He pushed the blankets to the floor and climbed onto the cot. A moment later he was asleep.

Mary was done an hour or so later. She ran through the animation repeatedly, comparing frame-by-frame with the photos. It surely could have been done this way; maybe it wasn't, but it *could* have been. Good enough to submit to try to claim the prize. She got up and stretched, hit the 'save' button, and shuffled back to the desk area to find Phil. She stood, silent, and watched him sleep for a few minutes, then walked to the desk and turned out the lamp.

Phil dreamt he was in a crowd of strangers, a crush all around him. He fell to the ground, and others fell on top of him. He could breathe, but he couldn't get up. He was conscious of pressure, pressure on his hips, on his chest, then removed, then pressure on his lips . . .. He woke, uncertain of where he was. He barely saw a shadow, a figure straddling him. Did she just . . .?

"Phil . . . Phil, it worked," Mary said. "We've got it."

"Fantastic," he said, "can I see it first thing in the morning?"

"That works for me," she said. "You owe me big-time,

buddy boy."

She sat down again, still straddling him, and the pressure returned to his hips. "Guess I'll have to hang around," she whispered. She sat for a moment, then searched out his hands with hers. She found them, and slowly guided them along her thighs and then up under her sweatshirt. She wore nothing beneath it.

His hands skimmed her abdomen and stopped at her breasts. He felt her, warm and round and full, and clearly aroused. He heard her breathe more deeply, through her mouth, and though Phil couldn't see them he sensed her eyes had closed.

"Are you sure this is what you want," he asked softly.

"Well, it's a damned good start," she replied. She released his hands and peeled off her sweatshirt and dropped it on the floor. Then she stood up, and Phil heard the pop of the top button of her jeans.

CHAPTER SIX

Phil awakened to the faint sound of his watch alarm. As he lifted his arm from around Mary's waist he kissed her on the back of the neck, then rolled over and pressed his watch buttons to silence the alarm. He had slept well, though briefly, his body cupped to her back and his nose buried in her hair. She stirred and said something unintelligible under the pile of blankets and clothes, then sank back into sleep.

They had at some time during their festivities abandoned the cot for the floor. That made things easier then, but now Phil felt the stiffness of joints and muscles unaccustomed to hours on a hard surface. At least he had had an air mattress when he went camping. But it was warm there next to her, and he didn't want to leave her for the cold of the room. Four o'clock, not even dawn yet, time to get up and go open the store. He got to his feet in the darkness and felt his way to the desk where he turned on the desk lamp. With its glow he extracted his clothes from the pile where Mary lay, and dressed. He studied her as she slept, on her side with one arm tucked under her head and all the intensity gone from her face. Quite a nice body, he thought, great shape and good tone. A shame to keep it hidden under sweatshirts and jeans all the time. And the enthusiasm and creativity she brought to her work she also brought to her lovemaking. Where does she live? How she gets to and from work? Does she even drink coffee? Important questions. It will be fun finding the answers. He pulled a blanket over her and then made his way to the bathroom. After a brief wash-up he put on his jacket and cap and left, locking the office door behind him.

Phil went through his opening routine at the Chocolate Shoppe in a pleasant daze. After the first rush of customers had passed he grabbed the wall phone and dialed the detective office. It rang six times.

"Yeah . . ."

"Hey," Phil said, "g'morning. Want me to bring you something? Coffee, danish, bagel, whatever?"

"Umm, hi there," Mary said. "No thanks." She yawned into the phone. "What time is it?"

"About nine."

"Christ! I've gotta get moving! I'll be back right after lunch and we can go over that model and figure out what to send in to claim that prize."

"Are you sure? Why don't you stop by the store and let me treat you to today's special."

"Can't. Wouldn't be a good idea, I'd be late for class. Besides," she laughed, "I thought I already had the special."

Phil blushed and smiled. Damn, he liked this woman. "You can have specials any time you like, trust me. Do you need a ride?"

"Thanks, no, gotta go. See you later."

Mary hung up. After a quick stretch she dialed a number and spoke. "Hey, it's me. Didja see my roomie last night? Good, thanks. Would you mind checking on him right now? I'm not home yet, and he gets ornery if I'm not there first thing in the morning . . . Yes, but I'm about 45 minutes from being there . . . No . . . Yes, it was *very* fine, thank you; I'll tell you about it later. Bye." She hung up and dressed hurriedly. She searched in vain for a rubber band for her hair, then combed its thickness with her fingers before tying a red bandanna around her forehead. A quick stop at the bathroom, then another at her computer table for her keys and wallet, and she was out the door and onto the street.

Phil sat down in the back room and started making a list. It began as a list of all the stock that needed replenishment, then the stock that they'd need for the last couple of days of Homecoming product for this weekend. There was always a rush on this stuff prior to the game on Saturday. His thoughts drifted to Mary, where he let them stay for a while, then to the murder. He wrote 'interior carillon plans' on the paper.

Ellen knocked at the office door and came into the room. "Phil, was that information what you were looking for?" she asked.

"Oh, what? What information?"

"The information that I left you on your cell voicemail." She looked disappointed.

Phil plucked the cell phone off of his belt and looked at it. Too long without a charge, it had expired some time ago. "Sorry, dead battery. No wonder it didn't ring. Why don't you tell me right now."

"Well," she began, leaned over and lowered her voice. "I talked to a couple people from the Homecoming Committee." She paused and looked left and right around the office.

"Ellen, there's nobody else back here. Go ahead."

"Okay. They said that there's an Alumni Committee that has been involved in the funding of the Homecoming events. They put up the money to sign the entertainers, make deposits to hold equipment rentals, submit fees with permit applications, make initial payment on insurance contracts, and retain lawyers. They're reimbursed to some degree by the Student Association funds and proceeds from ticket sales."

"Go on."

"The Student Association picked the magician for the Homecoming Week kickoff show. The Alumni paid the up-front money for it. The challenge to a local private investigator or a cop to figure out the main trick is a regular part of the magician's act. The Alumni Committee puts up the prize money, which the magician keeps if the trick isn't solved." She paused for effect. "It was the Alumni Committee that suggested your uncle for the job." She straightened up. "There! How'd I do?"

"Great," said Phil. "And for extra credit, you didn't by

any chance happen to get the names of the people on the Alumni Committee?"

She reached into her pocket, pulled out a piece of paper and laid it on the desk in front of Phil. "I thought you might ask for that next," she said.

"Nicely done, Ellen. Thanks. Tell you what — why don't you take the rest of the day off."

"Gee thanks, but I'm done for today anyway. I just work morning rush on Fridays, remember? Oh, that was a joke, wasn't it! Good one, Phil. See you next week." She turned and left.

Phil looked at the list. There were about a dozen names on it, most of which he didn't know, but Lars Jackson was on the list. He expected that there might be a fair number from this list that also appeared on the sponsor list for the Ball, but that was back at Dave's office. He'd crosscheck that later. The same group of 'entitled' locals would be likely to get involved in both events for the prestige, publicity, and business connections.

He pocketed the list and made a few phone calls to suppliers to order his replacement stock, then went to help with the mid-morning rush. He got there in time to mediate a dispute between Lisa and Pat over the huge coffee splash that was running down the back of Lisa's white blouse. That settled, customers again became priority one. Bagels running low? He went back to the kitchen and boiled and baked another couple dozen. A hundred gallons of ice cream arrived, coming in through the front door. Thirty-three tubs, twenty-four-pounds each; Phil got Albert to help him muscle them into the walk-in freezers. Phil was elbow-deep in the sink washing some cookware when Sam arrived for the afternoon shift.

"Hey," she said, "I'm glad to see that you still know how to work around here."

"I'm fine, thank you very much for asking. And how are you today?" He continued to scrub.

"Ooh, a little touchy today, are we? Didn't we get enough

sleep last night?" She donned an apron, grabbed a towel and started to dry. "I hope you haven't forgotten our 'date' tomorrow. And I hope you remember how to dance."

"Whoa, dance?" Phil replied in mock horror. "Who said anything about dancing? We're going there on a mission, remember?"

Sam shook her head. "That's what happens at a ball. You dance. It's required by ancient Wisconsin Statutes. Oh, boy, maybe they'll play the Chicken Dance!"

"I cannot foresee any circumstance that would get me to do the Chicken Dance. Period."

They finished their kitchen duties and went back to the office. Phil pulled together the shipping invoices and bills that had come in that morning while Sam opened the safe and put together the bank deposit.

"Phil, I'll do the accounting after the noon rush is over; I've got to get out front now and help. Could you do the deposit? It's ready."

"Sure," Phil said, "I'll do that now, then I've got some other things I've got to do this afternoon." He plugged his cell phone into the charger. "No cell this afternoon; call me at Dave's office if you need me."

"Just what do you find to do over there all by yourself?"

"You wouldn't believe me if I told you." Phil picked up the bank bag containing the deposit.

"Try me," Sam called after him as he left the office. "Please," she added, after he was gone. She joined the crew at the counter.

Phil took care of the bank deposit at the 1st National by walking through the drive-through lane. It was the only way to beat the bank lobby crowd over the lunch hour. Trudy, the octogenarian teller, gave him holy hell about it but she processed his deposit anyway. Must have been that raisin bagel that he slipped into the pneumatic carrier with his deposit bag.

He skipped lunch. It was more an omission than a decision; his thoughts were focused entirely on the investigation as he walked down State Street. He met Mary at the bottom of the stairs, coming from the opposite direction, and they climbed together to the office on the second floor. Once inside the waiting room they shared a moment of awkward silence while jockeying to open the inner door, then Phil grabbed her by her arms and drew her into a long, hard kiss. He could feel initial tension in her biceps through the college letter jacket she wore, and how that tension melted away.

After a few moments she pulled away and smiled. "Mmmm . . . hello to you, too. I hate to ruin the thought, but we've got an absolute ton of stuff to do today." She worked the inner door open and headed for the computer. "C'mon. You've got to see this."

Phil followed and watched while Mary typed in the password *Excalibur.* "I never turn it off," she said, "it takes too long to boot up." She launched the modeling software and ran through the animation of the magic trick.

"That looks terrific," he said. "I'll draft a letter asking for the prize and giving an overview of how it was done. Can you print out a dozen selected frames that outline the key stages and sight lines? Then I'll put it all in an envelope and drop it in FedEx."

"Then we're back to the names you brought yesterday?"

"Right. And I've got another list too." He found the piece of paper with the Alumni Committee names on it and handed that to Mary. "These are the people who brought Dave into the magic trick. I think we need to compare the three lists and concentrate first on the names appearing on all three, then pick up any others that we can. I want to know what these people do, where they live, who their friends are. And if possible, what they look like. And I need it by noon tomorrow."

"What's the rush?"

"I'm going undercover," Phil said. "I'm going to that Ball tomorrow night to see if I can meet some of these people and press them for a little information. Maybe there's nothing more than coincidence involving these people, my uncle, Scotch and magic tricks, but maybe there is. My story is that I'm looking to set up a Scotch and cigar bar business here and I'm looking for partners and future customers."

"Do you need any help tomorrow night?"

"No, thanks. Actually, Sam's agreed to go with me and pretend to be my date so I won't look quite so conspicuous."

Mary frowned and prodded at a list of names with her pencil. "Phil, I don't know that this is such a great idea. Why don't you skip the Ball and we can do a bit more careful background digging before we start getting fancy."

"Nope," he said, shaking his head. "I'm already committed. And really, it's not any more than I'd do if I really were going to open a drink-and-stink. They just don't know that I have another motive behind it."

"Whatever. Just watch yourself. Remember what always seemed to happen to Jim Rockford. You know, *The Rockford Files*?"

"Yeah." Phil didn't remember much about the show but he wasn't going to admit it. Plus, he really didn't want to know. "You were going to tell me about some of the things that Dave had you researching."

"Oh, right," Mary said. "He had me pull a bunch of stuff. A lot of maps, plat layouts of the whole downtown, from Mendota to Monona. And he had me find commercial real estate listings and sales for the past thirty-six months. And then there was the tax payment logs, also for commercial properties."

"Maybe he was looking to move this office. What did he have you do with it?"

"We didn't get a chance to do anything with it, it's around here somewhere. I'd just been dumping it into boxes and waiting for him to say that we'd reached 'critical mass.' He liked that term. The next step would be to haul it all out, enter some of the data into the computer, and post the visuals all around the room. Kinda get immersed in the details, then sit back and try to synthesize something from it. Use the power of the subconscious." Mary paused and looked up. "I think he had something that he was looking for, but he didn't clue me in. That would have come at 'critical mass' time."

"And he didn't have any files or notes on this at all? No case name or anything?"

"I don't know of any," she said. "But there are lots of papers and notes on his desk. Maybe we'll find something there. Anyway, let's package the trick solution and get that out of the way, then dive into names."

Phil got his letter and explanation drafted by the time Mary had printed off all the graphics. She keyed his work into the computer and printed it out while he dug through some items at the roll-top desk.

"Here." Mary held two file folders, extended for him to take, and his letters on top of them.

Phil looked up from his papers. "And these would be?"

"The two open cases. Those domestic surveillance deals. Do you want me to go through them with you?"

"Nah. I'll read them tonight." He took the folders from her and tucked them into his leather portfolio, and put the letters with the graphics printouts to mail.

"You sure?"

"Yeah, thanks. I'll call you if I have a problem. Oh wait, I don't have your phone number, do I."

"No, you don't." One corner of her mouth curled up, and she turned and sauntered back in the direction of her computer.

Phil frowned, realizing that he was going to have to beg for it, play a game. She'd volunteer herself but not her phone number. Sheesh. Then he laughed at his own frustration. He left for the local FedEx drop box with his portfolio and all of the other materials, plus a copy of Dave's offer letter and the magician's address.

"Okay," Mary said to no-one, "let's see just who we have here." After pulling off her letter jacket she set her keyboard aside. Then she arranged the Alumni Committee list, the brown paper bag with the Ardbeg buyer list, and the Ball sponsor clipping from the newspaper side by side on the desk.

One at a time she took a name from the buyers list and scanned the alumni list for it, marking each list to denote a 'hit', and then did the same on the sponsor list. Then she took the alumni list a name at a time and scanned the sponsor list with her finger, again marking each list for each 'hit'. Of the six on the buyer's list, two were on the alumni list and four on the sponsor list. Of the dozen on the alumni list five were on the sponsor list. The nine 'hits' on the sponsor list were spread among six names.

"Round one," she said, and put her keyboard back in position. She straightened her glasses then fired up the web browser and began her search.

Phil settled down on his sofa. The tumbler of Scotch was just within reach under the lamp on the end table. Earl Garner's piano came from the stereo, just loud enough to drown out the sound of sitcoms coming through the wall from the apartment next door. The first thing Phil looked at was Dave's personal notebook. It was quickly apparent that it would be of no help, as Dave wrote in it in some sort of incomprehensible code or shorthand. He tossed it aside. Now for the Anderson file.

Inside the folder was a loose collection of documents, some typewritten. They really were typewritten, with malformed and filled-in characters, and the uneven letter spacing of an old and worn manual typewriter. It looked like a basic transcription of somebody's notes or rambling dictation. Dave's notes, and by the looks of it, Dave's typing. He must have had an old typewriter sitting around the house somewhere, as it wasn't at the office. Phil began to read.

8/25. Marsha Anderson came to the office. Blonde woman, 40's. Thinks **husband** Tim is fooling around. Tim, 40's, accountant at Silby & Fredricks, west side office off of Mineral Point Rd. See photo. Her suspicions rose when she called his office and he'd left for the day, but hadn't arrived home - a 20-minute drive. Happens every day now. Typically doesn't get home for two hours. Claims he's working late. Agreed on $100 an hour

```
plus expenses.
```

Phil skipped ahead. It was pretty boring stuff, recorded in a day-to-day diary format. Dave had sent Mary to follow the guy after he got off of work. She followed him for a week, his Taurus leading her each night to a local chain restaurant. Anderson would spend about an hour and a half there, alone on a stool in the bar room pounding down tequila shots. With lime, no salt. Doctor told him to cut down on salt. He basically ignored all the barmaids and the other women in the room.

```
    8/30. Mary fucked up again. Third night in a row
she got plowed in the bar while waiting for Anderson to
do something. She even sat next to him, gave him a
chance to hit on her. Nothing - if he won't go after
Mary dressed like that the guy's only appetite is for
tequila. She got pulled over for DUI on the way home. I
got it fixed downtown, but if it happens again she's on
her own. And she forgot the receipts for her drinks
again - so I can't bill them to the client as expenses.
I keep telling her - club soda or ginger ale on the
rocks looks like the real thing, so don't lose your
head undercover. Rookie mistake.
```

Phil chuckled to himself and turned the page. There was a partial accounting of hours, Dave's and Mary's. It totaled to twenty-two hours that could be legitimately billed. A bittersweet answer for Mrs. Anderson – no infidelity, at least not yet, but certainly a budding alcoholism. This one gets billed, and Mrs. Anderson will have to get a phone call.

Time for a freshening. He set the Andersons aside and took his tumbler to the kitchen where he added some ice cubes and splashed another ounce of Scotch over them. Then, to the stereo; Garner had quit playing some time ago. Phil found Coleman Hawkins hiding behind Ella Fitzgerald, and loaded him into the CD player. He grabbed the other file folder from his portfolio on the way back to the sofa.

Tilburton. That's what the tab said. The materials inside said something else entirely.

```
    9/10. Met with Ted Essinger, head of the Foreign
```

Studies department. Thinks his wife is having an
affair, wants her followed. Wants pictures, not just
narrative. Adamant that we follow her, whoever she's
with, wherever she goes. Accepted for $125 an hour plus
expenses.
    9/11. Mary began surveillance. Nobody left the
house all day. I did evening watch, nothing.

Essinger. The name sounded familiar. Maybe from the list
of names on the Alumni Committee? Phil took a drink and
continued.

    9/14. Mary began surveillance again at noon.
Essinger came home at 4. At 7 Essinger left with Mrs.
Essinger in Mercedes 450SL. Mary followed them to
restaurant in Maple Bluff. I met her in the parking
lot, got the camera and telephoto from her and put on
magazine with infrared. She went home. Essingers came
out at 9. Followed them to big lakeside house on north
side of Mendota, off of County Hwy M, 15972
BurningTree. I left car off of main road and walked in.
Took cover 30 yards from 2 parked cars. Second car was
black Lincoln Town Car. Found Essingers and 3 unknown
men talking in driveway. Too far away to hear
conversation. They opened both trunks. Essinger
inspected Lincoln trunk, clearly snorted something,
then nodded. Small package passed around, all took a
hit. Men exchanged the box in the Lincoln's trunk for
the box in Mercedes' trunk. Closed trunk lids, shook
hands with Essinger. Then Mrs. Essinger hiked her skirt
and leaned over the Lincoln's trunk. All 4 men had sex
with her, Essinger first. I then concluded that this
was not Mrs. Essinger. I got it all on film, nice and
clear.

Phil laughed and choked on his drink and set the glass
down on the end table, then continued to read.

    Two possibilities. The woman was with Essinger at
his house, Mrs. Essinger's whereabouts unknown. Or Mrs.
Essinger went to the restaurant and stayed, and Mr.
Essinger left with the unknown woman. Either way, it
was dark and the unknown woman bears close enough
resemblance to Mrs. Essinger in height and build that
we couldn't tell the difference from a distance.
    9/15. Called Mary and told her not to go on

```
surveillance. She knows nothing of what happened at
that house. Called Essinger and told him that we could
no longer work the case. He insisted on wanting to know
why. I told him that it was a personal problem. He not-
so-respectfully expressed doubt as to my sincerity.
```

That was it. No more entries, no infrared photos. Just a page with a tally of hours for Mary and for Dave, through 9/14. Nice number of hours, but this was one case that Phil wouldn't bill out.

Phil tossed back the last of his drink, So – what happened to the film? Did Dave pass the film or his notes to the police? And did Essinger figure out the real reason for Dave's calling it quits? That was more than enough for tonight, he decided. Phil left the folders on the sofa.

CHAPTER SEVEN

Phil had been a forty-long since his senior year in high school, and he had maintained his six-foot, one-hundred-seventy-pound frame in much the same condition that it was then. It wasn't as easy now; his metabolism had started to betray him. He couldn't eat whatever he wanted anymore; in his college days it was pizza and beer to the point of near-nausea with his friends, laying on the floor to recover while watching reruns of *Charlie's Angels*. If he did that now he'd gain five pounds by the next morning and then spend the next two weeks working it off. He checked his look in the mirror. Better than most guys my age, he decided. He combed his thinning blond hair, studied the well-earned creases and wrinkles encroaching on his lean face, and sighed. At least the tux fit well. Black, traditional style, with the ribbons of black satin trim down the outside leg seams. He had chosen the red patterned vest rather than the cummerbund, atop a white-on-white collared shirt with a black tie. Red and white: UW colors.

Satisfied with his presentation he turned off the bathroom light and walked into his living room. After laying his tux jacket on the arm of the couch, he put a Mingus CD on the stereo and poured a finger of Scotch with a splash of water before settling into a chair with a folder of papers. It was too early to leave for the Ball, and a good opportunity to review the material that Mary had put together for him. She had hustled him out of the office on Friday and had given him strict orders not to reappear until Saturday noon. He had hindered her investigation by reading over her shoulder as she crawled through dozens of sites and documents on the web, by offering suggestions, and finally by just sitting and staring at her while she worked. He was content just to watch the subtle movements of her breasts under the white tank top with 'Rocky Horror Picture Show' lips on the front. She couldn't concentrate with his eyes heavy on her so she banished him. He returned to the office Saturday at noon sharp, and found the folder she had left for him.

Mary had profiled six people in varying degrees of detail and commentary. Once back at his apartment Phil had read the descriptions repeatedly then closed his eyes and tried to recall the key points of each. Then he opened his eyes again and reread, correcting his mistakes. When he was comfortable that he remembered the names and highlights without struggling he planned his strategies for conversations with each person. Then he got himself ready to go to the Ball. And now, glass in hand, he reviewed Mary's character sketches again as a last 'cram' before the final exam:

James Bradley. District Attorney for the past twelve years. One of the Ardbeg buyers. Undergrad degree at Michigan. Law degree at Northwestern. Had a law practice in Madison for five years prior to joining the DA's office as a prosecutor, and worked there for four years before becoming the DA. Married, four kids. Lives three houses down from the Governor's mansion in Maple Bluff. Drives a BMW 530. Possible political aspirations, either Democrat or independent. A picture from the newspaper – mid-fifties, black guy, little mustache, nice look.

Beth Talbot. Realtor, lists both commercial and residential properties but does most of her business in commercial. Also an Ardbeg buyer but not one of the UW alumni. Trim, professional, dresses well by the looks of the MLS picture. Makes her firm's million-dollar roundtable each year. No info on her educational background. First record of her in Madison about ten years ago when she began showing up as part of Allen Properties, a small local real estate broker. Now with a big national brokerage, works out of a downtown office. Lives in a condo on the west side, not married, mid-forties.

Lars Jackson. UW undergrad, UW law grad. On Alumni Committee. Old, old family in the area. Probably gets the shakes if he ever has to leave Dane County. Joined his father's law firm right after graduation, following his older brother into the family business, and has been there ever since. Younger brother joined four years later. His old man opened the practice in that same second-floor office thirty years ago. Non-drinker; now, anyway. Married for the second time, lost his first wife in a car accident shortly after they were married – he was driving the car. One son, from his second marriage, in high school. Forty-three years old. Plays basketball in a city 'over forty' rec league.

Ruppert Taylor. Owner and general manager of the largest local radio and TV stations by day, and chairman of the city council by night. Consummate political animal, 'Rup' maintains a stranglehold on the city's business. If he doesn't want it, it doesn't happen. It's been this way for thirteen years. His opponents call the mayor 'Rupe's kid.' On the Ardbeg list. UW undergraduate degree in business. Alumni Committee list. Married, no children, fifty-three years old. Lives lakeside at the edge of Shorewood Hills. Belongs to the country club, is a golfer, got a hole-in-one last year at Blackhawk. Now plays mostly at the UW course on the southwest side. Unknown how he got to own the stations – maybe family money.

John Smith. Yes, his real name. Owns an import shop on State Street – 'Importante' – that does a huge business with the college crowd, been there for about seven years. Belongs to the State Street Merchants' Association. Ardbeg buyer. UW undergraduate degree in international relations. Was treasurer of the Student Association while in college. Unknown where he was between graduation and the opening of his shop – about fifteen years unaccounted for. No known spouse. Lives above his shop at the campus-end of State Street. Thin, blond hair, intense nature.

Bobby 'Moose' Mikleski. Owner of Mikleski Construction, a firm known in the city for their ubiquitous construction barricades. Does lots of street work for the city, and also builds office buildings and other medium-sized commercial structures. 'Moose' is a still-celebrated UW grad, former All-American offensive tackle for the Badgers in the fifties. Played pro ball for a few years with the Minnesota Vikings until he went down with a bad knee injury. Came back to Madison and bought out a construction firm that he had worked for while in high school, and spent the last twenty years building up the business. Picture came from his Viking days – crewcut, no neck, and maybe two hundred fifty pounds then. Married thirty years, two daughters. Sixty years old. Lives in Monona. Alumni Committee list. Credit report shows some recent problems, probably due to construction slowdowns in the past year.

Phil closed the file folder and set it on the coffee table, then drained the last of the Scotch from his glass and considered how he was going to coach Sam. He decided he'd introduce her using her full name, "Xiamorha," rather than just 'Sam.' "Shya-moor-hah", he practiced aloud, faster, until he could do it without sounding forced. It'd be best if he led the conversations and she stayed focused on the purported goals of finding reactions to the business plan for the Scotch and cigar bar. That was all she knew anyway, so it should be easier for her to play her part honestly. If he had to go a bit out of bounds on the conversation he'd have to separate from her for a while to avoid confusing her.

It was time to roll. He got up and put on his tux jacket, turned off the stereo and patted himself down for wallet, keys, and cell phone. Then he retrieved the corsage from the refrigerator, turned out the lights, locked his door and headed for the parking lot.

He was fortunate to find a parking spot for his pickup just off of State Street, around the corner from the Chocolate Shoppe. At seven on the dot he walked into the store with the corsage box. Sam hadn't arrived.

"Well, would you look at this!" Judy said loudly from

behind the counter, and elbowed Aaron in the ribs. She put two fingers into her mouth and wolf-whistled. The rest of the crew and the few remaining customers looked around and, catching sight of Phil, joined in the chorus of compliments and catcalls.

Phil blushed, shook his head and walked back to the office. He sat for only a couple of minutes before Judy's face, wearing a smile so big it must have hurt, appeared at the doorway.

"'Scuse me, Phil?"

"Yes?"

"She's here. Just a second." She disappeared, and in a moment Sam walked through the door.

Phil stood up and said, "Holy . . ." and could go no further. He stared at her.

"What? What's wrong?" Sam asked, and looked down and around herself for anything that might be amiss. "Do I have a spot or a hole or something?"

He shook his head. "No, nothing's wrong," he finally got out. "Far from it. You just look . . . fantastic. Flat-out fantastic!"

She wore a blood-red spaghetti-strapped full-length dress with red sequin accent patterns. Silk, and fitted to show off all her petite curves. A slit ran up the side of her left leg almost to her thigh and gave her just enough room to move. On her feet were matching red high heels; nearly four-inch stilettos. The bodice was low-cut and gave her cleavage that Phil hadn't thought possible for her. She had an oriental-print shawl or scarf that she had draped over one arm, around the small of her back, and finished draped over the other arm. A tiny red sequined purse with a long red string strap hung from her shoulder. She wore her jet-black hair down with a red-and-white UW barrette fastened over her left ear. A little blush on the cheeks, long black eyelashes. And that red, red lipstick. Classy. Sophisticated. Amazingly sexy.

"Are you sure it's okay?" Sam asked.

"Absolutely! You're gorgeous."

She smiled. "Thanks."

"I could go naked to this thing and nobody would notice me standing next to you. So how come you never dress like this for work?"

"It never occurred to me. Say, you are lookin' pretty fine yourself. Are you going to hold that corsage all night, or are you going to pin it on me?"

Phil fumbled with the box, and then with corsage in one hand and a pin in the other he approached her. He paused, trying to figure out just how he could pin it on without being charged with sexual assault. "Ah, some help?" he begged. He felt like he was in high school again, junior prom. Sara Dickinson. He shook that thought out of his head.

She laughed. "Here," she said, pointing, "just go ahead and stick your fingers in there so that if you poke somebody, it's you rather than me." She waited patiently while Phil slid three fingers of his left hand into her dress, tight alongside her left breast, and held the corsage in place with thumb and forefinger while wielding the pin with his right hand.

"There," he said, withdrawing his hand, "that will do it."

Sam pinned the boutonniere that she had been holding onto Phil's lapel, then brushed a stray bit of lint from his shoulder. "Very handsome. Time to go?"

"Time to go," Phil agreed.

On the way to the Monona Terrace Convention Center Phil told Sam about the people that he wanted to speak with, and coached her about the Scotch and cigar bar concept and the kinds of things he wanted her to talk about if she had the opportunity. He kept stealing glances at her while he was driving, and if he had been watching her head he would have seen her nodding while he talked.

He parked in the ramp adjacent to the Terrace, and they walked through the clear night air to the main doorway. He picked up the tickets and surrendered them a moment later to the doorman. Just inside they paused to pick up Phil's preprinted nametag and to fill one out for Sam. He stuck his on his tux breast pocket; Sam peeled her tag off of its backing

70

and pressed it to her chest just above her corsage. She took his arm again, and they moved toward the main ballroom.

The bar was in the hall outside the ballroom, along its side and running its full length. There were eight bartenders working but not making much of a dent in the throng that stood five-deep along the bar. The hall also contained three six-foot-high cheese sculptures of Bucky Badger that dominated tables of hot and cold hors d'oeuvres. Early-arrivals had staked out their territory there, grazing continuously and working together to block out competition for the smoked salmon, caviar, and shrimp cocktail. Phil and Sam made their way into the ballroom.

Once inside Phil decided that he had grossly underestimated the task of finding six people in a crowd of this size and density. The large ballroom was already packed; this was not a fashionably late crowd. Fashionable, yes; but late, no. An eighteen-piece big-band orchestra occupied the far end of the room and pounded out a credible Duke Ellington medley. The dance floor was large and almost completely hidden by a middle-aged population of dancers. A large mirrored ball rotated slowly in flashes of red, white, and blue lights over the dance floor. There were few ball-goers of student age – this was more an event to separate wealthy alumni from their cash, as any proceeds exceeding costs went to charity. Around the dance floor was a fringe of eight-person round tables with white tablecloths and large floral centerpieces in UW colors. The exterior wall of the ballroom was entirely glass; doors led out onto a terrace that overlooked Lake Monona.

Sam pulled Phil's arm to bring his ear down to her mouth so she could be heard. "Where do we start?"

He put his mouth to her ear. "Not sure. How about we try the terrace?"

They dodged their way through the ballroom crowd and found an open door to the terrace. The crowd was less dense there, probably due to the cool temperature. Waiters with trays of hors d'oeuvres orbited around a small bar planted in the middle of the terrace. The stars were out, terrace lampposts had been strung with white Christmas-tree lights, and the placid lake held a gigantic gold reflection of the moon. Lights flickered around the shoreline.

"It's so beautiful," Sam said.

"Yes, it is."

"This is the first time I've been here. Nice setting, and a beautiful building."

"Wright's style is unmistakable. Have you been to Spring Green? Taliesin? His home and architectural school?"

"No."

"I'll take you there sometime." Phil scanned the crowd, then looked at Sam. "You cold? Do you want my jacket?"

She looked down at herself, then back at Phil. "Gee, pretty obvious, isn't it. No, keep your coat." She straightened up and arched her back even a little bit more. "These are my keys to conversation and a few dances." She sighed. "Men are so shallow."

"And women are so manipulative," Phil retorted. "Thank God." They laughed.

Phil caught a glimpse of Lars Jackson in a small group at the other end of the terrace. "There's Lars, my lawyer. Let's practice on him." Sam slipped her hand around Phil's left arm and they sauntered across the terrace to Lars.

Jackson saw them coming and turned from his group to greet Phil, hand outstretched. "Phil! Nice to see ya," Lars said as he grabbed Phil's hand and pumped it. "I was planning to call you next week and give you an update. If I do it here tonight I won't be able to charge you. And," he said, looking Sam up and down, "who might this be?"

"Lars, I'd like you to meet my . . . friend, Xiamorha Sang. Xiamorha, Lars Jackson."

Sam extended her hand. "*Very* pleased to meet you, Lars," she said, tipping her head down a little and gazing up at him with wide-open brown eyes. Then a flash of her little smile. She had him already; it was that quick.

"Oh, the pleasure is all mine," Lars replied with a strange look on his face. He took her hand and held it.

Shit, thought Phil, it's a good thing Barbara isn't watching; ol' Lars would be dead meat. Where did women learn such techniques? "Lars, I'd like to talk with you about a business idea I've got. Might need you to help me with the setup."

"Yeah, Phil, sure. Xiamorha, how did you and Phil come to know each other?" Lars was still gazing at her, a death-grip on her hand.

"Oh, I work with Phil at the Chocolate Shoppe," she said, and retrieved her hand from his grasp. "I manage staff, do some accounting, you know. A little of everything."

"I should really come down and see the place again, it's been a long time . . ." Lars' voice trailed off. A plump woman in a black sequined jacket and skirt appeared at his side. She didn't look happy.

"Barbara," said Phil, "It's been too long. Barbara, this is my friend Xiamorha Sang. Xiamorha, Barbara Jackson."

Sam gave Barbara a genuine smile and a handshake. "Nice to meet you," she said. Barbara nodded frostily.

"Xiamorha," Phil said, "I think it's time for a drink. Can I get you something?"

She nodded. "But let me get them. You and Lars have some business."

"Okay, I'd like a wine, please. Whatever would look best on my tux."

"Got it." Sam glided away toward the bar. With one last glare at Lars, Barbara turned and disappeared into a group of sequins behind them.

"Jesus Christ, Phil," Lars began. "Where did you find that girl?"

"She's a woman, not a girl," Phil said.

"Yeah, whatever. You havin' some of that?"

"Lars, she's an employee. A friend."

"Sure. Whatever. You were saying something about a business idea?"

"I want to open a Scotch and cigar bar on State Street or maybe the Capitol Square. I'll need a separate business entity. Permits. Liquor license hearing. Can you help?"

"No problem. Just let me know when to get started."

"I need to find a realtor to start looking for possible locations. I thought maybe that Beth what's-her-name-"

"Talbot?"

"Talbot, that's it, the one who advertises all the time in the paper. She seems to do a lot of this kind of property. Do you know her?"

"I've worked with her a few times on some deals. She's good." Lars jerked his thumb back over his shoulder. "She's right back there, why don't you talk to her about it?"

"Maybe I will. Would you mind introducing me?"

"Let's do it." Lars started to walk.

"Just one more thing before we go. My uncle did some casework for your firm over the years. Did he have anything going with you when he died?"

Lars stopped. "Nope, why do you ask?"

Phil studied Lars' face. "It seemed like he was into something. I can't figure it out. Maps, tax records, and no identified client. I wanted to let the client know that he won't be working on it anymore."

"Forget it. If there is somebody, they'll call eventually."

"It's a shame," Phil mused, "he was probably too busy on the magic act to follow up with his other clients. How'd he ever get involved with that magic gig anyway?"

"I have no idea."

Odd, Phil thought. Ellen had said that the Alumni Committee recommended Dave, and Lars was on the Committee. "Did Dave make any enemies while working on cases for your firm?"

Lars looked at Phil for a long time before answering. "You're good with coffee and ice cream, Phil. Leave the cop stuff to the cops. Dan Daman killed your uncle. Now, let's find Beth."

Sam was still stuck in line at the bar, so Phil followed Lars to the corner of the terrace to a clique of five women with long evening gowns and up-do hairstyles. Lots of jewelry, probably real, Phil thought. Lars reached in and pulled one woman out by the arm and Phil recognized her face from the MLS listings.

"Beth," said Lars, "I want you to meet Phil Bardo. He owns the Chocolate Shoppe on State Street. He may be interested in doing some business with you."

"Well, I'm always happy to meet someone who wants to do business," she said and grabbed at Phil's hand.

She had a sales seminar handshake, Phil thought. Firm and practiced to make an impression. "I feel like I know you," Phil said. "I've seen your picture many times in your ads. Looks like you've got a big downtown trade." Lars waved and left.

"I do all right," Beth smiled.

"I want to open a single-malt Scotch and cigar bar on State Street or Capitol Square, and I need to find a space. Do you think there's a market for this, and do you have anything that might fit well for it?"

"Sure there's a market. Upscale." She dug in her purse for a business card. "That's a trendy kind of business, and there's lots of people downtown that want to be trendy. I'd go for the Square, though. Those legislators are good marks for this, lots of disposable income and time. You could even do a second floor walkup or a basement. It is less than prime space for anybody else, but cool for something like this. The inconvenience adds cachet." She handed her card to Phil.

"So, would anybody you know go to such a place?"

"I might go, and I know a few others who are into that sort of thing."

"You like Scotch and cigars?"

"Yes to the former, and occasionally to the latter. Does that surprise you?"

"I don't know many women who like Scotch, let alone the single-malts. And, usually not cigars. I thought this kind of place would appeal mostly to men."

"Dark wood, leather, that kind of place?"

Phil blushed. "That was my first thought, but now I'd like to hear your thoughts on the kind of interiors that appeal to women."

"The kind of interiors that appeal to women are the kind that have men in them," Beth laughed. "As far as locations are concerned, I'll have to look in the listings. The only spot I can think of right offhand is that old strip club on the Square. Give me your business card and I'll call you in a couple days."

Phil handed her his card, and she dropped it into her purse. "I have to watch expenses on this," he said. "Would you know of any properties that are in foreclosure or owe back taxes?"

"No, I don't follow those. You can find those yourself through the City Clerk."

"Thanks. Say, my late uncle had a business near State Street, and I think he was planning to move it. Did he contact you? His name was Dave Helms."

"No, not that I recall."

"Thanks, Beth," Phil said. "I look forward to working with you. Have a nice evening." He shook her hand again, then turned and walked back toward the bar. Beth watched him go, then dove back into her group.

Phil found Sam with a glass of wine in each hand, surrounded by a half-dozen thirty-something lawyers. It made him feel odd, watching her with the young studs circling. Had she worn pheromone perfume tonight or what? She was in full flirt when Phil broke into the circle and said, "She's only fifteen. Beat it." The lawyers vanished.

"Hey, no fair!" Sam complained. "I was just practicing. And, they were so cute! Besides, I can't pass for fifteen, I'm over twice that." She handed Phil one of the glasses. "I chose red, it matches my dress better. I think he said it's a Cab."

"Thanks, that'll do."

"Any luck?"

"Yes, so far people seem to think that it's a good idea."

"Good. So what's next?"

"I don't know yet. Let's see who else we can find."

They made a casual trip around the terrace but Phil didn't see any of the other names from his list. They wandered into the ballroom in time for the orchestra's first break. A man in a cutaway tux approached the microphone; the University President was there to read the list of sponsors and fawn over them. Phil listened carefully, and when Ruppert Taylor's name was announced he spotted Taylor at a table near the wall. He had a large entourage with him, including one very large older gentleman. Unmistakable Moose Mikleski.

"Sam, let's try this." He told her some of Taylor's and Mikleski's backgrounds. "Actually, there's one more thing that I want to find out while we're here. I want to know how my uncle came to be picked for that magic act. Taylor and Mikleski were on the committee that recommended him."

"So that's what this is really all about." She had a bit of a pout started.

"What?"

"Your uncle. There's no Scotch and cigar bar, is there? It's a cover. You could have told me."

"Well, I-"

"Never mind. How do you want to approach them?"

"We'll go in and suck up to Moose and work our way into an introduction to Taylor. Taylor apparently likes Scotch. So, we need to open with Taylor about the Scotch and cigar bar, and work around to asking about Dave. This is the 'command performance.' Okay?"

"Okay, I guess."

They picked their way to the table and approached Mikleski. Moose was big and loud, a caricature of an old football player and a construction man, with a lumpy red-veined nose and puffy, scarred face. Phil broke into the conversation asking for an autograph, and got the older man started telling stories from his Viking days. Mikleski rambled on like a broadcaster afraid of dead-air and Phil was stuck, unable to move the conversation in the direction he wanted it to go. The orchestra resumed, and Moose turned up his volume and drew a small crowd. Phil watched Ruppert Taylor out of the corner of his eye, afraid that he'd disappear. Moose's bladder finally got the better of him and he excused himself and lumbered away. Free at last, Phil looked again for Taylor –

gone. No, he was on the dance floor. With Sam.

Taylor had Sam crushed to his ample belly, and as he wheeled her around the dance floor crowds parted for him. He was a good dancer, and he made sure everyone knew it. He had removed his tux jacket, and sweat soaked his shirt. Phil could see them talking and laughing as they danced. That funny feeling came again as he sat, waiting and watching.

The orchestra launched into a more contemporary tune. Sam broke away from Taylor and waved-off other potential suitors, then plopped down in a chair next to Phil.

"Hooooo! Now *that* was an experience! Give me your handkerchief," she demanded. Phil handed it to her and she stuck her hand down the front of her dress to dry everything off, then handed the handkerchief back to Phil. "God! That bastard literally drooled and sweated right down my dress. Gross! You owe me, Phil Bardo."

"Yuck. And?"

"And it worked," she beamed.

"How in the world did you do it?"

"While you were having your football fantasy with your buddy Moose, I wandered close enough to Taylor so he'd notice me. He introduced himself, and asked me to dance. I said yes. Simple."

"And what did you two talk about?"

"Oh, after I convinced him that he couldn't have me for a mistress we talked about the Scotch and cigar bar. He does like Scotch, and he thinks he's an expert. He liked the idea. I got him to brag about how big and powerful he was, with the radio and TV stations and the city council, and being on that Alumni Committee and all. I told him I was here with you and who you are, and who your uncle was, and he seemed to know the name. Then I told him that I knew the Committee recommended Dave for the job and I wanted to know how that happened."

Phil rolled his eyes. "Sometimes you're not very subtle."

She ignored him and continued. "Anyway, he said that Lars Jackson recommended Dave for the job. That's what you wanted to know, right?" She waited. "Didn't I do well?"

"Better than you know," Phil said. Lars? And he'd said nothing about it! "Can I get you a drink?"

"Sure. Same as last time. Cab."

"Be right back."

Phil fought his way to the bar in the hall. By the time he returned to the table, Sam was back on the dance floor, slow dancing with a baby-faced lawyer. Phil sat and watched, and drank his glass of wine. That feeling came to him again. Not a worry, not an illness either, he thought. Damn. He knew what it was, and he hadn't felt that in quite some time. Jealousy. He drank Sam's glass, too. He hadn't figured on this. Here he was, starting *some* kind of relationship with Mary – Mary, the first time he'd thought of her that evening. He hadn't figured that one out yet. And now, this thing with Sam? Phil loosened his tie and collar. This can be nothing but trouble, he mused. But for now, he needed to get rid of this feeling. Phil stood and approached the dance floor.

"May I cut in?" he asked, and the lawyer retreated. Phil bowed to Sam. "May I have the rest of the dances?"

"You may," she replied.

Phil took her hand and drew her close. The orchestra played a nice long set of slow dances, and Phil and Sam drifted easily, comfortably around the dance floor. She leaned her head on his chest. He had his right hand on the small of her back, guiding her; he was acutely aware that he had never touched her there before; it was all strangely new. Sam discreetly pulled the pin from her corsage and let both fall to the floor, then peeled off her name tag and let that drop, too. Then she pressed up against him, tightly.

They ran out of energy around eleven p.m. The orchestra was still playing, but Phil and Sam left the ballroom and made their way back toward the parking ramp with a few other worn-out guests. The night air felt good but Sam chilled quickly and Phil draped his tux jacket over her shoulders. They rode the elevator to the third floor of the ramp and meandered down the aisle to Phil's pickup. They climbed into the cab and sat, tired, with ears ringing.

"Sam," Phil began, "you were great tonight, in every way." She sat in the passenger seat, looking straight ahead, and Phil could see the left corner of her mouth turn up a little. "It was unfair of me to get you involved in all this, but I'm very glad I did. Thank you."

"You're welcome. I enjoyed it."

"We've known each other now for what, maybe three years?"

"Yes, three."

"It's weird, but I thought I knew you. Now I think there's so much more to know. I'd like the opportunity. To get to know you better." Phil heard himself say the words as if he were hearing someone else.

"I'd like that."

"I know there's this employer/employee problem, but I want to spend some time with you, talk, go places." This must sound stupid, Phil thought. Or threatening. Too late now. "Sam, I don't know where this is going, I can't promise-"

"Phil, it's okay. Shhhhh." Sam turned her head, her eyes closed and lips slightly parted, and leaned toward Phil as he bent to meet her.

They neither heard nor saw the van with its lights out that rolled to a stop behind Phil's pickup. The side door opened and two men dressed in mechanic's coveralls and Halloween masks climbed out with baseball bats and moved along opposite sides of the pickup. Their first swings shattered the pickup's rear window, spraying glass. On follow-through one bat caught Sam with a glancing blow to the head and knocked her to the foot-well. The next swings broke the windows in each door and drove glass into Phil's face, then a bat made contact with his left shoulder and laid him down across the seats. The last swings made a mess of the windshield, but its plastic core held the glass in place. The men returned to their van and left.

"Sam! Sam!" Phil reached down for her, his face and shoulder throbbing. He touched her back; she didn't move. He pulled himself closer through the broken glass on the seat and reached down with both arms. "There, I've got you," he said, and grabbed her under both arms and pulled her to his lap. She was limp, lifeless. He laid her head on his shoulder with his left hand and laid his right hand on her chest. There's the heartbeat. Good, now where's the breathing. His hand shook. Okay, she's breathing, thank God. He shifted her, and when his left hand came away from her head he could feel something warm and sticky running down his wrist. She was bleeding, and in a big way. He opened the passenger door with his right hand and wriggled out from under her, then laid her down across the seats and crawled back in beside her, kneeling on the floor. The truck cab started to spin, and he grabbed the steering wheel to steady himself. He searched his tux jacket pockets and found his handkerchief, then reached forward and cradled her head with both hands to find and staunch the blood flow. He felt a tremor, then another; her seizures had started.

"Oh, God no, please." He held her head and laid his on her chest. "Please, God, please. No, Sam, don't die on me. Please don't die. I'm so sorry. Please don't die. Please . . ."

He kept his hands pressed on her head wounds, and her seizures continued. "C'mon, Sam, you can do it. Don't die. Please, God, please don't die . . ." His tears stung the cuts on his face, and he barely heard the muffled voices and the sounds of people running in the parking ramp. Then there were hands grabbing at him, but he wouldn't let Sam go, and whatever it was that people were saying, he couldn't understand. Forever or an instant, he couldn't tell how much time had passed, and then a siren grew louder and lights flashed, and he felt more hands on him. He lost his grip and his hands were empty, and then there was a pinprick in his arm and a burning there, and the little consciousness he had left vanished.

CHAPTER EIGHT

The fog was lifting, and Phil could hear.

"He's coming around. Finish up that one there, would you please." A little squeaking, a rolling noise, something tugged at his face and then there was a snip-snip sound.

"Mr. Bardo," a voice said, by his ear. "Phil, time to wake up."

Phil opened his eyes. To his left a round face peered at him, and to his right a pair of gloved hands withdrew. Bright lights. The face smiled.

"Whu, wha . . ." Phil tried to talk but his lips and tongue wouldn't behave.

"It'll be a few minutes before you can talk. We numbed your face pretty well before we worked on it, just in case you woke up before we were done. Those paramedics gave you some nice stuff, though. It's Sunday morning, about two a.m. You're in the Madison General Hospital emergency room. I'm Dr. Gritz, your host for this evening, and my able assistant here," he nodded across Phil's body, "is Laura Roundtree. You came in here covered with blood, multiple cuts on your face, and a nasty contusion on your left shoulder. In shock, too. We've cleaned you up a bit, gave you some stitches, and x-rayed your shoulder. Nothing's broken, but it's going to be mighty sore for a while."

"Ggg, gul . . ."

"Hmm? Oh, 'girl.' The woman brought in with you? She's here, but a bit more worse for wear. Major scalp lacerations, bled like a sonofabitch. Big bump on the head and a concussion. Maybe a skull fracture; we can't be sure yet. She had some convulsions due to the head trauma, but that's settled down now. Doesn't appear to be any bleeding in there. She's got cuts on the left side of her face. Had to pick the glass out of 'em. Your girlfriend?"

Phil nodded. No point in explanations.

"Well, what a cutie! She'll be okay, she'll just need to take it easy for a bit. We'll keep her here for observation until later this afternoon, but then she can probably go home as long as there's someone around to help her for a few days. She can lay in bed at home just as well as here, and it costs a lot less." Gritz snapped his rubber gloves off and dropped them in a hazardous waste container. "Now, why don't you just relax for a few minutes and let those shots wear off." He walked away.

Phil closed his eyes again, and fell into a half-sleep. Time passed; no way to know how much.

"Mr. Bardo, there are some gentlemen from the police department here to speak with you."

He opened his eyes and saw Laura Roundtree with two uniformed policemen. He tried his voice. "Okay, thanks." He focused on the policemen. One he had never seen before, but the other was a semi-regular at the Chocolate Shoppe. "Carl, fancy meeting you here."

Carl brandished a clipboard. "Phil, you've never looked better." He balanced the clipboard on his stomach. "I need a statement. Can you do it now?"

"Yeah, I think so."

"So what the hell happened?"

"We were at the Homecoming Ball. It must have been shortly after eleven o'clock when we went back to my pickup in the parking ramp. We were just sitting there, talking. Then the rear window glass exploded, and the side windows blew in, and I saw a baseball bat. I heard them smashing the windshield but I didn't see them, I was down on the seat by then. I tried to help Sam. She was bleeding and unconscious, then she started having seizures." He stopped and thought for a minute. "I don't know what happened next."

"What happened next was you got lucky. Some other

folks heard the glass breaking and came to find out what was going on. They dodged a dark colored van with no headlights racing through the ramp. There were a couple of guys in it with masks on. No license plates. Then they found you and called 911. So, you didn't see the van or the guys?"

"No."

Carl handed Phil his wallet. "Anything missing – cash, credit cards, whatever?" Phil looked in it and shook his head.

"Can you think of any reason why somebody would do this to you?"

"I can't imagine."

"It wouldn't have anything to do with your uncle's murder, would it?"

"Next time I see those guys, I'll ask."

"Smartass."

"Any chance you'll find them?"

"I doubt it. You haven't given us anything to go on." Carl signed the form on the clipboard and handed it to Phil. "Read it over and sign it." Phil read it and signed it, then gave the clipboard back to Carl.

"We'll talk to Sam later – she's not with it yet," Carl said and frowned. "Phil, this wasn't a random act. If you don't want to tell me what's going on, fine, have it your way. But whatever it is, it doesn't look too healthy. If I were you I'd back off before somebody else got hurt, or worse. Your truck's still in the ramp. Have it towed out of there today or somebody else will. Take care." Carl and his silent partner left Phil's bedside and walked out.

A nurse appeared, also with a clipboard, pushing a wheelchair. "Here's your discharge papers and prescriptions for pain meds and antibiotics. You'll have to get them filled somewhere else, as our pharmacy won't open until nine a.m. If you'll just sign here . . . and then over here . . . we had your health insurance numbers on file from the last time. Any changes?"

"No."

"Good, then you're all set. You can leave."

"And Ms. Sang?"

"Oh, she won't be able to leave until later this afternoon. Will you be picking her up?"

"Yes."

"Could you bring some fresh clothes for her? Something with buttons would be best, not a pullover."

"I'll need her keys so I can get into her apartment for the clothes."

The woman pulled a plastic bag out of her lab coat. Sam's sequined purse was in it. "Maybe they're in here?" She offered the bag to Phil.

He reached in and opened the purse. It held a single key, her driver's license, and a lipstick. "Here it is," he said and held up the key. He returned the purse and bag to the nurse.

"Can I see her?"

"Oh no, not right now, she's getting another CAT scan. Some of the sections didn't come out the first time. Okay, now please have a seat in the wheelchair. Hospital regs – I have to wheel you out."

Phil was too tired to argue. He got up and collected his keys and cell phone from the counter. His tux jacket was missing; either still in the truck or with Sam, he guessed. The nurse wheeled him out of the emergency room and parked him under the awning outside. "Could you call a cab for me?" he asked. She said that she would and went back inside.

He checked his watch. almost four o'clock in the morning. Good thing that we don't open the store on Sunday as early as we do during the week, he thought. Still time to get cleaned up and get down there to let the crew in.

The cab came up the drive and stopped. Phil climbed in the back seat and gave the driver directions to his apartment. The driver started the meter and switched on the radio as the cab rolled away. The community-sponsored radio station came on and the DJ, a local who went by the name 'Trashwoman,' was finishing her nightly stint of commentary and music. Volume low, they cruised down John Nolan Drive and crossed over the deserted Beltline Highway. There wasn't even a glow of dawn yet on the eastern horizon. After winding through side streets they entered an apartment complex and pulled up to building E. Phil paid the driver without comment, got out and headed for the stairwell. At 206 he pulled out his keys, unlocked the door and stepped inside.

"Oh, shit," he said aloud. The place had been tossed. Someone had had a real good time doing it, too. The living room furniture was overturned and the cushions were scattered. His CD collection and all his books were pulled from the shelves and strewn on the floor. His prints and framed animation cels were yanked off of the wall and thrown to the floor, glass broken. Phil walked through the mess, then detoured into the kitchen. The refrigerator and freezer doors were open and the food was on the floor, defrosting. The cabinets were open and their contents shoved around. He threw the food back into the freezer and refrigerator and shut their doors. Then he opened the refrigerator door again and took out a can of beer, still cool. He opened it and took a long, deep drink.

Down the hall the linen closet door was open and all the sheets and towels had been pulled out and dropped on the floor. In the bathroom a few items had been pulled out of the sink cabinet and the toilet tank lid was on the floor next to the shower stall. A few steps down the hall clothes had been pulled from the washer and dryer and thrown together on the floor. "Damn," he said, "they mixed colors and whites." He stepped on them on the way to his bedroom.

The bed had been stripped, and the mattress and box spring overturned. All the dresser drawers had been removed and dumped. His hanging clothes had all been yanked from their hangers and dropped, and boxes from his shelves pulled down and emptied. Phil took another long pull from his beer and set the can on the nightstand. "Oh, screw it," he said, then tugged the mattress to an almost level position atop the debris on the floor and eased himself down onto it.

His cell phone woke him; he retrieved it from his pocket.

"Hello," Phil croaked.

"Phil, this is Aaron. Where are you, man? We need somebody to let us in. We've been waiting an hour."

Phil checked his watch; it was 11 a.m. He should have been there at 9 to start the Sunday opening, then to let the crew in at 10.

"Oh, sorry, it's gonna take me an hour to get there. Please have everybody wait."

"Hey, Phil, will-"

"Yeah, yeah, I'll pay you for the time you've spent standing around." Phil hung up. He rolled to his left to get up and a stabbing pain ran through his shoulder. He slowly worked his way to his feet, pulled off his bloody formal clothes and lurched to the bathroom. The face in the mirror looked familiar except for the railroad tracks of black stitches on his cheeks, chin, and forehead. Swelling had started. His left shoulder was a mass of blue-black-purple.

The long hot shower felt good. He found his jeans and a clean Chocolate Shoppe polo shirt and put them on while calling a cab. A strawberry Pop-Tart in one hand and his bomber jacket and hat in the other, he met the cab at the curb and they headed for State Street.

"Sorry I'm so late. Just coffee and ice cream today, folks, no fresh baking." Phil announced to the staff as he arrived to unlock the door.

"Phil," Judy said, staring. "What happened to you? No, that's fake, right?" She reached to touch one of the sets of stitches.

He recoiled from her touch. "It's real, believe me. We had a little accident last night. Sam's in the hospital, but she'll be okay and she'll be getting out this afternoon. She won't be able to work for a few days, so I'll need you all to carry some extra load." He swung the door open. "Okay, let's get it rolling."

As the day wore on Phil found himself tiring, and the pain in his shoulder and face bothered him. The pain prescriptions were unfilled, in his tux trouser pocket back at his apartment; he downed aspirin and ibuprofen begged from his staff. At three he called the hospital; the nurse said Sam was sleeping so he couldn't talk with her, but she was doing fine and would be discharged as planned. It was time to pick up Sam's clothes and get back to the hospital.

He had been to Sam's apartment only once before, two years earlier. It was a small, plain ten-unit concrete block building on a residential street just off of University Avenue in Middleton. The cab stopped in front of the building and Phil told the driver to wait, then he walked to the last unit on the right, ground floor. She had plants, lots of them, lining the windowsills and the drapes were drawn behind them. They looked wilted; maybe he'd give them a quick drink. He unlocked her apartment door and went inside. It was a studio apartment, a long rectangle with a bedroom/living room at one end and the kitchen, dining alcove, and bath at the other. She, too, had had visitors. Someone had searched her place like they had his, emptying drawers and turning over furniture. He stepped over some of Sam's clothes and went into the kitchen. Cabinet doors were open. There were two empty bowls on the floor, and a litter box. He hadn't seen a cat but it must have been hiding, and for good reason. He filled one bowl with water and after some digging in cabinets under the sink, found a box of dry cat food and filled the other bowl with it.

The cabby honked the horn. "Yeah, yeah, hang on a minute," Phil grumbled. He filled a large glass with water and walked to the front window, pulled back the drapes and watered the plants. He saw the driver looking toward him, and Phil held up his spread hand to ask for five minutes. The cabby waved and got out of the cab for a smoke.

Phil turned toward the piles of clothes on the floor. He tossed clothes back and forth until he found some baggy tie-waist white cotton pants and a green button-up blouse. There, a cardigan sweater, and then some underwear, a pair of socks, and a pair of slippers. He carried his finds to the kitchen and put them in a plastic grocery bag. Surveying the scene again, he realized he couldn't bring her back to her apartment. He found a large plastic garbage bag and scooped several armloads of assorted clothes into it, then took a quick trip to the bathroom to collect her basic toiletries. He grabbed his bags, turned out the lights and locked the door behind him.

The driver crushed out his cigarette as Phil approached and said, "Madison General, please." As they drove, Phil worked on what to do. Sam had no family nearby, and she needed help for a few days. He could do that himself, but not at her place – that had to get cleaned up. Same with his place. And whoever did it knew where they both lived, and could come back. And if he wasn't there . . . he didn't want to think about what could happen to her under those circumstances. They passed a flower shop on University Avenue, and Phil made the cabby circle back and wait while he bought a bouquet of cut flowers. They rode on again, and he realized he had forgotten to get his truck towed, and that he really could use a car. Dave's car! At Dave's house. That would work; he'd take her to Dave's place for a few days and take care of her there.

Pleased with himself, Phil let his mind wander. Girlfriend, he had said to the doctor. What else fit? Friend? True, but implies too little. Girlfriend? Too much, too soon. Besides, what does she think their relationship is? He looked out the window as they drove down Park Street. His cell phone rang.

"Hello."

"Phil? Where've you been? I tried your apartment, the Chocolate Shoppe, and the office. How'd things go last night?"

It was Mary. He had completely forgotten about her. "I've got a lot to tell you," he said, "but I'll have to call you later. I'm in the middle of something. Where can I reach you? At the office?"

"No." She gave him a number; home or cell, he wondered.

"Thanks. I'll call you later tonight." He hung up and pocketed his phone as they drove into the hospital's circular drive. And just what was Mary to him? Girlfriend? So much mystery about her, so smart, so confident, and so . . . mmmm. Jeez! What a mess. He paid the cabbie and told him to wait, and got out with his flowers and plastic bags.

They had kept Sam in the emergency room, awaiting

discharge. Phil identified himself to the LPN at the front desk, and she led him to Sam's bed. Sam's eyes were closed, head wrapped in a gauze bandage, with a large ice pack taped to the left side of her skull. She had cuts on her face and some on her arms, dressed with simple bandages. She wore a hospital gown; her red dress, shoes and Phil's tux jacket were in a plastic bag on the counter next to the sink.

"She's ready to be discharged," the LPN said. "She needs lots of bed rest, but she can get up and walk to the bathroom every now and then if somebody helps her. Her body will let her know what she can and can't do. If her speech gets slurred or she can't be roused, get her back in here right away by ambulance. I'll go get the paperwork and her prescriptions."

Phil set his bags down as the LPN left. He held the flowers in one hand and grasped Sam's hand with the other. "Sam . . . Sam," he said, massaging her hand to wake her. "How are you doing? C'mon, wake up and talk to me."

Her eyes fluttered, then opened. He saw her struggle to focus on him, and her eyes filled. Then the tears rolled down her cheeks.

"It hurts," she whispered, "my head hurts, really bad." She cried silently and squeezed Phil's hand, and closed her eyes. She looked so small and vulnerable in that bed with that big ice pack.

"I brought you some flowers, and some clothes. They say you can go."

She opened her eyes again and glanced at the flowers. She managed a tiny smile. "Thanks." Then, some breaths later, "What happened . . . oh, no . . ." She reached out carefully with one hand to touch Phil's face, the cuts.

"I'll tell you everything later. I'm going to take care of you for a while. Everything will be okay."

Sam closed her eyes again.

The LPN returned with papers and a paper sack. "They filled the initial meds from the hospital pharmacy. Sign these, here. Do you have some clothes for her?"

"In this bag."

"Good, I'll get her dressed. Stand over there, please."

The LPN pulled the privacy curtain and spent the next few minutes dressing Sam. Then she pulled the curtain open again; Sam was sitting on the bed in the green blouse and white cotton pants. The ice pack was gone. "I'll tuck that hospital gown into the bag," the LPN said, "it might be easier for her to wear at night. And here's some more gauze and a few new ice packs. Keep her head iced down for the next 24 hours." She helped Sam off of the bed and into a wheelchair that had been standing in the corner. Then she set the flowers on Sam's lap and pushed the chair toward the exit. Phil gathered up the bags of clothing, the medications, gauze, and ice packs and followed.

The cabby loaded the bags into the trunk while Phil and the LPN maneuvered Sam into the back of the cab. Phil got in, and Sam lay down with her head in his lap. "Bassett and Wilson," Phil said.

The Wilson Street house looked just as Phil had left it nearly a week ago. Dave's car was in the driveway. Phil ran up to the front door and unlocked it, turned on the lights and did a quick walk-through. Everything was in order – no visitors. He ran back outside, and he and the driver helped Sam out of the cab and slowly up to the house, down the hall and onto the bed in the back bedroom. Phil made another trip to the cab for the bags of clothes, paid the fare and tipped the cabby fifty-percent.

Alone with Sam, Phil whacked an ice pack to get the chemical reaction started and then used gauze to bind it to her head. She lay down again without speaking and went to sleep while Phil sat in the living room and read her medications to figure out which came next and how frequently. Then he called the Chocolate Shoppe.

"Aaron, it's Phil. Can you put Judy on? . . . Judy, can you and Lauren open tomorrow? I know you've done it a few times with Sam and me, and it would really be a big help . . . okay, great, thanks. I'll drop off the key in a few minutes. No, that's okay, I've got to go out anyway."

He went back to the bedroom to check on Sam; she was sound asleep. Phil left the house and drove Dave's car to State Street. After giving the store key to Judy he drove to a small market on Gorham Street where he bought several bags of groceries. Back at the Wilson Street house he set the bags in the kitchen, then went to the back bedroom to check on Sam. She was still asleep. He unpacked the groceries and put them away.

Night had come, and there was a chill in the house. Phil checked the thermostat and made sure that the old oil furnace would kick in at about 72 degrees, then went back and laid a light blanket over Sam before returning to the living room. The remains of a log rested in the tiny fireplace at the end of the living room. Phil found a newspaper and some matches, opened the flue and got a fire started. He prowled around in the kitchen and found no Scotch, but located a partial bottle of Grand Cayman gold rum. He poured some in a glass, kicked off his shoes and sat in a living room chair with his cell phone. He dialed the number Mary had given him.

"Hello?" she said.

"Hey, it's me."

"Phil, I was beginning to think you weren't going to call after all. Now, what the hell's going on?"

He gave her a detailed run-down of everything he could remember about the Ball. The start at the Chocolate Shoppe, the Ball setting, the people, the conversations that he and Sam had had, what they did, the orchestra, the food, everything. Everything except the revelation of his feelings about Sam. Mary listened and punctuated Phil's briefing with 'uh-huh' and 'God!' and a laugh here and there, and an occasional 'slow down a sec.' Phil realized she was taking notes. Then he got into the story of the parking ramp and the hospital.

"Christ, Phil, are you really okay?"

"Yes, just some artful designs on my face and a shoulder that feels like hell. Sam will be okay in a few days."

"Man, I was afraid something like that might happen. You hit somebody's nerve, Phil. Somebody you talked to, something you said." She paused for a few seconds. "Or somebody who knew you were going to be there. Shit. We'll have to think about this."

Then Phil told her about what he found at his apartment, and at Sam's. Mary interrupted from time to time to ask questions. As he talked he thought about the people who had known he was going to the ball. Anybody at the ticket processing office. The Homecoming Committee would have the guest list. ". . . and I've got Sam with me – she needs somebody to help her for the next couple days . . ." The tux store manager. His employees at the Chocolate Shoppe. Customers – he didn't know the ones that had hung around and watched him leave with Sam. The guy at the car wash, Jason, his nametag had said. And . . . uh-oh . . .

"So, where are you now? Your place?"

"No, too much mess, and I'm a little worried about returning guests."

"Sam's, then."

"No, same deal."

"Well then, where?"

Phil paused. His stomach felt like it was full of lead shot. Mary, too, had known they were going to be at the Ball. "The Mayflower Motel, South Park at the Beltline," he lied.

"Oh. The one with the sign – '$9.95 All You Can Eat.'"

"That's it."

"Good sign for a cheap motel. Anything I can do for you? Bring you something, stay with Sam or whatever?"

"No, thanks, we're okay for now. I should be able to get out for a while tomorrow, so I'll meet you at the office at one o'clock. All right?"

"Yeah. G'night, Phil."

He didn't want to think about it anymore. He got up and went to the back bedroom and helped Sam to the bathroom, then back to the bed. She lay without speaking and waved off Phil's question about changing into the hospital gown. He got a glass of water and her next round of pills, and helped her sit long enough to swallow them. The ice pack was still cold on her head, and he covered her up with the sheet and blanket to ease her shivers. He bent and kissed her on the forehead, just below the gauze.

"Phil . . . don't leave," she said. He could see tears again on her cheek.

"I'll be right back."

He went back to the living room and poked the ashes in the fire, then gathered the cushions from the couch and walked to the back bedroom. He lined the cushions up on the floor next to the bed.

"Sam."

"Hmm?"

"I'm on the floor, right here."

"Mmm." She shifted herself a little to allow her arm to dangle over the side of the bed so her hand could touch him.

CHAPTER NINE

"Good mornin', Mayflower Motor Hotel and Lounge."

"Hi. Could I please have Phil Bardo's room?"

"Who, ma'am?"

"Phil Bardo."

"Sorry, ma'am, nobody by that name here."

"Are you sure? He checked in yesterday."

"Ma'am, ain't nobody checked in here yesterday."

"Oh. My mistake, sorry." Mary hung up and shook her head. Damn. Damn! She picked up the phone again and dialed.

"It's me," Mary said. "I lost them, thought you ought to know . . . I don't know . . . I *said* I don't know . . . Don't worry, I'm supposed to re-connect this afternoon . . . yeah . . . yes, sir." She hung up. Crap, she thought, this was not the way to start the day. She checked her watch, then made her way to the shower.

The night had gone well. Phil had gotten up twice to change Sam's ice packs and feed her the painkillers and other meds, and they both went back to sleep easily. Mid-morning Phil woke, got up and showered, then made a call to the store. Things were well under control, or so Judy said. Lauren and Lisa were in the kitchen making the Halloween cookies for the day. The cops were in place at their table. Judy had done inventory and had a list, and Phil approved the items and asked her to call the suppliers and get same-day delivery.

"No reason for you to come in," Judy said. "I can handle this, just let me show you. I'll open again tomorrow, too."

"You're sure?"

"Positive."

"Well, okay. Thanks, I really appreciate it."

Phil busied himself in the kitchen and made omelets, toast, and coffee. A little real butter on the toast, and a side of strawberry preserves. He loaded the food on a cookie sheet he found in a cabinet and carried it to the back bedroom.

"Man, that smells good," Sam said.

"I'll help you with it in a second. Here." Phil eased her into a semi-seated position and wedged more pillows behind her back and head. Then he moved the food to the bed. "Do you want me to feed you?"

"I think I can do it – just scoot it up a little closer." She reached for the fork and carefully started to work on the eggs.

"So, how are you feeling?"

She replied between mouthfuls. "Head hurts, not too bad lying down, but standing up's a b- . . . Get dizzy standing . . . Seeing blurry, double . . . I feel slow, in a daze . . ."

"That sounds normal for a concussion. Saw a few of those playing high-school football." This girl can really pack it away for someone her size, he thought as Sam finished the eggs and toast.

She sensed his thoughts and as she reached for the coffee cup said, "I've never had any problems with appetite. You should see me drink."

"I'd like to," Phil said with a laugh, "but not today." He took the makeshift tray, leaving the coffee cup with her, and delivered it to the kitchen. Then he returned to the bedroom with his own cup and sat in a chair to one side with his feet on the foot of the bed.

"So what's going on – the ChoSho closed today?"

"No, Judy's handling it. Don't worry about it."

"I'm ready now. Tell me what happened, where I am, how I got here. I'm just gonna lay back and listen." She closed her eyes and folded her arms across her chest.

"Okay." Phil started with their walk back to the parking ramp. He didn't know how much she remembered of that night, of their talk in the pickup, of the almost-kiss right before the attack. He didn't know if she still felt the way she did that night or if she ever would again, and at that moment he was afraid to find out. He skipped to what he remembered of the attack and of the hospital. Then he told her what he found at his apartment and at hers, and his decision to bring her to Dave's house.

"Sam, if you want some fresh clothes they're in the black plastic bag next to the dresser. I'm going out for a while. I'll drop by and feed your cat again, and I've got to spend some time at Dave's office but I'll try to make it as quick as I can. I'll leave my cell here for you; call me at the office if you need me. Okay?" He felt her ice pack. It was still cold.

She nodded. She was tiring, ready to sleep again.

"Sam, I . . . I was afraid I was going to lose you."

She reached out her hand, and Phil took it. She squeezed his hand, hard, and let it go again. "Phil, who's Mary?"

"Uh . . ." This was not the conversation Phil wanted to get into, not now. Phil had added Mary's name to the payroll program; Sam must have seen it. "She was Dave's employee, and I'm paying her to do some things to close that business."

"Is that all?"

"I think so." His words felt awkward. They didn't sound convincing to him; he could imagine how they must have sounded to her.

She rolled to her right side and settled in for a nap.

The mail and the FedEx deliveries arrived at about the same time at Premier Entertainment. Margaret sorted through the envelopes, packets, and junk mail and separated them into piles for each of the agents. The stack for Casey Simmons was the largest, so she picked that pile from the desk and lurched down the hall to his office. She bumped his office door open with her hip, and the door smacked against the wall. He was on the phone – was always on the phone – and he ignored Margaret even when she dropped the pile onto his desk, right on top of the papers he was reading. She straightened her skirt and puffed out of his office and back to the reception desk.

"No, Blaine, there's no way they'll go to Toledo for that amount. Double it, maybe, or give 'em a percentage of the door on top. Call me when you return to the real world. Christ!" Simmons hung up the phone, then tugged the papers he was using out from under the mail stack and dropped them into the wastebasket. He glared at the stack, then pushed it away from him until it nearly dropped off the edge of his desk. He selected the FedEx package from the top and opened it.

The cover letter came from a detective agency in Madison, Wisconsin. As he read he half-turned his desk chair and pulled the file cabinet drawer open and fished out a folder and set it on his desk. He dumped the rest of the package contents on the desk and spread it out before him. There was a detailed text description of a magic trick, and a series of color images - perspective drawings of some building and shrouding in different positions, and a diskette. The last paragraph of the letter asked for payment of a $5,000 prize for figuring out how the trick was performed. He opened the folder and shuffled through the papers, then paused and read a few. Stephano was in Provo now, according to the tour schedule. Simmons looked at his watch and subtracted two hours, then hit the 'speaker' button on his desk set and dialed a long distance number.

"The Peaks Hotel, how may I direct your call?"

"To Steven Patch, one of your guests."

"One moment, please . . ."

"Yyyello?"

"Stephano. Casey Simmons. How're things in beautiful Utah?"

"Simmons, no more northern states after August, you got that? I can't take this shit. It's freezing and there's fuckin' snow on the ground."

"Yeah, yeah. We gotta talk about that gig you did in Madison. I get this thing in the mail today claiming the prize for figuring out how you made their carillon disappear. Some guy named Phil Bardo, representing Discreet Detective Agency."

"Well, how does he think it was done?"

Simmons read the written explanation aloud, and then he described the color pages that showed the stages of the trick.

"Simmons, that's just about right on. I'm not gonna do these big disappearing things anymore. Too many people have seen Copperfield do them, and have seen the 'how do they do that' shows on TV."

"We've got a problem here, sport. He's demanding payment."

"Then pay him."

"That's just it. You used the prize money to get your rigs to Utah."

"Oh. Well, there's got to be some angle we could work. How about we just ignore him?"

"That might work for a while, until he starts calling. Then what?"

"Can't we just tell him that he's wrong?"

Simmons had been a lawyer prior to becoming an agent. He pondered that straightforward suggestion for a minute. "Elegant in its simplicity. However, if he took us to court to make us prove it he'd win a big judgment, a lot bigger than the five grand. Not worth the risk, either in cash or bad publicity. Hang on a second. Maybe we can find a nondisclosure problem."

He dug through the papers in the file and pulled out a few pages. "Hmmm. Nope. Here's the nondisclosure agreement signed by that detective, the Helms guy that got killed. It binds the whole company to nondisclosure. So we can't refuse to pay due to an invalid nondisclosure and risk of loss of trade secrets." He flipped some pages and stopped to read one. "Okay, I'm reading the contract for the challenge, hang on." He read, paused and looked at the ceiling.

"I'm growin' old here, Simmons," Stephano groused.

"Yeah, keep your shirt on." He thought awhile longer, reread the contract again, then set it on the desk with a smile. "I'm so damn good and I didn't even know it. When we filled out that contract for the challenge prize, we filled it out for David Helms."

"So?"

"Not for the Discreet Detective Agency. The contract was with him personally, not with his company."

"Spell it out for me."

"We'll claim that Helms is the only one who can submit an answer and collect the prize. And he sure won't!"

"Not bad. You're a magician in your own way, Simmons. But what happens if this other guy gets pissed and goes to the press?"

"Let him. If we're lucky he'll spill how the trick was done, and then we'll sue his ass and collect under the nondisclosure agreement – which *is* with Discreet Detectives. Hell, if you're not going to use the trick anymore, we should provoke him into violating nondisclosure. That might mean we'd actually make some money on this god-forsaken tour."

"Okay, let's do it. Do you write a letter or what?"

Simmons nodded at the speakerphone. "Yeah. I'll write the letter and send it today. Make a snowman for me, will ya?" He cut off Stephano's reply with a poke at the phone. Another poke at the phone and Margaret's voice came over the speaker.

"Sir?"

"Margaret, dictation, please." Simmons hung up and waited for her arrival, humming to himself.

Sam's cat was hiding somewhere. Phil knew it was still in the apartment because the food and water dishes were empty. He refilled both. He decided that he'd do a little straightening of the mess, and after a few days the cat might show itself.

The kitchen was quick to fix. The bathroom really hadn't been disturbed. Next he set the major furniture pieces back on their legs and put the cushions in place on the chairs and sleeper-sofa. He put the drawers back into the long dresser, but the tangle of clothes and whatever on the floor didn't appeal to him, so he elected to leave that for the next visit.

He checked the latches on the windows – all locked. On the way out the door he inspected the lock and doorframe. There were no signs of damage, scratches or pry-marks. Phil locked the door behind him and went to Dave's car. He checked his watch; the work at Sam's place hadn't taken very long, so he still had time to run to his own apartment and pick up a few changes of clothes to take to Dave's. A left on University Avenue and a few more blocks took him to the on-ramp of the West Beltline Highway.

As he drove the western and southern perimeters of the city he agonized over Sam's question and his answer. Was she asking about the business duties, or was she really asking a question about a personal relationship? Most probably the latter, he decided. And his answer? Weak. Shit. He really don't know what his relationship was with Mary; how could he have answered any differently? And now he don't know what he has or might have with Sam. If he'd said 'no' he would have had to explain something that he didn't understand and would have ruined whatever it was he had with Sam; and if he'd said 'yes' he would have been lying to Sam outright and he just couldn't do that. Shit! Grow a spine, pick one woman, or at least be honest with both of them. No; too early, he decided. He really need to learn more about both of them.

He dodged around a slow-moving dump truck and took the off-ramp. His apartment was a couple blocks from the Beltline, and he was there within a minute. There was someone parked in his assigned spot, so he pulled into Sally and Kyle's. They both worked during the day so it shouldn't be a problem, he thought, unless they came home for a 'nooner.' He checked his mailbox in the first floor hallway – nothing. Upstairs he examined his doorframe and lock for any unusual marks. Nope, looked fine. He went inside.

The condition of his apartment depressed Phil; the mess was too big, too much. He decided to ignore it and walked back to his bedroom where he selected a large sports-bag from the pile on the floor and collected enough clothing in it to last a week. He took a last quick look around, then hoisted the bag and settled the strap on his good shoulder and walked out.

Twenty minutes later he arrived at the red brick building and parked Dave's car in the back. Mary hadn't arrived. Phil sat down at the big roll-top desk, then slid out of the chair and onto his knees to get to the phone. Gotta splice some wire on here and put this on the desk, he vowed; this arrangement was too much like praying to the phone company.

"Chocolate Shoppe."

"Hey, Judy, its Phil. I don't suppose Aaron is in, is he?"

"Yep, just a sec." Phil could hear Judy call for Aaron through the muffled receiver.

"Yo, boss," Aaron said. "What's up?"

"Aaron, how'd you like to do a little something special for me, a few extra hours. Paid."

"Sure."

"Great. You know where Dave's detective office is, don't you?"

"Yeah."

"After you get off at three o'clock today, I want you to get close enough to Dave's office to watch it. Sometime after three, maybe much later, I expect that you'll see a nice looking brunette, medium height, good build, probably wearing a sweatshirt, leave the office. I want you to follow her without being seen, and tomorrow you can tell me where she went. I want to know where she lives."

"Uh, Boss, why don't you just ask her?"

"Tried that once, and it didn't work."

"Isn't this, like, stalking or something?"

"No, it's really a human resources issue. She's an employee, and I think she has some problems and I'm just trying to figure out how to help her."

"Oh, okay."

"And don't tell anyone about this – it's a privacy thing, you know."

"Gotcha. I'm on it."

"Thanks." Phil hung up, then dialed another number.

"Terry's Car Care? Is Will there? Will, it's Phil. I've got a problem. My truck got trashed Saturday night in the ramp at the Monona Terrace. It's either still on the third level, or it's been towed away. Could you send somebody to find it, tow it back to your place and fix it? Great, I appreciate it. Thanks." He replaced the receiver and returned to the desk chair.

Phil heard the outer door to the office open and close. He stood up and waited, leaning on the desk. Mary came around the corner in jeans and sweatshirt, and when she caught sight of Phil and his rows of stitches she gasped and ran to him. She threw her arms around him.

"Oh my God, are you really okay?" She released him, and then held her hands close to either side of his face, wanting to touch him but unable to do so. "Does it hurt a lot?"

"Only when I smile, eat, or talk."

"Man! Didn't I tell you that was a bad idea to go to the ball?" She had her hands on her hips, and she was mad. "When are you gonna start listening to me?"

"And who's the boss around here, anyway?"

"Okay, okay, point taken. But, really. These people aren't playing games, and you don't have the experience."

"And you do?"

"Uh, well, no, but I've been in this business longer than you have." She went and sat in the leather chair and pulled her legs up under her. "And how's your 'friend' doing?"

"Sam? Oh, she's doing better, she'll be fine in a few days."

"Say, that motel has to be crowded and uncomfortable. Anything I can do for you or bring you?"

"No, we're fine, thanks." Phil sat again in the desk chair.

"Sure? I could come out . . ."

"No, really, it's okay. Before we do another debriefing on the Saturday events, could you find those boxes of research items that Dave had you round up? I'd like to take some with me and look them over."

"Be right back with 'em." Mary got up and disappeared into the stacks. Phil could hear her rustle between the stacks, stop, move some materials, then move on to other portions of the room. She reappeared empty-handed and looking genuinely puzzled.

"I don't know what to tell you. They're gone."

"Gone?"

"Gone. Vanished. Disappeared. Missing."

"Maybe Dave took them."

She shook her head. "No way. I was putting stuff in those boxes on the day of the murder. He didn't come to the office that day."

"Well, that's just great. We've been ripped off. I guess it's an indication that you were on the right track. Anything else missing?"

"Not that I know of."

"I don't suppose you remember where you got all that stuff? I think we'll need it."

"Most of it I got through the Internet anyway, and some of it is still on my hard drive. I can get most of it back pretty quickly."

"Then that will be the task for today. Oh, and there's something else. The Carillon drawings you had, the ones you used to build the wire-frame model. Do they have interior layouts?"

She shook her head. "No, exteriors only. But I can probably find some interiors in a day or two. Why?"

Phil shrugged. "Understanding the murder scene may help us understand the murder."

"Good point. I'll see what I can find."

"Okay, now let's do that debrief again." Phil again went through the events of Saturday night as Mary took notes and asked questions. They went into great detail, much more than they did on the Sunday phone call. They finished at about three-thirty.

"I've got to get back to check on Sam," he said. "Say, why don't you wrap up early too and get on that research tomorrow."

"Thanks, I'll stay just a bit and maybe get some printing started, stuff I already have on my machine."

Phil rose to leave. "Sounds good, I'll see you tomorrow afternoon."

"Take care," Mary called as he left. When she heard the outer door close she walked to the waiting room. As Phil's car left the lot and pulled out onto the street she jerked the office door open, stepped outside, closed and locked the door and ran down the stairs. She unlocked a mountain bike from a nearby light post and rode after Phil's car.

When Phil entered Dave's house he found Sam lying on the couch in the living room. She had changed clothes and wore an un-tucked long-sleeved plaid shirt and a pair of black jeans. Gauze was still around her head, but no ice bag.

"Up and around? Must be feeling better," Phil said.

Sam stretched and yawned. "Yes, it's a little better this afternoon. I felt pretty good around one o'clock so I got up to take a shower. 'Bout halfway through I got really dizzy, and I had to crawl on my hands and knees back to bed so I wouldn't fall over. When that passed I got dressed and came out here."

"Why didn't you call me?"

"I knew you were busy, and besides, I didn't take your cell into the shower with me."

Phil took his sports bag of clothing into the front bedroom and dropped it on the floor, then went to the kitchen and took an ice pack from the freezer.

"You're supposed to be wearing your ice pack." He put the pack carefully to the side of Sam's head, then wrapped the gauze to hold it in place and tucked the free end into the folds of the bandage.

"Phil, I found your tux jacket in a bag with my dress. Don't you have to return it?"

He settled down in a chair. "Crap. I forgot about that. The rest of the outfit is back at my apartment. It's probably ruined, all full of blood, and I didn't buy the damage insurance. I guess I'll have pay for it. Sorry about your dress. The dry cleaners won't touch it."

"We'll see how bad it is. Maybe I can save it – I know some ancient Chinese laundry secrets." She was silent for a moment. "What's going on, Phil? Why would people try to kill us?"

"I don't think they were trying to kill us. If they had

wanted to they could have finished us off easily. I think they were trying to scare us."

"It worked, for me anyway. But why?"

Phil sighed. "I owe you an explanation. Remember I told you that I wanted to know how Dave got the magic act gig? Well, I wanted to know because it is part of an investigation. I don't think that he was killed by that assistant professor. I want to know who really killed him and why. I feel I owe it to him to find out."

"And that's-" Sam began.

"What Mary and I are working on at Dave's office. I'd guess that somebody didn't like our questions and is trying to scare us away."

"Well, maybe you should listen to them."

Phil shook his head. "Can't, not now. If we hadn't gotten anywhere I probably would have dropped it. But now, they've confirmed that there's something out there to be found. I miscalculated by asking those questions so soon, so publicly. Now they know that we know something, and they know where we live. They wanted us to know that they know; that's why the attack and why they trashed our apartments. They hope that they can scare us into backing off. He looked over at Sam and shook his head. "I'm sorry to have gotten you into this."

"Yeah, me too. So what's next?"

"Dinner." Phil got up and headed for the kitchen. "I hope you like clams. While I get things ready would you call Judy? She's still got my key, so I'll need her to get there for opening tomorrow but I'll come in, too, for a while."

Phil got busy, first preparing a red clam sauce to simmer. As he worked he could hear Sam talking on the phone. Sam finished and came to sit at the kitchen table and watch. "She'll be there," Sam said, breathing deeply. "Mmm, this must be what heaven smells like."

"At least the Vatican's section," Phil responded. He put some water into a pot and put it on the stove, then washed and cut lettuce for a salad. The water began to boil and he added the linguini to the pot. He opened the wine and set the bottle and two glasses on the table. "Would you pour? I like a Cabernet with this, besides I neglected to buy a Chianti." Then he lit the broiler and set garlic bread under it. The linguini was done and he drained it and put it in a bowl. "Never rinse; drain and dress with a little extra-virgin olive oil."

"Extra-virgin is good?"

"Only in olive oil." He smiled at her, pulled the bread from the oven and cut it into chunks on a cutting board. Last, the sauce went into a bowl and was set on the table.

"Oh, man," Sam said through the pasta, "I take back what I said about being sorry you got me into this. I had no idea you could cook. I thought all you bachelors just drank beer and ate hot dogs with macaroni and cheese."

"I was saving that for tomorrow night." Phil was pleased that she liked the dinner. "Somebody told me that I should learn how to do one dish really well and I'd have everyone thinking I'm a gourmet."

"Yeah, I'll bet you do more than one thing really well. Pass the bread please?"

When they were finished Phil rinsed the plates and set the pans in the sink to soak. Dave didn't have a dishwasher, so there was more work for Phil to look forward to later. He refreshed the wineglasses and escorted Sam to the couch in the living room. Phil took a seat in one of the chairs.

"So, Sam, do you really have a cat? I haven't seen it yet."

"Oh yes. He's shy. He found a way into the base of the kitchen cabinets and hides in there when strangers are around."

"Does he have a name?"

"Gato. That's 'cat' in Spanish. I didn't have much imagination when I named him."

"Why Spanish? Do you have some Spanish somewhere in your family?"

Sam laughed. "Hardly. My dad is Chinese and my mother is Tahitian. I was born in Hong Kong."

"How the hell did you wind up in Madison, Wisconsin?"

She sipped from her glass. "Well, if you really want to

know, I'll tell you. But if I tell you my life story you've got to tell me yours. Deal?"

"Deal."

"Okay. Like I said, I was born in Hong Kong. The part of Chinese society that my dad aspired to did not accept mixed marriages or mixed children, so my parents never married. I lived there with my mother until I was about six, being supported by my father but not living with him. Then we became too much of a liability for him and he cut us off, so my mother and I moved to Tahiti to her home village of Haapiti and lived with her sister's family."

"And your father?"

"Never heard from him again."

"I'm sorry. Go on."

"We stayed in Haapiti until I was fifteen. It was great, but my mother realized that if I was ever to get a real shot at life I needed a better education than what was possible there. She brought me to the States, to Kenosha, where we lived with her cousin. My mom worked in a tractor factory and married a nice guy she met at work. I went to high school there and got my U.S. citizenship, and when the time arrived for college I came here."

"Your mother is still in Kenosha?"

"Yep. We're very close." She put her wineglass on the end table. "I better stop with the wine or I won't be able to walk to the bedroom. Anyway, I got my undergrad degree in hotel management, of all things. After graduation it seemed that jobs in this field for women, particularly women of some color, all seemed to start and end in housekeeping. I didn't find that appealing so I took odd jobs to make ends meet while I figured out what I wanted to do. Then three years ago I started working for you."

"And have you figured out what you want to do?"

"Sort of. I decided that I want to open my own business. That's the only way to have any real control over your own destiny. What kind of business, I don't know. But I know that I need some cash to do it so I've been trying to live cheaply and save up some money. But I'm beginning to think that I'll never get there. Fascinating, huh."

Phil smiled. "Actually, yes. Now here's the tough question: if money was no object and you could do anything at all you wanted to do, what would that be?"

Sam sat for a minute, thinking. "Oh, I don't know if I can tell you. It's kind of embarrassing."

"Why? We all have dreams."

"Remember, you've got to tell me yours, too."

"Absolutely. Now confess."

She hesitated. "Oh, all right. If I could be anything at all I wanted to be, I'd be a backup singer for Jimmy Buffet. You know, one of the girls that stand under the fake palm tree. I'd be singing that chorus from 'One Particular Harbor,' the bit that's in Hawaiian or Polynesian or something. Oh, God, I feel silly." She covered her face with her hands.

"It's not silly at all. I never would have guessed that, but there's nothing wrong with it." Phil could see her, slim and soft in a sarong with a hibiscus lei around her head instead of the gauze bandage. Barefoot. He saw the sand and island forest; he smelled a blast of flower perfume mixed with humid sea air. He tasted salt crystals on her golden skin. The island had forested peaks, a village with thatch roofed houses. A lagoon with brilliant, blue-green water.

"Phil?"

"Sorry, Sam, I was lost there for a minute. So why didn't you pursue it?"

"Two reasons. The first is lack of vocal talent. The second reason is more complicated. I absolutely love music, and somehow it is hardwired right to my emotions. Maybe it's a childhood thing, I don't know. We used to sing a lot in Tahiti. Anyway, with good songs I can't get through them without tearing up and my voice cracking to pieces. I can't even hear them, talk about them, or think about them without it happening. But it doesn't make me sad at all. Weird, huh." She wiped her eyes with her sleeve. "See?"

"It's not weird. I think it's great." Phil felt good that she had dared to share that with him. He hoped he could relax enough to reveal himself to her with similar candor. And he was surprised at the richness of the images she had created for him without knowing.

"I even have problems with this when I see someone really nail a good performance," she sniffed mightily. "That's it, that's all you get from me tonight. I think it's time for drugs and sleep. Tomorrow night it's your turn to tell stories." She got to her feet and moved toward the hall. "Thanks, Phil, that was a great dinner. And I liked talking with you. Oh – day after tomorrow is Halloween. Could you pick up a pumpkin, a candle, and some candy at the store tomorrow? Thanks." She turned and disappeared down the hall.

"Sure." Phil got up and went to the kitchen. There was still some wine in the bottle; he emptied it into his glass and returned to the living room to sit and do a little reading. He was asleep on the couch two pages into one of his uncle's books.

CHAPTER TEN

Judy told Phil that he had to work in the back office in order to avoid scaring the customers.

"But it's not that bad, and the stitches come out Friday."

"Well then you can come out Friday, too," she said. "And I guess it would be okay for Halloween."

So he worked in the office, a productive morning catching up on the computer and paperwork, payroll and payables.

"Phil," Judy said, standing in the office door. "I thought you were going to keep Sam resting."

"That's what I thought she was doing."

"Well, take away her phone. She called me twenty times yesterday about one thing or another. If she's gonna do that, she might as well be here – that would be less distracting than running to the phone every two seconds."

"I'll talk to her."

"The staff's worried about her. And about you too, by the way. We don't want you guys to overdo and bust a stitch or something."

"Judy-"

"Everything's fine here. We had a staff meeting yesterday to settle everybody down and get the schedules straight. What's the plan for Halloween? You know the downtown parade is tomorrow night, right?"

"I want to close at five o'clock, before the weirdness starts. The staff can wear costumes all day tomorrow. Are we set up for the 'pumpkin or alternative-vegetable-of-your-choice' carving contest?"

"Yes, and I think we'll have good participation this year.

Veggies in by nine o'clock, we'll tally customer votes at four o'clock. I assume you're not doing that Halloween Charity Fun-Run this Saturday?"

"Why not, Judy? I do the 5K every year."

"Oh, I just thought that maybe due to your accident . . . well, I'll put out the pledge sheet again." She ran off down the hall to answer the phone ringing at the cashier's station.

Phil called Terry's Car Care. They had found his pickup and bailed it out of impound early that morning. Will was working on the insurance estimate but was having trouble finding anyone interested in cleaning blood out of upholstery and carpet.

The tux place was not sympathetic when he called them about the blood damage to their inventory. Phil wound up buying the outfit under their 'used' price structure. Good for a Halloween costume, he thought. At least they didn't charge for the extra days he kept it.

Aaron came in just before Phil left the Chocolate Shoppe office. "007 reporting in, M.," he said.

"Hi, Aaron. What've you got for me?"

"Damn good thing I had my car," he said. "You left in somebody's car, and she was right after you on a ten-speed."

"You mean she left right after me."

"Yeah, and she followed you."

That was interesting. "Go on, Aaron."

"The only reason she could keep up was you kept missing the lights. She followed you to some house on Wilson and watched you go in, then she took off again. She locked her bike near a bus stop and hopped a bus, and got off in a neighborhood off of Odana Road. It was a small house at, wait, I've got it here," he handed Phil a piece of paper with an address written on it, "and that was it."

Phil noticed messy black stains on his skin. "What happened to your hand?"

"Oh. I sat on my pen, and it leaked." Aaron half-turned, showing Phil the big black ink spot on the back pocket of his jeans. "I waited there awhile, like to see if that was really her house, and she didn't come out again. Finally some big dude, looked like a football player, came along walking a bulldog and let himself in the front door. Then I had to leave."

"And you're sure she didn't see you?"

"No way, man, I was stealth personified."

"Aaron, thanks! Write up those hours and put it in my box to sign."

Phil's trip to Sam's apartment was uneventful. He called "Gato, Gato . . ." to no effect, then refilled the empty bowls again. Next he picked clothes from the floor and sorted, folded, hung, and put in drawers as he saw fit. She'd rearrange everything the way she liked it anyway, he knew, so it didn't pay to worry about it. He felt odd handling her underwear and bras. The last items left on the floor were the things that had apparently occupied a brick-and-board bookshelf; some art pieces, solid glass with surreal embedded fish; large hardcover books on Japanese and Chinese prints and the works of Gauguin. A softcover book about yoga. 'Train Your Cat in One Hour.' Travel guides to Hong Kong and French Polynesia. High school and college yearbooks. Within an hour he had finished setting everything right, and the apartment looked acceptable for her return whenever she was able.

Phil drove the Beltline to his own apartment. His place was still a disaster and he didn't have time to do anything about it. He collected the rest of his tux outfit in hopes that Sam could tell if any of it was salvageable, and gathered a few other items. Then, he left for the Discreet Detectives office.

Mary was already at work when Phil arrived. She had succeeded in getting some internal diagrams of the Carillon from somewhere, and was in the process of building a computer model of them.

"Hey," Phil said, approaching her computer table.

"Hey, yourself." She swung her chair around to face Phil. She had an enormous furrow of a frown on her forehead. "So who's the fathead who had me followed yesterday?"

Busted. "Ah, that fathead would be me." So much for

Aaron's 'stealth personified.'

"Thanks so much for invading my privacy," Mary fumed. "What were you thinking?"

"Ever since I've known you, you've been evasive and secretive and I had to know more about who I was dealing with. And if you knew you were being followed, why'd you go back to your house? Isn't that kinda stupid?"

"What makes you so sure that it was my house?"

"Uh . . . because you let yourself in with a key?"

"Could've been a good friend, or a relative. It is mine, by the way. That is, I rent it. If I thought I was being followed by a professional I sure wouldn't have gone there. I like to keep my private business private."

"Speaking of invading privacy, who was the fathead who was following me?"

"I had to follow you. You lied to me about where you were staying, and I was worried. I can't help you if you lie to me."

"How the hell did you know I lied?"

"You've really got to watch more detective shows. I called the motel. They never heard of you, and nobody had checked in."

Phil felt his face flush. "I figured the fewer that knew where we were, the less likely there'd be a slipup and we'd have visitors again." Damn, he thought, he'd have to think these things through more carefully from now on. "How'd you know I was the one who had you followed?"

"You just told me," Mary said. "I figured it was you but I didn't know for sure. That 'fathead' line was a bluff to make you think I already knew. It worked. You gotta work on your lying skills, friend, if you're gonna be in this business."

Phil decided that he really must have had a dumbfounded look on his face after that remark, because after a moment of awkward silence Mary lost her composure and burst into a full-blown gut-wrenching tears-down-the-face can't-get-air laughing jag, and Phil caught it too. He finally had to sit down on the floor and look away from her to regain self-control.

"Whew, it's been years since I've had one of those!" she said at last. "Oh Phil, I'm sorry. You're a sweet guy and you're trying, and I really don't want to make fun of you. Actually, if I were you I'd have done the exact same thing." She pulled off her sweatshirt-of-the-day revealing a GreenPeace t-shirt, and fanned herself with a handful of papers from the table.

Phil was mad at himself. Mad for being so easily tripped-up. Mad for still being attracted to this woman, mad for being fascinated by her abilities, mad for enjoying the verbal sparring. Mad for being dependent upon her in this case. Mad that he couldn't drop his feelings for her and concentrate on Sam.

"Okay, I'm better," she said, "I'll give you one question. Ask me one question and I'll answer it honestly and completely, and then we've got work to do." She waited.

"Who's your roommate?"

"Hoover. The love of my life for about four years."

Phil got to his feet. "Oh. Sorry, I didn't know."

"What do you mean? What's the matter with you?"

"I . . . I wouldn't have . . . how you could betray him so easily with me last week?"

"Huh? Who are you talking about?"

"My spy saw him go into the house. He was out walking the dog."

"Time-out. Hoover's my dog. J. Edgar Hoover. All bulldogs look like him."

"So who was the guy?"

She studied Phil for a moment. "The guy is my next-door neighbor, Kevin. He walks Hoover for me, takes care of him when I'm gone. He's a UW student living at home and he can use the extra bucks."

"Really?"

"Yes, really! I'm not living with him. Why, you're jealous, aren't you?" She stood up and walked over to Phil and planted a big kiss on his lips. She held it until he started to return it, then she broke it off and smiled. "Thanks, I'll take that as a compliment. Now we've got some work to do." She plopped back into the chair in front of the computer. "C'mon, let's get to it. You can have another question tomorrow. One of these days I'll have some questions for you."

Phil had lots of questions for her, and for himself, but they would have to come later.

"See," Mary pointed to a spot on a printout of the Carillon floor plan. "This is what I'm working on now – the location and size of the staircase."

Phil studied the diagram. "So we've got what looks like a narrow wooden staircase going up along a wall to – where's the side elevation? – okay, thanks – to, ah, a platform. It turns and goes up again and arrives at a landing."

"That's where the Carillon player sits and plays."

"And then a tight spiral stair, probably iron, goes up from there for access to the actual bells."

"There are fifty-six bells. They range from five to sixty-eight hundred pounds."

"Great, thanks. And when you enter the Carillon Tower, the stairs are to your immediate right. I can't tell – are these open stairs?"

"No," Mary answered, "the stairs are enclosed by a wall; drywall or plaster."

"Okay. So, is the space under the first flight of stairs open or enclosed by the wall?"

"I'm not sure; I think it might be enclosed."

Phil looked at what Mary had laid out on the computer. "I think the stairs occupy more of the ground floor space than what you've got there." She made an adjustment. "Okay, that looks more like it. An enclosed staircase, with the first floor landing right in the corner. Somebody coming down the stairs can't even see someone on the ground floor until they get to the very bottom. What about window openings in the exterior walls?"

Mary checked the exterior plans. "Nothing on the ground floor. There's a couple at the level of the player, and some further up."

"And there's, let me see, eight steps to the platform, then eight more to the landing. Just for fun, let's say a normal person under normal circumstances might climb or descend at one second per step. So sixteen seconds for the stairs and maybe two seconds for the landing – let's round to twenty seconds. In a hurry maybe they'd go twice as fast – ten seconds. Or faster."

"But not in the dark. They cut the lights during the trick. They didn't come on again until after the door was opened."

Phil wrote some notes. "Okay, and what was the sequence of events again right around the shots?"

"The Carillon was playing but stopped when the explosion happened. The curtain fell from the top down, and immediately started to rise again after hitting the ground. At that point the shots were heard."

"Let's check your photo sequence. You were shooting what, one frame per second? So, here, the curtain starts falling, one, two, three, four, five to the ground, then six, at seven it starts going up again, probably at eight or nine seconds the shots happen."

Mary nodded. "So Dan Daman is sitting at the keyboard, using both hands to play. He doesn't know exactly when the explosion is going to occur and when the lights are going to go out. When he hears it he stops playing, finds his gun, feels his way to the stairs, races down the stairs without falling, takes a moment to locate your uncle in the dark, and shoots him. All in the space of eight or nine seconds. Not too likely."

"Maybe he had a flashlight."

"Still, it's a stretch. And he couldn't save time by shooting your uncle from the stairs; the wall's in the way. Besides, the angle of entry of the bullets was wrong for someone shooting from the stairs. He would have had to come all the way down to the first floor landing and either crouch to shoot or hold the gun at waist height to get that forty-five degree upward angle."

"And then Daman yells out something, goes and hides the gun so well that nobody can find it, and comes back and gets into position next to Dave. And he does that in the dark and in-" Phil shuffled through the remaining sequence of photos, "in the thirty seconds it took for Stephano to get the curtain raised and the door opened. Again, not too likely. But Daman didn't have any blood spatter on him. Let's look at the area of the ground floor. With the stairs taking up so much space, and Dave taking up some of the rest, where could he be and not get splashed?"

Mary shook her head. "I couldn't see where your uncle was on the floor, and we don't know where the bullets hit, so it's hard to figure out where he was when he was shot or exactly where the shooter was."

"The cops told me that the bullets were deformed by hitting the stone wall. So we know that Dave couldn't have been standing with his back to the staircase wall or to the door. He had to be along a stone wall somewhere over here – " Phil outlined with his finger on the layout, "or here. And we know the shots came from in front of him. That means that Daman would have had to be here in front of the door, at the base of the stairs, or in front of the stairway wall. Let's see if we can narrow it down. On your 3-D model let's put in horizontal planes at the approximate height of each of the bullet entry points. Dave was five foot eleven, so the bullets were probably at five foot two and four foot four, based on what the cops showed me."

"There. Now what?"

"Let's assume Dave wasn't standing tight against the walls. So lay in vertical planes parallel to each of these two walls but in about a foot."

"Okay, basically bringing the walls in. So we're assuming Dave had to be standing along one of these two planes."

"Right. Now we'll put in planes for the bullet paths. A forty-five degree downward sloping plane from the line where these vertical and horizontal planes meet."

Mary fiddled with the diagram. "There. And then another forty-five degree plane from the other wall. The gun had to be somewhere on one of these two planes."

"Or close. Chances are neither Dave nor the killer would have stood exactly parallel to the walls or tight in the corner."

"I suppose we could round it off a bit."

"Good. Now, how far away do you suppose Daman would have to be to avoid getting splashed by blood from the shots?"

"I dunno. Maybe five or six feet?"

"Let's say six. Can you measure off six feet on each forty-five-degree plane?

"Give me a minute on this one, okay?" Mary stared at the computer screen as she gave the mouse and the numeric keypad a workout. Sweat appeared in tiny beads on her upper lip. Phil watched them collect and then a drop fell and landed on her inner thigh. Her jeans were nice and tight, he observed.

"Okay," she said, wiping her lip with a forearm, "I think this is it. So assuming that the end of the six feet represents the position of the gun, the killer would have had to be *inside* the stairway wall over here, have the front door *open* to stand here, or . . . would be crouching or kneeling right in this area."

Phil sat back and thought, and his left hand played with the ends of some stitch threads on his cheek. "Interesting. I guess that location doesn't make a case for or against Daman. I'd like to see it in person. When do they let the general public in there?"

"They do a mini-concert every noon. Anybody can walk in there and go up and watch the guy play."

"I guess I'll become a music lover tomorrow noon. Anyway, based on our time sequence analysis today I don't think Daman could have done it. Let's package up our thoughts on this and send it to the police and the DA. Give me a print of that model there and I'll do a write-up."

Mary clicked the 'print' icon and the printer moaned. "The next obvious question," she said, "would be if not Daman, then who? And how?"

"There had to be somebody else in there. I don't know how the police could miss him, though. And he would have to go out through the same door that the police were coming in. If he ran up the stairs to hide he would have run smack into Daman coming down."

"The door is unlikely; a heat flare would have shown up

on our infrared shots if someone had opened it," Mary said while thumbing through the photos.

"Maybe ol' Stephano is in on it. Magicians get people in and out of locked boxes all the time. Maybe he got somebody in and out somehow."

"Doubt it. Most of those tricks involve custom-made boxes with false sides or bottoms and secret doors. The Carillon is a big pile of rock, no back door."

"Just the same, maybe we should talk to him. That is, if he'll talk to us." Phil collected the paper from the printer. "Bring up the word processor, and let me drive the computer for a minute. I'll knock out that write-up."

Mary launched the word processor software and relinquished her seat to Phil. She stood amused, watching over his shoulder. "Are you sure you don't want me to do that?" she asked, observing his struggles with the Windows machine. "You could dictate. You'd be a dictator; you'd probably like that."

"No, no, I've got it under control," he lied. "I've got an Apple at work, and the software is very . . . damn it. How do you – never mind. Found it. Here we go. Now why don't you go somewhere for a half hour or so."

"Gee, thanks, but no. I'll just sit quietly over here and watch." Mary made a point of settling into the side chair, tipping it back and propping her feet up on the corner of the computer table. She laced her fingers across her flat stomach and smiled.

She watched him as he worked; he wasn't a bad typist once he got started. Every now and then she saw the tip of his tongue appear at the corner of his mouth, then disappear again. She guessed he didn't even know he did that. Her eyes followed the contours of his biceps under the denim shirt, his lean legs in the khaki trousers. She tried to see down into his lap but the keyboard tray was in the way. The night she seduced him in the office he was good, she recalled. He had patience, timing, and consideration – a maturity not found in the young ones. It was the difference between just 'having sex' and 'making love.' And stamina; he seemed to be in good shape, too. Uh-oh, she thought, feelin' a little warm in here. Nerve endings heating up, blood rushing around. Better change the subject.

"Phil, how do you stay in shape? If I worked at a shop serving ice cream and bakery products I'd be so big I'd have to grease myself to get out the door every day. Do you run or something?"

"I worry. It's guaranteed to keep the weight off. I run once a year in the Halloween race."

"Oh, yeah? That's this Saturday. You going this year?"

"Yeah."

"Can I join you? I was going anyway, and I'd rather go with someone I know."

"Yeah, sure. I only go 5k, though."

"Thanks, 5k is fine."

"Thought you were going to be quiet."

"Sorry."

He's smart, confident, funny and sometimes a little naïve; for this business, anyway, she thought, and he needed her whether he knew it or not. Seems to care about people, clearly cares about Sam. Mary knew she needed to find out more about her, and him. And whether there's a 'them.'

"Done," Phil announced, "a masterpiece. They'll have to let the guy go after this." He clicked on the 'print' icon and the printer started to warm up. "We have only one set of photos, so I guess I'll just send the whole package to the DA." He collected the pages from the printer, the photos, and the sheet showing their 3-D model of the murder scene. "Your computer is yours once again." He set off for the desk.

Mary sat down again in front of her computer. She saved Phil's letter to the hard drive, then she brought up her email program and created a new email. She attached the letter, the carillon graphics file, and a half-dozen other files to the email and clicked 'Send.'

"You still here?" Mary wandered into the desk area and

sat in the leather easy chair.

"Not for long," Phil said. He pulled a file from his portfolio and laid it on the edge of the desk. "I read the Anderson file."

"And?"

"We've got some hours to bill."

"That's it?"

"Yes."

"You aren't going to tell me I screwed up?"

"I figured you already knew that. The bottom line is that you got the information you needed, and the target had no idea he was being watched. Right?"

"Uh, right."

"But I'd suggest you be more careful. A different case, a different target, you plastered, and you could have gotten into big trouble. And I'm not talking about the cops."

"I know, I know. I've already heard this lecture."

"I don't want to see you get hurt."

"That makes two of us. By the way, how's our health insurance plan?"

"You should be asking about life insurance."

"Did you ever decide what to do with that other file?"

"The 'Tilburton' file?"

"That's the one."

"No. Maybe you should read it, then we can talk." Phil retrieved the file from his portfolio and handed it to Mary. She sat on the cot and read, and her face showed no surprise at the contents. She handed the file back to Phil.

"You aren't surprised?" he asked.

She shrugged. "No. Just because Dave didn't tell me what happened doesn't mean I didn't know."

"You followed him that night, didn't you. You followed Dave to help him in case he got into trouble, and you saw the whole thing too."

"I wish, but it wasn't so dramatic. I just read the file a couple days later."

"So why the secrecy? Why 'Tilburton' instead of

'Essinger'?"

"A security thing. Nobody looking for 'Essinger' stuff is likely to find it under 'Tilburton.'"

"Was he worried about somebody breaking in?"

"Apparently. Maybe he thought Essinger might come looking for it."

"Maybe he did. Where are the photos?"

"Uh, I don't know."

"You don't know? Did you ever see them?"

"Yeah, they were in the file when I read it the first time."

"And you put them back?"

"No, Phil, some of 'em were pretty erotic so I took 'em home."

"You're joking."

Mary rolled her eyes. "Of course I'm joking. They weren't *that* good. Maybe Dave, you know, sent them somewhere – to the cops, or the DEA or somebody."

"Maybe Dave destroyed them."

"Look around," she said and swept her arm in an arc. "Does it look like he ever threw anything away?"

"No. Maybe Essinger got in here and took them."

"If he found the file to find the photos he would have taken the file, too, don't you think?"

"I suppose so. I would have."

"What's the big deal? Why are you so hot on this?"

Phil leaned back in his chair. "It hit me that this Essinger guy could be involved in Dave's murder. He apparently didn't buy Dave's excuse for quitting the case. So what would he do if he figured out that Dave might have seen something he wasn't supposed to see?"

"Kill him to keep him quiet about the drug deal? It's possible."

"So why wouldn't he kill you, too?"

"He wouldn't know about me unless he found the file. And if he found the file, it wouldn't still be here."

"All right. So if he doesn't have the photos, and you don't, and they're not here, and let's say Dave didn't send them to anybody, then who might have them?"

"Somebody else. Somebody who found them. One of the other men in the photos? The hooker? Whoever processed the film? Maybe somebody decided to blackmail Essinger with them."

Phil sat up straight. "There we go! Somebody blackmails Essinger with the photos, probably even uses Dave's name to do it! Essinger kills Dave to end the blackmail, but guess what – the blackmail continues after Dave's death."

"That works. But there's another possibility."

"Go for it."

"Maybe *Dave* was blackmailing Essinger."

"Yeah, right. Or maybe *you* were blackmailing Essinger."

"Maybe I was. Maybe I still am. You just never know, do you?" Mary got up. "Let me know what you decide to do about this. I'm starving – it's time for my next feeding."

"I'll see you tomorrow. I'm off to the post office and then I'm going to see Mrs. Anderson."

Phil left the Anderson home with a check in his pocket. Mrs. Anderson had been somewhat indifferent to the news that, at least for the time he was under surveillance, there appeared to be no other woman involved with her husband. Phil had thought that a bit strange; he had expected a happier reaction. Then he had gone into the subject of the apparent alcoholism and she fell apart. It was then that it had hit him.

"You never really thought he was seeing another woman, did you."

She shook her head.

"He was sober for how long this time?"

"Two years."

"I'm sorry. Why didn't you just ask us to check for that?"

"I was . . . hoping it was another woman. That would be easier to fix."

Phil had told her to keep the money and use it toward rehab but she had insisted that he take it, so he did. Any job has its downside, he reasoned, but at least you usually feel good when you get paid. This one didn't turn out that way.

Phil bumped his way through the front door, a medium-sized pumpkin under his left arm and a grocery bag under his right arm.

"Hey, did you bring the stuff I asked for?" Sam called from the back bedroom.

'Got it," he replied as he kicked the door closed. He went into the kitchen and set the goods on the table. Sam shuffled down the hall and appeared at the kitchen door. She was wrapped in an enormous terrycloth bathrobe that must have been Dave's.

"This will do," she said, examining the pumpkin. Then she said "Oh" and grabbed for the table, and then sat down hard in a kitchen chair. "Still dizzy when I get up and walk around. But the headaches are better."

"Then maybe you shouldn't walk around. The gang's been worried about you. They think you're not resting enough and that I should tie you down on the bed."

She laughed. "I know what you're really trying to say - get off the damned phone. Poor Judy couldn't wait for you to tell me. I apologized to her, and I promise I'll be good tomorrow. I won't call her more than twice. It's just killing me to sit on the sidelines and not be in there with the team. And I can't get into daytime TV."

"Now you've got something to do tomorrow – carve the pumpkin."

"And roast the seeds. Gotta have roasted pumpkin seeds, otherwise it just isn't Halloween." She reached for the grocery bag and dug through the candy that Phil had bought. "These are good. So are these. Oh, and I love these, too. But these, yuck! I'll get rid of them first."

"You planning on eating all that candy by yourself?"

"No, I plan on handing it out for trick-or-treat. I'll eat the leftovers. I have my costume planned and everything." She unwrapped one of the candy bars and took a bite. "So what are you going to be tomorrow?"

"I thought maybe I'd pretend to be a businessman."

"Sorry, nobody will be fooled."

"Hey!" Phil feigned offense. "I think you're getting better; the sass levels in your bloodstream must be getting back to normal. Let me look at your head." She wasn't wearing the ice pack, and the swelling looked like it had diminished. He unwrapped the gauze bandage and examined the long line of stitches, clotted blood, bruising, and lump. The sight made him a little queasy. "Eewwww, I gotta put this back on before your brains fall out," he said as he wrapped her up again. "Seriously, how's it feel?"

"Really much better. I can get around okay by myself. I should go back to my apartment."

"I'd like you to stay and rest for a couple more days. Please."

"Thanks, I appreciate it, but we'll see. What's for dinner? Didn't you say this was hot dogs and mac and cheese night?"

"I have a confession. I can't tolerate those things anymore; too much of them in my poorer days. And I don't have a dinner plan yet, so how about a pizza?"

"Your confessions come later. Pizza's good. I'm gonna go get dressed and start my day." She rose and turned to go, then said "Whoa . . ." and groped for the table. Phil caught her arm and steadied her before she fell.

"Yeah, you're doing just great," he said. "Ready to be on your own." He scooped her up in his arms. "Can I give you a lift?"

"Why, yes, thank you sir. I live just around the corner," she said and pointed down the hall.

It was a fine pizza, New York style with large floppy pieces. They ate in the living room on the floor, and when the box was empty Phil used it as kindling to start a fire in the fireplace. The beer was cold and good with the pizza, and they each opened a second bottle for dessert in front of the fire.

"Still no cat," Phil said. "I don't believe you have a cat. Just an obese mouse somewhere."

"You know, animals have a sixth sense. He probably detects hostility, a threat to his position in the pack. He probably thinks you've replaced me, or that you're going to replace him."

"The latter isn't a bad idea. By the way, I finished picking up your place today but I'm sure it's all wrong."

She smiled. "I'm sure it is too, but thanks anyway. I would have hated to see it all messed up. I have a dominant 'neatness' gene from my mother."

"Have you called and told her about your head?"

"No, she'd just worry too much, and God forbid, she would come up here; she'd drive me nuts." Sam laid back and rested her head on Phil's leg. "Tell me your story. You promised, remember?"

"What? I don't remember anything of the kind. You were delirious last night, as I recall. You just imagined it."

Sam reached back with one hand and pinched Phil hard just above the kneecap.

"Ow! Okay, I give. You must know most of it by now anyway." He took another long pull from his beer. "It's been a long and middle-class life, a mid-western life. Born and raised in the suburbs of Milwaukee by middle-class parents who were products of the depression. We lived in middle-class white-bread neighborhoods, in ranch houses. My folks drove station wagons, had good honest jobs, and we went on driving vacations two weeks each year in the summer. Went to church on Sundays, and I belonged to the Boy Scouts. Traditional family values. Safety and security, minimal risk. The worst we had was 'duck and cover' drills in school during the cold war and the occasional bully."

"Sounds nice and peaceful. What's wrong with that?"

"Well, nothing really. Except that instead of learning how to deal with adversity, you only learn how to avoid it. My folks' motto was 'don't try something different, you might not like it, or you might fail.' On the rare occasion when they did try something new and liked it, then that would become the thing they did all the time. Safe again. It took me years to figure this out and then to learn how to take chances in life. I'm still learning."

Sam turned and looked at him. "That's why you started your own business, and why you take 'adventure' vacations. You create your own adversity; take risks to feel alive."

"You've got it. Had enough yet?"

"More, please." Sam turned her face toward the ceiling and closed her eyes.

"Condensed version. I came here to the University and got a degree in food science. Then I went to work for a series of large dairy firms. After disappearing into the corporate world for a number of years I came back to Madison and worked for some small family operations. I liked that, but I learned that to get ahead I'd have to be part of the family. So I started my own family business. And somewhere along the way I found someone smart, cute, ambitious, sassy, and with boundless energy." He looked at Sam; the corners of her mouth were twitching. "But she didn't work out, so I hired you."

"Pah! And you were doing so well there for a minute!" she laughed, reaching for his kneecap pressure point again. "You will regret that remark! You have no idea . . ." She gave up trying to fight through his blocks and settled down again. "And you're all alone now?"

"Yes. My folks died in a car crash ten years ago. No brothers or sisters. My mom's only brother was Dave Helms, and I spent some time with him while I was in college and then again after I came back to Madison. Plaza-Burgers and beer every Tuesday night. And he became a regular part of our revenue at the Chocolate Shoppe."

Sam felt around for her beer bottle, found it and took a drink. "And now you've got two businesses to run."

"Well, not really. I figure on closing the detective thing; I'm just using it now to try to find out what really happened to Dave."

"Do you like it?"

"Well, I don't know. I guess so. It's different."

"Tell me about Mary. Be honest. You can't escape this time."

Phil sighed. "I don't know very much. She says she'd been working for Dave a year. She seems to know the business pretty well. She's smart and attractive. She's also funny, headstrong, secretive and irritating. Provides plenty of adversity." He watched Sam for a reaction and waited for a follow up question. None came. He let the silence hang. "She also owns a dog."

"Oh, a *dog* person," Sam said, flatly. "Are you a dog person or a cat person?"

"I'm sort of in the middle. I like them both." Again the silence. Longer this time, he thought.

"So," Sam resumed, "If you could do anything that you wanted to do and money was no object, what would you do?"

"I think I'm doing it. Owning your own business is a thrill-ride. It's never dull, it consumes you completely, and you answer to yourself instead of some bean-counter in a corporate accounting department. When your decisions work, there's nothing like it. When they fail, there's nothing worse. And it is fun working with people, both employees and customers – a constant variety, very satisfying to see people happy and growing, to motivate and mentor them."

"C'mon. Stretch. What's your far-out dream that you wouldn't admit to anyone? Who do you want to sing back-up for?"

Phil laughed. "Oh, you just want to even the score, offset the blackmail, huh. Okay, let me think. I'm well past wanting to be quarterback in the Superbowl . . . I've always liked detective stories, mysteries. I'd like to try to be a detective, like Dave was."

"I kinda guessed that. Anything else?"

"Write a book. I don't know if that means being a successful author on an ongoing basis, or if it just means what it says – write one book. But I've always wanted to try it. To create, and then to see my work in print. I just don't have the time."

"Or maybe you find excuses not to try, for some reason."

"Maybe."

Sam drained the last of her beer and they watched the fire. The log was a little green in some places and liquid oozed to the surface and hissed in the flames. Phil thought Sam might have fallen asleep, and he was reaching out to touch her shoulder when she broke the silence.

"You've never married."

"Nope."

"Girlfriends?"

"Sure."

"But?"

"Not the right ones, I guess. And in recent years my work has pretty much occupied all of my time."

"Phil, is it weird that our dreams don't specifically involve other people? They were about us as individuals, doing something."

"I think the way the question was asked led to that kind of answer. Besides, each of our dream activities would involve people in some way."

"That's not what I meant."

"I know. Maybe there are still some things that we don't want to admit to each other. Or to ourselves."

She nodded, her head still on his leg. "It worries me, Phil. I'm already thirty, and I feel like I'm always just getting started. I'm treading water, not getting anywhere."

"There's more, isn't there?"

"I don't want to be alone."

CHAPTER ELEVEN

"And here," Judy pointed to the display case, "are the body-parts cookies that Lauren, Ellen, Josh, and Nick baked yesterday afternoon. I think they'll sell well today."

"They look pretty good," Phil said. "Let's see, arms, legs, hands, feet, ears, noses, wait a sec – here's a body part that we can't display . . . and here's another one." He handed the offending cookies to Judy. "Sort through the case and pull out any more of these, okay?"

"Darn. Guess we'll just have to eat 'em ourselves."

"Yeah, that's a real shame." Phil came out from behind the counter and toured along the windows. There was a line-up of carved pumpkins on the window bench facing State Street. In between them were a few carved green peppers, one butternut squash, a cantaloupe, and an enormous eggplant. Chocolate Shoppe customers were viewing the entries and dropping their receipts in the baskets beside their favorites. Later in the day the vegetable receiving the most receipts would win something. The prize had yet to be determined.

The weather was ideal for the State Street Halloween Costume Party. The skies were clear, ensuring a cool evening. It usually drew around forty thousand, but with good weather the number could be closer to fifty-five thousand. Free musical acts would play from two stages, one set up at the Capitol Square end of the street and the other at the campus end next to the Memorial Library. Nearly all cross-streets would be blocked and the bus lanes shut down later that afternoon to turn the entire length of State Street into a pedestrian party mall. The merchants on State Street either loved or hated this event based on past experience – usually the bar owners did a huge business, and the non-bar owners shut their doors early to avoid shoplifting and general harassment or damage. This was Madison's Mardi Gras, Fantasy Fest, Oktoberfest, and Gasparilla; a once-a-year opportunity for dressing inappropriately and behaving inexcusably. It was a blast.

That morning Phil had put on his usual Chocolate Shoppe polo shirt and khaki pants. At work the staff informed him that he lacked imagination, and they persuaded him to put on white pants, an apron, a chef's jacket and toque for the day. Judy wore white face paint with blackened eye sockets atop a man's black suit and white shirt – a zombie. Aaron was decked out as Superman, tights and all. Nick came as a tampon, encased in a white cylindrical tube with a rope coming out of the top. "Nick," Phil fumed, "turn that thing into a giant cigarette right now, or go home and change." Lisa wore a straw hat, sunglasses, bikini top, a grass skirt and flip-flops – until Phil realized that her bikini top was composed exclusively of body paint. He put on his best frown and told her to cover up immediately. "This is a family-oriented business," he scolded.

"Phil, families know better than to come to State Street on Halloween," she argued.

"Maybe so, but this isn't negotiable."

Lisa was back behind the counter ten minutes later, wearing a very pointy bikini top that she'd made by tying two waffle cones together with string.

Back in the office Phil worked on his accounting, then called Sam to find out how she was feeling.

"No problem," she said. "I'm being careful, lying down and resting every now and then."

"Good."

"I've got the pumpkin almost done, then I'll roast the seeds. They probably don't start trick-or-treating in this neighborhood until six so I've got plenty of time to get ready."

"I might be a little late tonight. I'm going to be here for our early close, then I'm going to check out some of the costumes. Traffic will be a mess getting out of here."

"I'll have plenty to stay busy."

"Say, you never told me about your costume."

"Let's just say you've seen it before," she replied.

Aaron appeared at the office door and knocked. "Sam," Phil said, "Superman just showed up. I've got to go, so I'll see you later." He hung up.

"Phil, just wondering, man, is there anything you need from the ultimate crime fighter? Need anybody followed or anything?"

"No, Aaron, not right at the moment, but thanks for asking. I hate to tell you this, but you weren't as stealthy as you thought last time."

"What? How do you know?"

"The woman you followed called me a 'fathead' for having you follow her. She obviously saw you."

"Oh, man . . ." Aaron deflated, as if Phil had handed him a piece of kryptonite. "And I was so careful . . . I can do this, Phil, I really can. I just need practice. Give me some tips on how to do it. Maybe if you had me do that stuff regular, like, instead of so many hours here."

"I've never followed anyone myself so I can't tell you how to do it," Phil laughed. "If something comes up I promise I'll give you another chance. Maybe you could just practice on your own time for a while. Just don't get arrested for stalking."

"Right, Phil, thanks man. I won't let you down next time." Aaron left and Phil picked up the phone and dialed.

"Mary?"

"Yeah, Phil. What's up?"

"Can you meet me at eleven-thirty at the office? I'd like you to go with me to the Carillon at noon today."

"Sure. Do I need to bring anything special?"

"Just a tape measure and a notepad. And you in a costume."

"Ugh. Costume, eh."

"Yeah. I'm not going to be the only one embarrassed."

"Hmm. Okay, I know what I can do on short notice. I'll see you at eleven-thirty."

Phil sat on the stairs that led to the detective agency. At eleven-thirty-five Mary rounded the corner and arrived at the bottom of the stairs. She was dressed in a white scoop-necked t-shirt and khaki jungle shorts with cargo pockets, hiking boots, and a belt holding a leather side-arm holster. Round-lensed wire-rimmed sunglasses and her hair in a ponytail completed the picture.

"Lara Croft, I presume," Phil said. "That's a good look for you. I need a shot of this!" He took her picture with his cell phone, then reached out and squeezed the holster. "Where'd you get this?"

"No, there's no gun in there, just a tape measure, and I got it from a friend." she said. "But I bet every cop we run into will want to feel it up, too."

"Yes, I'm sure . . ."

"So tell me, Phil, do you wear that chef getup every day?"

"No, just on days when the health inspector is stopping by. Let's get going." Phil got up.

Mary looked hopeful. "Bus? Cab?"

"You can't be serious. We walk."

It was about a mile between the office and the Carillon Tower, down State Street and up and over Bascom Hill. Phil paused at the statue of Lincoln, and looked back and forth between Lincoln and Mary. After a few moments of this, Mary rolled her eyes and gave Phil a backhand whack on the arm and said "Christ, Phil, he's never going to stand up for *me*."

The Carillon concert had already begun before they arrived. There were a couple of undergrads sitting on the terrace planters, listening. The front door to the Carillon Tower was unlocked so Phil and Mary walked in and the door closed behind them.

A single bare bulb in a ceiling fixture lit the ground floor. After a quick glance around they climbed the staircase to the platform where the Carillon player sat. He occupied a large bench in front of a Rube Goldberg contraption of wooden levers and tensioned rods. Phil watched as the man followed the music score and reached out with his fists, pushing down on the levers with exaggerated effort. Phil was surprised by the delay – there was over a second between the pressing of a lever and a corresponding bell ring, an awkward bit of timing for a musician. Phil and Mary walked back down the stairs, counting the steps and timing how long it took to reach the bottom.

Back on the ground level they shuffled to one side to let other visitors up the stairs, then Mary pulled out her tape measure and handed Phil a pencil and notepad. They did some quick measurements between the interior walls and examined the stairway wall. There was no storage area under the stairs. They looked at the stone walls and found a few spots on the wall opposite the stairs that could have been where bullets had lodged, but they couldn't be certain.

"It's so stupid." Phil said quietly. "Nobody would be able to figure out the magic trick from inside this cave."

"Yeah, Dave knew that, but it was an easy paycheck. Just show up and collect a few bucks. And by putting me outside we had a chance to figure it out and get the bonus. Stand over there and hold the end of the tape. Over a little more. Now hold the tape to your chest. There." She backed away from Phil with the other end of the tape. She peered at the markings on the tape. "This is six feet." She crouched down until the tape was at roughly a forty-five degree angle. "Now this is the most likely area." She scuttled back and forth in an arc until she bumped into walls in either direction. "Right in here." She stood up and let go of the tape, and Phil reeled it in and took a couple steps toward her.

"What's that back there?" Phil pointed to a dark spot on the floor behind Mary at the base of the wall.

She looked over her shoulder. "It's a metal grate set in the floor. Heating duct or something." She turned around and examined it, stuck her fingers through the grate and tugged. "Maybe two feet long, and a foot wide. Tight, cemented in. Nobody came in through that."

"Who said they had to come in?"

She looked up at Phil and smacked herself on the

forehead. "Duh! That's it! They did it right through the grate! But how would somebody get down there? There sure aren't any trap doors in here."

They went outside and blinked in the sunlight, then circled the Carillon Tower in search of any other doors that might lead to a basement or a utility room below. They found none.

Phil pawed through the shrubs at the base of the carillon. "Aren't you supposed to find and push some secret panel in the rock and a door mysteriously opens in the wall revealing a stone spiral staircase?"

"The real Lara Croft does that, Phil. I'm a fake."

"Some help you are." They sat on the edge of a planter. "There's got to be a way," Phil said. "Somebody's got to be able to service whatever it is that's down there. They're not going to rip up a stone floor to do it."

"And it isn't likely that some murderer would be able to chip that grate out of the cement, crawl down there, put the grate back in place, wait for who knows how long, shoot your uncle, wait for everyone to leave, climb out, cement the grate back in place, then make an escape all without being noticed or heard by anyone."

"I agree. There's got to be some way to get down there. We need to look at the plans again. Maybe talk to somebody in the Facilities Department." He stood up. "Let's wander back, shall we?"

They walked back over Bascom Hill, then down the Library Mall and past the band tuning up on the stage. As they passed the 'Importante' storefront, John Smith was closing up. Phil nudged Mary and said, "There's Smith. I haven't gotten a chance to talk to him about the scotch and cigar bar."

"Wonder what his hurry is."

"Let's find out." Phil set off across the street with Mary in pursuit. "Hey, John," Phil called, "closing' early today?"

Smith looked and nodded over his shoulder as he cranked up the window awning. "Hello, Bardo. Nobody's buying anything today anyway. Who's your friend?"

Mary stuck out her hand. "Lara Croft."

"Yeah, whatever," Smith said, ignoring her hand. A young man appeared at the window balcony above. "John, hurry up," he called down to Smith.

"John," Phil said, "I wanted to ask you about a business idea-"

"Look," Smith interrupted, and cocked his head toward the balcony. "He's got a complicated costume for tonight and I've got to start getting him ready. Stop in and buy something sometime, Bardo. You too, Croft." Smith finished securing the awning and went back into his shop and locked the door behind him.

"A friendly sort," Mary smirked. "Not!"

"He's usually nicer than that. Can't imagine what's bugging him today."

They continued down State Street. The cops were setting up the barricades for the evening and it was only mid-afternoon. When they reached the Chocolate Shoppe Phil stopped on the sidewalk.

"Mary, I've got to work for a couple hours and do the early close. Why don't you come in and let me treat you to a coffee. And I think I've got some special cookies that you might like. Then we can catch the street action as it gets started and call it a day."

She nodded. "I'd like that. Let me buy a newspaper first so I'll have something to do while I wait." She trotted across the street to a paper box and bought a paper, then came back to Phil. "Ready."

They went inside. Mary picked a table next to a window in the corner and settled in with her paper. Phil went behind the counter and caught Judy by the elbow, then pointed at Mary. "Please give her anything she wants, on the house. And a plate of those cookies we confiscated this morning." Then Phil went back to the office.

Within two minutes Superman was at the office door. "Phil, she's here! That woman you had me follow is right here in the ChoSho!"

Phil looked up. "Yes, I know. I brought her here."

"Oh. Well. I just thought you ought to know, y'know, in case. And man, she's - wow. Did she tell you how she knew I was followin' her?"

"No, she didn't. Why don't you go and ask her yourself?"

"Really? Well, okay, I guess."

An hour passed. Phil finished his back room work and went out to the counter. Superman was at the corner table and Mary was entertaining herself by making him uncomfortable. She leaned forward with her elbows on the table, biceps pressed tightly against the sides of her chest to force more cleavage into view. She stared at him over the tops of her sunglasses, and between bits of conversation she put one of the special shaped cookies deep in her mouth and slowly withdrew it from between her lips. Superman squirmed on his chair. Mary saw Phil watching and gave him a wink. Phil filled a coffee cup and brought it to her table.

"Coffee?" Phil asked.

"Yes, please," Mary said. Then, to Aaron, "I think your job here is done, Superman."

"Uh, yeah. Thanks for the tits-uh, tips." Aaron got up and hurried away.

Phil shook his head. "Man of steel?"

"He certainly is now," Mary laughed. "Nice kid, I was just havin' a little fun."

"You are incorrigible. Try to behave; we'll be out of here in an hour."

The streets were beginning to fill with costumed pedestrians. Phil and the staff counted the ballots in the carving contest and the winner turned out to be Lisa's eggplant. The last of the customers left except Mary, then Phil shooed the staff out the door and locked it. "This will give them no end of speculation tomorrow," he said. He busied himself with the counting of cash, final cleaning of tables, and emptying of the trash containers. Mary read her paper and watched the early partygoers arrive out in the street. Phil turned out all the lights but the one in the hallway leading to the office and said, "We're done. Let's go."

The street had grown thick with people in costume. Traffic was packed on the two cross-streets in a rush-hour horror. The bands at both ends of State Street started to play and people began to move toward the sounds. Cops were out in force and meandered through the crowd with bemused looks on their faces; no rowdies yet; there hadn't been time to consume enough beer. There were costumes of every imaginable type: homemade ones of cardboard, duct tape and paint; rental costumes, rubber faces of famous people, risqué, grotesque, pious, and everything in between. Body paints. Goths with their special party piercings. Pregnant nuns. Pregnant priests. Star Trek characters. Dogs with their fur painted. A couple, each wrapped in nothing but cellophane. Two guys in suits with 'IRS' in big letters on their briefcases, clearly the most frightening of all.

"I'm in the wrong damned business," Phil said to Mary, observing all the cups of beer being carried in the crowd. They walked to the Capitol Square end of State Street and stopped to get a cheese steak sandwich at a street vendor's cart and listen to a set from the band. Then they walked all the way down to the Library Mall end of the street. Along the way people were flinging Mardi Gras beads from open windows and second-floor cast-iron balconies overlooking the street. Mary received offers of beads in exchange for lifting her costume top but she politely declined. They listened to a set from the band on stage and watched the cops chase people out of the Library Mall fountain.

"I think I've seen enough for tonight," Phil said, "how about you?"

"Yeah, I guess so. I used to come down for this every year and stay until bar-time, but I'm not that young anymore."

"I don't think I was ever that young. Can I give you a ride home?"

"Sure, thanks."

"My car's behind the office."

They pushed their way through the crowd and back down

State Street, and turned down the side street. As they approached the red brick building the door to the Discreet Detective Agency opened and someone emerged dressed in a Phantom of the Opera costume.

"Hey! Stop!" shouted Phil, and the figure shot down the stairs, ran down the block heading away from State Street and turned left at the next corner.

"Go that way, cut him off!" Phil pointed back toward State Street, and Mary took off running. Phil reached the corner, turned, and caught a glimpse of the figure halfway down the block. As he sprinted down the block Phil saw the figure turn left again at the next corner and head back toward State Street. Phil puffed to the corner, his lungs and legs aching. *This does not bode well for the 5k*, he thought. Rounding the corner he forced himself to pick up the pace again. He lost sight of the Phantom as he approached State Street – he had gotten into the crowd. Damn it! Phil slowed to a trot, then saw a figure on the sidewalk trying to get up.

"Are you okay?" Phil called, running up to Mary.

"Shit!" she said as she wobbled to her feet. "That sonofabitch ran smack into me! I saw him coming, and I gave him the 'stop or I'll shoot' thing." She demonstrated with spread legs and both arms outstretched with the heel of one hand cupped in the other as if she was steadying a gun. "He never even slowed down. Bam, right into me. Knocked me flat on my ass and kept going. I'm sure gonna feel this tomorrow."

"Are you sure you're okay? We should go to the emergency room. They know me well and you'll get right in."

"Nah, I'm fine." She brushed herself off and hunted for a moment before finding her sunglasses in the gutter. "We'll never find him now."

"We could get lucky. Let's just take one quick stroll down State Street. Okay?"

She shrugged. "Sure."

They entered the crowd and worked their way in the direction of campus. There were a couple of false alarms, people who from a distance looked like they might be wearing a Phantom costume but proved to be bullfighters or vampires. The band at the Library Mall was playing reggae at sonic-boom levels. Phil felt his inner organs vibrating inside his ribs.

"There, look," Phil said. "Next to the stage."

Mary looked. "That could be him."

"You swing to the left a bit, in case he tries for the side street. I'll go head-on and we'll see what happens."

Mary moved off to the left and took up a station on the corner. Phil moved from one knot of partygoers to the next and worked his way toward the stage. Then the crowd in front of him evaporated and Phil was uncovered twenty feet from the Phantom. He saw Phil and turned and ran, not toward the side street where Mary was waiting but toward Bascom Hill.

"Damn," Phil said, "here we go again." Phil took off after him. Mary saw the Phantom make his break and she ran after him, too. They chased him to Park Street where he dodged between cars coming from both directions, and then he headed up Bascom Hill with black cape flying from his shoulders. Phil stayed on the sidewalk behind him, and Mary was to his left on a flanking maneuver behind the buildings. This hill is a killer to walk, let alone run, Phil thought, as he pushed himself to keep going past the old Music Hall, and then the Law building. The Phantom passed South Hall and made a left turn, and Phil was sure that Mary would be there to bottle him in from the other side. Phil wheezed around the corner of South Hall. Mary was already there, bent over with her hands on her knees, panting. But there was no Phantom.

Phil staggered to a stop, then sat down on the ground. A few minutes later he was able to talk.

"Okay, so how'd you let him get away *this* time?"

"Me? Hell, Phil, I came 'round the corner just before you did. Nobody home. I figured you lost him on the other side."

"Nope. He came down here." Phil stood up and looked around, then checked the bushes. "I'm sure he came down here. But there's no place for him to go without our seeing him."

"Well, he's not here now. I think I've had enough fun for

tonight."

"Yeah, okay. Youngster like you can't handle a little exercise?"

"Shut up. I'm just afraid I'll have to do CPR on you if we run any more tonight."

They walked down the hill, then back through the crowds on State Street. When they got to Discreet Detectives Phil climbed the stairs and quickly checked through the office. There didn't seem to be anything missing or disturbed. He locked the door. "Tomorrow I'm going to go to Bill's Key Shop and get this lock replaced," he announced.

Phil pulled into the driveway on Wilson Street, dead tired. Sam's pumpkin was lit in the front window. He walked to the front door and rang the bell. The door opened.

"Trick or treat! Jeez, Sam, what the-?"

She stood in the doorway in a hospital gown, gauze bandage around her head, with rivers of blood soaking the bandage and running down onto the gown. She had a bowl of candy in her hand.

"C'mon, Phil, it's ketchup. Get in the spirit! And you would be . . . a chef, or a baker. A sweaty one, by the look of you."

"Yeah, well, I've been busy."

"I like a man with lots of dough. You can come in."

CHAPTER TWELVE

Sam appeared in the kitchen fully dressed while Phil was finishing his toast. "I'm coming in with you," she said.

"Oh, no you don't. I can't have you passing out in front of the customers."

"I'm fine, really. Check it out."

He unwrapped her gauze bandage and found that the swelling on her head had gone down to almost nothing. The wound had fully closed and stopped seeping, and her scalp was a little puckered where the stitches entered the skin. "Hate to admit it, but you're almost perfect again."

She carefully combed her hair over the gash. "See? There's no reason for me to sit around here any longer."

"Painkillers?"

Sam put her hand in her right jacket pocket. "Check."

"Antibiotics?"

She put her hand into her left jacket pocket. "Check."

"Promise me that you'll take it slow. No skipping breaks, okay? Or I'll send you home. I mean it!"

"Yes, sir! I may need a longer lunch hour – I want to go out to my apartment."

"You can take my car."

Sam did well through the opening routines, and when the morning crew arrived they made a great fuss over her. She made them focus on the customers with the pledge that during the slack time they'd exchange stories of all that had happened since the previous Saturday. Phil wondered how Sam would treat the subjects of the Ball, the attack, and their evenings at Dave's house. What would the crew say to her about his closing-time guest? Last night Phil had told Sam about his trip to the Carillon, the intruder at the detective office, and the futile chases. He hadn't left Mary out of the story but he hadn't dwelt on her, either. Sam had listened, silent, fingers playing with the seam of her hospital gown. When Phil had finished Sam had said, "I'm glad for you. You're getting the chance to live your dream," and retired for the night. He had sensed that maybe she wasn't really all that glad. She was right, though. He was getting his chance, though not under the circumstances he would have chosen. Opportunity didn't always wait for the right circumstances. You take it anyway.

At the break Phil left to do his errands and to avoid eavesdropping on the telling of tales; this was Sam's time to get reconnected with the team.

"This is what that lock of yours looks like on the inside." Bill set a demonstration model with clear Plexiglas side panels on the counter. "It's a decent lock, not something you can slip with a credit card. And it's not easy for an amateur to pick, so it was most likely somebody with a key. It would be a shame to change out the whole lock."

"But it is possible that somebody could have picked it."

"Somebody who knows what they're doing. A professional. But somebody like that will get past almost any lock, including any new one you'd put in."

Phil picked up the model and examined it, then played with the key and watched how the key cuts positioned the spring-loaded pistons. "I suppose it would make more sense just to re-key the lock. I don't know how many keys Dave had made and who he gave them to."

"And it's a lot cheaper than replacing it. Shall I write up a work order?"

Phil nodded. "Please. Could you drop three new keys at the store when you're done? I'd appreciate it."

"Will do." Bill wrote on his order pad. "I'll send my apprentice over this morning to do it. Smart kid, university student in architecture. He catches on fast. Gene?"

A curtain covered the doorway that separated the front desk from the back workroom. It parted and Gene appeared in the doorway, the same young man who had called to John Smith from the 'Importante' balcony the day before.

"Gene, this is Mr. Bardo. I need you to re-key a lock for him this morning." Bill tore the work order from the pad and handed it to him. Gene accepted the work order and nodded at Phil. "I'll get right on it," he said.

"Oh, Phil," Bill added, "can we have your key? Saves us a little time."

"Sure." Phil pulled his key ring from his pocket, removed Dave's office key and handed it to Bill. Bill gave it to Gene, who pocketed the key and the work order and retreated behind the curtain.

"What did the cops say about it?" Bill asked.

"I haven't told them," Phil replied. "Nothing is missing as far as I can tell, and there's no damage. And I have no description that would be of any help. There's really nothing that they could do other than file a useless report."

"Well, I'd tell 'em anyway. You just never know."

Mary's head drifted slowly toward the desktop. Just before impact she snapped awake again, sat back, and glanced quickly to either side to see if anyone had noticed. The man was boring; really boring. Monumentally boring, she decided. Social and economic impact of post-war monetary policy on neo-socialist blah blah . . . yeeeaaauuuckkkk. Why Phil wanted her to sit in on a class and check him out was . . . uh-oh.

"Ms. – I'm sorry, I don't recall your name. Are we not sufficiently entertaining for you?" She looked up; Dr. Ted Essinger stood at the edge of the stage, pointing directly at her. "Yes, you." There were scattered snickers echoing in the lecture hall.

"Sorry. Just checking out the class for next semester," Mary said.

"And?"

"No fuckin' way!" She got up and grabbed her backpack,

then beat a retreat up the aisle and out the rear doors of the lecture hall.

After Bill's Key Shop, Phil made his way down the block and around the corner to Terry's Car Care to check on his truck. It was still in one of the service bays. The windshield, side windows and rear cab window had been replaced and all the broken glass had been vacuumed out of the carpeting and seats. The upholstery was gouged and scratched but nothing that cut through the fabric backing. Sam's blood had stained the seat fabric and carpet; the steam cleaning had helped, but hadn't gotten it all out.

Phil found Will, the owner, in the shop's office talking with a thin goatee'd man in his 40's. "Sorry to interrupt," Phil said, "I'd just like to know when you'll be done with my truck."

"Phil! C'mon in. We've just got to give you an oil change and new wiper blades and you should be good to go. This is my not-so-silent partner, Ken Sullivan. Ken's also deep into Urban Design. You know, that big development group that's always fucking everything up downtown."

"We're going to be presenting a proposal at next Monday's Downtown Development meeting," Ken said. "They're also going to reveal the master plans for stage four of State Street and the expansion of the Monona Terrace project."

"You should go to the meeting, Phil. I'm going," Will slapped his hand on his wallet, "to find out what all this is going to cost me. It's going to be at the City-County Building, seven p.m."

Phil nodded. "I'll plan to be there. Who puts on this meeting?"

"City Council and the Regional Planning Commission. Ruppert Taylor chairs it."

Phil got back to the Chocolate Shoppe at the second lull, just before the lunch hour. Sam and the staff were huddled around a table at the back of the store. They stopped talking and looked at him when he entered.

"What?" he asked. No one offered any explanation, and they drifted away from the table. "Okay, fine. Don't tell me," Phil said in mock hurt. Sam borrowed his car keys and disappeared to do her apartment run. As he went to work behind the counter he could feel things gradually returning to normal. Business picked up speed at the lunch hour and he became too consumed to care what had transpired at the back table. He was jostling and teasing the staff, cajoling customers, cup by cup and scoop by scoop, and it felt good. Phil retrieved fresh three-gallon tubs of ice cream from a walk-in freezer, made waffle cones and cleared tables. He cleaned the grinders, refilled the whole bean bins, inhaled the aromas of the different beans and admired their dark, slightly oily skins.

Sam returned. "Go," she said, "I'm fine, I've got it covered here." He collected the keys that Gene had dropped off that morning, hung his apron on a hook next to the cash register and headed for the door. On his way out he took a quick look back – Sam was watching him. She took his apron and tied it on, then turned and dove into the action in front of the espresso machine.

At Discreet Detectives he tried the new keys in the lock and they all worked perfectly. He wandered the office again and tried to determine if there were any items disturbed or missing, and found nothing obvious. Mary's computer sat where it always had. The roll-top desk and the contents of its drawers seemed untouched from the day before. Phil sat at the desk and contemplated the next move. The 'who' was still completely unknown, and the only thing he was ever more certain of was that Daman wasn't the 'who.' The 'how' was becoming clearer. It was possible that the killer could have shot Dave from beneath the grate – the trajectories made sense; they just had to show that it was possible for someone to get down there to do it. The killer carried the gun away with him. The 'why' remained as much a mystery as the 'who.' Maybe the two had to be discovered together.

Phil sorted through the mail and picked out an envelope

and opened it. It was from Stephano's agent. He read it and threw it down on the desk in disgust. The front door opened and closed, then he heard footsteps and a 'tick, tick, tick, tick' on the wooden floor. Mary appeared, and at her side was a rumpled mass of bulldog. "Phil. this is Hoover," she said, pointing at the dog. "My neighbor can't let him out this afternoon, so I brought him along. Hope you don't mind."

"That's okay," Phil said. The dog stood at her side, then he walked stiff-legged to the desk and pushed his way past Phil's legs and into the kneehole of the desk where he sat down. He took up a large portion of the kneehole.

"He and Dave bonded," Mary said. "He likes you, too. I can tell."

"Sure. Hey, is that a black eye?"

Mary touched the area under her right eye. "A little one. A souvenir from last night. You should see the bruises on my back. And I've got to show you this beauty right here . . ." She started to unbutton her jeans.

"Not now, thanks." Phil backed his chair away from the desk. "By the way, Stephano's agent sent us a letter denying our prize due to some legal technicality about the offer being made to Dave, not to Discreet Detectives."

"That's crap."

"Maybe so, but it's not worth the energy right now. Maybe I'll give him a call tomorrow."

"Hey, I sat in on Essinger's class this morning."

"How'd it go?"

"Well . . ." Mary described her run-in with the Foreign Studies professor, and Phil dug his thumbnail into the knuckle of his index finger in hope that the pain would keep him from laughing.

"That wasn't quite what I had in mind," Phil said and forced a stern face while he tapped a black BIC pen on the desktop.

"No kidding. Me neither. So what's next? Obviously I can't go undercover with that guy after this."

"Obviously. We'll have to try something else. Tomorrow

maybe you can find out who lives in that house out on BurningTree."

"All right."

"Let's leave Hoover here to answer the phone. I think we need to visit the University's Facilities Administration Department."

"Mr. Hanley will see you now." Nancy, a student in a work-study program, got up from her desk and led Phil and Mary down a basement corridor in the old Engineering building. She showed them into a small office and left.

The office was crowded with rolls, racks, and stacks of architectural drawings. There were dozens of ring binders with manufacturers' names on their spines. Promo coffee mugs – 'Pierson Piping,' 'Manson Brick and Tile,' and many others half-filled a bookshelf. A beefy, red-faced man in his sixties commanded the cluttered desk.

"Hanley," he said, and stuck out his hand. It was big, with thick fingers and rough with scars and calluses. "What can I do for ya?"

"Phil Bardo and Mary Haiger," Phil said as they shook hands. They moved some papers off of two side chairs and sat. "We won't take up too much of your time. We have a question about the Carillon Tower."

"Oh? I did this just a couple months ago. Setup for Homecoming. Wait-" he dug around in a pyramid of rolled up drawings, "here it is." He unrolled a drawing and spread it on his desk. It was an exterior layout of the Carillon Tower. "Gave a copy of this to that magician, so's he could plan his trick. He had to get the scaffolding approved through me to make sure he wouldn't damage the building. Nobody does nothin' like that without me approvin' it."

"Thanks, but that's not what we need," Phil said. "We're curious about a grate in the ground floor. What's it for, drainage?"

Hanley rolled up the drawing. "Why the hell would ya want to know about that?"

"We just like to know the practical side of how things work."

Hanley's eyes narrowed. "Well, I don't know. That's facilities infrastructure. Important stuff. Not just anybody can see it. Gotta be careful, what with terrorists and all." He reached into a drawer and brought out a handful of papers. "Ya gotta fill out these request forms and these background checks, both of ya, and they gotta be notarized. Then ya send 'em in. They'll be processed. The review board will check 'em and either approve or deny 'em. If they approve 'em you'll get a notice in the mail. If they don't, you won't." He held out the papers.

"Mr. Hanley," Mary said, "this is ridiculous and you know it! This is a state institution, paid for by the taxpayers, and covered by the State's open records laws. We are taxpayers. You can't withhold information. You might as well give it to us right now the easy way, otherwise we'll request every stinking detail of every building on this campus and you'll be pulling drawings until you retire!"

"Honey, simmer down, ain't nobody withholdin' information. It's just procedure. Do ya want it or doncha?"

Phil turned to Mary. "Darling, I think we went about this the wrong way. Maybe we should have called Moose first and asked him-"

"Moose? You a friend of Moose Mikleski?" Hanley asked.

"We had a nice long talk with him just last week at the Charity Ball. Well, sorry to bother you, Hanley, we'll call Moose." They rose to leave.

"Wait just a second." Hanley put the sheaf of papers back in the desk drawer. "I can maybe help ya a little." He turned around and flipped through a four-foot stack of drawings piled atop a cabinet, then tugged out one multi-page set and laid it on the desk. "This should cover it. The terrace infrastructure." He put his half-glasses on the end of his nose and studied the diagrams. He traced some paths with his finger, and turned the page. "Yep. See here. The steam tunnel runs underneath. That grate just lets warm air from the tunnel get up into the tower.

The tower was never plumbed for radiators or nothin', gets pretty damn cold in the winter."

"Steam tunnel?"

"Yeah. They're all over campus. All the older buildings are heated with steam, with radiators. We got a steam plant just off of University Avenue, and the tunnels have steam pipes that run to each of the buildings. We also use the tunnels for electric, phone, coax, and now fiber optic cables. Some ya can walk through, some are just big enough to pull somethin' through with a pull-tape."

"How big is the one under the Carillon?"

"Oh, that's one of the older ones. It's big enough to walk through in some spots."

"How do you get into these tunnels to do repairs and run cable?"

"There are more than a hundred access hatches on campus, in buildings and just scattered around the grounds."

"Mr. Hanley, you've been more than helpful. Thank you." Phil rose. "C'mon, Dear, let's let Mr. Hanley get back to his real work."

"Hey – when ya see Moose . . ."

"I'll tell him how big a help you were," Phil said. "Thanks again."

"That," Phil said when they got outside, "was perfect."

"*Honey? Darling? Dear?* Thought I was gonna puke!"

"Sorry, you weren't getting anywhere with threats and intimidation. I had to get him comfortable again, and that meant setting the women's movement back to something he was familiar with. You should just be happy I didn't ask you to unbutton your shirt for him."

"How'd you know to use the Moose connection?"

"It occurred to me that they were about the same age and in somewhat related businesses and might know each other. Plus, he had his autographed picture on the wall. Figured it was worth a shot."

"Well, bravo. Now we know how the killer got in and out."

"Yes. Now it's just a matter of who and why."

They walked back through campus, and Phil led a detour up to Bascom Hill and around South Hall. "I wonder . . .," he said as he searched around the base of the building. "Ah. Come look at this."

Mary worked her way between two bushes to stand next to Phil. There was a square concrete box behind the bushes next to the building. Set in the top of the box was a grate with hinges on one side and a hasp and lock on the other. There were footprints in the dirt next to the bushes.

"Care to guess what this is?" Phil asked.

"A steam tunnel access hatch?"

"That would be my guess. Maybe we ran into Dave's killer last night."

Back at the office Phil and Mary composed another letter to the DA. They described their theory on where the killer was when Dave was shot and how he got away, based on the steam tunnels, the grate, and the angle of the bullets.

Phil proofread the letter. "This will do it, for sure. I'll bet Daman will be cleared of charges and out of jail by sometime next week." Phil folded the letter and tucked it into an envelope. He applied a stamp and addressed it, and prepared to leave while Mary answered some emails.

"Here's a new door key – I got the lock re-keyed. Do you and Hoover need a ride home?"

"No, thanks. I've got a car today, it's out back."

"Do I get to ask a question?"

Mary folded her arms across her chest. "Well, I suppose. Go for it."

Phil watched her facial expression as he spoke. "Is it true that you aren't, and never have been, a grad student here at the UW?"

She was impassive, no clues, no surprise displayed, and she said "That's right."

"Why-"

"No," she interrupted, "you've had yours for today." She

unfolded her arms and ran her fingers through her hair. "I'll see you tomorrow."

Phil mailed the letter and went back to the Chocolate Shoppe. Sam had already left. He stayed to help with the nightly close, then got into Dave's car and headed back to Wilson Street.

"Sam?" he called, once inside the house. There was no response. Phil walked to the back bedroom where he discovered that all Sam's clothes were gone, even the bloody red dress in the plastic bag. He checked the washer and dryer – her clothes weren't there, either. She had gone. He wandered back to the kitchen and took out a bottle of rum, and poured a half-glass. When he settled down in a chair in the living room he noticed the small envelope leaning against the lamp on the end table. He opened it and read.

"Phil, thanks so much for everything. It means a lot to me, more than you know. I need to sort some things out and maybe then we can talk some more. I'm going to cook dinner for you right here, at seven o'clock, exactly one week from today. Be there! Sam."

CHAPTER THIRTEEN

The Walk-Up Clinic wasn't very busy that morning. Phil had to wait only fifteen minutes before he was shown to a treatment room. The young female physician put on some rubber gloves and found a sterile tweezers and a pair of small surgical scissors.

"I was going to do this myself," Phil said, "but I figured I'd mess it up and have to come in here anyway."

"What'd you do, cut yourself shaving? Time to change your blade, man." She began cutting the sutures and pulling the threads from the cuts on Phil's face. It didn't hurt.

"Broke a car window with my face."

"Oh. Next time, roll it down first." She tossed the instruments into a bin for sterilization. "All done. Those cuts will heal nicely. Should hardly be noticeable after a few months. You might have to be careful shaving around a couple of those, as the skin there will be bumpier than it used to be."

Sam had decided to go to her own regular doctor for the stitch removal and a check on her concussion. Phil had offered to go with her to the appointment, but she had declined. "Thanks, but there's no need," she said, "I'll see you later at work." He had hoped to go so he could see her outside of work. Her abrupt departure Thursday and her note about sorting things out made him feel distanced from her, a setback after they had gotten so much closer.

Phil returned to the Chocolate Shoppe. When Sam came in she went straight back to the office and checked Phil's face. "Mmm, not bad," she said, turning his head back and forth in the light. "And maybe just enough scarring to give you that slightly dangerous look."

"Your turn," he said. She sat down in the chair, turned the left side of her head to the light and lifted her hair with her spread fingers. Phil turned her head a little and moved some more hair and found the cut in her scalp. It was a good three inches long and a bit ragged, but the swelling was gone. "Looks much better," he said, "but if I were you I wouldn't plan on going to the 'bald' look. That's a shame – you have such a nicely shaped head."

"There go my plans to become a Tibetan monk."

"And the dizziness and headaches?"

"Gone and gone."

Phil stepped back and leaned against the desk. "Sam, did I do something this week . . . if I offended you . . ."

"No, no offense," she shook her head. "But you did do something. You got me thinking about some things, and I just had to go . . . it was time, anyway." She stood up. "I haven't figured it all out yet, and I can't explain it now, but when I'm ready I'll tell you about it." She smiled. "Now, I've got to get to work and you've got to go figure out who did this to us." She walked away, all slim hips, angular shoulders and black hair swinging. She wore black twill pants and a simple white cotton blouse, neat and back to normal. He felt warm again; he had felt cold since reading her note.

"Dale, I'm looking for a car." Phil leaned on the table, bringing his head close to the policeman's.

"Don't spill my coffee. There's a bunch of dealerships out on the south Beltline."

"I'm looking for a *particular* car. A black Lincoln Town Car, with a partial license plate of something-Z-something-1-something-something-2."

"I know this couldn't have anything to do with a certain murder investigation."

"Of course not."

"Because that would be a really bad idea for you to get involved in that."

"Absolutely. The guy dinged my door in the lot at the mall."

"Yeah? Which one?"

"Passenger side. Can you help me out?"

"Anybody with you?"

"No."

"Then you probably wouldn't have seen a ding on the passenger door, huh." Dale wrote in his notebook. "I'll call you. Was that a Wisconsin plate?"

"Oh. Sorry, I don't know."

Dale sighed and put away his notebook. "Just tell me what you find out, if there's any connection. Maybe I can help you stay out of trouble."

The Post Office attendant was happy to tell Mary the time when the mail was usually delivered to the houses on BurningTree – between ten and eleven o'clock every weekday, and usually about an hour later on Saturdays. Anything else they could do for a prospective homebuyer out there? No? Then, have a nice day!

She parked her car on County M. The mail truck passed her at ten-fifteen and disappeared down BurningTree, then reappeared five minutes later and moved on to the next street. Mary drove down BurningTree, past the house, and saw the mailbox screened from the house by a large cluster of bushes. The street was deserted; she turned around and drove back and rolled down her window. She opened the mailbox and pulled out a handful of mail, junk mail; even rich people get it. Some real mail, too, addressed to Mr. George King. She stuffed the mail back into the box and threw gravel with her tires as she drove off. George King. Should be easy to remember.

The phone on the nightstand rang, and the little red light next to the receiver flashed. He cursed, then said "Sorry, babe, remember where we left off," and rolled away from the girl with the creamy white skin and bleach-blonde hair; it was a wonder he could find her at all on the sheets. He snagged the receiver with his left hand and held it to his ear.

"What?" he demanded.

"Stephano? Casey Simmons."

"Oh, Jesus. If I had known it was you I wouldn't have answered."

"Thanks a lot."

"You've caught me at a delicate moment."

"Now? It's got to be only eleven a.m. out there! Too bad. I don't give a shit who or what you're doin', as long as she's of age. She *is* of age, isn't she?"

"Yeah, sure. In this state."

"Oh, lord. Anyway, I've got Phil Bardo on hold. He wants to talk to you, so I'll put him through."

"Whoa! I'm not talkin' to that guy! He'll be trying to get us to pay up on that disappearing Carillon trick."

"Relax, I took care of it. He's agreed not to take us to court if you will just talk to him about that night."

"You got that in writing?"

"Absolutely."

"Fuck." He looked over at the girl, who was busy trying to figure out how to operate the remote for the hotel TV. She'd wait – she's paid by the hour, anyway. "Oh, all right. Put him through."

The phone clicked. "Stephano?"

"Yeah."

"Phil Bardo. I want to talk to you about the night of October nineteen."

"Make it quick. You're holding up a business deal."

"When did you first meet my uncle?"

"About three o'clock that afternoon. He signed the contracts and I told him when to show up at the Carillon."

"When did you see him next?"

"At showtime."

"Did you search the Carillon before the trick?"

"If you mean 'was there anybody else left in there prior to the trick' the answer is no. My crew made sure there was nobody in there until we unlocked the door for that guy –

Thelma, Telman, whatever-"

"Daman."

"Okay, Daman, and your uncle."

"But you didn't search it yourself?"

"No."

"And your road crew-"

"They've been with me for two years. I don't use locals. The setup is too precise and requires too much rehearsal to use unskilled labor."

"You having any trouble with any of them?"

"The trouble they get into usually isn't with me, it's with the local cops after the show. I pay 'em too well for them to give me any grief personally."

"Did you have any input on my uncle's selection?"

"Not a bit."

"Do you know who did?"

"Nope, and I don't care. That selection was made before I got to town. Turn that thing down!" he said to the girl, and she stuck her tongue out at him, but she cut the TV volume down to a whisper.

"Did you meet with the Alumni Committee?"

"No, just with the student Homecoming Committee. But there were a couple members of the Alumni group who sat in with them."

"Do you remember who?"

"Some lawyer – Johnson, or Jackson or something like that. And there was a college professor, can't recall the name. Maybe a German-sounding name. He didn't say anything anyway."

"Did anything go wrong with the trick, or different from the way it was scripted to go?"

"Well, let's see, there was a murder . . ."

"Thanks, I'm aware of that. Anything else?"

"No."

"What happened after you heard the shots?"

"We ran the curtains faster than usual so we could get in there, and I unlocked the door."

"You were the first inside?"

"Yeah."

"What did you see?"

"Your uncle on the floor, and Daman next to him."

"What did you do next?"

"Pushed Daman out of the way and did CPR."

"Thanks for trying. Did Dave ever regain consciousness, did he say anything?"

"No. Are you about done?"

"Soon. Did you see a gun laying around anywhere?"

"No."

"Did you see Daman or the cops or anybody else pick anything up off of the floor?"

"No."

"What was Daman like?"

"In shock. Nearly non-functional."

"Who came in with you?"

"A couple of cops were the first in behind me. They helped with CPR and cuffed Daman."

"Do you know their names?"

"No."

"And then?"

"The ambulance showed up and took your uncle away, and the cops pushed everybody out and sealed the Carillon."

"Did they take statements?"

"Oh, yeah. Repeatedly. It was a lot like this, actually."

"What about the crowd. Anybody acting strange out there?"

"They were pretty quiet, except for one girl. She freaked out when they took your uncle out to the ambulance. She seemed to know him. I don't know, but I think they might have had to sedate her."

"Anything else I should know?"

"Yeah. You owe me a new costume; I can't get the blood out of the one I wore that night."

Stephano hung up the phone and turned his attention back to the girl. "Okay, darlin'," he said as he took the TV remote from her hand and dropped it to the floor, "time to get back to business."

She looked at her watch and frowned. "I'll hafta charge ya for another half-hour."

"But we haven't really done anything yet!"

"It's not my fault ya wasted time talkin' on the phone. That's the rule."

"But I have a coupon . . . two for one."

She giggled. "Silly, we don't take coupons . . . do we?"

By the time Mary arrived at Discreet Detectives that afternoon Phil was mid-way through a call with Beth Talbot about real estate. He set up an appointment to meet with Beth the following Monday to lay out more guidelines for the Scotch and cigar bar property and tour some available spaces. Mary threw her backpack on the side chair and sat cross-legged on the wooden floor in her jeans and sweatshirt. She waited for Phil to finish.

"I don't know where I'm going with this," he said after hanging up. "It's just a fishing trip. We've got to figure out why Dave was interested in real estate so I can get a focus for the meeting."

"Your face looks good."

"Huh?"

"I said your face looks good. Maybe better than before."

"Couldn't do it much harm, I guess. Now, Talbot said Dave hadn't contacted her. I wonder if he talked to any other realtors."

"How's Sam doing?"

"Fine. She moved back to her apartment yesterday."

"Good! I mean, I'm glad that she's better."

"Back to real estate. Why would he be interested? And he wasn't going to move the office; this has to be the cheapest rent around. He asked you to research old sales, not currently available properties?"

"Well, actually he wanted the current ones too."

"And have you been able to dig up any of the material

you had before?"

"Jeez, Boss, you've been keeping me so busy wearing costumes and running around the countryside . . . yeah, I have found some of the stuff. Speaking of running around, are we still on for the 5k tomorrow?"

"Yes, we are," Phil laughed. "Noon at the band shell at Vilas Zoo. Now, are you just about done getting off of the subject?"

"No, not yet. I'll meet you there at noon. Carry your cell so I can find you. Okay, now I'm done."

Phil sighed. "All right. Let's assume Dave was looking for a pattern of some sort. Why else would he ask for so much data over several years?

"So what kind of pattern do you want to look for?"

"Location, location, location. But that won't tell us much all by itself."

"It's a start. Do you want to spring for a mapping program? We could plot all the commercial sales from the last two or three years on a map by address."

Phil shook his head. "Good idea, but cash is tight right now. Let's just mark them on a city map spread out here on the floor."

"Think about it for a second, Phil. If we use a mapping program and plot from database data, we can add and subtract sales from the map based on related data values. It will be a lot quicker to explore patterns and correlations that way."

"I love it when you talk techie. You mean that we can add or subtract sales of, say, a certain square footage."

"And/or within a price range, or for a particular seller or buyer. Or realtor. It all depends on whatever data we put in the database. It would take days to do those kinds of visuals manually on a hardcopy map. With the right software it will take seconds. And that will be a lot cheaper when you consider my time. I'm *very* expensive."

"Yes you are, in so many ways."

"You know I'm right, so cough it up."

She was right, and Phil knew it. "Tell me what you need

and where to find it."

Mary got up and took a black pen from the desk and wrote the name of the software package on a slip of paper she plucked from the wastebasket. "Here," she said, "make sure you get the 'Windows compatible' version. You can find it at the University Bookstore." She beamed. "You won't regret this. While you're gone I'll work on rounding up more data. Oh, I almost forgot. I found a name for that house on BurningTree this morning. George . . ."

"George. George what?"

"I'm working on it. It was short, kinda familiar. Some kind of royalty. George . . . Earl. No. Duke? That's not it."

"King?"

"King. King George. George King. That's it, I'm sure."

"Next time write it down. George King. I think he's the guy that does those awful locally produced commercials for that refrigerator company, CoolKing. He owns the company. They do a huge business in custom commercial units and also high-end designer home units. He's a refrigerator magnate!"

Mary said nothing.

"Refrigerator magnate?"

Still nothing.

"Get it? Magnate? Magnet?"

"Yeah, I get it. I'm trying not to encourage you. My dad makes jokes like that. Now aren't you supposed to be going to get my software?"

Phil left the office and went to Terry's Car Care to retrieve his truck. It was ready and waiting, freshly washed, and he settled up for his deductible with a credit card. Inside the cab he ran his hand lightly over the remaining bloodstains on the seats and wondered how Sam was doing. Maybe she'd be ready to talk again in a week? He was glad he hadn't had the seat covers changed. The overhead door went up and he drove out of the service garage into the street. It felt good to be driving the pickup again, and it seemed like it had been a lot longer than just a week. He parked in the ramp around the corner from the bookstore and went in search of the software.

The sales clerk was helpful and soon his charge card was another few hundred nearer his limit.

"Hey, it's about time," Mary said when Phil reappeared.

"Had a little detour. Picked up my truck."

"What is it with boys and trucks?" She grabbed the box from him and gave him a hug around the waist. "That's the one. Thanks!"

"I know women like things in small boxes, but somehow I didn't think it was software."

"I'm not your average woman."

"I noticed." He felt a flash of heat, sparked by the contact and fueled by the conversation. He knew that if anything were to get done that day he'd have to leave. "Anything I can do for you?"

"No," she said, releasing him and waving the box in the air, "I've gotta install this, and I've still got a bunch of data to dig up. I think Sunday afternoon or Monday we'll be ready with data and everything. So you go rest up for that 5k and leave me alone to compute!"

"Okay, I'll go, but how about today's question?"

Her shoulders sank. "Not today, I want to ride this software high for the rest of the afternoon. You can have two tomorrow, okay? Please?"

She really wanted to be let off the hook. She had a passion for everything she did, even when it came to computers. Nothing halfway, Phil decided. "It's a deal," he said. "I'll see you at noon tomorrow."

"Good. Now get out of here before I do something that we'd both enjoy."

Phil cleared his throat. "'*You'll regret it. Maybe not today, maybe not tomorrow, but soon and for the rest of your life.*'"

"Oh, man, you're not making this any easier. Go!"

That made it even harder for Phil to leave, but he did.

CHAPTER FOURTEEN

Saturday brought perfect weather for the races, cloudless skies and cool temperatures in the low sixties. The routes started and ended at the band shell at the Vilas Park Zoo and the 5k and 10k shared both beginning and ending. A large banner hung from the band shell saying "Halloween Charity Run" and taped music played over the PA system while the racers pinned on their numbers. The 5k racers had red numbers, the 10k'ers black. Every vertical object, every tree, telephone pole, fence post, or trash can had racers pushing against it in a stretch. A large white wall-less tent stood beyond the finish line and prominently displayed the name of a local beer distributor.

Phil wandered the crowd near the band shell looking for Mary. He wore a 'Halloween Charity' t-shirt over Nike jogging shorts, cross-training shoes and a Chocolate Shoppe ball-cap. Around his waist he carried a black nylon butt-pack containing his wallet, keys, and cell phone. People he knew from the State Street business community were there, some to race and others for moral support. He saluted toward some and said a few words to others as he moved through the throng. Will from Terry's Car Care sported a red number; John Smith from Importante wore a black one. The Funnel Cake vending cart was drawing a good crowd and had attracted some local cops and paramedic personnel.

"Gotcha!" he heard as he felt someone grab his elbow. Mary had arrived. "Hey, I'm glad you brought that pack. I was afraid I'd have to carry my keys in my hands the whole way. Do you mind?" she asked as she unzipped the flap.

"Would it matter if I did?"

"Not really." She stuffed her keys into the pack and zipped it up again.

"You're looking good this morning," Phil said. He thought she looked the happiest he had seen her, with the possible exception of the moment when he had delivered the mapping software to her. She looked fresh, smiling and clearly in the best of moods. Her short-billed biker's racing cap was on backwards and a stub of ponytail stuck out from underneath. Large wrap-around sunglasses hid her eyes, and the shoulder strap of a red sports bra showed in the neck opening of her sweatshirt. On her bottom half she wore a black Lycra knee-length running skin and running shoes.

"Thanks."

"Is that just a costume or are you a regular runner?"

"I run, but I try not to make a habit of it."

"What do you make a habit of?"

"Outside? I like to bike." She pulled off her sweatshirt and tied it to a tree with its arms, then produced her number from her waistband. "Would you pin me?"

"Gladly." Phil took the number she offered and attached it to the back of her sports bra with its safety pin. He pinned slowly, admiring her physique. This has been worth the trip already, he thought. She was lean, well-toned, and what body fat she had was apparently concentrated on her chest – one-hundred-percent natural, he knew. No belly button ring, no tattoos. There were still a few bruises and scrapes on her back from her Halloween night collision on the sidewalk. He could see that her appearance was not lost on the other men in the vicinity; their heads had turned in her direction. When she trotted to a cooler to get a paper cone of water she was approached by a 10k'er. Phil couldn't hear what the man said to her, but he clearly heard her say "Fuck off, asshole" before coming back, laughing.

"What was that all about?" Phil asked.

"You really want to know?"

"Sure."

"He suggested that I should 'lose my father' and run the race with him. Among other things." She studied Phil for his reaction. "Does that bother you?"

"What do you think?" Phil leaned over and kissed her, long and hard on the mouth and she gave back as good as she got. He could see the 10k'er watching, and when they finally separated Phil faced the man and gave him a large grin. "Age isn't everything," Phil commented.

"There's something to be said for experience," Mary said. She glanced down and saw that her nipples stood out rock-hard from the cold and Phil's kiss. "Hello," she said and crossed her arms on her chest, "I need that sweatshirt for a while."

"It would be a damned shame to put that on. Let's stand in the sun and watch the opening ceremony."

They walked to the band shell and stood as the local dignitaries lined up on the stage. The mayor was there, as were Ruppert Taylor, the police chief, the race coordinator, and the beer distributor. They took turns at the microphone. "The weather . . . great event for the city . . . thousands of dollars for charity . . . largest registration yet . . . dedicated volunteers . . ." Phil heard only bits and pieces of the standard speeches as he daydreamed, one arm draped across Mary's shoulders. Then the 10k'ers gathered at the starting line. The police chief drew a starter's pistol and fired into the air, and the group lurched ahead, down the broad walkway for a pass through the outdoor animal exhibits and then out onto the street that led to the arboretum.

As the 10k spectators melted away into the zoo areas, the 5k'ers assembled at the starting line. Mary and Phil stood about two thirds of the way back in the pack, and when the gun sounded they had to wait a few seconds for everyone in front of them to ripple into motion before they could move. The 5k had many more participants than the 10k, many of them novices or partnerships; husband and wife of differing experience, mom and kids, grandma and grandpa, college kids. There were also some walking and a half-dozen wheelchair participants.

Mary and Phil ran comfortably and dodged through the crowd like determined shoppers at the mall during holiday season. They made it into the front half of the group and settled into a gap where the runners had spread out. Phil could feel sweat working its way under his cap and down onto his forehead. He looked at his companion; he could see dark wet areas advancing on her sports bra.

"You're sweating," he said.

"I don't sweat, I perspire. You need me to call 911 for you?"

"Not yet."

"Or maybe carry you for a while?"

"I'll let you know."

"So, Phil, what do you do for fun?"

"I work. But I try to get away once a year. Do an adventure vacation somewhere."

"Like what?"

"Kayaking on Lake Superior. Sailing to Catalina Island. Shark diving in the Bahamas. Camping in Tahiti. Climbing Mayan temples in Mexico."

"Cool. You go alone?"

"Sometimes. I have a travel buddy that I've gone with other times."

"And who's he?"

"She. An old friend."

"Sam?"

"No."

Mary was quiet for a few minutes. "Tell me about her."

"My travel friend?"

"No, Sam."

Phil thought before he continued. "She's been an employee for about three years. My 'right-hand man.'"

"I bet she'd love that phrase."

"She's great with the store, and the staff loves her. Smart, fun to be around."

"C'mon, you can do better than that. You know what I'm

asking."

He glanced sideways at Mary, met her gaze, then turned back to face the street. "We've become closer. Recently. When I think she might have died in that attack, I . . ."

"You in love with her?"

"I care about her a lot."

"That's not what I asked."

"No. I don't know. Maybe. We're friends, just starting to figure things out."

"Friends."

They ran on in silence. They rounded the three-kilometer mark and followed the road through one of the older neighborhoods, past a golf course, and headed back in the direction of the zoo. Phil had slowed, feeling soreness in his legs, and though he had crossed into his 'second wind' of energy his lungs were aching. Mary seemed to be unaffected other than having completely soaked her top with sweat.

"Your turn," Phil said. "What do you do for fun?"

"I go out sometimes. Dance clubs, concerts, but that's about it. My philosophy is 'enjoy the moment' because that's all I can afford. By the way, that was question number one!" She laughed and took quick sidelong glances at Phil.

"Do you have family here?"

"My folks and my brother live in DC. I've got a sister in Denver. That was number two." She looked at Phil again. "That was the best you could do?"

"Sorry. My brain's tired."

"You didn't make me work hard at all."

"I could ask a third one."

"Too bad – you'll have to wait until tomorrow."

Phil smiled. He didn't know why she played this question game, but he enjoyed it. He had many questions that he wanted to ask, some leading to answers that he wanted and needed to hear. Others – he was afraid to hear those answers. His low-ball questions stretched the game; he didn't want it to end. And he didn't want to force her to lie to preserve the real secret she held, whatever it was.

They re-entered the zoo and crossed the finish line, still ahead of about sixty-percent of the 5k runners. They watched the rest of the pack come in, and when their breath returned they got beers from the tent and drank them while waiting for the 10k runners to show. Mary retrieved her sweatshirt from the tree and put it on.

"What have you got going for the rest of the afternoon?" she asked.

"My apartment," he said. "I've run out of clean clothes at Dave's, and I can't put off cleaning up the mess at my place any longer."

"Hey, let me give you a hand with that. It's the least I could do."

"Why do you say that?"

"Never mind. It'll go a lot faster with two."

"You think so? Seems to me you have a talent for causing distraction."

"Yeah. It's part of my charm. Consider it an adventure vacation."

Phil shrugged. "All right, if you really want to." He unzipped the butt-pack and handed Mary her keys. "My apartment's down off of-"

"Don't worry, I can find it!" She turned and jogged off in the direction of the parking lot. Phil watched her. He wished he had her energy level. She wanted to spend time with him; now that was a good thing. He felt his legs stiffening so he did a few stretches and then walked to his pickup.

Mary arrived at Phil's apartment building about five minutes after he did. Phil had waited in the parking lot for her, and they climbed the stairs together to the second floor. Once inside Mary stood in the middle of the living room with her hands on her hips and looked around at the mess. "Oh mother," she said, then stripped off her sweatshirt and biker's cap and threw them into a corner. "Where do you want to start?"

They began with turning the furniture upright and setting

it back in position. Then it was bending, stooping, squatting and reaching to pick all the items from the floor and return them to their places on the bookshelves and tables. They worked up a sweat in the living room and when they finished there they paused for beers that Phil had bought at a convenience store on the way. Phil turned on the stereo and found the Badger football game – they were playing a team in a western time zone and the game had started later than usual. The kitchen was next. They cleaned the refrigerator and pulled everything from the cabinets and cleaned, then put it all back again. Phil washed the clothes that had sat on the floor in the hall for the past week. In the bedroom they put the dresser drawers back into the dresser. After returning the overturned mattress and box spring to the bedframe they made the bed. Then it was down to putting things away, with Phil giving directions on what had to go back in the closet and what went in which dresser drawers. Finished, Mary collapsed face-down on the bed, tired at last. Phil stood leaning against the doorframe.

"Thank you so much for helping. I would have been at this all weekend if I had to do it all myself."

"Yr wlcm," she said into the quilt.

"Let me take you out for dinner as a thank-you."

She rolled over onto her back. "Okay, do I get to pick the spot?"

"Sure. You think it over, I've got to take a shower."

Phil went into the bathroom. He stripped, climbed into the shower stall and turned on the water, nice and hot. He had a large tiled shower stall, and it had great water pressure and a seemingly unending supply of hot water. He stood, eyes closed, and let the stream pound on him. He was almost asleep standing up when he felt a hand on his hip.

"Care to share some of that water?" He turned sideways and let Mary edge under the spray with him. She held onto him until she was well soaked, then she backed out of the spray and took the rubber band off of her ponytail and shook her hair loose. Then she ducked back under the water. "I could use a shampoo – would you mind?" Phil handed her a bottle. She left the spray again and poured a palm-full of shampoo and put it on her hair. "Well?" She waited for him with her back turned.

"Do all your men do whatever you ask?"

"Pretty much."

"They don't mind?"

"It's funny. Nobody's ever complained."

He reached out and began to work the shampoo through her hair, working up a lather and kneading her hair with both hands, then massaging her scalp. Her head was tilted back and her eyes were closed, her breath almost a purr. Phil detached the hand-held showerhead and rinsed her down, chasing the shampoo suds down her back with the water. She turned and leaned on the tile wall, her forehead against her forearms on the wall. "Soap me now, please."

"Yes, ma'am." Phil took the bar of soap and started at her shoulders, rubbing the bar on her muscles and massaging them with his other hand. He worked down her back to her waist, then rubbed up a double handful of lather and set the bar on the holder, then reached around her with both hands. He started at her collarbones and moved his hands down her chest to her breasts, gently massaging them. Then lower, feeling her taut abs. She watched, head down, breathing through her mouth. He went back to the bar of soap and worked up another lather, then he placed one hand on her lower abs and the other on the small of her back and worked them both lower, kneading, lower still, following her curves until his hands met between her legs. Her eyes were slits, and her breath came in shudders. Phil moved down her legs, massaging all the way down to her ankles, then rinsed her off.

"That," she said, "is the way to take a shower. She turned to face Phil, and confirmed with her eyes and hands that his blood had indeed arrived where she had expected it to. Lacing her fingers behind his neck, she said "Lift me." Phil caught her under her buttocks and lifted, and she wrapped her legs around his waist and locked her ankles behind the small of his back.

He lowered and entered her, and they began to move in concert, breath by breath. Her breasts danced against his chest as she moved up and down, slowly at first. Then faster, harder as she rocked her pelvis, and she opened her eyes and stared unblinking into his. Faster and harder, and the water beat down on them and they moaned together, louder, and then they could stand it no longer and her back arched and he held her deeply down on him, their hearts pounding and their bodies in spasm together. He leaned into her, spent, her back against the wall of the shower. Gasping, she released her ankles and he set her down. They both leaned against the tile wall with legs shaking.

In the next moment the bathroom door burst open and three policemen with guns drawn threw back the shower stall door. All three drew beads on Phil.

"Hands on your head! Phil Bardo, you're under arrest for the murder of David Helms!" Phil and Mary stood open-mouthed, frozen. "I *said*, hands on your head! *Now!*" Phil complied. "Denny," one cop said, "you and Bob take him to the bedroom and get him dressed for downtown. The girl stays here." Two cops reached into the shower and each grabbed Phil by an arm and pulled him out, then escorted him to the bedroom.

Phil dried himself with a towel that one of the cops had brought from the bathroom, and began to dress. "This is a joke, right?" Phil asked. "Who put you guys up to this?" One of the cops pulled a card from his pocket. "You have the right to remain silent . . ." Phil heard the shower turn off and bits of conversation from the bathroom.

"Miller, you stupid son-of-a-bitch, what the fuck do you think you're doing?" Mary demanded.

"Haiger, nice to see you again." He looked her up and down, the blush of her orgasm still on her chest. "And I mean that sincerely. By the way you should be thanking me; the boys wanted to come in five minutes ago, but I made 'em wait until you were done."

"Goddamnit, you've fucked up everything! Jesus! You

have no idea. Give me a towel!" She snatched the towel Miller handed to her, and dried herself furiously. "He had nothing to do with it. Nothing! I *told* you guys that."

Miller laughed. "The DA thinks otherwise. Seems you're not credible – wrong team, plus he thinks your impartiality is compromised. Can you believe that? He signed the arrest warrant this afternoon. Oh, and the downtown crew executed a search warrant today at Discreet Detectives. Found some interesting stuff."

"Jesus, oh, Jesus," Mary said, "you guys are *so* fucking dumb!" She wrapped the towel around her and pushed past Miller to the bathroom door. She got to the door as Phil was being led away in handcuffs by the other two cops. He looked at her as he went by, his eyes dead.

"Phil, God no, this isn't what you think. It really isn't! Give me a chance to explain. Phil, please . . ."

Lars took the call in his office at home. The office was small and just off of the dining room behind a pair of French doors. He had taken care to be sure that it looked like a stereotyped lawyer's office; floor-to-ceiling bookshelves were packed with large bound hardcover volumes marked *Law Review* and *Wisconsin Statutes* on their spines. A mahogany desk sat on an oval rug in front of the window, a leather cornered desk blotter with a green felt insert protected the desktop, and a brass accountant's lamp with a green glass eyeshade stood on one corner of the desk. The multi-line phone and answering machine sat on the other corner. The chair was high-backed, red leather, with ornamental brass nails. Behind the chair and under the window stood a faux antique credenza, oriental style, with a fax machine and a printer on it. The one wall space not covered with a bookshelf held an English print of a hunting scene, noblemen riding horses in pursuit of hounds.

Barbara was asleep on the family room couch, the television still on in the corner of the room. It was nine p.m. when the call came in and she roused at the ring and picked up the portable handset. "Hullo? Just a minute. Lars," she called with one hand over the mouthpiece, "line one!" She listened until he picked up, then she listened a little more and then hung up and reached for the remote.

Lars punched the speakerphone button. "Lars Jackson," he said, and leaned back in his chair.

"Lars, it's Phil Bardo."

"Phil, how's it going? Hope you had a good time at the Ball last week."

"Lars, I need your help. I'm in the city jail. They've arrested me for the murder of Dave Helms."

"What? You've got to be kidding!" Jackson rocked forward in his chair.

"No joke. I'd like to get out of here. What can you do for me?"

Jackson rubbed his face with both hands. "Not much, I'm afraid. They won't do arraignment and assign bail until Monday. They do it on weekends for drunk and disorderly, but not capital murder. Oh, man." He rubbed his face again. "You're in there until Monday. At least."

"Can you handle the arraignment for me? And how about defending me?"

"I can do the arraignment. But Christ, Phil, I do so little court work . . . "

"But you do criminal cases, right?"

"Mostly corporate law. A little criminal work now and then, you know – vandalism, petty theft, small stuff for old clients with bad kids. But murder . . . that's out of my league."

"Lars, please! Think it over. Or at least help me find someone."

"Yeah, we'll see. I'll come see you tomorrow and we'll talk through what happened, and I'll fill you in on what to expect on Monday. Bail. I'm assuming they won't deny bail. Do you have any cash available?"

"Lars, you know better than that. I can pledge some assets, but I don't have much cash."

"Then you'd better be thinking about where you might get some. Friends, whatever. Make some calls tomorrow."

"I will. Please come by in the morning."

"I'll be there." Lars hit the disconnect button. He reached into the briefcase standing next to his desk and found his Day-Timer. He flipped through the address section and located a phone number, then picked up the handset and dialed.

"It's Jackson. What's the meaning of this? . . . You know what I'm talking about . . . No, it was goddamned stupid . . . He just called me . . . Wants me to get him out and defend him . . . I told him no . . . What? . . . No, that puts me in a very awkward position . . . No, morals and ethics . . . Very funny . . . I said no. He's an old friend and client, for God's sake, I can't." Jackson listened and drummed his fingers on the desktop. Then his drumming slowed to a stop, and Jackson's face grew slack and lost color. "You bastard . . . I can't believe . . . Well, I guess I don't have much choice, do I." He hung up the receiver.

"What's wrong?" Barbara stood at the door. Lars had no idea how long she'd been there.

"They arrested Phil for murdering his uncle."

"Oh, no! He didn't do it, did he?"

"No, of course not. Don't wait up for me – I've got some work to do tonight."

Mary sat in the fiberglass bucket chair in front of the glass window, second carrel from the left, on the third floor of the City-County building. There was a narrow counter in front of her and the glass reached from the countertop to the concrete ceiling. A wall phone hung on the left side of the carrel. The setup on the other side of the window was a mirror image. She didn't know what to do with her hands. They shook, and she tried to quiet them by rolling them up in the bottom of her sweatshirt. She shifted her chair on the dirty gray linoleum floor. The visitation room was empty except for a guard at the far end; it was not yet time for the Saturday night rush. The bare fluorescent lights hummed overhead.

She heard a door open somewhere, then the sound of footsteps. Phil appeared dressed in an orange jumpsuit, and sat in a fiberglass chair on the opposite side of the glass. He sat expressionless, staring at her.

Mary picked the phone receiver off of the cradle and held it to her ear with both hands to keep it from shaking. She waited.

Phil sat, arms crossed, and made no move to pick up his phone. He could see her lips form the word 'please.' Her eyes glistened and the corners of her mouth trembled. He slowly reached for the phone.

"Phil, I didn't set you up! Really. You've got to believe me."

"Sure. Look where believing you has gotten me so far."

"I know what it looks like, but you're wrong. We'll get you out of there and I'll tell you everything. Oh God, I can't believe this happened!"

"I'm such a sucker. I'll bet you and your friends have had a good laugh."

"Stop it, it's not like that!"

"BA in radio, TV, and film, eh. You didn't mention acting classes, but I should have guessed. You're pretty good. It's over, you can drop the act now."

She cast her eyes down at the countertop. "I suppose I deserve that. There's no act, not now. But I need to explain, and maybe you'll . . . but I couldn't before, and I'm not supposed to now, but-"

"If you've got something to say, just say it."

"Okay." She released the phone with one hand and dug in the back pocket of her jeans. "This is going to go badly anyway, so let's get it over with." She produced a slim black leather card case, flipped it open and pressed its face against the window.

It was an ID, and next to Mary's picture and name Phil read 'Special Agent, Federal Bureau of Investigation.' Phil put his phone receiver back on the cradle, rose, and walked away from the window. Mary heard the sound of a door in the distance, then the hum of the lights.

The Sycamore Pub was having a typically slow Saturday night. The green neon sign was lit. The portion of the sign saying 'Mike 'n' Oscar's' was out, but the name 'Sycamore Pub' and the bushy tree symbol were bright. The pub was a block off of campus to the south, nowhere near the chaotic nightlife on State Street. On a little island of buildings that split University Avenue and Johnson Street, it usually saw most of its business over the lunch hour.

"Mike, still got some of that Guinness?" Oscar asked. He gestured over his shoulder. "Lady in the corner wants it. And lots of extra napkins."

Mike leaned over and dug in the chest cooler behind the bar. He found a bottle of Guinness and dried it on a bar towel, then popped the cap off and grabbed a glass and a handful of napkins. "If you don't mind I'll take this one myself."

He walked to the dark back corner of the room and set the napkins on the table, then poured a half-glass of the stout leaving a creamy, bubbly half-inch head. It always reminded him of pancake batter. He set the glass and the bottle on the table and then pulled a chair over from the next table and sat down.

"So, what are you here for this time?"

"Therapy," Mary replied.

Mike grunted. "Someday I'd like to see you come in here when you're not having a problem."

"You wouldn't recognize me. How's Annie?"

"Good, real good. Her practice is picking up. Maybe you should go talk to her again instead of the St. James Gate Brewery."

"I'll give that some thought."

"Yeah, sure you will."

She took a long drink from the glass and wiped the foam from her lip with a napkin. "There's this guy. He's in a lot of trouble, but it isn't his fault. He thinks it's my fault, but it's not. Mostly not, anyway. And he won't let me explain . . . shit, it's starting already." She wiped her eyes with a bar napkin. "I thought we had a chance, but now . . ." Her lips trembled.

"Does he know how you feel about him?"

"I don't know. I thought so, but . . . damn." She wiped her eyes again. "He doesn't believe anything about me anymore."

"A hazard of your profession. Anything I can do?"

She shook her head. "No, I just need to be alone, but not too alone. Know what I mean?"

"Yeah."

Mary held the bar napkins to her eyes. "I've got to figure out how to fix things. I've . . . uh-oh, here we go . . . put something sad on the CD player."

"Yep." Mike got up and went back behind the bar. "Oscar, put on 'Blue' for me would you? And turn it up." As the music started he watched the young woman collapse on the table, body racked with sobs. He checked his watch. "I've gotta take a walk. I can't watch it again. I'll be back in an hour. She'll be okay by then." Mike took off his apron and left it on the bar as he walked out the door.

"Can I use your phone?" Mary laid the Guinness bottle, her glass, and a wad of used napkins on the bar. "My cell is dead. Along with everything else in my life."

"Sure," Oscar said, and set the phone on the bar. "Is it really all that bad?"

"Oh, yeah. And it's about to get worse." Her face was red and puffy, but she had pulled herself together. The breakdown and rebuild was complete. She took a piece of paper from her wallet and looked at it, then dialed the phone.

"Sam? This is Mary Haiger. Sorry to bother you this late, but we've got a big problem. We need to talk. Right now. I'm coming to your place. Yeah, I know where it is. I'll be there in fifteen." She hung up and scooted the phone toward Oscar. "Thanks."

"You okay?"

She nodded. "Tell Mikey I rallied. That was just what I needed. I figured out my game plan. Thanks for putting up with me." She took a ten-dollar bill from her wallet and laid it on the bar.

"Hell, you went through more than that in napkins. Keep it. It's on me."

"You sure?"

"Yeah. Now git, before *I* have a breakdown!"

She laughed and slid off the barstool and went out the door.

Oscar rang up a tab and took some bills from his pocket and put them into the till, then cleared the bar. Mike walked in a few minutes later and after looking around joined Oscar behind the bar.

"Well?"

"You called it. She was back in business about five minutes ago."

Mike nodded. "Good."

.

CHAPTER FIFTEEN

The deputy searched Lars Jackson and his briefcase, tape recorder, and laptop computer. Satisfied, he escorted Jackson to a private conference room, bare except for a metal table bolted to the floor and two wooden chairs.

Lars set his tape recorder and a legal pad on the table and waited. The door opened and Phil entered wearing his orange jumpsuit. The guard closed the door and locked it from the outside, then watched through the small window in the door as Phil took his seat at the table.

"Nice outfit," Lars said.

"Thanks. My fashion coordinator picked it out for me."

"Phil, I've thought it over. I'll defend you, if you still want me."

"I'd like that. And you can add others to the team if you need to, but I need you to lead it. Somebody I can trust."

"All right. Let's start with the arraignment hearing tomorrow. I'll be there with you, and you won't have to say a thing. The judge will read the charge against you and ask for your plea. The charge will be murder in the first degree. I'll enter your plea of not guilty, and the prosecutor will ask for bail to be denied. He'll make something up about how dangerous you are to society, or that you are a flight risk. I'll counter that, and the judge will set bail. Then all you need to do is put up the cash for bail, and you'll be out by noon."

"How much will the bail be?"

"That's a good question. There are no bail guidelines in this state; the judge has complete discretion. If you were a famous local, you might just get away with a signature bond.

180

For a person of your means, your first offense, local small businessman with strong ties in the community, not likely to flee or commit another murder, I'd guess one to two hundred. You get it all back if you show up for all your court appearances."

"One to two hundred. Thousand."

"Yes."

"Holy . . . I don't have that kind of cash laying around. Can Dave's account or the insurance-"

"Nope, you can't use that, it isn't yours yet. Talk to your friends or your bank. Wisconsin doesn't permit bail bondsmen."

"I'll get to work on rounding up some cash today. What's next?"

"Next we talk about the case." Lars started the recorder. "I talked with the prosecutor's office this morning and I got the basics of their case. For motive they've got your inheritance from Dave. Remember we had to file preliminary probate with the court on his assets? That included the life insurance policies. It's all public record. They got a warrant for your bank balances and your store's accounting records, and they show that you're not exactly flush."

"Go on."

"Opportunity. They'll need to show that you could have been available to do the killing, and you'll need to have some alibi that shows you couldn't. Where were you on the Friday of the murder?"

"I was camping and kayaking on the shore of Lake Superior."

"Any witnesses? Anybody see you up there?"

"Not that I can think of. It was a rustic camp, nobody around – late in the season. I reserved and paid for the site over the Internet; there'd be a record of that."

"Gas, food. Did you buy gas or go to any restaurants with a credit card? Your statement would show dates and locations."

"No, I paid cash. I suppose some people saw me, but I

wouldn't know who."

"How about cell phone calls? We could get a trace of the call paths through the cells. That would prove where you were."

Phil thought about that one. "Yes, I called the store Thursday, the day I left, and again on Monday. That's when I found out about Dave."

Lars shook his head. "No good. You could have gone out of town Thursday to set an alibi, come back and done the deed Friday, then gone out of town again to complete the alibi. We'll leave that for now and come back to it later." Lars rearranged himself on the chair and leaned on the table. "They think they've found the murder weapon."

"Really? That's fantastic! Where?"

"They got a search warrant yesterday for Dave's office. They found a .38 in the desk. It has your fingerprints all over it. They swabbed the inside of the barrel. It's been fired recently."

"Oh, shit." Phil thought back to that day in the office when he had examined the gun. "I picked it up and looked at it, it never occurred to me . . ."

Lars doodled on his legal pad. "They also found some other interesting stuff. Diagrams of the Carillon. Photos. Looks like somebody's been casing the place. They confiscated a computer and are searching that now."

"But we were using those to figure out the trick and how the murder was done! We submitted a claim to the magician for solving the trick!"

"We? Who's 'we'?"

"Me, and Mary Haiger. She's an employee; she was Dave's employee. Turns out that she's with the FBI. She's probably part of the prosecution's case. Probably set me up."

"But if she testifies honestly about how those documents were being used, she might be very useful to us. What else can you tell me about her?"

Phil hesitated. "Well, I don't know much about her, but we had a relationship . . ."

Lars groaned and slammed his pen down on the legal pad.

"No, please tell me you didn't fuck her. Please." He stared at Phil. Phil didn't answer. "Great. Just great," Lars said. "Any testimony she gives that appears to help you will be discounted on the basis that she's lying to protect her lover. Jesus!" Lars fumed for a minute. "I'll have to talk to her anyway, maybe we can make something out of this." He made some notes on the paper. "Do you have anything else you can tell me?"

Phil shrugged. "Maybe a couple things. You know that Sam and I got beat up after the Charity Ball?"

Lars nodded. "Yes, I saw the police report this morning."

"That same night somebody broke into our apartments and searched them."

"Oh? Where are the reports on those?"

"I never called the cops. Didn't appear to be anything missing."

Lars wrote notes and shook his head.

"And Halloween night Mary and I saw somebody coming out of Dave's office, but he got away."

"And again, I suppose you didn't call the cops."

"No."

"The prosecution tells me that you sent the DA some things. They're going to have to give me copies, but I haven't seen them yet. Tell me about them."

"I sent two letters. The first one to prove that Daman couldn't have done the murder. And the second to document how it was done via the steam tunnel under the Carillon."

Lars put his pen down. "So you took it upon yourself to play detective and ruin the DA's case against Daman, and then provided him with everything he needed to build a case against you."

"Kinda looks that way, doesn't it."

"Need I remind you that you don't have a PI license or training? You don't, do you?"

"No. But I'm not doing cases for hire, so I don't need a license, right?"

"Right. So now instead of being a snoop, you look like a criminal." Lars turned off the tape recorder and leaned forward. "You didn't do it, did you?"

"Lars, don't be an ass. Of course not."

He sighed, and pressed 'record' on the tape recorder. "Tell me a little about the arrest. Maybe we'll be lucky and they screwed it up."

"Didn't you read the report?"

"Yeah, but I want to hear it from you."

"It was yesterday at my apartment, around six p.m. We were in the shower-"

"There's that 'we' again. Was it that 'Haiger' woman?"

"Yes."

"That's funny. There's no mention of her in the arrest report. "

"She was there. I guarantee it."

"Probably some deal between the FBI and the police department. Maybe we can use that. Then what?"

"They pulled their guns on me and hauled me away."

"Did they read you your rights?"

"Yes."

Lars packed up his legal pad and recorder. "I don't know, Phil. This doesn't look good. It's circumstantial, but that's usually enough to convict. If I were you I'd give serious thought to a plea bargain. You'll do time but not as much as you would under an outright loss in court."

"I can't do that, Lars. I'm innocent. If I go to jail on a plea bargain or on a conviction my life's over."

"Think about it." Lars stood up and walked to the door. "I'll see you at nine tomorrow in front of the judge." He knocked on the door. The guard unlocked and opened the door and let him out, then motioned to Phil.

Mary sat on the floor in her living room, leaning back against the couch. Hoover sprawled on the floor in front of her with his head on her lap. She held the phone to her ear with one hand while scratching the dog under his jaw with the other.

"Richard," she said, "that doesn't cut it! I expect more

from you than that! First you let his uncle do your work for you, then Phil. And when he gets into trouble, you walk away."

"It's a local murder case," said the voice on the phone. "We've got nothing to do with it. If we get involved now we'll jeopardize the real investigation."

"We already are involved," she replied, "I'm sure to be called to testify. I sent you what we had; you know Phil isn't a murderer. Lean on the DA. Call him and tell him that Phil is clean."

"No. This is the way it's going to go down. You'll give a sworn deposition and you'll leave the Bureau out of it. I'm transferring you back to Chicago. This has gotten personal for you, and you aren't any good to us there. Pack up, I want you here in my office Wednesday morning."

"I don't think so, Richard! You're damn right this is personal!" She hung up and worked her way out from under the bulldog's head. She found a Post-It at her desk and wrote the date and "I quit" on it and signed her name. Then she dropped it in an envelope along with her FBI identification card. On the front of the envelope she wrote 'Big Dick' Butler, and the address of the FBI office in Chicago. She applied a stamp, and it was ready to go in the mail.

The wind bit into Tom's face as he worked on the north fence line. Something had happened overnight in the atmosphere; the jet-stream had dipped and spilled a mass of Canadian air over the border. It had been in the sixties the day before, but now he guessed the temp was in the forties. The wind came unobstructed across the bare fields on the farm just north of the city, and pushed the wind-chill down into the twenties. He struggled with the roll of snow fence as he unrolled it along the barbed wire fence line. He hoped his work would keep the snow in the barnyard a little more manageable and the driveway to the house more clear. Last year he hadn't gone through the effort, and the wind drove snow dunes halfway up the sides of his old two-story farmhouse.

He caught a faint whistle. He turned his head in the

direction of the farmhouse and he could see a small figure waving something in the air. Nancy was calling him in. It was just as well; he could use a break from the cold. Tom pulled the hitch pin to separate the utility trailer from the tractor, then climbed onto the frigid steel-pan seat and started the old Massey-Ferguson. It rattled and shook, and Tom eased it into gear and drove back to the farmhouse.

"Phil's on the phone," Nancy said when Tom entered the kitchen. "He said it was really important. Now Joseph," she said to the back end of a teenage boy scavenging in the refrigerator, "it's almost lunchtime." He ignored her and continued to dig.

Tom picked up the handset. "Yo, Phildo, what's goin' on? No, I haven't heard anything, I've been out in the yard. Whoa, say that again?" Tom grabbed a kitchen chair by the back and spun it around, then sat straddling it backwards. "No. No way. I don't know how you get yourself into these messes." He pinched the handset between his ear and his shoulder as he worked his coat off and let it fall on the floor behind him. "Anything you need, just . . ." Tom glanced at Nancy. "Wow, that's a lot, but yeah, I can do that . . . call me when you know exactly how much . . . City-County building. Right. See you tomorrow." He hung up and turned to Nancy. "We've bailed each other out so-to-speak for almost forty years. Now he really needs to be bailed out – he's in jail. He needs a loan for bail." He waited.

"Do it," she said, "whatever you need, do it. Just don't tell me how much."

Sam was seated at the visitation carrel when Phil arrived. She wore a leather jacket, open, and had a purple knit scarf bunched up in her lap. She smiled when Phil sat down and she held up the front page of the Sunday *Wisconsin State Journal* so he could read it through the glass: 'Police Scoop Up Chocolate Shoppe Owner in Murder' was the second story headline. They each picked up their handsets.

"Hey," Sam began, "any publicity is better than none. We

had more customers than usual this morning. Brilliant marketing scheme, Phil."

"Trust me, this was not in my plans. This was a set-up, Sam. I had nothing to do with Dave's murder."

"I know that. We'll find a way to prove it. Somehow." She put the paper down. "This is serious stuff. I hope it doesn't happen a lot when you play detective. Now, when are you getting out of here?"

"Tomorrow, I hope. Should get bail assigned in the morning, and I've got someone lined up to pay it. Maybe I'll be out by the afternoon."

She nodded. "Don't worry about the ChoSho, I'll take care of that. Is there anything else I can do?"

"Talk to the staff. Tell them that I'm innocent."

"I already have. I called them all last night."

"Last night? But the paper didn't come out until this morning. How'd you find out last night?"

"Mary called and told me."

Phil slumped in his chair. "Shit, Sam, she was in on it. I don't know how or why, but she was part of the set-up."

Sam shook her head. "No, I don't think so. You really need to let her explain. You were quite rude to her last night."

"Sam, she's an FBI plant! She fed them information, set it up to incriminate me for some reason. She betrayed me!"

Sam leaned forward and put her elbows on the counter. "No. She was blindsided as much as you were. She came over last night and told me everything."

"What?" Phil sat bolt upright. "She came to your apartment? And told you everything. How much of 'everything?'"

"Everything-everything. At least you were really clean when you got to jail."

Phil slammed his fist on the counter. "Damn it! Sam, I'm so sorry, this is the last way I would have wanted you to find out."

She waved her hand. "You don't owe me any apologies."

"I'm not a murderer now but I might be after I get out of

here!"

"Please, Phil, listen to me. You need to let her explain. She's on your side, and you need her help to get out of this."

"Bullshit."

"Damn it, Phil, the least you can do is hear her out! She abandoned her career to help you!"

"How do you know that?"

"She told me." Sam nodded over her shoulder. "She's outside, waiting to talk to you."

"Yeah, her credibility is at an all-time high right now. What makes you think she's telling you the truth?"

"All right, name one time when she actually lied to you. Just one."

"She said she was a grad student."

"That's pretty harmless, you have to admit. Part of her cover. Any time when she lied to you about anything important?"

"Well, it wasn't as much lying as it was not telling."

"There's a big difference. Please, Phil, don't blow it this time. Let her explain."

Phil studied Sam's face, looking for – well, exactly what, he didn't know. Hurt, perhaps betrayal. Disappointment. But what he saw was purpose, determination. Confidence.

"Okay. I'll talk to her."

"Good." Sam got up and collected her newspaper and scarf. "Don't you dare let me down," she warned, and hung up the handset. She turned and left the room.

"FBI," Jackson said into the phone, "he said she works for the FBI! I suppose you knew that . . . Well, thanks *so* much for sharing. Jesus!" He took his handkerchief from his pocket and wiped his forehead. "I don't like this, not at all . . . Yes, I'm defending him . . . It's not that simple, especially now with the FBI poking around . . . Yeah, yeah, I heard you the first time."

He punched the disconnect button on the desk set. Then he opened the bottom right drawer on his desk and reached down between the hanging files. His fingers closed on a small glass bottle, and he brought it up to the desktop. He stared at the bottle of vodka, then cracked the seal and poured some into the glass on his desk.

Mary came in and sat in the chair Sam had vacated. She picked up the handset as Phil began to speak.

"Why'd you have to get her involved? Of all people, why her?"

"Oh, right, that's *my* fault, Phil. Let me remind you who took her to the Charity Ball and got her head bashed in. She's been involved, she just didn't know it. All I did was give her information so she could make an informed choice. Besides, you need all the help you can get."

"Thanks to you."

"Look, I owe you an explanation. I hope you'll shut up and listen this time."

"You mean we don't have to play twenty-questions today?"

"No games today, Phil. I'm not in the mood."

He glared at her, and she began.

"I got my undergrad degree here at the UW. I went to a job fair on campus and got recruited by the FBI. It was something I'd always wanted, since I was a kid watching old movies and detective shows. I went through a year of training in DC, then I was assigned to the Chicago office as a resource agent. That happens a lot to women with strong computer skills. I was only there a few months when I got sent to Madison, my first field assignment. They needed someone to blend in with the University community, to help with research on an investigation. There was no other agent assigned here." She paused. "That's when I started working for your uncle."

"Why him?"

"Dave had stumbled across something that bothered him, something that bothered him enough to call the FBI. They wouldn't assign a regular field agent, but they did send me. To help Dave, to do background research for him. And to have him tutor me."

"C'mon, that seems pretty irregular. A PI doing investigation for the FBI? And tutoring an agent?"

"Phil, how do you think Dave got into the PI business?"

Phil was silent.

"He was ex-Bureau," she continued. "After he retired, he opened Discreet Detectives. And he did favors for the Bureau now and then."

"So what was the investigation?"

"Well, that's the problem. I don't exactly know. My orders from Chicago were to just do whatever Dave wanted me to do. Dave didn't explain what was going on – he'd ask me to find data on things, do research – we've already talked about that part. I think he was just trying to gather enough raw material first, then we were going to try to put it together. Another week and I would have known what he was working on. But he died, so I stayed on with you to try to figure it out."

"Why the hell didn't you tell me?"

"When you're under cover you're generally not supposed to go blabbing the details of your assignment."

"I get it."

"I sure hope so. I sent them information about the murder as we discovered it, because I'm convinced it's all connected. Either somebody in the Bureau or somebody at the DA's office wants you to butt out and turned this thing around on you."

"And the Bureau won't tell you about the investigation?"

"They wouldn't tell me before, and they certainly won't now. I'm no longer on the team. I quit."

"Why? Why give up everything you've worked for?"

She hung her head. "They were going to ship me back to Chicago this week. Make me give a sworn statement in case somebody asked for my testimony in your murder trial. And it wouldn't have been one that mentioned the FBI investigation or helped you." She looked up at Phil. "They don't give a rat's ass about you or the murder. They don't think you did it, but they don't want anything to disturb their precious investigation. They'll assign someone else to pick up where Dave and I left off."

"So you could have walked away-"

"And left you high and dry. But I didn't. I couldn't. Do I have to fuckin' spell it out for you?" She glared at him. "Do you honestly think I jump into bed with just any guy who comes along? Or that I would do it on orders from my boss?"

"No. At least I hoped not."

"For the record, what we did had everything to do with you and me, and nothing to do with my goddamned job!"

She dropped the handset and it bounced and rattled on the counter. Her hands shook as she looked away and combed her fingers through her hair. Phil gave her a minute, then rapped on the glass. She picked up the receiver again.

"And Sam. You told her everything."

Mary nodded. "Yes, everything."

"Why'd you have to do that?"

"She wanted to help, and she needed to know all of it. She's an adult - she needs to know what she's getting into, and who she's up against. Somebody had to be honest with her, and it didn't look like it was going to be you."

"Well-"

"Wait, there's one more thing. Your apartment. Sam's apartment. That was me."

"What?"

She sighed. "I thought you were moving too fast, getting in over your head. I didn't know what to do. I figured maybe if you thought somebody was onto you, you'd back off a little. So I trashed your places. Sorry."

"And the batting practice?"

"Not me. No way."

"I don't know what to say."

"Don't say anything, not now, just don't shut me out. Please. After all that's happened I don't think I could handle that." Mary hung up her handset and headed for the door without another glance at Phil. He was still holding his handset when the door banged shut.

CHAPTER SIXTEEN

It was over by ten minutes after nine, just as Lars had predicted. The judge set bail reasonably at seventy-five thousand, in spite of the prosecutor's arguments. At Phil's call Tom came in from the farm, withdrew cash from his account and put up the bail. Phil was dressed in his street clothes and walking out of the City-County building by noon.

"Where to?" Tom asked as they got into the cab of his pickup.

"My apartment. I've got to wash the jail off of me, get into some fresh clothes, and pick up my truck."

They drove in silence around the Capitol Square, edging from light to light in the lunch-hour traffic. Tom turned down King Street to Wilson, then followed that to John Nolen Drive for the ride south.

"Tom, how'd we get so old all of a sudden?" Phil asked.

"Huh? I thought doing jail time hardened a guy. What are you doin', getting all soft and philosophical on me?"

"Dave's murder started me thinking."

"Dyin' will do that."

"I woke up one day last week and realized that I'm just a few years from being fifty. I'm not ready to be that old."

"Being fifty sure beats the alternative. And fifty isn't as old now as it used to be."

"I suppose. But I feel like I'm still in my twenties or thirties in my head. I think I've been so focused on my business I've missed out on a lot."

"Keep your nose to the grindstone too long and all you wind up with at the end is a flat nose?"

"Something like that."

"You know you can't do it all. It's mutually exclusive choices, every day. You're always goin' to miss out on somethin'. You can't know what it's like to live in the same small town your whole life and also know what it's like to live your whole life in Manhattan."

"So, your secret to a happy life is learning to make the right choices."

"Not necessarily. That can result in paralysis, and no choices get made. The real secret of happiness is learnin' to believe that the choices you make are the right ones."

"Subtle. The ol' Country Philosopher strikes again."

"If you're acquitted you won't just go back to the same old thing you've been doin'?"

"No."

"Hah! We'll see about that."

"But if I go to jail on this murder I may not be eligible for parole until I'm nearly seventy. And there's people I want to be with, things I haven't done that I want to do, and all that will be gone. I don't want to give those up."

"Then you've got no choice, do you? You have to beat this." Tom drove on, past the Dane County Coliseum. "So who is she?"

"Who is who?"

"Hey, remember who you're talkin' to. I've seen the signs before. It isn't just Dave's murder or getting older, and it isn't just about the trial. There's a 'somebody,' too. Anyone I know?"

"No. And it's not that simple. There's one I've known as an employee for years. I think I'm seeing her in a new light."

"Oh? Does she see you in this new light, too?"

"I don't know."

"Well, don't waste your time or hers. You'd better find out."

"And there's another one. It's there physically with her, but-"

"Two! Do they know about each other?"

"They do now."

"No shit! That should be fun. You do have something to motivate you. If you had to choose between them right now, which one would you pick?"

Phil shook his head. "I don't know, not yet. I don't even know how to know. You've been married a long time; how did you know that Nancy was the right one?"

"There's no easy answer to that." Tom pulled a toothpick from his jacket pocket and stuck it between his lips, then worked it back and forth with his tongue. "One day you just know. Maybe it's when you have to talk to her every day, *have to*, even though you may have nothin' new to say. Or when you realize you'd give up everything you've got for her and she'd do the same for you, but neither one would ever ask that of the other. Maybe it's when goin' through life suddenly seems pointless if she's not there goin' through it with you." Tom thought for a minute and shifted the toothpick. "I don't know, Phil, I suppose it's different for everybody. For some people it's probably enough just to have great sex."

"And the perfect one has it all."

"There's no 'perfect.' It's stupid to wait for perfect. If everybody waited for perfect nobody'd ever get married. You'll never find it, even if you could figure out what it was. I'll bet you twenty bucks you can't really define your perfect woman. Besides, perfect would be pretty damned boring. Discovery, adaptation, adjustment, compromise, acceptance – that's all part of the fun, keeps it interesting."

"You're not much help."

"On the contrary, I think I've outdone myself. So which one of 'em is it?"

"I don't know. I need more time."

"There's no time left. Warden's closing the cell door. Which one makes you sickest to your stomach when you think about what could have been? Or when you think about her taking up with some bozo while you're sitting in jail?"

"I . . . know. For now, anyway. Thanks for the ride and the bail-out, Sigmund." Phil got out of Tom's truck in front of his apartment building.

Sam dug deep into the Dulce de Leche Caramel with the scoop. She started with four rapid scrapes to build a nice tight coil of ice cream, then slower pulls to roll the cold ball thicker. At the right size, she added one last scrape and then mashed the ball into the waffle cone that she held in her other hand, firm enough to set the ice cream without breaking the cone. She wrapped a couple of paper napkins around the base of the cone and exchanged the cone for cash with the customer.

"Next, please?"

"Two scoops of Moose Tracks in a dish, please. With sprinkles."

She had to lean far into the freezer case and stretch to her full length to reach the Moose Tracks pail. The customer reminded her of Mary. *Two nights ago at Sam's apartment door, Mary with her letter jacket over her sweatshirt and jeans, hair down, her mouth a thin grim line. Sam let her in, and she came in and sat cross-legged on the floor. Gato inspected her, sniffed her up and down but refused to let her pet him.* Two scoops, Sam reminded herself, and deposited scoop number one into a light plastic dish. Almost enough for scoop two; another couple draws. "Sprinkles, ma'am, I asked for sprinkles." "Sorry, here you go. That'll be two-and-a-quarter, please." *Sam offered a soda or beer; Mary said no, thanks, and then she said Phil was in jail but he didn't do it, and that she was worried and that Sam needed to worry, too. That was an understatement. Sam worried from the beginning about this whole detective thing.* "My change? I gave you three bucks." "Sorry." *She said she was sorry, she didn't see it coming. You couldn't have, Sam said, and then Mary said she wasn't what she seemed. Then she explained about Dave and the FBI.* "Small Jamaican Blue Mountain and a single scoop Turtle, sugar cone." She filled the hopper with the single serving of Blue Mountain beans and ground them into the filter. Brew start and cone – waffle? No, sugar. Sugar. New scoop, where's the Turtle? There. Damn, she dragged her elbow in a new pail of Strawberry. *Guilty until proven innocent. Mary insisted they'd have to solve the case to prove Phil's innocence, and he needs her but won't talk to her. That, she said, was where Sam came in; to get Phil to come around, to let Mary explain. He'll listen to you, Mary said. Save his life.* Plastic lid, napkins, "That's three seventy-five. Out of five, here's a buck and a quarter. Next, please." *There's more to this, otherwise he'd listen, Sam insisted. Okay, Mary said, if you are going to trust me you need to know the whole truth.* "Excuse me, I said Snap-O-Lantern, one scoop in a dish, and one of those cookies. Right, those." Clean scoop and a dish, and start to dig. Dish full, cookie – wax paper square, nice big cookie, this one. *Relationship was the word Mary used next. And then* – Sam turned and crashed into Lauren, sending dish, ice cream, and cookie to the floor.

"Oh, Sam, I'm sorry, let me help you," Lauren said. Sam knelt on the floor and stared at her hands covered with Snap-O-Lantern and crumbs. "I'll get the customer's order. Lisa!" Lauren caught Lisa's eye and pointed at Sam.

Lisa helped Sam to her feet. "C'mon, let's go in the back and get cleaned up," she said. Sam nodded, eyes filling. "It's okay," Lisa said on the way to the washroom, but it wasn't. They mopped what they could from Sam's blouse.

"I need to sit for a while," Sam said. Lisa left her in the office and returned to the counter. She stopped Lauren and whispered "She's not quite right yet, is she?" and then went to clean tables.

Sam leaned back in the office chair and closed her eyes. She tried to think of ice cream, of the rush to come that afternoon, of the accounting that needed to be done, but she couldn't escape the playback in her head. *Relationship, you mean you're . . . Yes, Mary had said, twice; the last time was Saturday right before he got arrested. The cops broke in on them in the shower.*

Sam felt that same hole in her stomach again. She pictured that woman naked in the shower with Phil. *You need to leave now, Sam had said. But that hadn't been enough for Mary, who asked if Sam liked him or perhaps even loved him. Sam said she didn't want to talk about it, and Mary replied that she didn't much care about what Sam wanted at that moment; that she knew Sam liked him, and that she liked him too and that it did neither one of them any good if Phil went to jail. Then Mary said that she didn't expect Sam to like her, but that she was the best chance Phil had to get out of the mess and she couldn't help him if he wouldn't work with her. Sam had to make him do it, to help all of them; that it was on Sam to talk to Phil into listening, to let Mary explain. Then Sam asked what would happen when it was all over, and Mary said she didn't expect either one of them to step aside — at the end Phil would have to choose. That's when Sam told Mary to get out. And Mary had left without another word.*

Later, after calling the Chocolate Shoppe employees Sam had called her mother. They talked of the past, of China and Tahiti, of her childhood and her father. The crowded streets of Hong Kong, how they hid from her father's friends and business acquaintances. The peace of the island, acceptance in the village, her first young boyfriends. Canoeing inside the reef, fires on the beach. The flight to America. Her fear of the big high school, of being different again. The naturalization process, the tests and interviews, and the triumph of the pledge. Every time her mother asked of current things, her job and friends, Sam changed the subject. Her mother had asked what was wrong, and if she was pregnant. Don't worry, good things come from being pregnant, she'd said. Sam told her no, she wasn't pregnant, though sometimes she wished she was, and that somehow with that things would be different. Wishing doesn't help, her mom replied; that doing helps, and Sam had always been good at doing. Don't stop now, whatever it is, her mom said. That Sunday morning Sam had decided what to do. She walked to the visitation room with her newspaper, and Mary, waiting in the hall, stopped her and told her about quitting the Bureau. All right, Sam had said, and went in to see Phil.

The office phone rang and shook Sam out of her thoughts.

"Hello?"

"Sam, I'm out. I'm at my apartment," Phil said. "How are you doing?"

"I'm not fully with it today for some reason, but I'll make it. Everything's fine here."

"Good."

"Is there anything I can do for you?"

"No, I just . . . wanted to call. I'm going over to the office this afternoon to start to work on figuring a way out of this.

Do you want to come over?"

"No, not today. I need to get back into action here. But I would like to help in any way I can. Let me know what you need me to do."

"Okay, thanks. I will."

"And say 'hello' to Mary for me. Promise me you'll do that."

"Uh, okay."

"And Phil, don't forget Thursday, seven o'clock. I'll need a key. I've got some things to get ready."

"I wouldn't miss it, not for anything. See you tomorrow at the store."

Sam hung up. That awful pit in her stomach was gone and her energy had returned. Back behind the counter she surveyed the landscape of customers; the cops at the table, the shoppers in line at the cashier station. Lisa clearing tables, Lauren grinding and brewing. The afternoon sun cut through the windows.

"Next, please?" Sam said.

Mary sat in her chair at her computer table, rocked back and put her feet up. She laced her fingers across her stomach and closed her eyes.

"Sleeping?" Phil had come in quietly; she had not heard him approach.

"Meditating. My computer. They took my goddamn computer, and everything else that I had re-researched. Now I need to re-re-research, but I don't have a machine." She pulled the rubber band from her hair and shook the ponytail loose, and ran her fingers through her hair. "I'm getting faster each time I do it, but I still need a machine. They won't give mine back for a while, maybe not until after the trial. You got room on your credit card? Or a couple thou in cash?"

"Maybe we can pick one up tomorrow; I have to go meet with that realtor this afternoon. But, I hate to lose the day. What do you need, just something to get onto the Internet?"

"Yeah, for now."

"I'll call Sam at the store. You can go over there and use the one in the office today. It's an Apple, but you should be able to figure it out. Or Sam can help you."

"Oh, I'm sure she'll be real happy to see me."

Phil shrugged. "She made me promise to say 'hello' to you for her. I think she's okay with you."

"She did, huh? I know what that means. Phil, c'mon now, she's-"

"She's what?"

"Never mind. It will do for today. Just give her some advance warning." Mary picked at the Bucky on her sweatshirt. "What about you? Are you okay with me?"

Phil hesitated. "If feeling deceived is okay. But I admit I need your help. Maybe we can work our way back to where I can almost trust you again."

"Now that's an inspiring vote of confidence."

"Did you really quit the FBI? To help me?"

"Yeah. And yeah."

"If that's true . . . well, let's get busy. I've got to go to this meeting, and then tomorrow we really need to talk about a strategy. And my lawyer wants to talk to you."

Phil went back to the roll-top desk and called the store. He talked to Sam and explained the situation and asked for her help in getting Mary onto the Mac. He could detect no obvious signs of resistance, so he told Mary to go over to the Chocolate Shoppe whenever she was ready.

Phil left Discreet Detectives and walked to Beth Talbot's real estate office. The receptionist took his name and directed him to the waiting room, where he paged through staple-bound booklets of residential and commercial listings, Beth's picture prominent on both front and back cover pages.

"Mr. Bardo! I didn't expect to see you," Beth said when she entered the room. "I saw the paper yesterday."

They shook hands. "Yes," Phil said, "I wasn't sure myself that I'd be able to keep this appointment."

"You're sure you want to pursue this right now?"

"I'm innocent, and I've got to keep going on with my

plans otherwise I'll miss an opportunity, won't I?"

"Well yes, I guess so. Let's go back to my office and look over the map."

Beth led the way down the hall to an office mid-way between the reception area and the fire exit. She took off her gray tweed jacket and laid it on a chair, then took her place behind the desk. Phil sat in a vacant side chair.

"Now, you wanted a place for a Scotch and cigar bar. How many square feet did you have in mind?"

"Not too big, maybe about a thousand. I'd like to have first right of refusal on adjacent space to the side, above, or below, it doesn't matter. In case business really takes off."

"Do you want to lease, or do you want to buy a building? Or build on bare land?"

"I'd prefer to lease, but I'd consider buying."

"Okay." Beth took a map from a drawer of her desk. "I found a few lease spaces last week after we talked at the Ball. They're around that size, give or take a little. You had said State Street or Capitol Square? Let me show you." She spread the map on the desk, referred to a printed listing, and touched the map with her pencil. "There's one right here on State Street, just a couple blocks off of the Square. Ground floor. Used to be a restaurant. But that's premium dollar space and a little close to Antoine's, and they've got a quasi-Scotch bar. And then there's one here on the Square, the place that used to be a strip club. That was a really popular spot when the legislature was in session. There's a third one, a basement deal, a block and a half off of the Square to the north. Right there." She circled the spot. "It's in the basement of a building that used to house the University Press. Upper stories are used for warehouse space now, but the basement is open and there's a nice, quaint stair access from the street."

Phil nodded. "I'd like to see those. Are there any other places in the downtown area that I should consider? Like where there's upscale development going on?"

Beth frowned. "Like where?"

"What about around the Monona Terrace? With business

picking up in that facility I'd think that upscale businesses would be gathering in the blocks around it."

"No casual foot traffic. You need people walking from work to the parking ramp, or walking to dinner, or leaving from dinner. Near some night life and other bars."

"But with the conventioneers there each week, and performances booked there four or five nights per week . . . it caters to the thirty-to-fifty-year-old crowd, just the age bracket I need. Students aren't going to drink expensive Scotch and smoke cigars. And there's a parking ramp."

"Really, there's nothing available there anyway, lease or buy. Let's go look at these first three and see what you think." She put away the map and stood and slipped her jacket over her arms. "They're all just a few blocks from here. Let's walk."

When Sam noticed Mary standing in line at the counter she dried her hands on her apron and caught her eye, and motioned toward the back of the store. Sam led the way down the hall to the office, then sat in the desk chair and logged onto the computer.

"There you go," Sam said, and vacated the chair for Mary.

"Thanks. This is uncomfortable for both of us. I'll try to stay out of your way."

"You do that," Sam nodded, standing legs apart and arms crossed. "I want you to know I'll do anything."

"I know you will. You'll have to, if you want to win."

"You don't know who you're dealing with."

"Neither do you."

Sam returned to the counter and Mary began her work on the Internet. The first thing she did was to log onto her email provider and check her inbox. The emails with file attachments that she had sent to herself were still there. She had done that as a backup of some of the files she had retrieved earlier. Apparently the police had yet to crack her password and gain access to her email. She saved the files to the Apple under obscure file names, and then she closed her email window and launched a search engine. Back to the online records of the

City Clerk's office. Real estate sales. This was going to be a long and boring afternoon.

She dug through hundreds of file links, opening files and copying and pasting tables of data into a spreadsheet that she created. Her database was growing again, and this time she found some information that had eluded her in the first passes. She had hacked into the MLS database with her computer a week ago, but she couldn't remember the passwords. Just as well, she thought; she shouldn't hack using the Chocolate Shoppe computer. Save that one for tomorrow.

Mary heard raised voices, the sound of some clanking, a mug dropped and broken on the floor. She got up from the desk and wandered down the hall to check it out. It was about time for some caffeine anyway, to spark the afternoon.

There was a large man behind the counter with the Chocolate Shoppe staff, a student by the looks of him. Ellen and Sam were pushing at him, shouting at him, trying to move him out but he laughed and moved his bulk like a linebacker fending off blockers. Judy stood to one side with the phone receiver in her hand but the cord ended in bare wires.

The man's back was toward Mary, and she waited for an opportunity. When he let one arm dangle for an instant Mary grabbed it with both hands, twisted it with her full strength and pushed it as far up between his shoulder blades as she could reach. He grunted in pain and raised up on his toes, and Mary leaned into him and toppled him forward against the freezer case. She held his arm with one hand and slammed her other forearm against his neck, grinding his face into the top of the case. It was a stretch for her given his size, and she lost her leverage. He growled, reared up and drove backward and crushed Mary against the coffee machine, spilling the coffee that was coming through the filter and knocking the filter baskets loose and to the floor. Mary lost her grip, slipped on the grounds and fell. From the floor she tried a leg-sweep to knock him down, but it was like trying to kick over a pair of telephone poles. He grinned and swatted at Sam and Ellen who had resumed their frontal attack. Then he saw the bagel knife on the cutting board and grabbed it. Sam swept Ellen behind her and stood her ground, bouncing slightly on the balls of her feet, fists clenched and close to her chin. "Aw, ain't that cute," the man said, and reached for her. Sam lunged between his arms. Her jab reached full extension at the moment of contact with the man's throat. His face registered surprise as he stumbled backward grabbing his throat, then he fell over Mary and his head made a "thok" sound as it bounced on the tile floor. He lay still.

Sam reached for an arm and felt a pulse and looked to make sure he was breathing. "Packing tape!" she shouted. "Quick!" Judy ran to the storeroom and returned with fiber-stranded tape. Sam pulled the man's ankles together and spun tape around them. Then she and Mary rolled the man to his stomach and pulled his wrists together behind him, and taped those as well.

"Okay, Judy, 911," Sam said. Judy ran back to the office. Sam sat on the floor, panting.

Mary stood up, soaked in coffee and grounds. "Where the hell did you learn that? Some Chinese martial arts-"

"High school in Kenosha," Sam interrupted. "I thought you were going to stay out of my way."

"I said I'd try. And if I hadn't laid on the floor right here you'd still be dancing with this goon."

Sam stood up. There were half-a-dozen customers standing, watching open-mouthed. "Folks," she said, "the police will be here in a minute, and we'll need some witnesses. Please wait and give statements. Coffee's on the house."

She turned back to Mary and said, "Thanks."

"It was fun. Let's do it again sometime." Mary walked back to the office.

Phil stopped by the store after his tour of properties with Talbot finished. Dale Nivek was there, writing in a notebook and talking with some of the customers.

"Phil," Dale called, and excused himself from the customers. He walked over to Phil. "Your ladies hog-tied a big drunken football player in here a while ago. He got a free ride to the hospital. He got behind the counter, broke some stuff, and threatened them. You'll press charges?"

"Yes, we'll press charges. Is everyone okay?"

"The drunk was the only one hurt. He got knocked out when he hit the floor, and his throat is pretty swollen where Sam hit him."

"Sam hit him? She took this guy on by herself?"

"She and Ellen and . . . what's her name. 'Bout this tall, sweatshirt, good lookin' . . ." Nivek checked his notebook. "Mary Haiger. I've gotta finish getting statements from these customers. See you later; I want to talk to you about your latest problem." He went back to the group of waiting bystanders.

Phil found Sam doing the end-of-day cleanup.

"Sam! Are you all right?" Phil grabbed her by the biceps and turned her from the sink so he could look her in the eyes. "How'd this happen?"

She shook him off. "Relax," she said, "everything's fine. Just some dumb jock out of control. We took care of it."

"Sure, no big deal, happens all the time. Weren't you scared?"

She smiled. "Sure, but more mad than scared. And then there was the adrenaline rush. It all happened so fast that we really didn't have much time to think about it. He ripped out the phone cord and broke some mugs . . . You should buy Mary a new sweatshirt; that one's pretty badly coffee-stained now."

"She's okay? Is she back in the office?"

"She's fine. She left about twenty minutes ago. Now I've got to get back to this or I'm going to have to stay late."

"Yes. Well. Thank God you're okay." Phil gave her a hug. "You've got to tell me more about it later. Now I've got to run to the Downtown Development meeting."

Phil left and walked to the City-County Building. He arrived five minutes before the scheduled start and found a seat in the back row. He could see people trying to look at him without being conspicuous about it. Though the auditorium was nearly full, no one sat in the seats next to him.

A large screen stood on the stage, flanked by long tables set with water pitchers and tabletop microphone stands. A projector on a table with telescoping legs was planted in the middle of the audience and some cords snaked over the chairs to the stage and up to a laptop computer on a podium. Floor-standing microphones were waiting for audience questions at the ends of the two aisles. Then people with papers in-hand began to wander onto the stage from the wings and take seats at the table. He recognized a few: Ruppert Taylor, the City Council chairman, and Moose Mikleski, of course. Also, Will's partner, the developer. Phil didn't recognize the dozen or so others that filled in the remaining seats.

He saw Beth Talbot going down the far aisle and squeezing into a row near the front of the auditorium. Phil looked around the audience and was able to pick out more of his acquaintances from the State Street area; storeowners and managers, those whose businesses weren't open after six p.m. John Smith from Importante. Colin McDermott from McDermott Books. Suzanne of La Boudoirderie. Dominick. Will from Terry's Car Care. Standing in the back along the wall were some of the cops with State Street beats.

Taylor pushed a switch on the microphone in front of him and the PA system burped to life. "This meeting of the Downtown Development Council will come to order," he announced. "I'm Ruppert Taylor, Chairman of the City Council. The agenda for this evening includes Stage Four of the State Street Plan followed by the Monona Terrace Development District Plan and a few miscellaneous proposals. But before we get to that, let me introduce my colleagues. To my left are Bob Bulgar of the Regional Planning Commission, and . . ." He introduced all the people at the tables on the stage, people who were either presenting plans at the meeting or who were part of the Downtown Development Board of Directors. Politicians, developers, builders, planners and a few business owners, all with vital interest in returning people to the downtown area and reversing customer flight to the suburban malls and strip shopping centers.

First was the presentation on Stage Four of the State Street Plan. The first three stages had taken roughly thirty years to accomplish, and had started with the basic conversion of the street into a pedestrian mall split by bus lanes. The prohibition of cars and trucks hadn't lasted too long, as it was nearly impossible to service the businesses without them since few of the buildings had rear access through alleys. A gloomy-looking public servant stood at the podium and drove the presentation from a laptop, projected on the screen, while one of the board members narrated. Plantings, repairs, sidewalk expansion, relocation of bus shelters. Artists' color drawings of the current and new looks, block by block. The man droned on and some of the audience drifted out. Phil wished he hadn't grabbed that large coffee on his way out of the store and prayed for deliverance by intermission. Finally the lights went up and the man at the podium broke open some cardboard boxes and handed out stacks of papers to rows of audience members. Taylor called for questions from the floor. Four or five people lined up at each floor mike.

The first question clearly showed that the person asking it had paid no attention to the presentation, so Phil made his escape to the men's room. Standing two-deep behind the urinals Phil found himself in line next to John Smith.

"Hello, John, how was the 10k?"

"Phil," John nodded, "it was good. I didn't expect to see you here tonight. A bit tacky, don't you think?" They each stepped up one more spot in line.

"No, I don't. I'm innocent, John. It's all a big mistake."

"Sure. So are you ducking out now?" They made it to the porcelain.

"Ahhhh. Didn't think I'd make it. No, I'm staying for the Monona District. Thought there might be some interesting opportunities over there. I've been thinking of opening a scotch and cigar bar. What would you think about that?"

He shrugged. "Might work. That niche isn't overcrowded here."

"You a Scotch drinker?"

"Occasionally." Smith finished and zipped up. "Catch you later." He left, and Phil finished. He washed his hands and fished for a paper towel from the dispenser – empty, of course. He dried his hands on his jeans and returned to the auditorium.

The question and answer session had ended and the guests on the dais had taken a short break. They were returning to their seats when Phil re-entered the auditorium. The crowd had thinned so Phil moved up into the middle of the seats to get a better view. He found Beth Talbot and sat next to her, nodding to her in greeting. Taylor brought the meeting into session and turned the mike to Bob Bulgar of the Regional Planning Commission.

"To understand where we're going with the Monona Terrace District you need to know where we came from," he began. "Fifteen years ago the Monona Terrace area was a blighted swamp along the shores of Lake Monona, a series of empty rundown warehouses along the shore hemmed in by the railroad tracks and John Nolen Drive. Once upon a time there was actually a tiny fishing industry here but that died and the shallow shoreline silted in." He waved at the man at the podium, who clicked on the PC and a color-coded map of the area flashed on the big screen. "The railroad served the warehouses on both sides of the track." He came out from behind the table and stood next to the screen. "The warehouse district extended from here," he pointed to a spot on the screen, "to here in an arc following the shoreline, and inland beyond Wilson Street near the railroad yard." The screen flashed and the map was replaced by a 30's-era drawing of a modernistic building. "This was the original design for the Monona Terrace Convention Center, proposed by Frank Lloyd Wright. It was intended to be built on fill land out into Lake Monona, and anchor the end of Monona Avenue coming off of the Capitol Square, a real nice sight line. As you know, under Ruppert Taylor's leadership the City finally acquired land and built a modified version of this original design as what we now know as the Monona Terrace Convention Center."

Phil leaned toward Beth. "How did the city acquire the land?"

"They bought some, and the rest they condemned under eminent domain laws," she whispered.

The screen flashed again and an aerial photograph of the convention center appeared. Text along the bottom of the slide read 'Convention Center – Mikleski Construction.' There was a smattering of applause from the audience. Bulgar waited for it to subside. "That was the initial phase. The intent has always been to continue the redevelopment of this district, to expand on it using the convention center as the centerpiece of a master plan that makes use of the natural beauty of the shore and creates economic development opportunities and enhances the tax base." The next slide to appear was another map, more detailed, of the shoreline. "The next phase of the plan calls for the construction of a small municipal marina and what is called 'The Boathouse,' a multipurpose building also based on an original design by Frank Lloyd Wright. That would be right here." Bulgar pointed to an area on the screen. "Then phases after that would be economic development areas here," he waved his arm in the arc following the shoreline to the northeast, "and here." He pushed his hand inland, to the north of the railroad tracks. "Developers are being asked to submit plans that include both commercial and residential development; the commercial development being hotel, retail, entertainment and service oriented, not heavy industry. Residential would be apartment and high-rise condo."

Phil leaned toward Beth again. "These are the types of areas I was talking about. Upscale development where a Scotch bar would fit right in. Who owns all this land now?"

"The City owns some, the railroad owns some, and the rest is in private hands."

Bulgar continued. "The plans should include rail as a key asset. We foresee that rail will be an increasingly important method of passenger travel as well as freight, and that a new passenger station in this development district will help deliver customers to this area and benefit downtown as a whole. We believe that this plan will provide Madison with one of the premier convention facilities in the upper Midwest, a preferred location with vast economic benefit to the area."

The next ten slides were spreadsheets showing the projected costs and economic impacts of the next phases of the development. Bulgar read each one, each number. Phil felt his eyes glaze over.

When it was time for questions Suzanne was first in line at the audience microphone. "What about the impact of the development of the Monona District on the State Street and Capitol Square merchants?" she asked.

"Our studies show that Monona will create more demand rather than take customers from State Street," Bulgar replied. "With the residential development as part of the package, there will be more people in the downtown area which should benefit State Street and Capitol Square businesses, too."

"But the residential development isn't until the later phases. Won't we get bled of our customers until then?"

"We believe that this area will draw people into the region, and if any areas are negatively impacted it will be the far east-side and west-side malls for the first couple years as people come downtown again."

From the expression on her face Suzanne didn't appear to be convinced, but she relinquished the microphone and sat down.

There were a half-dozen people waiting to ask questions, but Phil was antsy. The areas that were depicted in the maps were part of the areas for which Dave had been collecting information. The timeframes made sense too; the data collection that Mary had been doing covered years beginning with the start of the convention center planning.

"I'll call you in a few days," Phil said to Talbot as he stood, then he made his way to the aisle and out of the auditorium. He felt a little guilty not waiting for Urban Design's presentation. But a possible Monona Terrace tie-in? He'd not be able to concentrate on Urban Design anyway.

Xiamorha sat on her floor in a t-shirt and drawstring pajama bottoms. She placed a small votive candle in a simple glass holder, lit it, and set it on the floor in front of her. She pulled her legs into the lotus position, rested her hands on her knees and sat with her back straight and eyes fixed on the candle.

Her eyelids narrowed as she breathed and concentrated. Her pulse rate slowed, she could feel her heartbeat and the push of the blood in her arteries. Then she no longer heard the traffic sounds outside or the stereo in the apartment next to hers. Inhale; she contracted her pelvic muscles and began to visualize air being drawn in through her pelvis, filling her lungs from the bottom up, rising higher, air spilling up into her throat to her head. Then exhale; relax the pelvic muscles, imagine pushing the air back down through her body and out.

It started on the inhale, the tingle that accompanied the air rising and filling, climbing her spine from the base and up her back. Then, out, that tingle fell with the imaginary column of air, down her body and out. The tingle grew stronger and raised goose-bumps on her arms and legs. Her nipples grew erect, and her mouth fell open as she breathed slowly and deeply. The heat started, pooled in her groin, and the current shot through it to her spine and back again. It was all she could do to avoid shivering as the electricity traveled and grew larger each breath cycle. The heat grew, burned in her, and beads of sweat appeared on her forehead. Concentrate. In and up, out and down. Finally the heat exploded up her spine, wrenching her backward, and she gasped as she reached back to catch herself. Her insides were on fire, contracting in rolling waves in a delightful overload. She lay back on the floor, exhausted, concentration gone.

When her breathing returned to normal she sat up and got her legs out of the lotus cross, then dried her forehead with the bottom of her t-shirt. She marked her place in the book that had been open on the floor beside her – 'The Tantric Guide to Sexual Performance' – and tossed it toward the bookshelf. Then she got up and put the candle on the table next to the bed, rolled Gato out of the way and crawled under the covers. She blew out the candle, and the room was dark.

CHAPTER SEVENTEEN

Lauren sat in her car on the street across from the Essinger house in University Heights, working a crossword puzzle. Phil's instructions had been pretty vague – watch for anyone leaving the house and find out where they go. "What are we looking for?" she had asked. "Not sure," he replied, "maybe we'll know when we see it."

Someone had left the house but hadn't gotten very far. A trim blonde woman in a down vest, about five-foot-ten, had come out to work in the yard. She picked up sticks, raked leaves, and pulled dead annuals out of flowerbeds. It was a decent day, temperatures in the sixties, and Lauren had her window rolled down as she struggled with fifteen-down and twenty-three across. Something had to be wrong with the clues; either that or she had misspelled foie gras in eleven-down. 'French garden painter' – had to be Monet. Or Manet. She had had trouble keeping the two straight during the impressionism portion of her art history class.

A shadow passed over her puzzle and then she felt something cold and sharp pressed against her neck. It was a three-tined garden hand-fork, held by the blonde woman.

"Now you listen, and you listen carefully," the woman hissed. "Ted's done with you, so you can just crawl back into that hole where he found you! What was the name of that place – 'Jiggles?'"

Lauren froze, eyes wide. "Hang on, you've got it all wrong-"

"There's no point in your waiting around here for him. It's over. I've got him by the balls now, and if he forgets to ask

212

permission to breathe, I just squeeze . . ."

"But-"

"If I ever catch you here again, or anywhere near Teddy, I will make things most unpleasant for you. Now, get out of here!" She withdrew the hand tool and Lauren started the car and hit the gas.

Phil was at the cash register Tuesday morning when Dale Nivek walked up. "Hey, Dale," Phil said, "you said you wanted to talk to me about something?"

Dale leaned forward. "Not here. Give me a medium mocha." He passed a couple of dollars to Phil. "Meet me in fifteen minutes at the corner of State and Frances." He took the coffee and some napkins and left. The rest of the beat cops were still at the table near the window and they watched Dale's departure.

Ten minutes later Phil pulled Sam aside. "It sounds melodramatic, but Dale wants to meet me down the street to tell me something. I'll be back in a few minutes."

"Right," she whispered, "and don't forget the secret handshake!"

"You're not taking this seriously."

Phil left the store and turned right, dodged some customers heading for his door and set off down the sidewalk toward Frances Street. When he reached the intersection he spotted Dale standing on the opposite corner. Phil waited for a bus to pass, then cut diagonally across the intersection.

"That's jaywalking," Dale said when Phil reached him.

"Yeah, like that's the biggest of my worries right now."

"I shouldn't be talking to you, especially not about this. Jesus, Phil, why'd you have to keep diggin' around that murder?" Dale looked around casually, watching for any other blue uniforms. "Word at the copshop is that the DA is pretty pissed at you. He had a nice neat case all tied up and you wrecked it for him. So he went after you and squashed any real investigation."

"Isn't he interested in the truth?"

"Phil, think about it. We're heading into an election year, so he's interested in appearances. What office do you suppose is on the ballot?"

"I have no idea. Tell me."

"State Attorney General. Bradley's running for it. He needs the case solved quickly so he can get his campaign off to a good start. And he had that until you got in the way."

"Well now, that *is* interesting."

"If you had either let Daman take the fall or leaked that stuff to the press instead of sending it to him maybe you wouldn't be in this fix. But now, he sees you as his ticket to the election. Haven't you heard his first campaign commercials?"

"No. Where are they running?"

"On Ruppert Taylor's stations. A tough-on-crime message. He'd look pretty silly if he cut Daman loose and had nobody else to hang. We don't get that many murders in this town. People like to see justice done. To somebody."

"So who's backing Bradley anyway? What are his chances on unseating the incumbent, ah, what's his name?"

"Kleinstern. I think Bradley's chances are pretty good, since his primary backer is the Taylor Group."

"He's another one of Rupe's kids?"

"Maybe. He sure seems to spend a lot of time at Taylor's office in the City-County Building. Hey, you didn't hear any of this from me. If the Chief even thinks that I'm talking to you I'll be pulling midnight basketball duty or working private security." Dale looked around again. "If I get any more I'll try to let you know. You've always been a good guy, Phil, and I really don't want to see you take the fall. I also got the scoop on the Lincoln; it was a rental."

"No."

"Yep. Belongs to 'Luxury Wheels' in Milwaukee."

"Did you find out who rented it?"

"No, Phil, you never gave me a date."

"Damn, Dale, I didn't, did I. There's a lot of stuff to remember in this business."

"It takes practice. If you give me a date . . ."

"September fourteenth."

"I'll see what I can do."

"Thanks, Dale, you don't know how much I appreciate this. If I get cleared you've got a free pass at the store."

"Shit, now I've got to write you up for trying to bribe an officer. On second thought, get outta here while I'm still in a good mood." Dale gave a nervous laugh. "See you later."

Phil clapped Dale on the shoulder and walked back to the store. Dale's buddies were finishing up at the window table. Sam saw Phil enter, and she grabbed him by the arm and steered him down the hall to the office. "It's Lauren," she said, "she's ready to bolt. You've got to fix this."

Phil entered the office and found Lauren sitting in the desk chair with her knees drawn up to her chest and her arms wrapped tightly around her legs. Her face had no color in it.

"What happened to you?"

"Phil, you didn't tell me I could get killed doing this. A crazy woman, she put a–a–garden thing, a pitchfork or something, right here." She demonstrated with her left hand against her throat.

"Jeez, I'm sorry about that!" He put his hand on her shoulder and felt it shaking, then squeezed it. "I sure didn't expect it to go that way. You're okay now, just take it easy. Who did this?"

"A blonde woman, I think the woman who lives in the house, the wife. She – she threatened me, she thought I was – I don't know."

"Think. Exactly what did she say?"

"She said that Ted was finished with me, that I should go back to where he found me. Some strip club, I think."

"She named it? What was the name?"

"Oh, man. I – shit, I don't know."

"That's all right, maybe you'll think of it later. Anything else?"

"Yeah. She said something about having him by the . . . the . . ."

"I get the picture."

"And she squeezes if he doesn't get her okay to do anything. Her okay to breathe, she said."

"Wow, this is great stuff! Good job!"

Lauren shook her head. "I don't know if I can work here, Phil. I have to quit, I just – this is, like, way too intense."

"It's like your acting class, that's all. You played a part; it was like doing an improv."

"No. When you die on stage you can still walk away."

"Okay, don't worry, I won't send you on any more of this things. I know that's not what you signed up for. Just don't quit your job here. Please, we need you. Sam will never forgive me if you leave. You don't want to be responsible for causing me all kinds of misery, do you?"

"Well, maybe." She looked up, then laughed. "You deserve some, a payback for this." The color was returning to her face.

"Look, you go home and rest up. I'll pay you double-time for the hours you were scheduled to work today, and you come back tomorrow to work as usual. And forget this quitting talk, okay?"

"Double, huh?"

"Did I say double? Really?"

"Yes, you did. I heard you." Lauren released her legs and stood up. "Okay, for now. We'll see how it goes."

"Thanks, I really appreciate this. You did a good job today."

"Ah! It just came to me. 'Jiggles.' The name of the strip club was 'Jiggles.'"

Lars sipped from his coffee mug and listened to the phone receiver as his receptionist passed by his office door. Then he said, "I talked to the girl this morning. She's not with the Bureau any longer. The muzzle's off . . . her testimony should be enough to blow this out of the water." He got up and stretched to swing the office door closed, then sat down again behind the desk. "Oh really. I don't think you appreciate the difficulty of the position you've put me in . . . No, you don't. Let's review. Forget for a moment that this guy's a friend. You want me to be good enough so that he doesn't go get himself a real lawyer, but you want me to be bad enough so that he loses. We have an obvious witness for the defense, but now you want me to figure out some way to prevent her from testifying . . . No way, don't even think about that. It's got to look rational, like the right thing to do, so it won't be questioned by my client or the judge. Oh, sure, it's a piece of cake." Lars opened his bottom desk drawer and retrieved a bottle of vodka, poured some into his coffee, then screwed the top back on the bottle and put it back in the drawer. He took a drink from the mug and coughed. "Trial calendar? Hasn't been assigned . . . When? Oh, for Pete's sake . . . That doesn't leave me much . . . I don't give a rat's ass if he wins. I've got to be careful or I could get disbarred and then I sure won't be of much use to you, will I . . . Yeah. I've heard it before. Now you listen to me. I have a safety deposit box. In that safety deposit box is a nice long letter. You want to know what the letter says? . . . Yeah. Anything happens to me, guess what. Now let's just try to figure out a way to get through this without making things worse, shall we?" Lars took another swig from his coffee mug. "No, I'll call you when I feel like it." He hung up the receiver and drained the rest of the mug. Then he picked up the receiver and dialed.

"Chocolate Shoppe."

"Phil, it's Lars. I just found out; I thought we'd have several months to get ready, but it looks like they're pressing the case into the schedule early . . . I don't have the exact date yet but it is likely to be in about four weeks . . . I know. We can file motions, but . . . yeah. Do your Christmas shopping early. We need to get together this week . . . Thursday. Okay. Bye."

Phil climbed the stairs in the back corner of the Music Hall. There was no elevator in the old building and somehow the University had gotten around the ADA requirements to make all offices wheelchair accessible. The top floor was converted attic space, a small hall with just a few stifling offices built around the dormer windows set in the roof. The wooden floor creaked as he walked. The door was open to the last office on the east side of the building, and a man sat in a simple office chair with his back to the door. He was engrossed in some paperwork. The partly open window admitted a faint breeze, and classical music came from a small CD player on the corner of the desk.

"Dan Daman?"

"Yes?" The man turned around in his chair. He had dark hair, curly and thick, with some gray working itself in at the temples. Phil guessed he was in his thirties.

"Schubert, isn't it?"

"Why, yes, his Third Symphony. In D."

"Sorry to bother you, but I'd really like to talk with you for a few minutes. I'm Phil Bardo."

"Oh, oh, you!" Daman said, slack-jawed, pointing at Phil and rising from his chair. "Now don't do anything you're going to regret . . ." He backed away until he was pressed against his desk. His right hand moved cautiously behind him in search of the telephone.

"That's some gratitude. I'm responsible for getting you cleared of murder charges, you know."

"Yes, yes, I am thankful for that, to be sure. But you, now you're . . ."

"Charged with the murder. Yes, but I'm just as innocent as you are."

"Well, isn't that what anybody would say?" The hand continued its search for the phone.

"I suppose so, but in this case it's true. I'm not here to hurt you. If I were, I would have done it while your back was turned. That would have been a lot easier. I just need to ask a few questions. Back a little further and to your right."

"What?"

"I said the phone is back a little and to the right from where your hand is. If you want to call someone, go ahead. I'll wait." Phil leaned against the doorframe.

Daman finally found the telephone. He picked it up and

held it to his ear, and studied Phil for a reaction. Phil stood, impassive, and looked Daman in the eye.

"I guess some conversation couldn't hurt," Daman said, and put the receiver back on the cradle. "Just stay over there. Now what do you want?"

"I want to hear your story about what happened that night, and maybe ask a few questions. It might help me catch the real killer and clear myself of the charges."

"I told my story to the police."

"A fat lot of good that did you. And how likely do you think it would be that they'd share it with me?"

"You have a point, Mr. Bardo."

"Phil."

"Okay, Phil. I suppose I do owe you something."

Fifteen minutes later Phil was on his way back down the stairs. Daman had relaxed a bit by the time he finished telling Phil his story, and he had even managed to choke out a thank-you for Phil's efforts in getting the charges dropped. Daman hadn't met Stephano prior to the afternoon rehearsal of the show, and he met Dave for the first time at the evening performance. It had happened pretty much as Phil and Mary had envisioned, Daman feeling his way in the dark down the staircase and discovering Dave Helms dead on the ground floor. The feel of warm blood and the smell of death and gunpowder; that was a new image provided by Daman. He had never touched a dead body prior to that night, and he had clearly been shaken by the experience.

Daman said that the gunshots were loud and echoed in the enclosed space of the Carillon. "Like someone slamming a door right behind you. And each was punctuated immediately by a metallic 'clank.' The pitch was about like the G above middle C." Daman had reached for a small portable electronic keyboard and pressed the key, to illustrate. "Then when I reached the bottom of the staircase I heard a scraping, a scuffling sound."

"Footsteps?"

"Perhaps. Like the third clarinet shifting his feet on

stage."

"From where the body was found? Maybe Dave was moving around."

"No, he wasn't; the sound came from nearby."

"How can you be sure?"

"I lead an orchestra class – Orchestra 3201. With my eyes closed I can tell you which chair in which section just turned a page of sheet music. I know my sound, Mr.- er, Phil."

The sounds Daman had heard reinforced the steam tunnel theory; the kick from the shots probably knocked the gun barrel against the grate, and the scuffling sound could have been the killer making his escape through the tunnel below.

Phil was certain that Daman had absolutely nothing to do with the murder. He found no new leads from Daman's story, nothing that might be a clue to the real killer's identity or whereabouts. He hoped that the very absence of other clues might be a clue; he just had to figure out what it all meant.

He reached the ground floor, opened the door and stepped outside into the sunlight.

Mary and Phil spent hours at the Computer Superstore later that afternoon. She wouldn't even consider an Apple product, much to Phil's dismay. But she was the one who was going to have to use the machine, so . . . They decided on a floor-standing tower. She insisted on the fastest processor, an enormous amount of memory and hard drive space, and a separate solid-state drive for backups. "An investment in your future," she said with a laugh. "Plus, I need it so I'll be happy while I work. You want me to be happy, right?"

"I wouldn't want you any other way."

While the hardware department was busy configuring the machine to her spec Mary led Phil through the software department. They collected boxes of software to replace what had disappeared with the confiscated evidence; database, graphics, and statistical analysis packages. The tab for the whole thing, hardware and software, came to well over three thousand dollars.

"A 'couple thou,' she says," Phil said as he pulled out his VISA. "I hope I've still got enough room on this to buy gas on the way back."

"Don't complain, it's a capital asset for your business. You can depreciate it over the next three years."

"If I have three years. And it's still cash going out now. We don't have any cash coming in, remember? Depreciation expense reductions to net income don't help much if you have no income to start with."

"Oh yeah. So maybe accounting isn't my strongest suit." She waited. "This is where you're supposed to say that all my other good qualities more than make up for that."

"You're right."

"That my other good qualities make up for my accounting?"

"No, that this is where I'm supposed to say that."

They carried all the boxes up the stairs to Discreet Detectives and piled them around Mary's table. She took off her letter jacket and flung it in the corner, then rolled up the sleeves of her denim shirt.

"I'll get busy with this," she announced. "I plan to be here all night. By daybreak we'll be back in business. Would you mind ordering a pizza and some kind of soda with lots of caffeine?"

"What kind?"

"Make it a 'garbage' pizza, with everything on it. I don't care what kind of soda. Man, I'm pumped! This is almost better than sex."

"You've *got* to be kidding."

"I said almost. Yeah, I'm kidding. But it is pretty damned good."

"There's help now for people like you. A twelve-stepper for the technology-addicted."

"But I don't *want* to be cured."

Mary got to work opening the boxes and Phil ordered the pizza and sodas. He paid for them when they arrived, and he carried them to Mary's table. She was surrounded by empty boxes. The hardware was connected and powered up, and she was busy adjusting cache sizes and setting up directory structures.

"There," she said, and pointed at a stack of boxes without taking her eyes off of the screen. Phil closed the flaps of a box to form a table. He set the pizza down and opened a can of soda for her.

"Here you go."

"Mmm. Okay." She stuck her right arm out and felt around for the soda without looking. Phil moved the can so that her hand came in contact with it. She picked it up and drank, then set the can next to the keyboard. "Thanks."

"Can I help you with anything?"

"Hmm? Nope."

Phil took a seat in the extra chair. She was totally immersed, staring at the screen with fingers flying on the keyboard and mouse. Her mouth was partway open. He watched; her lips moved but no sound came out. She was talking. To him? To herself? No, to the computer.

"Y'know, I thought maybe I'd just burn this place down. Torch it. Maybe tomorrow. Whadayathink?"

"Sure, Phil. Whatever."

"Did you hear that the Pope got married today? To a fourteen-year-old."

"That's nice."

"Kids. I thought we would have five kids together. Okay?"

"Mmm. Maybe next week."

Phil gave up, unable to break her concentration. His guard had slipped; it was hard for him to stay angry with her. He got up and zipped up his jacket. "Thanks again for helping Sam yesterday. See you tomorrow."

"Sure. G'night, Phil."

CHAPTER EIGHTEEN

Mary woke at five a.m. with a pain in her side – the cot had grown uncomfortable. She checked her watch and struggled to her feet, then tousled her hair with one hand and hauled up on the belt loops of her jeans with the other. It had gotten chillier in the office over the last several hours; she buttoned up the denim shirt that hung open and untucked from her shoulders. She shuffled barefoot to her computer table and sat, and put on her glasses. The series of database load jobs that she had launched had completed successfully. She launched the web browser and accessed her Internet email host. There were about fifteen emails there with file attachments. These were the last of the files she had sent herself from the Apple at the Chocolate Shoppe. She downloaded each of the files and saved them to a directory on her new machine, then began to reformat them one by one. She reached for a piece of leftover pizza, cool and soggy, and chewed absently while she worked. The half-can of 'Buzz' cola on the table was room temperature and flat but wet enough to wash down the pizza. Finally she prepared the database loader and queued up fifteen individual jobs in the job scheduler. She clicked on the 'run' button and watched as the first load job started. She stared at the queue list until the screen saver kicked in, then her stomach rumbled and she released a toxic belch of 'Buzz' and onions. "Oh yeah," she said aloud, "it don't get no better than this." She stood up, stretched, scratched her stomach and made her way to the bathroom, careful to avoid looking in the mirror. Then, back in the main office space she threw herself down on the cot and went back to sleep.

She dreamt, and she knew she was dreaming. There was a car, with people inside, their talking muffled. She pulled on the door handle to get in but the door was locked. It was an older car, a sedan. She saw people get into the car from the other side, but for some reason she couldn't go around to the other door. "This is stupid, this is a dream, just go around," she told herself, but she didn't. She tugged on the handle in desperation, then pounded on the window but the door remained locked and no one inside paid attention to her. Then she realized that she heard real voices, and she woke up.

Phil was seated in the wooden chair behind the roll-top desk and Sam sat in the leather easy chair. They were talking softly.

"Ohhhhhh," Mary groaned as she pushed herself to a sitting position on the cot. She held her face in her hands and rubbed her eyes.

"*It's alive, it's alive!*" Phil said.

"Funny, Dr. Frankenstein. Just remember, you made me this way." She looked up; Sam sat watching her, little Sam in her pressed white blouse, her little leather jacket, her neat creased black slacks, her damned perfect complexion and her big brown eyes. She's probably never looked or felt like this in her life, Mary decided. "What's the matter, honey, havencha ever seen a dead body before?"

Sam didn't respond.

"God. I'm really looking and feeling my best right now."

"We brought you coffee and doughnuts," Phil said, "the breakfast of champions." He brought the items from the desk to the cot. Mary took the coffee from him and sipped it, then fished in the bag for a powdered sugar doughnut. "It's ten o'clock," Phil said, "I thought we'd better get caught up and talk about strategy."

"Yythh," Mary said through the doughnut. She took a long sip of the coffee. "Computer's ready. File loads should be done by now. I just need to load the statistical analysis software and we should be ready to play."

"Okay." Phil took a pad of paper from the desk drawer.

"So how do we prove I didn't do it?"

"Reasonable doubt?" Sam asked. "You don't have to prove you didn't do it, you just need to do enough to make a juror think maybe you didn't, right?" Sam looked from Phil to Mary for confirmation.

"Right," Phil replied. "At least theoretically. So how do we do that?"

"Alibi," Mary said. "Show that you couldn't have been in town when the murder occurred."

"That's a problem. We haven't found a way to verify where I was on that Friday. We thought maybe phone calls, but we talked Thursday after I left and again on Monday. Friday, Saturday, and Sunday we didn't. Sure, some people had to see me, but nobody specific and no noteworthy events. Lars is working on the alibi research."

"I've had an initial meeting with him," Sam said. "He's calling all the Chocolate Shoppe employees and getting preliminary statements about you and what they remember from the days around the murder."

"He called me, too, yesterday morning," Mary added. "I told him everything I could about what we were doing with the investigation, the computer, and so forth. But that wasn't about the alibi, that was about explaining the circumstantial evidence."

"Explaining away the circumstantial evidence helps cast doubt," Phil said. "I think we can explain about all the Carillon drawings, as we've got the original 'challenge' letter and copies of what we sent to Stephano. The gun and my fingerprints, that's another problem. Apparently they can't prove that the gun was the murder weapon, only that it could have been. If I hadn't picked it up and looked at it, Mary's fingerprints would have been all over it."

Sam looked at Mary, eyebrows raised.

"It's a long story," Mary said. "And no, I didn't do it."

"Then there are our letters to the DA." Phil wrote on his notepad. "How do we show that they're the result of good detective work rather than the confession of some ego-driven nut that wants everyone to know how smart he was in commission of the crime?"

"I see only one way to do that," Mary said. "We've got to complete the picture. Tie the method to a motive. Show that there are other people involved; how and why they did it."

"And you don't need to find the real murderer?" Sam asked.

"It sure would help," Phil replied, "but even if we don't we'd at least raise doubt if we could prove some sort of plot that the DA can't explain, something that had nothing to do with me."

"What about the attack on us? And the break-ins?"

"Sam, there's no proof yet to tie the attack to any of this," Mary explained. "And the break-ins? Well, that was me." She looked at Phil. "Okay, so I didn't quite tell her *everything*."

"You deserve a good spanking," Phil said, shaking his head. "Sam, we also had break-ins here that aren't explained by Mary's juvenile delinquency. The preliminary research that Mary and Dave did is missing. And, Halloween night we surprised somebody coming out of the office. We can't prove that any of that actually happened."

Mary finished her coffee. "So we've gone full-circle. We're back to having to find the reason for the murder in the first place."

Phil nodded. "And there are two possibilities that we know of. The first is the Essinger drug case – you know, the UW prof, the hooker, the wife, and the coke. The motivation for the murder would be to cover up the drug dealing or maybe eliminate blackmail. Sam, this is the one that Lauren was on when she got jumped; the wife apparently thought Lauren was the hooker. We've got to find a way to get closer to these people."

"And the second," Mary said, "is a possible tie to the real estate investigation. If we can find a motive there maybe we can find the real killer." Mary's eyes grew wide. "'*Was you ever bit by a dead bee? Dead bees can bite ya, ya know, just about as bad as live ones. 'Specially if they was really mad when they died . . .*'"

Sam shot a glance at Phil. He rolled his eyes. "Rent *To Have and Have Not* – Bogart, Bacall, and Walter Brennan," he said to her. "I never have understood what the hell Brennan was talking about with that line."

"Me neither," Mary laughed, "that's what makes it so memorable. I'm going to load that software package. Then we can try what we've wanted to try for the last two weeks – to see if there's some correlation in the data that will give us a clue. I'll launch a series of jobs that look for repeated data values that occur in conjunction with each other." She brushed the powdered sugar from her hands and headed for the computer.

Phil and Sam sat, silent. Phil looked at his few notes on the legal pad, then he tore the sheet from the pad and crumpled it into a ball and threw it into the wastebasket. He leaned back in his chair, staring at the desk and the objects on it. The stacks of papers and notes. A few black BIC pens. The Ardbeg bottle. Too early for a drink, though he felt like he'd already been up for nearly a full day. It was only eleven o'clock in the morning. And, it wasn't Ardbeg, anyway.

"Sam."

"Huh?"

"Why would somebody drink out of a bottle and then fill it up again? With something other than what was in there in the first place?"

She shrugged. "When we were in high school we'd sneak drinks out of our parents' liquor bottles and top off the levels with water so nobody would notice."

"Exactly." Phil opened a desk drawer and took out a glass. He took a couple sheets of paper from the legal pad and wrapped one around the bottle and held it, then put the other sheet on top and unscrewed the cap with it. He poured a half-glass of the liquor, then re-capped the bottle.

"When my uncle drank Scotch, he drank this brand exclusively," he said. "This," he swirled the liquid in the glass, "is not his brand. Somebody drank his Scotch and refilled the bottle with some other brand. Why?"

"To hide the fact that they were here and drank his Scotch? In case somebody would notice that the levels had fallen in the bottle?"

Phil nodded. "Yes. To mask a clue. But maybe they left a couple behind." He held the glass up to the light of the desk lamp and watched the light refract through the amber liquid. "They didn't use water; they must have drunk up all or most of the Ardbeg. Just adding water would have looked and tasted too weak. And watered Scotch would attract attention; Dave certainly wouldn't have added water to the bottle. So they used Scotch, a cheaper brand. We need to pay a visit to Dominick." He put the glass down on the desk and got up. "Be right back." Phil walked through the stacks to Mary's computer table. "Got a bag?"

Mary dug around in one of the computer boxes and produced a plastic bag with some instruction manuals in it. She shook the manuals out into the box and handed the bag to Phil. "Thanks," he said, and returned to the roll-top desk. He wrapped a piece of paper around the bottle and picked it up and eased it into the bag. "I need to find Dale, too. Let's go for a walk."

He called out "Be back in a bit" and heard Mary's distant "Okay," then he and Sam left.

Dominick held the shot glass up to the light to examine the color of the Scotch. He tipped the glass to one side and then slowly back to neutral and watched the 'legs' of liquid wash down the inside of the glass. He held the glass beneath his nose and inhaled deeply, eyes closed. And again. Then he raised it to his lips and poured a sip into his mouth. Swishing the Scotch back and forth over his tongue, his eyes closed, Dom worked on the taste. Smokey, a little earthy. He spit into a wastebasket.

Phil and Sam stood and watched the ritual. Old Dom had been happy to try to help, and they didn't want to disturb his concentration. Phil looked at Sam and caught her eye and they raised eyebrows at each other, waiting. Dominick had been happy to see Phil, but he was positively thrilled to meet Sam. She had that effect on men, and did nothing special this day to create it. She waited, hands in her pockets.

"I can't say for sure," Dom began. "I don't think it's one of the cheap knockoffs." He lifted the shot glass and poured the rest into his mouth. He swished, opened his mouth slightly and sucked air over the pool of Scotch on his tongue, then spit again. "It isn't a single-malt. And it isn't terribly old – I'd guess less than ten years." He set the shot glass down. "Sorry, I can't do better without points of comparison. And unless you want to buy a lot of bottles, we're not going to do that here." He saw Sam's shoulders slump in disappointment. "Why don't you take your sample down to Antoine's. Tell him I sent you. Ask him to set up a shot of every kind of real Scotch whiskey that he's got, excluding the single-malts and the ones older than ten years. Then get him to help you compare color, smell, 'legs' and taste. Maybe you can narrow it down that way."

"Thanks, Dom, that's a good idea," Phil said. "And if we happen to come up with one, any chance you'd know if you've sold any recently?"

"Sure, but it would take some work. I've got inventory records and credit card receipts for the past several months. We could go through those."

"Fantastic! Thanks so much, we'll be back if we can narrow it down." Phil led the way out of the store and Sam flashed a big smile at Dominick before hurrying after him. Dom blushed, waved, and dried his shot glass on his shop apron.

They found Antoine's to be quite accommodating, especially after Phil said that Dominick had sent them. Antoine himself appeared and led Phil and Sam to a private curved booth in the corner of the bar room. Sam scooted in and Phil and Antoine flanked her on each side. The bartender came over and set a dozen shot glasses in a row on the table and a bottle of Scotch behind each one. On Antoine's instruction he disappeared into the back room for a few minutes and then reappeared with an eighteen-inch fluorescent lamp. He laid it down between the bottles and the shot glasses and plugged the cord into an outlet on the wall.

"Backlight is best," Antoine said. "Shall we begin?" He filled each shot glass with a shot from a corresponding bottle. Then he poured Phil's sample into a shot glass and slid it along the row, looking for a color match. The three of them examined the colors, debated, and moved the obviously wrong ones out of the way. Phil poured two more samples from his Ardbeg bottle so each of them could have one to use for comparison. They each held a sample in one hand and a candidate in the other, tipped them carefully together and watched the 'legs' on the glasses and how they compared. More debates, and a few more candidates were kicked to the side.

Then they began the smell tests. They sniffed over each of the shot glasses and their sample, comparing back and forth. "I'm having trouble," Sam confessed, "they're all starting to smell the same."

"Just wait, it gets harder," Antoine said. "Like your nose, your palate will be most sensitive at the very beginning. After a few tests, well . . ." He signaled to the bartender, who brought three regular glasses and a pitcher of water. "The water may help." They weeded out two more candidates.

Then it was time for the tasting. "Small sips," Antoine cautioned. "Roll it on your tongue. Inhale over your tongue. Then after you swallow, give it a minute and contemplate the aftertaste. You'll taste smoke, earth, grass, maybe faint barley. Then clear your mouth with some water and then do the same test with Phil's sample. Here, let's try first with something grossly different." He took one of their first discards and pushed the shot glass in front of Sam. "Go for it."

Sam took a sip and made a terrible face, but swished the liquid in her mouth, breathed as Antoine had suggested, and closed her eyes while swallowing. She sat, eyes closed, and followed the aftertaste as it first burned then grew cold and evaporated from her mouth. She repeated the ritual with Phil's sample.

"Whoa, there was a big difference," she said. "I really hadn't expected something so dramatic."

"It will be a lot more subtle with the ones we've got left," Antoine said. "Sometimes it might help to actually sip a little water with it; it explodes the taste. Let's get started."

They began. Antoine was right, the differences in the remaining pool were small and subtle. They debated, argued, repeated the tests, altered the sequence, cleared their palates with drinks of water, debated, and tested again.

"Shouldn't we be spitting instead of swallowing?" Sam asked, laughing.

"You could, but it isn't nearly as much fun," Antoine replied.

They worked it down to two final candidates. Phil and Antoine favored one brand, but Sam insisted that the other was the perfect match, and that she was always right. "Well, two is pretty damned good," Phil declared. He wrote the names on the back of a Chocolate Shoppe business card and put the card in his pocket. "We'll carry that back to Dom and see if we get any hits. Now what can we pay you for all this?"

Antoine leaned forward and pushed the shot glass discards back to the center of the table. "Tell you what," he said. "I've enjoyed this little exercise. Nothing better than having a nice drink with a lovely lady and a first-rate gentleman." He surveyed the shot glasses. "I don't think you want to pay me by the shot for all this. If you help me drain the rest of these, the whole thing is on the house."

"We can't refuse that offer, can we?" Phil said to Sam.

"No," she slurred, "that would be rude. And fistc-fiksa-fiscally irresponsible."

Fifteen minutes later all the shot glasses were empty. Phil and Sam bade farewell to Antoine, and rose to leave.

"Uh-oh," said Sam, and grabbed for Phil's arm. Phil braced himself with both hands on the table. "I agree," Phil said. "Everything is moving."

Antoine remained seated at the table. He laughed and said, "Note that this is a side-effect of standing up, certainly not a side-effect of drinking."

"Antoine, could we leave this sample bottle here with you?" Phil asked. "I don't want to risk dropping it. I'll pick it up later, or a cop named Dale Nivek will stop by for it. Okay?"

"Sure, no problem."

Phil and Sam, arm in arm, bumped their way between the tables to the door. The bartender held the door open for them. After debating who would go through the door first, Sam led Phil out onto the sidewalk. Antoine heard them laughing outside in the sunlight. He took Phil's bag holding the sample bottle to the back room and shut it in his safe, and then returned to the bar room to help the bartender clean up.

Phil held Sam up with his left arm around her shoulders and Sam grabbed Phil around his waist with her right. They set off down the sidewalk at an unhurried window-shopper's gait, though anyone watching closely would see impairment not attributable to shopping. Phil was certain that if he let go of Sam she'd tumble to the sidewalk, and he was uncertain how long he could keep his own feet if he stood alone. Sam wasted absolutely no thought at all on their condition; she watched the shop windows and kept veering toward them to examine things she saw. She was a nice drunk; she had reached a chatty stage and talked happily to Phil, herself, and anyone passing by about something; it was hard to determine the subject. The Scotch made Phil quiet, and he was generally not very talkative to begin with. He decided that the best word for him was 'bemused.' He felt good, his nose was numb, and he wore a constant slight smile. He thoroughly enjoyed Sam's animation and her contact; her clutching his waist, the bumping of her hips and legs against his, her shoulder rubbing on his ribcage. He steered them along, and when they got to the break in the buildings that housed a tiny park he guided them to a rough landing on one of the park benches. The park had two small grassy spaces bordered by concrete, and a few raised platforms with abstract sculpture affixed to them. Another bench held a homeless man, and in the back a mother watched a toddler put stones in his pockets.

"Three ibuprofen and all the water you can drink," Phil said, interrupting Sam's monologue.

"What?"

"That's my patented hangover preventer. Three ibuprofen and lots of water. Combats dehydration. Prevents the hangover."

"Oh. Okay, give 'emmm to me."

"I don't have any *here*. I'm just saying that's what we *need*."

"What do we need?"

"Never mind. We're going to sit here a while. Sooner or later Dale will come through here and I'll talk to him. Okay? Just let me do the talking."

"Oooo, Dale. I like Dale."

"I like Dale too. Just let me talk, ok?"

"Anything you say. Anything you say can and will be used against you in a court of law," Sam laughed.

"Yeah, don't remind me."

The homeless man woke up and approached Phil, his hands in his pockets.

"'Mornin', Phil."

"'Morning, Al."

"Any spare change for one of your cups of coffee?"

"Sure." Phil pulled out his wallet and extracted a couple of bills. "Here. But my stuff's too expensive. You can get twice as much for your money at one of the fast food places."

"Thanks, man." He accepted the bills and jammed them into his pants pocket, then nodded at Sam. "Say, you two seem a little extra 'happy' today."

"We've been doing research," she said.

He laughed. "I've got a Ph.D. in that kind of research. Let me know if you need any help." He wandered out to the sidewalk and disappeared.

They sat and watched as the toddler collected more rocks and the woman with him emptied his pockets. Phil let his eyes close, and he listened to the murmur of passing pedestrians and enjoyed the warmth of Sam's leg resting against his.

"Dale!" Sam proclaimed.

The officer in his winter leather jacket came through the park from the rear and stopped at the bench where Phil and Sam sat. "I don't normally find you two out here. Who's minding the store?"

"Judy's got it today," Phil said. Sam started to say something but Phil pinched her leg and she stopped. "Dale, I've got a really big favor to ask you."

"I don't suppose this would have to do with-"

"Yes, I'm afraid it does. There's a bottle being held at Antoine's for me. It's Dave's bottle, from his office. We found out that somebody drank it and refilled it with a different brand."

"So?"

"I'm sure it's got my fingerprints on it. But it might have somebody else's on there, too, somebody other than Dave. Whoever drank and refilled the bottle. And that person might be the key to keeping me out of jail."

He sighed. "Tell me what you want me to do, as if I couldn't guess."

"I'd like you to get the bottle and have it dusted for prints. And then if you could see if they're on file . . ."

"And just what case would I associate this with? I can't waltz in there and have just anything checked."

"Don't tell them it's my case. Tell them it's a breaking and entering. That's probably what it was, too. I'll even file a report with you – we are missing some stuff."

"Okay, okay. I'll stop by Antoine's this afternoon. This will take a couple days to get results. You've got a couple days, right?"

"Sure. I've got all the time in the world."

Dale snorted. "I'll see what I can do. Your car, by the way, was rented to Anton Zhuziewicz, a Polish national. No criminal record of any sort. The only address was a home address in Krakow." Dale picked at his teeth with a toothpick.

"So he's clean," Phil said, disappointed.

"Maybe he just hasn't been caught yet. Or it could be that

he's got a record under another name. Care to tell me what this is all about?"

"I have no proof other than Dave's notes, but it looks like Dave might have accidentally witnessed a drug deal on September fourteenth between Zhuziewicz and a professor named Essinger. Essinger had hired Dave to follow his wife, and things got mixed up. We're thinking that maybe Essinger realized that Dave knew about the drug deal and killed him to keep him quiet. Or, that someone was blackmailing Essinger with pictures Dave took, and Essinger killed Dave thinking that he was the blackmailer."

"So, Mr. Detective, where do you go from here?"

"I . . . don't know. Any suggestions?"

"I'd wonder if the prof owns a gun, and where he was on the night of October nineteenth. Well, I guess I'm off to Antoine's. You two want to walk down there with me?"

"No, thanks, we're just going to sit right here for a while."

"You sure? I think you should get up and walk with me." He winked at Sam. "You can walk, can't you? Maybe we should have Sam walk this line on the sidewalk."

"Sure!" Sam said and made a move to stand. Phil grabbed her leg and pinched again, and she sat down hard on the bench.

"Dale . . . I know this is a bit unusual," Phil said. "We were doing some research on the contents of that bottle with Antoine, and it got a little out of hand."

Dale waved him off, laughing. "I'm just giving you some shit. As long as you're not out here barfing on people or driving your car, what you do is your business." He looked at Sam. "Take care of this guy, will you?"

"Yes, *sir*!" she responded with a salute.

Dale walked away shaking his head.

"I think it's time we go back to the office," Phil said. "I think I saw some ibuprofen there, and maybe Mary's made some progress."

"I let you do the talking, didn't I?"

"Yes, you did. You were perfect." Phil pulled himself to

his feet using the arm of the bench, then helped Sam to stand.

"Peeeerfect! That's good," she said. "Can I talk now?"

"Sure. C'mon, Xiamorha, let's go." He put his arm around her shoulders again and guided her to the sidewalk.

"Xiamorha. I like that. I like it when you say it. Xiamoooorha," she said. She put her arm around Phil's waist and grabbed onto his jacket.

Sam slept noisily on the cot while Mary and Phil poured over some computer printouts.

"This is all summary-level stuff," Mary said. "We look at that first to see if there are any obvious areas of correlation, then we'll rerun and look at the correlated data values in those areas. Each data class is run against each of the others."

"Only two-way? Can't you do three or more classes at once?"

"Sure. We can try that after we narrow it down a bit with the two-way. Otherwise, there'd be so many possible combinations that this program would run for weeks. And the output would be so large that we wouldn't have time to evaluate it."

Phil used his finger to trace through the tables. He was having a hard time concentrating. The numbers on the printout wouldn't hold still. The ibuprofen and water would help in a few hours. He and Sam had drunk water until they were nearly sick – that was the key. He looked at her on the cot and wished that he were asleep next to her. "So . . . here, for example." He pointed at a box of numbers on the page. "It looks like there may be some correspondence between realtor and buyer; these numbers are higher than most of the others. This means that there are data values in these two classes recurring in combination?"

"Right," Mary said. "So we'll have to examine those classes in more detail. We'll run a two-way of these and display the correlation of the actual data values and see what we've found. If it looks significant, we then use those data values to run more correlations on other data elements and see what else shows up."

"I'd like to see the date distributions on those too," Phil said. "For each deal are there both buy and sell transaction records, or are they two different records in the database?"

"Just one record per deal, with both buy-side and sell-side information in it. It isn't a normalized database, unfortunate in some ways. But it makes for easier correlation with this software."

"Hmm. Looks like we've got some correlation between buyer and seller too."

"Okay, we'll start with detail on realtor-buyer and buyer-seller and see what we've got. I'll display the date and some other data too." Mary got up and went back to the computer to launch some more queries.

Phil called Dominick and gave him the names of the two Scotches that they had selected at Antoine's. "Good," Dominick said, "both are Scotch blends, less than ten years old. One's pretty common and the other we see occasionally. I sell them both."

"Any chance you might have sold either of them recently, up until about a week ago? And would you know who you sold them to?"

"It's probable. But we'll need to pull inventory records, then credit card receipts. Most people buy liquor on credit cards. Say, am I gonna get into any trouble with this?"

"No, Dom. I'm just trying to find out who really killed Dave, and this might be a lead. When could we check inventory and credit card slips?"

"I'll look at inventory transactions today. If I find something, I can dig out credit card receipts tomorrow, but I don't have time to go through them. You can come over and look at them here, though."

"Can I send someone else over to look through them?"

"That'll be fine."

Phil hung up the phone. It was a long shot. Phil realized that whoever refilled the Ardbeg bottle could have done so months ago, or could have done it two weeks ago with Scotch purchased two years ago. But it was also possible that they realized while drinking the Ardbeg that they had to cover their tracks, and quickly bought a lesser bottle of Scotch from the closest source. It was worth a try. He'd send Aaron over to look through the credit card slips.

"Hey," Mary said. "Take a look at this."

Phil shook himself out of his reverie. Mary stood at his side and laid a series of pages on the desk.

"This is the next lower level of summary correlation of realtor and buyer, sorted from lowest correlation to highest. What do you see?"

Phil ran his hands down the page, then flipped to the next page. "Nothing." Nothing jumped out yet; zero correlations. Realtors and buyers all different. He flipped another page. "Hello, Beth." Beth Talbot's name appeared, along with thirteen different corporate names for buyers. The printout showed the count of the number of deals done with each combination. Phil added them up; there were forty-seven deals spread among the thirteen buyers.

"What else strikes you about this?"

Phil looked again. "Beth does a lot of commercial real estate business. She's successful. But we knew that. Let's see." He flipped through the pages again. "She seems to do all her business with corporate clients, whereas other realtors do more with individuals. Is that it?"

"There's more. Do you recognize any of those corporate clients she deals with?"

Phil studied the names. "No."

"And do you see any of those names associated with any other realtor?"

"No, but maybe they have exclusive deals with her."

"Yeah. I think we need to find out who these corporations are, don't you?"

"That could be interesting."

Mary nodded. "We can look for the corporate registrations tomorrow. They're probably either Wisconsin or Delaware corporations. I'd bet on Delaware – fill out a form and mail it in with your check. It's just about that easy. And then we need to look at the dates and locations." She stretched. "I've got the buyer-seller running now. I've got to run home and shower and change, maybe get something to eat. I'll be back later to play around with it." She looked at Sam, still asleep on the cot. "Unless you want me to stay with her."

"No," Phil said, "why don't you go ahead. I'll make sure she gets home." Phil looked at Mary. "How are you doing? Do you need any cash to get by, now that you're working only one job?"

"I'm okay for a while," she said. "They still owe me a check. And you still owe me a check. Or two."

"What are you going to do when this is all over?"

"I dunno. Why don't you ask me that after they acquit you. And if they don't, well, you won't care." She smiled and patted Phil on the shoulder, then walked out.

Phil watched her as she left. He suddenly felt tired, old. He looked at Sam and knew he had to get back to his apartment and crash for the night. But first . . . he approached the cot and rubbed her arm.

"Xiamorha. Xiamorha! Time to go home."

A smile broke across her face and her eyes popped open. "Is it morning?"

"No. Early evening. Let's get you home."

"Okay."

Phil helped her to her feet. She was much steadier than she had been earlier. Phil took her hand and they left the office together.

CHAPTER NINETEEN

Phil woke up feeling great. He lay in bed for a few minutes, trying to determine whether he felt good because his hangover preventative had worked or because there was still alcohol in his bloodstream. He decided on the former, and got up and prepared to go in to the store. He dressed in regulation khakis and a polo, threw on a bomber jacket and a baseball cap and made the drive to the Chocolate Shoppe on dark vacant roads. His hands were cold on the steering wheel, and the pickup's heater was just beginning to pump out warm air as he turned into the little parking lot behind the Discreet Detectives building. He left the truck there and walked, shoulders hunched and collar turned up, to the Chocolate Shoppe.

His opening routine was comfortable, and took him miles away from murders and trials, lies and computers. The first of the staff arrived and he supervised them in the last stages of the bagel and bakery production for the day. They opened the doors as the sky began to lighten. Phil had time for a coffee and to watch through the window as Suzanne, wrapped in a down duster and a cloud of frozen breath, arrived to prepare her store for the day. Then the first customers were upon them and Phil boosted the thermostat to compensate for the heat lost through the door's frequent openings.

Sam arrived, cheeks reddened and eyes watering from the cold. Phil was surprised for an instant to see her, then remembered that she was to work an early shift to spell him to work on the case, and so that she could leave early to get ready for their dinner that night. Flowers; he needed to remember to pick some up on the way home.

"And how are you feeling this morning, Ms. Sang?"

"Dr. Phil," she began while strapping on an apron, "I thought about hating you while you were making me drink all that water. But I've got to say," she fluffed her hair, "it worked. I feel fantastic." She stretched up on her toes and gave Phil a quick kiss on the cheek. "I slept like death, in my clothes, and woke up right on time."

"A little miracle, isn't it."

"I'll say. I didn't do anything really stupid or embarrassing yesterday, did I? I think I remember almost everything and it seems okay to me."

"No, you were fine."

"Good. I really had a good time. Now, you haven't forgotten, have you?"

"What, is today your birthday?"

"No . . ."

"I know! The anniversary of your hiring!"

"No!" She laughed and whacked Phil on the arm with the back of her hand. "No more guessing! Today's my day, our dinner date! I'll expect you at seven. And I need your key." She reached out, palm up.

Phil laughed, too, and removed Dave's key from his key ring. "I didn't forget. I wouldn't miss this for anything." He placed the key in her palm.

She put the key in her pocket. "Now, run along and solve the murder. I've got it all under control here."

Phil stood in Lars Jackson's office, looking out the window. They had been over the alibi situation, but there had been no breakthroughs. There just weren't any corroborating witnesses to place Phil on the shore of Lake Superior on Friday October 19th.

"But there isn't anyone who can place me here in Madison that night either," Phil said.

"True, unless the prosecutor finds someone to lie. It's been known to happen." Lars sat in his chair, hands in his lap. "Let's move on to something else. You know I talked with

Mary Haiger, Xiamorha Sang and the Chocolate Shoppe employees for their statements."

"Yes."

"I'm worried about Mary's testimony."

"Why? Isn't she consistent in her story?"

"Her story's fine, but I think the prosecutor will do one of three things. He'll try to show that you used her to do research for your premeditated murder, or that you used her in a cover-up attempt. Or, more likely that you were both in on the murder together, from the beginning. I'm amazed that he hasn't had her arrested by now."

"That's ridiculous! She was with the FBI. They've got records of her involvement. And most of her research was done for Dave, before I even knew her."

"You can't prove when you first met, can you? The prosecutor will ask her whether she researched the Carillon. Then they'll ask other questions that will get her saying 'yes,' 'yes,' 'yes,' getting you two stuck deeper and deeper in circumstantial evidence. And when I ask her when she did the research and for whom, they won't believe her."

"Why not?"

"Because they will already know that she had a relationship with you, and they'll believe she's covering for you. She was with the FBI. *Was.* Why'd she quit? Because of a relationship with you. You can bet that will be the first thing the prosecutor waves in their faces."

Phil didn't say anything.

Lars continued. "There's no way to prove that the research was done for Dave. The jury and the press will love this. 'FBI agent falls for victim's nephew, works murder scam for love and inheritance.' Scandal. True love and true crime. Tabloid stuff."

"But her testimony is the only thing that can save me! You can counter all the prosecution's points."

Lars shook his head. "Phil, with what they'll do with her testimony . . . you'd be better off if she didn't testify."

Phil sat down in the chair in front of Lars' desk. "This

debate is pointless. The prosecution is sure to call her to the stand. We can't stop it anyway."

"That's not entirely true. There is one way to keep her from testifying." Lars picked up a pen and scratched lines on his desk blotter.

"Well?"

"In this state a spouse cannot be compelled to testify against a spouse."

"Excuse me?"

"Marry the girl, Phil. Do it quick, before they issue the subpoenas. If you wait any longer it will look just like what it is, a dodge to keep her from testifying, and it will make you look even worse."

Phil got up and began to pace. "No way. I can't do that."

"Think it over, Phil, but don't take too long. It gives us control over the situation. If you marry her and we don't want her to testify, then she doesn't. If we decide that she can help after all, then she can testify. But they can't force her." He stopped doodling and set the pen down. "It keeps our options open. And once this is all over and out of the headlines you can quietly get a divorce."

"No." Phil shook his head. "Besides, we're not 'together' anymore. We never really were. It was a passing thing, a mistake." And, he thought, what a mistake it would be to marry her now.

"I'm not talking about love and a lifetime commitment, Phil. It's just a practical matter. Marry her, the sooner the better. Pay her to do it if you have to, just make it in cash. You will have to live with her, and you will have to fuck her. That shouldn't be too unpleasant, given what I've seen of her."

"Now, hang on just a-"

"They'll ask about that in the hearings that will undoubtedly be called to try to disqualify her spousal exemption. If you aren't living with her and you're not fucking her, the court won't believe that this is a real marriage and they may refuse the exemption. It's too late to get her pregnant, though that would be the best."

"She'd never go for it anyway, it's like prostitution."

"Phil-"

"Find another way. We're done for today." Phil walked out the office door.

"Do it, Phil," Lars called after him. Lars drummed his fingers on his desktop, then pressed a number on the phone set. The receptionist answered.

"Hey, honey," Lars said. "I need you to set up a couple of meetings for me. Get Xiamorha Sang and Mary Haiger in here to see me on the Bardo case. Sometime in the next couple days. No, two separate meetings. Haiger first. Thanks."

"Dr. Essinger's office."

"Hi," Mary said. "This is Amy, calling from Dr. Krompholmostiger's office. I was hoping you could help me. I'm doing-"

"Who?"

"Amy. I'm doing his-"

"No, no, Dr. who?"

"Dr. K. Anyway, I'm doing his expense reports and I'm stuck on a couple dates. He says he thinks he was with Dr. Essinger on those dates, but he can't remember what they were doing. Do you have his calendar handy?"

"Yes, but-"

"Good. October nineteenth?"

"Wouldn't you rather just talk to Dr. Essinger? I can transfer you."

"No, no, Dr. K is a bit embarrassed about this; you know, it's a memory thing. A senior moment. He doesn't want Ted to know. Now, about October nineteenth."

"Dr. Essinger and his wife were supposed to be at a dinner speaking engagement in La Crosse that evening, at the University."

"And he made it?"

"Actually, no. His wife got sick and he cancelled."

"Do you know where he was instead?"

"I assume he was at home."

"And the other date I need to know about was September fourteenth."

"Let's see. It just says 'dinner, Le Mont Suisse, seven p.m.' Then 'King party.' Does that help?"

"Maybe that will help him remember. Thanks, and please don't mention this to Ted." Mary hung up the phone.

"'S'matter, Phil?"

"Had a meeting with my lawyer. It didn't go well."

"Oh, sorry. Do you have to glare at me like that? What the hell did I do to deserve that face?"

Phil broke his stare away from Mary and focused on some papers on the desktop. "I suppose you've never regretted doing something. Or not doing something."

"Oooh, I'm not sure I like the word 'regret' used in such close context with me."

"Never mind. It's nothing."

"Not true, but if you don't want to tell me, that's okay. Yeah, I've had an occasional regret. But I don't let 'em last. It doesn't do any good. Can't change the past; you can only change the future."

"Let's change the subject. Any good news?"

"I don't know if it's good news or not. The prof doesn't have an alibi for the night of the murder." Mary went into a detailed account of her phone activities.

"I'm impressed! Your ability to lie is surpassed only by your ability-"

"To lay?" she finished.

"Something like that." Phil rearranged his notes on the desktop. "So Essinger's wife gets sick and he bails on a speaking engagement. That sounds weak, and we don't know if they actually stayed home."

"She's got some sort of power over him, and knows about his fooling around. And specifically with whom. What's she got?"

"I can think of only one thing: she's got the missing photos."

Mary sucked on her lower lip. "Oh, man, that's clever. Dave wants out of this mess, so let's say he sends the photos *and the negatives* to Essinger's wife, anonymously. She's free to use them however she wants, so she cuts off his — use of the hooker. Maybe the drugs, too, or maybe not if she's into that sort of thing. But Essinger must know she's got the photos if she's got that much control over him."

"If Essinger wanted to kill anybody, wouldn't it be his wife?"

"You've got a point."

"Maybe I should bill Mrs. Essinger for the detective work and the photos. Anything else?"

"You've got to talk to the hooker."

Phil sighed. "I was afraid that was going to come up. Why don't you do it? You're a better liar than I am."

"Don't you think it might make just a little more sense for a man to talk to her?"

"I suppose so. Can you find me a photo of Essinger?"

"I bet I can. Ten bucks says I can find one in less than ten minutes."

"You're on."

Eight minutes later Phil had his photograph in hand and his wallet was ten dollars lighter. Mary had moved on to the real estate investigation and was waving some papers in her hand.

"Here's some interesting stuff," she said. "Those corporations buying the properties? Most of 'em were set up over the last ten years or so. Most are holding companies with P.O. boxes in Delaware."

"And the principals?"

"Nine of the thirteen have your friend John Smith as an officer and founder."

"Really?"

"I wouldn't lie to you. Not about this, anyway."

Phil shot her another dirty look.

Mary rolled her eyes. "I'm kidding, okay? Lighten up!"

"Looks like he didn't want to be identified as a real estate tycoon and tried to hide behind some corporate window dressing. What does he do with all those properties?"

"I suppose he sells 'em. Those same corporations are showing up in the detail of the realtor-seller correlation. Look at these." She laid some printouts on the desk in front of Phil.

"So he speculates in real estate. Lots of people do."

"Ah, but look at this!" She laid another printout on the desk.

"Buyer-seller," Phil said, running his finger down the page. "Looks like we've got some repeat performances."

"And those performances star-"

"Smith's companies as seller, and the City as buyer." Phil sat back and scratched his head. "Weird. That's not much speculation, is it, when you sell to the same people." He looked up at Mary, who stood with a Mona Lisa smile and her arms crossed in front of her. "I want to see a-," he began.

"Map with those property locations identified-," she interrupted.

"And a list of his buys and sells in date order-"

"With prices-"

"And appraised values. You're already working on these, aren't you."

"Yup," she said. "They're in the works."

"Good job. What about back-tax sales?"

"What do you mean?"

"Where the city seizes a property due to property tax delinquency and then sells it."

"Oh, yeah. No, I don't think those are in here."

"Add 'em," Phil said. "And repeats on the same property. Same place bought and sold multiple times."

Mary wrote some notes on a FLYN. "I'll put 'em in. Now we're cookin'," she said. "This could be quite interesting. I should have the stuff ready this evening. Are you going to hang around and wait for it?"

"No. I'm . . . meeting Sam at seven."

Her head snapped back. "Oh, really. Gonna get her drunk again? Her place or yours this time?"

"Stop it! You're way out of line."

"And you're not?"

"Mary-"

"Forget it! Just forget it." She hurried to gather the printouts from the desktop.

"Is there anything else? Anything important?" Phil asked.

"I had one more piece of good news, but it's gone now."

"What was it?"

"You had stopped glaring at me."

Dominick told Phil of the results of his inventory search. His records showed he sold three bottles of one brand and two bottles of the other in the past four weeks. "I've got the files of card receipts set aside," he said. "Send somebody over and I'll put them in my office where they can sift through them."

Phil called the Chocolate Shoppe and asked for Sam.

"Hey, Phil, what's up?"

"Guess what. Dominick sold some of the Scotch. I need to send Aaron over there to go through the credit card receipts."

"No problem. When do you want him?"

"I'd like to start him right now, then he can continue tomorrow until he's done."

"We can cover. Hang on, I'll get him."

Phil waited for a few minutes. He could hear the swoosh of the espresso machine frothing the milk, the rattle and clang of the old cash register, muffled voices and a baby crying.

"Hello?"

"Aaron, it's Phil. I need a favor."

"You got it, boss."

"I need you to go to State Street Liquors. Now. Ask to see Dominick. I need you to go through some of his credit card receipts and find the names of the people who bought two kinds of Scotch and the dates that they bought them. Dom will give you the brand names. If you don't finish today, go back tomorrow until you're done."

"Roger that. You need me to follow them or something?"

"No, just get me the names and dates."

"I've been practicing, Phil. I'm really good now. Nobody would see me."

"Great, I'll keep that in mind. But for now, just the names and dates."

"Okay."

"Put Sam back on."

"Can't, Phil. She just left for the day."

"All right. I'll talk to you tomorrow."

Phil hung up and checked his watch. It was nearly four o'clock, three hours before his Wilson Street date. He could hear Mary hammering the keyboard. The roll-top in front of him still held notes and papers that Dave had left. No time like the present, he thought, and he pulled a pile in front of him.

"I thought you had a date tonight," Mary said, breaking Phil's concentration.

Phil checked his watch. "Yow, it's seven-fifteen! Shit!" He dove for the phone, scattering the papers that he had been reviewing, and dialed the Wilson Street house. No answer.

"Damn. Damn!" He jumped up, grabbed his jacket and cap and ran for the door.

Mary walked to the front of the office and locked the outside door and then wandered back to her computer table. She talked to herself on the way. "Bye, Mary." "Bye, Phil." "Thanks for reminding me about the time." "No problem, glad to help." "You gonna be okay working here alone again?" "Sure, don't worry about me." "Maybe I should stay?" "No, really, Phil, go on. I'll be fine. I'll be just . . . fine."

Lights were on behind the window blinds at the house on Wilson Street. Sam's car was at the curb. Phil parked in the driveway behind Dave's car and picked up the flowers from the passenger seat of his truck. It was seven-thirty and he was lucky to have gotten there that quickly, with the stop at the Mom & Pop Shop for the flowers. He ran up to the front stoop, picked some mail out of the mail box, and went inside.

"Sam?"

"Hi," she called from down the hall.

"I'm really sorry I'm late."

"That's okay, I counted on you being late. I'll be out in a second."

The light Phil had seen coming through the windows came not from the lamps but from four clusters of small candles, held in assorted glasses and holders. A fire burned in the fireplace. There was a stereo boom box with a CD player on an end table, a stack of CDs next to it. An aroma from the candles, from the meal, or the fire hung rich and wonderful in the air. He breathed it in, then set the flowers and mail on the arm of a chair and removed his cap and jacket. He picked up the flowers when he heard footsteps in the darkened hall.

Sam emerged from the hall into the soft light of the living room. She wore the blood-red spaghetti-strapped dress, the low-cut one with the sequin accents, the same one she wore to the Ball. The slash, the red high heels, the oriental-print scarf, all the same as it was the night of the Ball. The UW barrette clung to her jet-black hair over her left ear. And that red, red lipstick. Phil felt the rush again, the sledgehammer of adrenaline or testosterone; the warmth washed over him. "Sam, you're just gorgeous," he said.

"Why, thank you," she said. "I thought we'd try this again, maybe get it right this time. I got most of the blood out." She took the flowers from his hands. "How nice! I'll put these in water. Why don't you go and change; I've left some things for you in the bedroom." She stretched up and brushed his lips with hers for an instant, and he smelled her subtle-sweet perfume. "Ground rules for tonight," she said, "no Chocolate Shoppe. No Discreet Detectives. And my name is Xiamorha." She headed for the kitchen and he watched her as she walked, rippling beneath the fabric of her dress.

Phil went down the hall to the bedroom and turned on the light. There he found his tux laid out. She had worked a miracle on the suit and the shirt, and though he could see the outline of some spots here and there if he really studied it, they wouldn't be noticed in soft light. He dressed, then returned to the living room.

"Nice job on the tux, how'd you do it?" Phil called.

"I told you I had an ancient laundry secret," she said from the kitchen. "Believe me, you don't want to know what it is."

"Anything I can do for you?"

"Punch 'play' on the CD player and open the wine."

Phil pushed the 'play' button and the beginnings of Miles Davis' *'Ballads'* CD filled the room. He went into the kitchen. Sam wore a long apron over her dress and was busy at the stove. She had set the kitchen table with a tablecloth, place settings, and wine glasses. He looked around and spotted a bottle on the counter. "Is this the one?"

"Yes," she said without looking, "I took it out of the fridge a few minutes ago. A white, I hope you don't mind. It goes better with what I'm making."

"And what are you making?"

"Seared sesame-encrusted fresh Ahi tuna steaks on a bed of julienne Chinese vegetables, with a soy/wasabi sauce. Rice. And a lettuce salad with a coconut-papaya dressing. An Asian fusion menu."

Phil found the corkscrew in a drawer. Not one of the new fancy ones; no arms to manipulate, no needle to inject air, no cams, levers, or blades. A wooden handle formed a 'T' on top of the spiral metal screw. He started the point of the screw into the wax seal and drove it down into the cork. Then a pull on the wooden handle and the cork came out cleanly, with a pop.

"Wonderful sound," he said, and examined the cork. It looked good, moist, no mold. The bottle was only a year old, made to drink young, so he would have been surprised to find any mold. "It drives me crazy," he said, "when you see people sniff the cork. Do they really expect to smell anything other than cork? You *look* at the cork, you sniff and taste the *wine*. *That's* the only way to know if the wine has corked or gone bad." He poured a splash in one of the wineglasses, swirled it for a moment, then breathed over it. He took a sip, then set the glass down and poured both glasses half-full.

A cloud of steam rose from the stove and Sam reared back to avoid a face scalding. "That was close," she said. "I hope you're not a connoisseur about everything."

"No, but I think I know quality when I taste it. Or see it."

"Done," she proclaimed. "Could you hand me the dinner plates please?"

Phil complied. Sam put a bed of the vegetables on each plate, topped with a block of the seared sesame tuna. A drizzle of wasabi sauce, a small mound of rice, a dish of extra sauce, and the main course was ready. She took salad plates of greens and dressing from the refrigerator and added them to the table. After surveying the scene one last time she untied and removed the apron, then sat at one of the kitchen chairs. Phil sat in the other, across from her.

"Oops, hang on," she said, and got up to get matches. She lit the two candles on the table, then turned off the kitchen light and sat down again. She was golden in candlelight. Phil watched as a little bead of sweat or condensed steam rolled from the base of her throat down her breastbone and disappeared into her cleavage.

"Sam-Xiamorha, this looks fantastic!"

She beamed, then raised her glass. "To getting it right." They touched glasses and drank, then set them down and cut into the Ahi.

They made small talk as they ate, but Xiamorha paid little attention to the conversation. She watched Phil, watched as he cut the rare Ahi and savored it. Some men were imprecise, hurried at their meal; Phil cut carefully, smoothly, appreciating the sensual experiences that came with each type of food. The give of the fish to the blade, the color and moisture on the newly cut face, the crunch of the hot sesame seeds with the soft cool center of the tuna flesh in his mouth. He didn't rush; he gave respect to every bite. Even the rice, the traditional stickiness rather than the modern commercial variety that won't hold together on a chopstick, he appreciated that, too. Her eyes teared, and she shut them.

"Xiamorha, are you all right?"

She blinked a few times. "Yes, fine. I just need a refill, please." Phil refilled both of their wineglasses.

"That was excellent," he said, finished. "You did a marvelous job. Where did you learn to cook like that?"

"I dated a sous-chef a few years ago. I learned some things." She put the last bite of Ahi in her mouth.

They got up and cleared the table except for the wineglasses. Phil stripped off his tux jacket and rolled up his sleeves and Xiamorha donned her apron. They filled the sink with sudsy water and washed and dried all the dishes, pots, and cooking utensils by candlelight. While they worked side by side Phil said, "Your note last week. Did you ever sort out whatever it was?"

"Yes, I think I did." She polished a plate with the dishtowel and put it in the cabinet.

"Good. And?"

"And that's all you need to know for now." She laughed and hung the dishtowel to dry, then took off her apron as Phil drained the sink. She held up the wine bottle. "This one's dead, would you mind opening the other?"

Phil retrieved the second bottle from the refrigerator and opened it, then topped off each of their glasses. While Xiamorha made a trip to the bathroom Phil carried the wineglasses and bottle to the living room. She returned and brought his tux jacket from the kitchen and held it for him to slip on. Then she restarted the CD on the boom box.

"May I have this dance?" she asked.

"You may have all of them."

They slow-danced through Miles Davis' *Ballads*. Phil added wood to the fireplace and Xiamorha refilled their wineglasses. She started a Paul Desmond CD on the boom box and Phil took her and held her, close. They danced, slowly, and she wrapped both arms around his waist and pressed her head to his chest. He buried his nose in her hair, smelled her perfume, the candles and fire. She moved with him but a little out-of-phase so that the fabrics rubbed, the flesh trailed, then rebounded. He traced her shoulder blades with his fingertips, tracked the spaghetti straps down her back. Her skin was warm and smooth.

About halfway through the CD Xiamorha stopped for a drink, poured another, then picked up a small candle and her glass and walked down the hall. Phil stood in the living room. He waited for a minute, and when she didn't return he filled his glass and followed.

He found her standing in the back bedroom, facing the bed with her back to him. The candle and her wineglass were on the nightstand, and she had pulled the comforter and sheets down to the foot of the bed. He set his glass on the dresser and as he approached he saw that her dress had been unzipped in back. He rested his hands on her shoulders.

"I thought you'd never get here," she said.

"Xiamorha, you don't need to do this."

"Yes, I do." She reached up and put her hands on his. "It wasn't right before. It couldn't have been. And I don't know if it can be or will be in the future." She paused and took another breath. "But what I do know is that it's right, right now." She hooked a spaghetti strap with the little finger of each hand, pulled them past her shoulders and dropped her arms. Red dress and sequins slipped over her skin and fell to the floor. She stood in the pool of red, naked except for her high heels and the UW barrette. Her skin shone golden in the candlelight, and Phil heard her breathing. He became acutely aware of his own breathing, too, and blood pounded in his ears. He felt a twinge of guilt – if Mary had a fit when nothing happened, what would she do when something did happen, here, tonight, as she obviously assumed it would? But it was over with her, wasn't it, there and gone. And then he felt guilt again; this was Sam's time, their time, and the start of what he hoped would be . . . and he felt a flash of anger with Mary and with himself. "Xiamorha," he said.

She found his hands again, and drew them around to her breasts. He felt her, round and firm, a scant handful each.

"I'm sorry," she said, "I'm not as big as Ma– as you might like."

"They're beautiful, just right."

Eyes closed, she smiled and leaned back on him. He traced her shape with his fingers, followed the curves of her breasts and teased her nipples until they were so aroused she flinched at his touch. He brought his hands to her waist, then slowly passed them up and down her sides. Not quite massaging, but feeling skin against ribcage, over hipbones, and the muscles in her buttocks and thighs. He moved his hands in front, over her pelvis and down; and he traced her there until she wobbled on her high heels. Phil scooped her up and carried her the three feet to the bed where he laid her down, then undid the buttons of his shirt and discarded it on the floor, and then the rest of his clothes.

She reached out her hand and he took it, and she pulled him onto the bed. They explored each other with kisses, soft and hard, and unhurried touches. Eyes open, they watched each other's reactions. The single candle gave everything a soft focus, and one skin blended with another. When he finally took her the first time, she on her back, he supported himself with his arms. He watched her face, her eyes and mouth, and her breasts as they shifted to his movement. He concentrated on his breathing and he brought her near her climax and then slowed, then brought her near again and slowed, and then her eyes grew wide and her mouth drew into an 'O' as he brought her and let her finish, her back arched and her insides twitching. Then, he was consumed with spasms inside her.

"Ohmygod," she said, panting. "Quick."

He rocked back on his heels, leaving her. She rolled to her stomach, then pushed up to her hands and knees and backed up to him. She reached between her legs and found him, still hard, and guided him again into her warmth and wetness. He moved inside her, holding her by her hips, carefully, slowly, and made sure she could take him fully, and she rocked in counterpoint to him.

Beads of sweat break out on the small of her back as they moved, and he reached around with one hand and felt her breast, bouncing, beating against his hand. He caught it and pinched the nipple, hard.

"Oh yeah," she blurted, "do it again!"

She sped her rocking and then she let out a loud cry and reached back with both hands, grabbing Phil around the thighs and pulling him into her with all her strength, and they came again together. Exhausted, they tumbled to their sides.

"Xiamorha, you are incredible."

She gave a tired laugh. "Thanks. You do pretty well yourself."

"Xiamorha-"

"Shhhhh. Feel the glow . . ."

She reached behind her and found his hand and pulled it around and settled it on her breast, radiating heat. Phil tucked his nose into her hair and breathed her perfume again and the candle and sweat and sex. They fell asleep there, together in the half-light.

CHAPTER TWENTY

Sam woke at the sound of the shower. She got up and put on Uncle Dave's big terrycloth robe, then went to the kitchen and hunted down the coffee maker, a filter, and some ground coffee. She sat on a kitchen chair and waited while it brewed and the aroma filled the room.

Phil entered the kitchen, dressed for work. As he passed her chair he let his hand drift across her shoulders. "Last night was perfect. Thank you." He poured two mugs and set one on the table in front of her.

"Yes, it was, wasn't it." She sipped at the coffee.

"Sam, I-"

"No, stop. Let's leave it right there for now, at perfect." She closed her eyes and breathed the coffee vapors from her mug. "I'll clean up here this morning, then I'll be in to the ChoSho by noon."

"I've got to go."

"I know. I'll see you later."

Phil left with his mug of coffee. Sam sat at the kitchen table and listened to him drive away into the darkness. She sipped her coffee and closed her eyes. Last night; it made her warm and tingly to think about it. She drained the last of the coffee from her mug and turned off the coffee maker, then shuffled down the hall and went back to bed.

Dominick's office was an old kneehole desk in the corner of a crowded stockroom. A bare light bulb hung over it and there was a green metal four-drawer file cabinet along one side. Aaron sat at the desk; on the desktop to his left was a pile of

257

accordion file folders with brown string ties. He had emptied the contents of one folder onto the desk and sifted through receipts. Dom still did things the old-fashioned way, writing out the credit card slips by hand, noting items sold, and running them through the card-press. He didn't even call in the card numbers to check limits. No fancy computerized cash register or card swipe for *this* guy. Aaron had to ask Dom to write the names of the Scotch brands on a sample card receipt in the peculiar shorthand he used, so that he could see what he was looking for. He taped the sample to the desktop. When he came across a card receipt that looked like it might be a candidate he placed it next to the sample for closer comparison.

Aaron had found the first of the receipts he was looking for late afternoon the day before. It had happened just ten minutes into his search, and had given him a thrill and the hope that he'd be done within an hour or two. He had carried the receipt to Dom's old copier and made a photocopy. The next morning Aaron had returned to State Street Liquors still hunting for his second hit, but the excitement of the chase had worn off. He knocked over his coffee and scrambled to mop up the spill with his sleeve and blot-dry the receipts. He found his second and third receipts by ten a.m., but by noon he was still missing the last two. Dom said that it was possible that they could have been cash purchases, or maybe put into the wrong week's folder. It was also possible that he just missed them. Aaron went back to the folder for the week in question, dumped the receipts onto the desk and started again.

"That's got to be just about the dumbest thing I've ever heard!" Mary shook her head in disbelief.

"Now just think about it for a minute," Lars said. "Do you agree that it's important for the defense to manage the witnesses?"

"Obviously."

"And you agreed before when we went through your testimony that it could quite possibly be turned against him."

"I said maybe. I don't know."

"Yeah, maybe. There's only two things that can keep you off of the stand. One, you disappear. Two, we work the spousal exemption."

"Three. Solve the case first."

"Oh, that's looking real likely, isn't it. And if you don't, it will be too late to do either of the other alternatives. You want to disappear right now?"

"No, I can't."

"All right, then. What are *you* gonna do about this? You got him into it, and then you made things worse by fucking him and quitting your job. Your credibility as a witness for the defense is zip."

"Shit. How'd this all get to be my fault?"

"That's the way it looks, honey. Look, this shouldn't be such a big deal. You've got something going with him anyway."

"Not any more, since the arrest. And besides, he's seeing Sam now."

"What? Are they-"

"How the hell should I know? You think I hide under his bed or something? Jesus!" She put her face in her hands.

Lars hadn't foreseen this wrinkle. He leaned back in his chair. He studied the woman in front of him, or rather, the top of her bowed head. He thought he was close, so close, to getting her to buy in. And now this Sam thing. Maybe it could still work. He waited.

Mary looked up. "Did you talk to Phil about this?"

"Yes."

"Does he know you're talking to me about this?"

"No."

"What did he say when you asked him?"

"He said no."

"Well, that's it, then."

"Not really. I think he'll come around if you talk to him."

"He would never listen to me on something like this. He'd think I've got some other motive. My credibility with him is pretty low right now."

"That's understandable. I'm meeting with Sam later today. She might be the only one right now who can talk sense into Phil, but I won't even talk to her about this if you won't agree to do it. Would you do it if Phil asked you to?" He waited again. "Are you willing to let him go to jail because you won't play?"

Mary sat, numb, and thought through the scenarios. As goofy as it sounded initially, Jackson did make a little sense. Could they afford not to do it? Phil and Sam . . . this could ruin them. She felt sick. But then maybe . . .

"What all would this involve?"

"It's simple. You get married, immediately. You live together. You do what it is that happily married couples do – *all* of it, understand? You've got to, to be credible when they ask you about it. And when it's over you get a divorce. It's like a long date with clerk's fees at the beginning and the end."

"All right. I'll do it if it will help keep him out of jail."

"Good girl!"

"But only if *Sam* asks me to."

Lars watched as Mary left his office. Nice piece, he thought, and if Phil wasn't doing her any more maybe he could work something out with her. Probably should wait until Phil's behind bars, though. He'd console her then. Boy, would he. Barbara would never find out, not like the last time. He fished around in his bottom desk drawer but all he came up with were empties. Time for a trip to State Street Liquors. He was glad he'd started drinking again, as it helped him ignore troublesome details like ethics and guilt feelings. He had a problem screwing Phil like this, but it was a matter of self-preservation. Better that it be him. He put on his coat. This Sam complication could be a challenge, but if she really loves the guy maybe she'd go for it to save his ass. Or so she'd think. He put on his hat and whistled to himself as he left the office.

"You were right," Dale said. "Your prints are on the bottle." He handed a brown paper bag to Phil. "We're done with this."

Phil took the bag containing the bottle and tucked it below the counter. "No surprise there. Anybody else?" He counted out the change and handed it to Dale.

"We found some of Dave's. And then there's some partials that don't line up to either you or Dave, but we can't match 'em to anything in the files."

"Well, at least there's proof that there was somebody else in the office. Probably the somebody who refilled the bottle."

"It doesn't prove anything. Those prints could be from whoever stocked the bottle on the store shelf, for all we know. There's just no way to tell. We'll hold the prints in the file in case something else comes up." Dale put his change in his pocket and picked up the coffee cup and the Danish, and left.

Phil wiped the counter and watched as Ellen poured a hot chocolate and Lauren ground beans for a latte. The staff seemed extraordinarily curious this morning. 'Have a nice evening, Phil?' 'How'd things go last night?' It's hard to keep secrets in any family, and he decided that they knew. They found out somehow that he and Sam were going to get together last night. He made a mental note to address this in a future staff meeting. Good or bad, the relationship could cause either reaction in the employees. He didn't know which way it was swinging them, and at this point he had no idea what to say about it. It is what it is, he decided, and they'll just have to deal with it.

Mary came into the Chocolate Shoppe around eleven o'clock and approached Phil at the counter.

"A double espresso to go." She seemed humorless, and her hands shook as she dug in her wallet for money.

"Well, good morning to you, too." He called out the order to Lauren, and turned his attention back to Mary. "No, no, I'll get this," he said. "What the hell is wrong with you?"

"Nothing. Caffeine withdrawal. Are you coming in today? We've got some good stuff to look at."

"I'll be over in a little bit. Are you sure you're all right?" He could only catch fleeting eye contact with her, which was unusual; she liked to look right into him, unblinking.

"Yeah. I've gotta go." She grabbed the espresso from Lauren's hand and headed for the door. As she disappeared down the sidewalk Phil caught Lauren and Ellen watching him. They turned, embarrassed, and hurried off to clear tables. Weird.

Sam arrived at noon, fresh and cold-air energized. She paused and chatted with some of the customers at tables before she shed her coat and headed for the back office. Lauren intercepted her and walked with her. After a few minutes they both reappeared, and Sam tied on an apron behind the counter.

"Hi, there!" she said to Phil with a grin.

Phil smiled back. "You're looking pretty cheerful. You must have had one pleasant evening last night, Xiamorha."

"The best. And here, it's Sam." She winked and handed him the key to the Wilson Street house.

Phil's pickup truck turned off of Highway 12 and came to a stop in the gravel parking lot of the 'Jiggles' club. There were three other cars in the parking lot. The club was located in an aging steel pole-barn building, formerly a feed store, just a mile outside of the city limits. Lower property taxes and lax enforcement of alcohol, tobacco, and adult business laws were undoubtedly a motivator for setting up here, Phil mused. Not much business in the afternoon, though. The illuminated sign by the road said 'Live Nude Girls.' Sure beats dead nude girls. Phil got out of his truck and went inside.

The place smelled of hay and beer, with a delicate hint of insecticide. On a small stage in front of him was a young red-haired woman, sitting topless on a wooden chair under a spotlight. Some country music played on a sound system, and when she saw Phil the woman got up and began a half-hearted dance around the chair. Phil headed for the bar in the corner, and when she saw him do that she gave up her dance and sat down on the chair again. There was one bartender on duty and one patron at the far end of the bar, a man, sitting motionless with a beer clasped between his hands.

"Beer," Phil said to the bartender.

"What kind?"

"Doesn't matter. Whatever's on tap."

The bartender filled a glass from the nearest tap and set it in front of Phil. "That's two bucks."

Phil took a ten-dollar bill from his wallet and laid it on the bar. "I was wondering if maybe you could help me. I'm looking for a girl."

"There's one right there," the bartender said, nodding toward the stage.

"No, not that one. There's a particular one, I think she works here. A blonde, kinda tall, like about five-ten or so. Medium build. You know anybody like that?"

"We got a lot of blondes. They don't come on until tonight. She got a name?"

"No." Phil pulled a computer-printed photo from his pocket and handed it to the bartender. "But she might be seeing this guy."

The bartender studied the picture and handed it back. "I think I've seen him, maybe a couple of times. But I don't know about him with any of the girls. Why don't you ask Misty?"

"Misty?"

"Misty Valley. On stage."

Phil left the ten on the bar and took his beer to a table next to the stage. He motioned for Misty to join him, and she got up and walked to the wooden steps and down to the floor. Phil held a chair out for her, and she sat down.

"Well, well, a gentleman," she said. "Don't see too many of those here."

"That's odd, isn't it? Misty, I was hoping you might be able to help me." Phil tried hard to keep his eyes on her face. She must use a tanning bed, he thought, as she was a mass of freckles and had no tan lines.

"Depends on what you have in mind."

Phil took a twenty-dollar bill from his wallet and handed it to her with the picture. "Have you seen this guy?"

Misty tucked the bill into her g-string, then looked at the picture. "Yup."

"I hear there's a blonde, maybe a dancer here, that's been seeing him. About five-ten, medium build. Maybe late twenties or early thirties. You wouldn't know anything about her, would you?"

"I might."

Phil took another twenty from his wallet and held it in his hand. "I'm not paying ten bucks a word."

"Yeah, yeah. She's a part-timer, fills in now and then. The rest of the time she works for an escort service."

"What's her name?"

"Dee. Dee Best."

Phil laughed. "Sure."

"That's her real name, buddy."

"What's the name of the escort service?"

"Temporary Trophies."

Phil stood up and let the twenty fall to the table. "Thanks, Misty."

"What, that's all you want?" She looked up in surprise.

"That's all."

"Hey, at least let me give you a lap dance or something for your forty bucks."

"Some other time. Buy yourself some sunscreen."

"Let's look at the map." Mary brought the map up on the screen. Phil stood behind her and looked over her shoulder. He put his hand on the back of her chair to steady himself as he leaned forward. She shifted away when his hand accidentally brushed her back. The map view came up, and it covered the whole isthmus from Lake Mendota to Monona, including State Street and all of downtown surrounding the Capitol building. There were dozens of yellow dots on the screen, overlapping and obscuring each other.

"The dots mark the locations of all the real estate sales that I could find over the last ten years," she said. "What we can do now is change what sales we display by altering the selection criteria for the sales." She clicked her mouse and a dialog box popped up showing the data items available for use as selection criteria. At the SaleYear field she typed 'where SaleYear > (CurrentYear – 5)' and clicked the 'go' button. Half of the yellow dots disappeared. "Neat, huh? Now it's only the last five years of sales. So where do you want to go from here?"

"Let's look only at Beth's sales."

Mary tabbed to the SaleYear field and deleted her criteria, then tabbed to the Realtor field and typed '= Talbot' and clicked the 'go' button again. The display changed, and more dots were gone. There were occasional dots on State Street and in the blocks surrounding the Capitol. There was a concentration of dots along and extending from the shores of Lake Monona north for several blocks.

"So Beth does a lot of commercial property downtown, and particularly extending south to Lake Monona. She's benefited from all the downtown redevelopment plans, both for State Street and for the Monona Terrace area. No surprise there." Phil pulled at the skin on his chin as he thought out loud.

"Let's drop Beth for a moment and look at Smith's companies," Mary said. She typed an extended series of criteria into the Buyer field then copied them to the Seller field. Click. "Look. These are deals where he's either buyer or seller." The dots appeared along the shores of Monona and for a few blocks inland.

"Okay, so he's smart enough and has enough resources to buy property where there's major development action going on. And he primarily uses Beth for a realtor. Nothing wrong with that."

"*Exclusively* uses Beth for a realtor," Mary corrected. "By the way, I included the back-tax sales you asked for. Let's look just at those." She made the changes and clicked on 'go.' Dots changed, but the pattern remained similar with more dots concentrated along the Monona shore.

"That was a blighted area," Phil said. "Again, no big

surprise. Owners walked away from their properties. The City seized them for back taxes and sold them. But why would the City sell them if they were going to need that land for the development of Monona Terrace and that new marina and boathouse? They just bought them back again later."

"Timing might explain it." She jiggled the mouse as she thought. "We need to get a timeline of events associated with the Terrace development district projects. Then we can mix in a timeline of the sales with those development elements. Maybe that will show us something that we can't see on the map."

Phil nodded. "Good idea. I know who can help us with the timeline. The guy at McDermott Books is an amateur historian. I'll run down and see him."

"I'll set up a new file to hold a series of dates and events, whatever you guys come up with. We'll merge that with the sales transactions and then sort them in date sequence and see what we get." She paused. "But there's got to be something else. Timing of legal real estate deals can't be enough to get a man killed."

"Money."

"Ms. Sang, won't you please come in. Nice to see you again." Lars stood behind his desk and gestured at a side chair. "Have a seat."

Sam entered the office and sat in the chair. The receptionist who escorted her set a thermal carafe of coffee and two mugs on the corner of the desk and left. Lars poured both mugs full and handed one to Sam, then took the other and stood, sipping, looking at her. Phil had good taste, he decided. This one wasn't quite so in-your-face sexy, at least not in that down jacket. Wish she'd take it off; she has a nice little figure, he recalled. She's so serious. She's got a quiet exotic beauty, and almost an innocence that he found very appealing. Maybe she'd need consoling, too.

"Can I hang up your coat for you? No? Okay, then let's get down to it." He sat down behind the desk. "I appreciate your coming over on short notice. We have a critical situation, and I think you might be able to help."

"I'll do what I can."

"Good. Let's talk about the testimony. I believe you know Ms. Haiger . . ."

McDermott Books was the best independent bookstore on State Street. Colin McDermott carried both new and used books, and he maintained such a unique inventory and an atmosphere of intellectual exchange that he had established a large set of customers who refused to shop anywhere else. He even lent used books to special customers who either couldn't make up their minds or who couldn't afford a volume. It was like Sylvia Beach's Shakespeare & Company in 1920's Paris, the literary soul of the community.

"Col, you want to buy some books? My uncle's got a few that I might like to sell."

"Phil!" Colin rose from his stool behind the cash register and reached out his hand to shake Phil's. "Aye, it's been an age, hasn't it, though. Good to be seein' ya. And about those books, well, I've seen 'em before and I expect I can see 'em again. Bring 'em by and we'll see what we can do."

"Great, I will. But that's not really why I'm here. I need your help, a history lesson. Recent history."

"Oh? Book history or real history?"

"Real. I need a timeline on the events around the previous and current phases of Monona Terrace. The Convention Center, and the coming marina and boathouse and key elements related to them."

"Facts or commentary?"

"Both."

"Aye, that'll cost you extra! And what to this might you be alignin'?"

"Real estate sales."

McDermott pursed his lips and looked at Phil from under one frowned eyebrow. "Thomas Mann said, '*There is nothing that is not political.*' Are you sure you want to travel this path?"

"I have no choice. You know that."

"You aren't the first, but 'twas not healthy for the last."

Phil searched his memory, then said, "'*Use your health, even to the point of wearing it out. That is what it is for. Spend all you have before you die; and do not outlive yourself.*' George Bernard Shaw."

McDermott nodded. "I can have it for you on the 'morrow, if I can find what I did for Dave. It's here," he gestured vaguely at a wall of papers and books, "awaiting rediscovery. Call before you come."

"All done?" Dominick asked as Aaron approached the front counter.

"Yeah, I guess. There's just one I couldn't find." He handed some slips to Dominick. "Here are the ones I found. I copied 'em. And here's the files." He dropped the accordion files on the counter. "Thanks, man!"

Dominick nodded. "Tell Phil good luck, and I hope this helps." He watched as Aaron went out the door, then he picked up the individual charge slips and looked at the dates so he could put them back in the right files. He took the first slip and found its corresponding accordion file and opened it, then casually paged through the slips. That had been a good week. People stocking up before homecoming. All manner of alcohol sales; lots of beer, wine, and the hard stuff. He flipped through more slips. Some were regular customers that he recognized, and there were lots of irregulars; one-timers, transients, and students. The fake IDs were getting harder and harder to tell from the real ones. He stopped at the last slip in the file, looked at it, sighed, then pulled it out and laid it on the counter. Nice kid, he thought, but not too observant. That last slip wasn't hard to find at all.

Two hours later Sam left Lars Jackson's office. Her face was ashen and mascara streaked, her eyes red. She walked quickly down the hall and past the receptionist, then out the waiting room door. The receptionist got up and charged down the hall and stopped at Lars' door.

"What did you do to that poor girl? She's a wreck, for God's sake!"

"Nothin', honey, nothin'. Now shut the door, I've gotta make a call."

"Well?" Mary looked up at Phil, who walked in carrying a paper bag.

"Nothing yet. Sounds like Dave asked him for the same information. We should have it tomorrow. This is our Ardbeg bottle."

"I'm sorta stuck until then. Any new ideas?"

Phil sat down in the side-chair facing Mary. "One thought did occur to me on the way back here. We never really inspected the scene of the crime, never looked for clues."

"What would you call all my crawling around on my hands and knees in the Carillon?"

"I'd call that several feet too high."

"Ooh, gotcha." She checked her watch. "It's only five o'clock. What's your plan?"

"Find an access hatch. When it gets dark, go in and try to make my way to the Carillon and see what I can find."

She rolled her eyes. "It's just that simple, huh? How do you plan to get in through a locked hatch?"

Phil smiled at her. "I know someone who was trained to pick locks. What's more, this person has God-knows how many other kinds of shady stealth skills."

"You sweet-talker, I thought you'd never ask."

"What would you recommend for this operation?"

"Wear dark clothing and rubber-soled shoes. Gloves. Bring a small flashlight. Meet me on the Lakeshore path below the Social Sciences building at about eleven p.m. I'll bring a flashlight, compass, notebook, and a few other tools of the trade. We'll find a close access hatch, hopefully one screened from the road."

"I have two areas I want to inspect: the Carillon and also the South Hall access where we lost our Phantom friend."

"In that case, let's do it differently," Mary said. "Meet

here at ten. We'll walk up Bascom Hill like a couple, then casually turn around South Hall and jump into the bushes and down that hatch just like he did. Saves us trying to find one in the dark."

"Make it nine, and we'll grab a quick something to eat down here first."

When Sam got back to her apartment she went right to the bathroom and threw up. She knelt, clenched the toilet seat with both hands and hung her head in the opening, stomach cramping; tears streaming down her face and dripping off of her nose into the vile water. Again. And once more, until there was nothing left. Gato came into the bathroom and picked his way over her legs, sniffed the air and then jumped into the empty bathtub. Sam pulled a hand-towel down from the towel bar and wiped her face, then curled up in a ball on the floor.

The phone rang, but she didn't answer it.

"Burger and fries with a soda. Bifteck et frites, avec eau de seltz. Sounds better in French," Mary said, finishing. "You really know how to show a girl a good time."

"Hey, I paid for it, so don't complain." Phil redialed his cell phone. Still no answer. He tossed down the last of his Coke and gathered up the remains of their meals. "Now it's time for you to earn your keep." He threw away the garbage and they left the restaurant.

They could have been taken for a couple coming back early from clubbing, either Techno or Goth, with their black outfits. They walked down the State Street sidewalk toward campus, Phil's arm around Mary's waist and her hand in his back pocket. Their act began on State Street and had to continue until they were safely in the tunnel. They stopped in front of South Hall to let other couples pass, and Mary pulled Phil's head down and locked her lips on his. No one paid them much attention; they just stepped around them.

"Hey," Phil said, breaking it off, "I'm really not comfortable-"

"Sorry about that," she said. "It seemed like the logical thing to do. We're acting like a couple, remember? Get with it. I think we're okay, nobody's near."

They ambled around the corner of South Hall, arms around each other, and entered the darkness along the side of the building. Seeing no one, they took out their flashlights and began searching behind the bushes for the entrance hatch.

"Next clump down," Phil said, and they moved to the next knot of bushes. "Here we go."

"Crap. There's a lock," Mary whispered. "You watch for people, I'll try to get it off." She unzipped her black jacket and reached into the inside pocket and withdrew some lock picks. She held her flashlight in her mouth as she crouched over the lock and worked her tools. Phil stood, back against the building, and swiveled his head first one way, then the other. No one. No one. No one. Uh-oh. "Cop," he hissed.

The university patrolman was walking up Bascom Hill on the same sidewalk they had used, and was swinging his flashlight beam along the buildings. He had just passed South Hall and was making the turn onto the sidewalk that would lead him right past them. Mary doused the flashlight and put down her tools, then grabbed Phil and locked him in another passionate embrace. "Grope me!" she whispered through the kiss, "now!"

"What?"

"Feel me up, for God's sake! Hurry!"

Phil parted her jacket with his right hand and began rubbing and squeezing her left breast through her black t-shirt. She moaned, louder than necessary he thought, and the beam of the flashlight passed the corner of his eye and lodged on the side of her face, then down. It paused where Phil's hand was moving. The officer stopped.

"Hey, you two! Take it inside!"

"Okay, officer," Mary said. She pulled back from Phil and straightened her jacket. "Let's go, darlin'." She took Phil by the hand and led him out of the bushes and down the sidewalk in the direction the officer had come. The cop watched them until they disappeared around the front of South Hall, then he continued on his way.

Ten minutes later they were back in the bushes alongside South Hall. "A few more seconds and we would've been in," she said as she removed the lock from the hasp. "Let's go." Phil lifted the grate and Mary found the metal ladder with her feet and climbed down into the tunnel. Phil followed, holding the grate with one hand and gently closed it overhead.

Once on the tunnel floor they shined their flashlights around. The steam tunnel was narrow, lined with pipes and wire bundles of various sizes and textures, just wide enough for one person to pass at a time. The ceiling was low, also lined with pipes and wires resting on hanging metal supports, and Phil had to duck. The floor and walls of the tunnel were composed of concrete and concrete block. There were light bulbs protected by wire cages every ten feet or so but they could find no switches to turn them on, so they traveled by one flashlight and kept the other in reserve. Mary strapped a diver's compass onto her wrist and she checked their direction. "We need to go north and west to get to the Carillon," she whispered. "The compass is a little goofy with all this metal around, but I think we're going in the right direction."

The tunnel ran straight north, parallel to the South Hall wall, and crossed under the green on Bascom Hill. Phil cracked his head on a low-hanging pipe support, and they stopped while Mary checked for damage to his scalp. None found, they moved on. There was another access to the surface at the side of North Hall – someone had spray-painted 'N. Hall' on the tunnel wall where some pipes made a 90-degree bend and disappeared into the wall. Mary and Phil continued north, and their tunnel dead-ended into a larger one that ran east-west.

"The main. It probably goes from the plant up Park Street to Science Hall, then west paralleling Observatory Drive," Phil said. It was still crowded, holding larger pipes, and the temperature was hotter from the big steam mains. The humidity was up too, and there was more water dripping. Mary peeled off her jacket and hung it on a valve handle. They turned left and, avoiding standing water on the floor, made their way west.

"Keep track of the turns on this," Mary said and handed a notebook and pen to Phil. "We'll need to reverse all the turns to get out again." The tunnel sloped up a little and they encountered a branch tunnel to their left.

"Has to be Bascom Hall," said Phil, "onward." The tunnel sloped down again, more steeply, following the contour of the hill.

"The Carillon and Social Science buildings should be on our right about now," Mary said, "but there's no tunnel."

"Keep going, there must be another branch up here somewhere."

They arrived at another "T." To the left ran a large tunnel, to the right the corridor grew smaller. The walls of the right tunnel were a mixture of block and brick.

"Turn right," said Phil. "This looks like an older section, like Hanley said." They went right, and the tunnel again took a downward slant, then bottomed out and came to another "T" where there was an access ladder to a grate above. Phil had been writing the turns on one page of the notebook and sketching them on another. "Flashlight, please." Mary pointed the light onto the notebook. "Left should lead to Elizabeth Waters, the women's dorm, and to the other old lakeshore dorms," said Phil. "Right should be Social Science and the Carillon." He took off his jacket and laid it on the floor. He could feel the sweat running from his head down the back of his neck. Mary's t-shirt was soaked, and she wiped her forehead with the back of her forearm. They set off to the right. The tunnel began to climb again, and it grew dramatically smaller in height and width. They turned sideways and crouched to get through some areas. They went to their hands and knees for others. Insulation had fallen from some of the pipes, and Mary's shoulders came dangerously close to the scalding metal. "Lower, get lower!" Phil advised. Then they felt some air movement, and at a 90-degree left bend in the tunnel there was a small chamber where they could stand. Mary scanned the room with her flashlight, and spotted a grate set in the ceiling several feet above them.

"I think we've arrived," she said. "But there's no ladder."

"Spread your legs."

"Ooooh, now we're getting somewhere."

Phil knelt behind her and put his head between her legs, then held her shins and stood up so that she sat on his shoulders.

"I kinda like this," she said.

"Shut up and tell me where to go. Hurry, I can't hold you very long."

"Okay, forward, forward, now left a foot, a little more. Stop. Now turn around." She had her fingers of one hand through the grate, and held the flashlight with the other. "I need to get my face closer. I'm gonna kneel on your shoulders. Left leg first." She leaned right and worked her left shin onto Phil's left shoulder, then leaned left and worked her right. Then she straightened up, pulling on the grate. "Ah. Perfect." She moved the flashlight beam around through the grate. "Phil, we were right! I can see most of the first floor. And the grate is wide enough that you could stick a muzzle through and get a good angle. They waited for the right moment, found him with a flashlight and shot right through here!" She worked her way back to a seated position, then Phil knelt so she could get off.

The flashlight was starting to dim. "We'd better look around quick and go," Phil said. "I left the other flashlight in my jacket back at the last junction."

Mary systematically moved the light over the walls, around the floor, and across the ceiling. There was nothing there that appeared to be evidence of any sort, other than a few scratches on the floor beneath the grate. "There," she pointed at the scratches, "maybe left by a ladder or something." They looked for any object that could be used as a ladder or stilt, but found nothing. The flashlight grew dimmer.

"Time to go. Ladies first."

Mary put the flashlight in her mouth and went back to her

hands and knees and re-entered the little tunnel going downhill the way they had come, and Phil followed. The flashlight died, and they felt their way through the blackness. Phil was trying to estimate their progress and about how far they had come from the junction when Mary ran into his jacket on the floor. She found his flashlight and turned it on.

"Much better." She stood up and handed Phil the jacket. "Why don't you lead for a while. You've got the map."

Phil took the flashlight and reviewed his notes, then set off backtracking their route. His notes and map were good, and they collected Mary's jacket from the valve handle where she had left it. Then it was back through the tunnel past North Hall, under the green, and to South Hall. There, under the access, they put their jackets on. Phil took a moment to shine the flashlight around the space. He scanned the pipes on the walls, the floor, and all the cable bundles running across the ceiling. Then he checked the ladder leading up to the access hatch. There was a little something stuck on one of the bolt-heads of the ladder support brackets. He reached for it. It was a piece of black fabric, torn, about an inch square. He turned to Mary and showed her the patch. "Did you lose any material on the way in?" She checked herself.

"No. Give me the flashlight and I'll check you."

"No need. I'm not wearing anything like this. Maybe somebody else we know lost it on the way down the ladder. Somebody who was in a hurry." Phil put the scrap in his pocket. "I don't know about you, but I'm ready to go." He climbed the ladder and turned off the light, then slowly opened the access grate and looked around. It was clear. He climbed out and held the grate open as Mary followed, then set the grate down again. She locked it in place.

They emerged from the bushes arm in arm and sauntered down the sidewalk, turned at the end of South Hall, and headed down the hill toward State Street.

It was almost midnight when Mary locked the deadbolt on her front door. She threw her jacket on the couch. Hoover woke, barely, opened his eyes to check to see who was there, then closed them again and was soon snoring from his spot on the rug. Mary picked at her t-shirt, sticky-wet with sweat, and had it half off when there was a knock at her door. She put her shirt back on and looked through the peephole, then unlocked the deadbolt and opened the door.

"Sam. C'mon in."

CHAPTER TWENTY-ONE

"When I couldn't get you on the phone I decided to come over and wait for you."

Mary nodded, and pointed Sam toward the couch. "Beer? Soda?"

"No, not right now."

Mary went to the refrigerator and found a beer, opened it, and returned to the living room. She sat on the opposite end of the couch from Sam, pulled her legs up underneath her and took a long drink. Hoover sighed loudly and went back to sleep. Mary took another drink and studied the woman at the other end of the couch. Her black hair and big dark eyes, the little mouth. Café-latte skin, flawless except for some small scars on her left cheek. She wore a neat white shirt, like a man's dress shirt but a woman's, buttoned except for the top button, with the outline of her bra faint against the fabric. A black woven-leather belt. Jeans, new, with faint creases. Black ankle-high boots with three-inch heels. She's a beauty, Mary decided, and on top of that what she's about to do takes balls.

Mary looked down at herself, at her sweat-soaked black t-shirt, her wet and muddy black jeans, and bare feet. I can be a white shirt, yes, but a man's white shirt, she thought. Untucked, and sleeves rolled up. A couple buttons unbuttoned, top and bottom. I'm no bra, no belt. I'm faded and frayed jeans. "I'm a mess," she said. "We were in the steam tunnels."

Sam looked down at her hands in her lap. "You know why I'm here."

"Yeah."

"Will you do it?"

"I don't know. You haven't asked me to."

"Why should that make any damned bit of difference to you?"

Mary laughed. "That's a good question. Maybe I've got an overdeveloped sense of fair play, and this seems like cheating. It isn't any fun to win when you cheat."

"This isn't a game. Not to me, anyway."

"I didn't say it was a game. It's more a competition, isn't it? Or maybe I figure that the three of us are bound together in this, like it or not, and we all need to agree if this is going to work. We're all going to be committing perjury together."

"That makes a bit more sense."

"Maybe I also need to see how much you really care about this guy."

"It doesn't seem right, or fair, I mean. It seems like I just woke up and figured out what I want, and now I've got to give it up to have any chance of ever getting it." Sam fussed with her belt buckle. "Are you in love with him?"

"Shit, Sam, I've known him maybe three weeks. It's a bit early, don't you think?"

Sam was silent.

"Like him, yeah, I like him a lot," Mary continued. "We have fun and I think we work well together. At one point I thought we might have possibilities. Maybe we still do." She watched Sam carefully for a reaction. "You do want me to be honest with you, right?"

"Yes. But why'd you have to come along now, and why did you-"

"Why'd I move so fast? When I see something that interests me, I go for it. Maybe the better question is what the hell took you so long? You've known him, what, two years?"

"Three."

"Three. Just where the hell have you been?"

"I'm asking myself the same question." Sam shook her head. "I don't understand how you can do this so casually. Doesn't getting married mean anything to you?"

"I've learned to do a lot of things, pleasant and

unpleasant, to achieve an end result."

"That would make me dead inside."

"It would make me dead inside not to." Mary took another sip of her beer and sat back against the cushions. She untucked one leg and rubbed Hoover down his back, and waited.

"If there's any chance that this could help save him . . . please." Sam looked up and met Mary's gaze. "Please do it."

"You know what that means? Jackson explained it to you?"

"Yes. Do everything you have to do."

Mary drained her beer and set the can on the end table. "Look. I know you're in love with him, and right at the moment he thinks he's in love with you. And knowing both of you, I'd guess that neither one of you has said it. That's your problem, not mine. And he's certainly *not* in love with me; not now." She leaned forward. "You know that the only way he'll go for this is if *you* convince him to do it. If you can do that, then I'll marry him. If we keep him out of jail and if I haven't been able to change his mind about which one of us he's in love with, I'll go along with the divorce. I can't be any more honest than that. Do we have a deal?"

"Okay. I'd like that beer now."

Mary got up and retrieved two cans from the refrigerator and opened them. She handed one to Sam and then sat on the couch again.

"Sam, if I were in your position I don't know if I could stand to do what you're about to do."

"It makes me sick to think about it. I don't like you, and I don't like what you've done to my life. But in an odd way you may have become my best friend today."

"Or your worst enemy."

When Phil got to the Chocolate Shoppe to do the open on that morning he found the lights on. Sam was there, the opening routines already nearly complete. She was in the kitchen checking the day's baking in the ovens. She had flour handprints on her jeans, an apron around her waist, and the sleeves of her white shirt rolled up past her elbows.

"Hey, what the hell's going on here?"

She wheeled around at Phil's voice. "Hi. I couldn't sleep, so I figured I'd do something useful."

He looked at her as she stood, smiling, wiping her hands on a towel. The top three buttons of her shirt were open and her bra pushed her breasts into partial view. Nice, he thought. He knew he was about to be manipulated, but he decided he might as well enjoy it.

"Good," he said, "I wanted to talk to you about something anyway." What he really wanted was to take her, right there, right then. On the floor, or on the stainless steel prep table, flour and dough crumbs and all.

"And I need to talk to you, too." She finished with the towel and hung it on the handle of an oven door. "You first."

"Ah. Well. I was wondering if you could get Judy to do Sunday and if you'd like to come over to my place and watch the Packer game. With me, alone. Nothing fancy, maybe we'll just grill some brats or burgers."

"I'd like that a lot," she said, "but maybe you'll change your mind after what I've got to say."

"Oh? This doesn't sound good."

"Let's sit." Sam pulled up a couple of metal chairs from along the wall and set them facing each other. They sat there in the kitchen and Phil waited for Sam to speak.

"I met again with your lawyer yesterday. He said some things that made sense."

"That's remarkable. The last time I talked to him he made no sense at all. I'm beginning to think I'm using the wrong lawyer."

"Shush. I need to get through this. Don't interrupt."

"Okay."

"He told me about Mary's testimony and how it could hurt you. And he told me about how important it was for him to be able to control whether or not she testifies. He told me about the only option available." She reached forward and took Phil's hands in hers. "I've given it a lot of thought. We need to use every trick. I want you to do it."

"You don't mean-"

"I want you to marry her."

Phil shook his head. He hadn't expected this and he felt confused, hurt. Maybe she didn't care for him after all. "I can't do that, Sam."

"Yes, you can."

"No! Besides she'd never go for it."

"She will. I've talked to her about it."

"What? When?"

"Early this morning."

"Sam, she's using you! Don't you see that?"

"She didn't engineer this thing. I know she'll try to use it, but I'm using her, too."

"No."

"Why not? She'll give you a divorce later."

"Sam, I-" he searched for words, "I-oh hell. Sam, I'm in love with you, not her."

She squeezed his hands. "You don't know how much I've wanted to hear that. I love you, too. I finally realized that I have for years."

"I can't do this to you."

"Phil, you can't *not* do it to me!" She released his hands and got up, then paced around the prep table. "I'm not happy about this, believe me. It tears me up inside to think about it, about you and her. *God!*" She slammed her fists down on the prep table and flour poofed into the air. "Things could have been *so* different, *so* much better. The time I've wasted!" She trembled and worked her hands open and closed on the table. She flicked hair out of her face with one hand and left flour streaks on her forehead. "But this improves your chances for staying out of jail, so you *have* to do it!"

Phil leaned forward and put his face in his hands. He said nothing.

"Phil, don't you understand? Damn it! You're not doing it *to* me, you're doing it *for* me. If you really love me, Phil, you'll do everything you can to stay out of jail. That's the only way you and I will ever have a chance." She took a deep breath. "Do it for me, Phil. If you won't, I'll walk away. Right now."

She stood, waiting, while Phil sat with his face in his hands. The timer on the oven rang. A truck went by in the street outside, brakes squeaking as it slowed for the cross-street. A thud announced that a bundle of Saturday papers hit the sidewalk outside the store. She heard her own breathing, felt her pulse in her neck. Her fingers clenched flour on the prep table. Phil raised his head, and she saw tears, silent, spilling down his face.

"Will you be my best man?"

Sam came around the table and sat down astride Phil's lap. She pulled his head to her shoulder and wrapped her arms around his neck and squeezed.

"It's got to be done as quickly as possible," Sam said.

"How quick is that?"

"Why not today? A civil ceremony is the way. Fill out the form, pay the money, and a court commissioner says a few words. Done."

"That's it?"

"Oh, the blood test. You both have to get a blood test first."

"How long does that take?"

"Used to be it took a few days to get the results back, but now they do it on-site at the clinic while you wait. Takes an hour or so."

"How'd you get so smart about all this?" Phil asked.

"I had lots of time this morning waiting for you to arrive, so I used the Internet." Sam pulled burned cookies from the oven and threw them away.

"And I suppose you know the hours and location of a walk-in clinic?"

"Nine to noon, East Washington at Highway 151."

"And the Court Commissioner's office?"

"Open until three today. They do a good business on

Saturdays."

Phil shook his head. "You don't leave much to chance, do you? I suppose we should call Mary."

"She'll be here at nine."

The ceremony, if it could be called that, was brief. They stood before the Formica counter under the fluorescent lights, opposite the commissioner. Mary held Phil's left hand and Sam his right. The commissioner stamped and signed the marriage license, pronounced them man and wife under the laws of the State of Wisconsin, County of Dane. Phil and Mary signed the license, then Sam signed as a witness. Phil paid and collected his receipt, and they were done.

"Gee," Mary said as they left the office, "you gonna get me a nice big diamond ring?"

"If this works and I stay out of jail, I'll get each of you whatever you want," Phil said. "Now we've got work to do."

They returned to State Street. Mary headed for Discreet Detectives while Phil and Sam went to the Chocolate Shoppe.

Phil had asked Sam to call a staff meeting. "They need to know, he had said, "they'll find out somehow anyway, so we'd better tell them what we want them to hear." As the staff assembled Phil sat at the desk in the back, trying to figure out what to say and how to say it. There was a knock at the door.

"Aaron, make it quick. I've got something I've got to finish here."

Aaron came forward and handed Phil some photocopies. "Here are the slips I found. For the Scotch."

"Four?"

"I couldn't find the last one. Must have been cash, or filed wrong. That guy's got a shitty file system."

"Thanks, Aaron. I appreciate it. Good job. Write down all your time on your card."

"Yeah, I will. Anything else you want me to do? Maybe check out these people?"

"I don't know. Let me think about it."

"Roger." He left and went back to join the rest of the staff gathering at the tables.

"I want to tell them," Sam said, appearing at the door.

"I should tell them."

"Yes you should, but I want to."

"Why?"

"I think they'll take it better from me."

"And why would they take it badly from me?"

Sam looked at the floor. "I believe some of them were hoping that you and I . . . I . . . I don't want them to feel sorry for me." She looked up. "If I present it, I can save some of my dignity."

"All right. What do you want me to do?"

"Just go out there, tell them how great they are, and turn the meeting over to me. And then go on over to your office and work with your wife on your case."

"I wish you wouldn't say it that way."

She walked back to the counter area.

Phil noticed that the light on the answering machine was flashing. Dominick's voice came over the speaker, saying that he had found the last of the slips. Phil wrote the name of the customer on a corner of one of Aaron's photocopies, and played the message twice to make sure he heard it correctly, and then deleted the message. Then he folded up the photocopies and put them in his jacket pocket. He pushed his chair back and stood up, put his cap on, and went out to the table area. There were no customers in the store; Sam had locked the front door and hung a handwritten sign on the door that said 'Closed for Inventory.'

"Thank you all for coming. I'll keep my part brief, and then I'll turn this meeting over to Sam."

Phil finished his remarks and let himself out the front door. Sam locked the door behind him. He waited for a bus to pass so he could cross the street, and he looked back at the store. Sam was sitting on the counter, legs dangling and swinging, and talking. He couldn't hear her. The bus passed, and he crossed the street. McDermott's was on the way so he decided to stop there.

Colin McDermott found Phil waiting for him when he returned to the front desk.

"Brother Phil! You didn't call."

"I was coming this way anyway, and I thought I'd save some time by just stopping in."

"'*Half our life is spent trying to find something to do with the time we have rushed through life trying to save.*' Will Rogers."

"My turn," Phil said. "*But at my back I always hear Time's winged chariot hurrying near.*' Andrew Marvell."

"Bravo, Phil." Colin laughed and clapped his hands, then reached under the counter to retrieve a manila file folder. "Here is that which you seek, the bulk of it the same as that provided your dear uncle. Only a little extra, for very recent political situations."

Phil accepted the folder. "Thanks, Colin. What do I owe you for your effort?"

He shook his head. "I climbed not very high in the tree for this fruit. Use it well; that will be my reward."

"I know this guy," Phil said. He held a newspaper photo that he had pulled from the file folder. "He's a regular at the store, has been for the last couple years. He always orders a double pistachio, in a waffle cone. Seems like a good guy." He handed the photo to Mary.

"'Attorney General Gary Kleinstern announces his bid for re-election.' So?" She handed it back.

"It's in here with the material about the DA who is campaigning against him. James Bradley." Phil paged through the other papers. "There's a few other articles in here, minor stuff. Looks like Kleinstern and Ruppert Taylor haven't exactly been best of friends. These guys see both sides of every issue – Kleinstern sees one side, and Taylor sees the other. No wonder Taylor is supporting Bradley."

"What are you supposed to do with this information?"

"I don't know. Maybe I just need to talk to Kleinstern the next time he comes into the store."

"Hand me the list of dates, please. I'll put all these into the database so we can sort them with the dates of all the property transactions."

"While you're doing that I'll read all the commentary and try to figure out how it fits in. Here," Phil pulled the photocopies with the Scotch buyers' names on them from his pocket, "these are the people who recently bought blended Scotches at Dominick's. The kind that might have been used to refill the Ardbeg bottle."

Mary took the papers and set them to one side. "I'll see what I can find on these later. The time line comes first." She adjusted her glasses on her nose and began to enter data.

Phil watched her. "I don't believe I thanked you for what you did today. Thanks."

She didn't stop, didn't turn away from her screen or pause but the corner of her mouth twitched up. "You're welcome. Now leave me alone for an hour."

Phil called Lars Jackson at home. Barbara answered the phone.

"Barbara? Phil Bardo. I'm looking for Lars. Is he in?"

"Hello, Phil. Lars isn't home yet. Have you tried his office?"

"No, I assumed he'd have gone home by now."

"Can I take a message?"

"Please. Just tell him Mary and I got married this afternoon."

"Congratulations! I'll give him the message."

Barbara hung up the phone and walked down the hall, through the living room, through the French doors into Lars' office. He was sprawled in his leather desk chair, snoring.

"Lars. Lars!" She grabbed his shoulder and shook it, but he continued to snore. She picked up the glass that sat half full of water and ice on his desk. She sniffed it, then took a sip. Definitely not water. She leaned over and pulled his shirt away from his chest and dumped the drink and ice between the buttons.

"Wha-wha-" he jerked awake, eyes flung open.

"Phil called. He got married."

"No shit."

"And you're getting divorced."

"Aw, Barbara . . ."

She turned and walked from the room. Two suitcases waited in the hall next to the front door. Her car was parked in the circle. She left the front door of the house open as she towed her bags to the trunk and put them inside, closed the trunk and got into the driver's seat. She closed her door and drove away.

Lars shook the ice out of his shirt. He had heard the opening of the front door, the clickety-click of the suitcase wheels on the brick pavers, the thunk of the trunk lid and the car door. He heard the car start and the roar as Barbara hit the gas and left the driveway. He got up, dripping, and walked to the front door and closed it.

Back in his office he mopped his chair with a golf towel then sat down and dialed the phone.

"It's me. He did it . . .yep, I told you it would work. Hope you're happy. It's all downhill from here, as long as nobody screws up. Bye."

He leaned back in his chair. She'll come back, he thought. She always comes back.

"Okay, here we go," Mary said. She clicked the 'go' button and in a few seconds they had a list of events and real estate sales transactions, sorted by date. They peered at the computer screen and scrolled down the list, then back up again.

"I'm sorry, I just can't see it like this. Too much data and too small a window. I need to take a few steps back. Can you print it?"

"Sure," she said, and clicked the print button. A few minutes later they taped the pages together on the floor in a long line in front of the roll-top desk. Phil searched the desk and found some colored markers. He got down on his hands and knees and went down the list, highlighting in yellow the dates and events associated with the announcement and development of the Monona Terrace and the marina/boathouse projects.

"Yellow are the Terrace project dates."

"Gimme a red."

Phil handed Mary a red marker, and she crawled down the list highlighting the deals for which Smith's companies were either buyer or seller. "These are Smith's real estate deals."

"Now politics. Blue would be a good color, don't you think?" Phil took the blue marker and went down the list again, marking such items as Ruppert Taylor's election as City Council Chairman, Bradley's appointment as DA, the new police chief, and the mayor's election. "McDermott said that everything had to do with politics, or something to that effect. There's got to be a connection here somewhere."

Mary took a black pen from the desk and wrote in the margin. "These are when I came to work for your uncle, when he was killed, the approximate date that our first research went missing, the charity ball, and our Halloween intruder."

They stood up and backed away from the paper. Phil stood to one side of the list and Mary to the other. They studied the placement of the colors as they moved back and forth along the sheets. Every now and then one of them would bend over or kneel to examine a patch of dates and events, then stand again.

"What do you see?"

"Mmm, not yet," Phil murmured. He took a green marker and went down on the list again. "These are the back tax sales. The ones that do a turnaround – City seizes, City sells, City buys back later." He highlighted, then drew lines to connect the deals related to the same properties. He stood up and backed away from the list.

"Yes. I think I see some things. You?"

She studied the sheets. "I'm not seeing it. But don't tell me, I want to figure it out. I just need a break."

"It isn't as much the data itself as it is the interpretation."

Phil got down on the floor and began rolling up the sheets. "We can look at this again later. I'm not going to leave it laying around here so it can walk off again." He got up and found a rubber band in the desk drawer and slipped it around the tube of paper. "It's getting late. We never decided . . . your place or mine?"

"How about mine. I've gotta deal with Hoover."

"In that case I need to stop by my place for some things." He tucked the tube into the inside pocket of his jacket. Mary went back to her computer table and put on her shoes and coat.

She grabbed Phil's hand as they started down the stairs. "Pretend that you like me," she said, "we're supposed to be newlyweds. You never know who may be watching." At the bottom of the stairs she pulled him into an embrace and kissed him, and then they walked to his pickup arm-in-arm.

"Where do you want me to put this?" Phil stood in Mary's living room with his duffel bag of clothes slung over his shoulder. Hoover stood before him, snuffling his jeans.

"Where do you think? The bedroom. Turn right at the bathroom, there." She nodded toward a small hallway. "You've got to put some effort into making this look real," she whispered. "If I were working for the prosecution, I'd be sitting in a car or in the bushes outside, watching our every move through binoculars. Taking pictures. I might have had the time to bug the house and your apartment. Or I'd have one of those laser eavesdropping devices, picking up conversations from the vibration of the window glass."

"Aren't you being a little paranoid? How could they possibly have found out so quickly?"

"Shhh! You have no idea . . . they could have had a tail on you ever since you got out of jail. Now c'mon, work on your acting skills. At least we can have a little fun along the way." She kicked off her shoes and tossed her coat onto a chair. She picked up the bag of sub sandwiches and the six-pack that they had bought on the way and collapsed on the couch. "Saturday

Night Live?" She reached for the TV remote.

"I'm so old I remember when that show was funny." Phil took his duffel to the bedroom and dropped it on the floor without turning on the light, then peeled off his jacket and dropped that, too. He returned to the living room and sat on the couch. "I was going to watch the Packer game tomorrow with Sam, at my place."

"Given the circumstances that's not such a good idea."

"I need to call her." Phil took his cell phone from his pocket and dialed Sam's home number.

"Hello?"

"Xiamorha, it's me."

"Hi."

"How'd it go?"

"About as I expected. They were shocked. But I was able to spin it the way I wanted. Don't be surprised if they get you a wedding present. Some of 'em are convinced that she's pregnant, but that wasn't my doing. None of them know what this really is."

"Good. I'm glad it went okay. Sam, about tomorrow-"

"No, I can't make it."

"Judy couldn't work?"

"She can, but . . . I just can't."

"Oh. Well, it's probably best that way."

"Yes. Are you . . . where?"

"At Mary's house."

"Oh. Look, I've got to go to bed."

"This isn't easy for me either, you know."

"I know. G'night, Phil."

He turned off his cell phone. Mary was busy flinging small chunks of bread from her sub at Hoover. He waited until a scrap nearly hit him, then he opened his jaws and inhaled the piece with a flash of movement. His jaws closed with a loud "clop" and his jowls shook.

"How does he keep from biting himself?"

"I have no idea."

They finished their subs and beers in silence while

watching TV. When the show ended Mary turned off the set with the remote and stood up. "She knows this is the way it has to be. She signed up for it."

"Yeah."

"C'mon, Phil. It's show time." She peeled off her shirt and stood before him, then turned and walked slowly toward the bedroom dragging her shirt by one sleeve. Phil stood up and followed. Hoover carefully inspected the sub bags for remains, then wandered back to the bedroom.

"Mary?"

"Yeah?"

"Does he really have to be in here?"

Mary sat up and leaned on one elbow to peer over Phil's abdomen. Hoover stood at the side of the bed, watching. "But he's so cute!"

"I feel strange enough about this without having your father watching us."

Mary laughed and got out of bed. "Hoover, out!" She steered him toward the door and closed it behind him, then took a flying leap back onto the bed. "Who's driving tonight?"

"Be my guest."

"All right, but you'd better fasten your seatbelt."

CHAPTER TWENTY-TWO

Phil woke up alone. It was early, and the sun was just beginning to lighten the window shades. He got up and pulled on his jeans and left the bedroom.

Mary had made coffee. Phil poured himself a mug and read the note she had left on the kitchen table. She had gone biking. He wandered back to the living room where Hoover lay on the braided rug. He eyed Phil, but made no other outward reaction. Phil sipped his coffee and paused in front of a bookshelf. There were some framed pictures, all of people he didn't know except for Mary in a couple shots. The others were – mom and dad? Brother? Friends? She had a whole life he knew nothing about. He examined her books. She had paperbacks, good for someone on a budget and someone who devours them rather than just reads them. From their condition Phil knew that she was a tactile reader; a cover-bender, a page dog-earer and a highlighter, getting the most out of the reading experience. Her authors were Raymond Chandler, Nora Roberts, John D. MacDonald, and Elmore Leonard. There were Dashiel Hammett, Danielle Steel, and Erle Stanley Gardner. Arthur Conan Doyle, of course. And John Grisham, Agatha Christie, and Patricia Cornwell. All the mysteries were together, but she didn't alphabetize them by title or by author. She wouldn't. Another shelf held textbooks on relational and object-oriented database design, systems analysis, and statistics. There was a PADI *Open Water Divers Manual* and Humann's *Reef Fish Identification* field guide. A world atlas, and a guide to movies on video next to a stack of DVD's: *Casablanca, To Have and Have Not, Judge Dredd, Married to the Mob, The Matrix. Twin Peaks* episodes one through five. *The Untouchables.* And, there were three unmarked DVD's. He popped one into the player, pressed 'play' and turned on the TV. A couple in the throes of energetic lovemaking appeared. He ejected the DVD and put it back on the shelf, and turned off the TV.

Hoover got up and stood near the door, tail-stump twitching. Mary came in a moment later, red-faced and sweating from her ride. She wore the same outfit that she had worn to the Charity 5K/10K.

"Good dog," she said as she scratched him on the head. "He's always so excited to see me." The only part of that dog that looked alive was the tail, Phil thought.

"And how are *you* this morning, husband? Are you happy to see me, too?" She bounded to Phil and stretched up to give him a kiss, and at the same time slid her hand down the front of his jeans. "Ooh, getting happier, I think!"

"Whoa!" Phil laughed, "a little early."

"Huh! Didn't know there was a time limit," she said, and removed her hand. "I make no apologies for my appetites." She lay down on the floor and Hoover came over to her and began to lick her face. "Is there any coffee left?"

"Yes, I'll get you some." Phil went into the kitchen and filled a mug. He returned and set it on the floor next to her hand. "Here you go."

"Thanks." Hoover finished washing her face and she got up on one elbow to drink.

"Who are these people in these pictures?"

"Which ones? Show me."

Phil held up a framed snapshot.

"Those are my folks. Leighton and Louise."

"And this guy?" Phil held up another picture.

"My brother, LJ. Leighton John."

"And these . . ."

"My sister, Marilyn, and her family. And the next one over – that's me and two college friends, Patricia and Patrice."

Phil put the pictures back on the shelf. "Tell me about

your folks."

"They live in DC now. I think I told you that before. They were embassy staff, overseas for years. I spent a lot of my childhood in foreign countries."

"Oh, they were-"

"Spooks."

"Still?"

"No, of course not. At least not that they'll admit."

"Have you told them about what's going on here?"

"No, not yet. They don't seem to agree much with my decisions."

"And your brother?"

"My brother. *Much* older than me. DC area, too. Works for the Bureau."

"So you were just going into the family business, so to speak."

"Yeah. I grew up with it; it was all I ever wanted to do."

"I feel bad that you quit on my behalf."

"Don't. It was my choice to end it the way I did. It was just as well. Some parts of the Bureau still have vintage ideas about what people like me can do."

"People like you?"

"Women. Women with opinions and brains."

"Oh. You certainly do have both of those."

"And I'm not afraid to let people know."

"You know, you might be more successful if you tamed that with a little tact."

"Nah, that'd ruin my charm." Mary finished her coffee and began some stretching there on the floor.

Phil watched her. He was never that flexible, probably not even in the womb. "Hey, I'm curious. What's with the sweatshirts?"

She laughed. "Oh come on. You think you already know. You tell me."

"Okay. Part of it is to look more like a college student, to blend in. Part of it is so that men will pay attention to what you're saying rather than to what's hanging on your chest. You take it off when you want distraction."

"Very good, Sherlock. All true. But that's not all."

"I don't know."

"You've missed the obvious. They're damned comfortable, and I get cold easily."

Phil shaved, showered, and dressed while Mary finished her stretching and ate some breakfast. He got on his cell phone while she was in the shower. Judy was doing the opening at the Chocolate Shoppe, and all was fine. Sam wasn't there and when he tried calling her apartment she didn't answer, so he left a message. He dialed into his answering machine at his apartment. There was one message; Tom inviting him out to the farm to watch the Packer game that afternoon. He called Tom and accepted the invitation, and said that he was going to bring a surprise. Then he called Lars Jackson and told him about the timeline of the dates of real estate sales and the Terrace development and set an appointment to meet him the next day downtown to go over it.

Mary appeared wrapped in a towel. "So what's the plan for today? I need to know how to dress. Sweatshirt or not?"

"I thought we'd go downtown for the rest of the morning and work on the case. Then we'll go to a friend's house and watch the game. Okay?"

"You're willing to bring me out of the closet so soon?"

"I thought you said we had to make this as real as we could."

"Yeah, but you seem to be having a problem with that."

"Well, I'm trying harder."

"Calm down."

"Shit!" Jackson said. "Don't tell me to calm down. It's all about to come apart!"

"Meet with him and find out what he really knows."

"Yeah, I will, tomorrow. But I'm telling you, all he needs to do is take one more step with this and I'm toast. It's happening all over again. I should never have gotten involved with you people. It's going to be every man for himself."

"Don't do anything stupid. Keep your mouth shut. We'll take care of it. We'll take care of you."

"Like you took care of it the last time? No thank you. Every time you guys take care of something it gets worse. I've had it with you. I'll take care of myself."

"Jackson, you're worrying me."

"Good. I'm glad someone's finally worried besides me."

He hung up. He took a swig from the open bottle on his desk, then booted his computer and launched the word processing program. The first lines he wrote were "Gary Kleinstern, Attorney General, State of Wisconsin. Dear Mr. Kleinstern: I am writing to you in regard to a case, #35417-201. I have certain knowledge . . ."

Phil and Mary had the papers spread on the office floor again.

"I've been thinking about this," Mary said. "Let me see if I'm seeing what you're seeing. There's a pattern here," she pointed to the list of dates, "and here. He buys property just *before* the dates when the City announces their area development plans."

"Yep. What else about the patterns?"

She studied the lists. "Some time after the announcement, maybe months or a year, he sells the properties."

"Yes. The property within the City's zone, the area needed for development of the public facilities, he sells to the City. The properties just outside the zone he sells to other businesses for development."

"Hey! I was just getting to that."

"What else?"

"Oh. The back-tax sales. The City seizes and sells the back-tax properties to Smith before the development announcements. And then, buys them back from him later to build the convention center and the new boathouse complex."

"Right. So what's wrong with this picture?"

"Looks like he's getting advance knowledge and/or preferential treatment from somebody in the City."

"Now we're getting to the meat of this. Why would somebody give him special treatment?"

She paused. "We don't have any data on this kind of thing."

"So what? What would you guess? Then we'll look for the data to support it."

"Hmm. The only thing I can think of is money. They clue him in early so he can swing some big deals. I'd assume he gives them a cut of the action."

"And how do you suppose they could make a sweet deal even sweeter?"

"Ah . . . ah . . . the appraisals! Undervalue the back-tax sale and over-value the later buyback? The City gets stuck for the extra bucks, Smith wins big, and somebody at the City gets a nice personal spiff from him under the table!"

Phil smiled, grabbed Mary's face in both hands and planted a big wet kiss in the middle of her forehead. "Congratulations! You've got it! We've got it. And we may have some data that could support this theory. Don't you have the sales price and appraisal values for all these deals?"

"Yeah!" She was flushed and grinning from her success.

"That's where we'll look next. And we'll try to find out who would have control over those appraisal values. There's one more factor. Care to guess?"

"No. Tell me."

"Look at the political events. None of this started happening until after Ruppert Taylor got in as City Council chairman and he got his protégé elected mayor."

"So? Could be coincidence."

"Could be. But whoever murdered Dave must have had a whole lot of something to protect in order to be willing to kill over a real estate scam. Money, power, or both. I'll bet on both. McDermott said everything was political. What is politics other than money and power?"

"Phil, these are good theories but we've got a lot to prove. So far it's all circumstantial. And we still don't know who pulled the trigger. We don't have a single lead. Not one."

"I know, but I think we're getting closer. We may have to stir things up somehow. Something will break. It has to." He gathered the printouts from the floor and rolled them up. "We've also got to check out these Scotch buyers. See if we can find out where they live. I'd love to know whether any of them have a nearly-empty bottle sitting around their place."

"Any theories on how that ties in?"

Phil stopped. "Yeah, actually I do. Two possibilities." He smiled. "Let's go, we don't want to be late for the game." He pushed 'redial' on his cell phone. The smile left his face. There was still no answer, and he left a terse "Call me" for a message.

Phil pounded the horn as he wheeled into the farmyard. He parked next to the house, and as he and Mary got out of the pickup Tom came out the back door.

"He said he was bringin' a surprise. Are you it?" Tom asked with a grin.

"I'm it," Mary nodded.

"Tom, this is Mary," Phil said. "My wife."

"Wha? Noooo, come on, now!"

"Go figure," Mary said, and extended her hand.

"Well, I'll be dipped in shi . . . Nancy, Phil's hitched!" Tom bellowed. He grabbed Mary's hand and shook it. "I am *so* glad to meet you. This is a surprise! How'd you get him to do it?"

Mary glanced at Phil and replied, "His other girlfriend made him."

"Huh? Haw, haw, sure. Well, come on in, it's too damned cold to stand around out here. Girlfriend made him! Sheee-iiit!" Tom led the way back into the house with Mary and Phil close behind.

Inside they made introductions with Nancy and tore off their coats. The house was warm, and the scent of the wood-burning furnace and freshly baked apple pie permeated the space. The game was starting and they all crammed together on the couch, beers in hand.

Back at Mary's house later, Phil put his cell phone down on the nightstand and crawled into bed next to Mary.

"Phil, I'm sure she's fine."

"You're probably right. It's just a bit unusual, that's all."

"Well, how'd I do today? Tell me the truth."

"Great. They loved you."

"Really?"

"Really. Tom paid you the highest of farm-guy compliments. He said you were the best of both worlds; just like one of the guys and a great piece of horse-flesh at the same time."

"Aw, that's nice." Mary rolled to her side and rearranged her pillow, then edged backward until she ran up against Phil.

"I've known Tom forever. Probably forty years." He raised Mary's Favre jersey and rested his hand on her hip.

"Does that bother you?"

"Yes, a little. I can't help but think that you'd feel like you were hanging out with your parents."

She rolled over to face him. "It doesn't bother me. I like older men."

"Why?"

"It's kinda like the difference between a puppy and a dog."

"You'll have to explain that one."

"Puppies are cute and funny, fun to be around for a while but you gotta train 'em and they get really annoying. They chew your shoes, shit on your rug, and run away. Are you listening?"

"I'm trying to follow your analogy. You must have had some odd dating experiences. Go on."

She ran her hand over Phil's chest, tracing the muscles and ribs. "Dogs, now, have gotten over those puppy problems. They know who they are, they're smart, they know their job, and they value their relationship with their human. They're strong, and they're just a bit protective. And sometimes they can be just a little dangerous."

"Wasn't Hoover-"

"Nah. He was a used dog."

"Used."

"Yeah. He's seven; I've had him for four years. Somebody else dealt with all that puppy crap."

"You're going to make a very interesting mother someday."

"Won't I, though!"

"You're already pretty well equipped for it, I see."

"Ohhhh. Thanks. I've got another one of those, you know."

"Ah. Yes, indeed. Equally fine."

"You know, I'm actually a very sensitive person. In many ways."

"I can tell. See?"

"Mmm. That's one way."

CHAPTER TWENTY-THREE

The construction foreman arrived a little late that morning to the condo construction site two blocks off of State Street. He walked the site quickly, carrying his clipboard of the project plan and the checklist of what the crews had accomplished the previous Friday. They had done the first pours for the six-foot-diameter pillars that were to run the height of the lobby. Today they were to do the second pours if the first were sufficiently cured. Three men followed him, carrying their coring drills and dragging a wheeled compressor. They stopped at each of the first two columns and used the equipment to drill into the columns and take core samples. They ejected the cores into carrying tubes and sealed and labeled the tubes. The building inspector would be coming by to verify that the concrete had cured enough, that the aggregate used wasn't too large, and that there were no apparent voids. At the third column the foreman noticed that the pour was much higher than it should have been for that day. He frowned; that wasn't good, and a decent building inspector would make him tear it down and do it over again. He had a fifty-fifty chance of getting a decent inspector. He marked the column for two cores, one low and one high, and moved on to the fourth column while his crew got to work on the third. The fourth column was the right height, and he marked it for coring.

"Hey Boss," a crewman called. "You'd better come have a look."

He walked back to column three. There was a small group of construction workers gathered around the two tubes of core samples on the ground. One sample looked like the ones from columns one and two. In the other the concrete looked fresher, less cured. And, there was something in it, fabric perhaps, and some jelly-like substance. There were irregular white flakes or chips in it, too.

"Shit," he said. "That'll never pass. Tear the fucker down."

The sirens split the air on State Street about mid-morning, right during the second rush of customers. The street cops had vacated their tables in a hurry after receiving calls on their radios, shortly before the sirens came. The people coming in through the door of the Chocolate Shoppe reported that a cluster of police and ambulance units had converged on a nearby condominium construction site.

Phil was working the coffee machine, and Sam the cash register. They had both come that morning to do the opening.

"Sorry I didn't call," she had said at her arrival, "I went to Kenosha yesterday, and I got back really late. My mama has a hard time letting me go once I'm there."

"I was worried. I want to talk to you every day."

"I needed some time. And honestly I just couldn't, couldn't talk to you right after . . ."

"Please, Sam, don't do that again. Don't run out without telling me where you're going."

"I am an adult, you know."

"Yes, I know. I know very well!"

Sam gave Phil a sharp elbow to the ribs and turned her attention to her opening tasks.

Later, about halfway through the noon rush, Gary Kleinstern entered the store. Phil took over the cash register in time for Kleinstern's approach.

"Double pistachio in a waffle cone today?" Phil asked.

"Yes, my usual."

"Even on cold days, huh."

"There's nothing like it."

Phil got a waffle cone and a scoop and began to dig in the

ice cream tub. "Aren't you Gary Kleinstern, the Attorney General?"

"That's right."

Phil scraped a good-sized first scoop and pressed it into the cone. "Good luck on the re-election. And thanks for your patronage over the years."

"Thanks, and you're welcome. You guys have good product here."

Phil dug the second scoop, one much larger than he prescribed for his staff to use. If they saw him deliver this one he'd never hear the end of it. "I'm Phil Bardo, the owner."

"Yes, I know who you are." He accepted the cone that Phil held out to him.

"Look," Phil said, "I have a problem. As a citizen, a taxpayer, a voter, I really would appreciate a few minutes of your time."

Kleinstern handed some bills to Phil. "Are you sure that's such a good idea?"

Phil made change and gave it to Kleinstern, who put it in the tip bucket. "Honestly, no. But I have to try."

Kleinstern took a bite. "Oh, that's good. First class." He wiped his mouth with a napkin. "Come to my office this week. Whatever you do, *don't* make an appointment. I'll be in all week. And I'll fit you in for a few minutes whenever you arrive. Bring a quart with you."

Dee Best left her ten-year-old Honda Civic at the valet parking stand and took her time walking into the lobby of the Edgewater Hotel. She was a few minutes early. It had been a couple years since she'd been in the restaurant, but only a few months since her last visit to the hotel. She loved staying there. The place did it right; they knew how to treat a guest. Her long blonde hair was pulled back and wrapped into a knot at the back of her head, and she left her sunglasses on. She adjusted the blue blazer on her shoulders and made sure that her tan camisole and cleavage appeared between the lapels. The wool skirt was a good match, and warm enough for a day like this.

She had worn low-heeled boots, not knowing how tall the men she was meeting would be; at her height she was careful not to add too many inches. To some it would be too intimidating; to others – well, you just never knew.

"I'm meeting the Valdez party," she said to the maître 'd.

"One moment." He checked his list. "Mr. Valdez has arrived. May I show you to his table?"

He led the way to a small table at the far end of the dining room. The table overlooked the lake, and a forty-something man sat there. He was nicely dressed and trim, with thinning blond hair. Definitely not Hispanic. He rose at her approach; he appeared to be about six feet tall. The maître 'd held her chair for her, and she sat, and Valdez sat after her.

"Mr. Valdez?"

"Yes, call me Juan. Dee Best?"

"Yes. That's not your real name."

"No, it isn't. And yours?"

"Real. Deirdre Best. Dee Best. How could I find a stage name any better than that?"

"Thank you for joining me for lunch."

"Where's the rest of your party?"

"It's just us."

He's nervous, she thought. Probably a first-timer. Or, there could be another explanation. "Are you a cop?"

"No."

"Prove it."

"How do I prove that I'm not something?"

"Come with me." They left their napkins on the table and she led him to the men's rest room in the lobby. Inside, she checked for other patrons as Valdez waited. "Okay," she said, "drop 'em."

"Now, hold on-"

"Cops can't expose. Drop 'em, or our nice lunch meeting is over." Valdez unbuckled his belt and dropped his trousers. "And the boxers," she said, and he complied. "Okay, sorry for the inconvenience. You can get put back together."

"Inconvenience," he grumbled as he hurried to get

dressed, "how about the embarrassment?"

"From what I can see you've got nothing to be embarrassed about."

Back at the table she relaxed. Now she could have some fun. It was always that first few minutes, especially when they use fake names, that bothered her. She'd been careful in her career, hadn't gotten busted yet and didn't intend to start now. She ordered raw oysters for an appetizer and Sauvignon Blanc by the glass.

"So, Mr. Valdez, if you're not a cop, what do you do?"

"I investigate things."

"Oh. A PI."

"Sort of. That's really what I want to do today. I want to talk to you. That's all, just talk."

"Oh? What's the matter, don't I appeal to you?" She slid an oyster down her throat and chased it with a sip of wine.

"It's not that."

"Well, maybe you'll change your mind later." This was a first, she thought. Usually it was hard to get them to talk, not the reverse. "Oyster?"

"No, thanks. Do you know this guy?" Valdez handed her a piece of paper with a photograph on it.

Dee downed another oyster, then took a look. This was not good. "Obviously you know that I do, otherwise you wouldn't have gone to all this trouble. We've done some business. He used to be a regular."

"Used to?"

"He stopped calling."

"Do you know why?"

"His wife. He said she found out about me and was putting the screws to him."

"Did he say how she found out?"

"No, but he was pretty upset about it."

"When was the last time you heard from him?"

"Oh, it must have been around the end of September or the first part of October. Why? He's okay, isn't he?"

"As far as I know. Did he ever say anything to you about

suspecting that his wife might be having an affair?"

"It came up a couple of times. He said he hired a PI to catch her – oh, you?"

"No, it wasn't me."

Their main courses came. She picked at her salmon salad. Valdez seemed nice enough, but she couldn't figure out what he had to do with Ted. Ted had some pretty unpleasant friends. "Do you know Ted?"

"No. Somebody I knew did, though." Valdez finished his veal scaloppini. "Do you remember seeing him on September fourteenth?"

Dee dropped her fork and started to rise. "Now, wait a minute, whatever's happened, I have nothing to do with it. You're-you're with- "

"No, please sit down," Valdez said. "I know what happened on the fourteenth, but I'm not with those guys. I've just got a couple more questions. Please, sit."

Dee sat down.

"Now," Valdez continued, "just who were they? The ones with the merchandise."

"I don't know their names," Dee replied. "Afterwards, on the way home, Ted called them the Polish Mafia. I didn't have anything to do with the coke. Really, I didn't!"

"I believe you. What did they have to do with the party?"

Dee shook her head. "Nothing. They just met Ted there in the driveway to do their deal. And after they were done, they left."

"After they were done with you."

"I guess you do know what happened that night. Yeah, after they were done with me. They never went into the house."

"And you and Ted?"

"We went in and partied for a while, then we left."

"So King didn't have anything to do with the deal?"

"I don't think so. Ted didn't even bring any of the coke inside."

"What does Ted do with the coke?"

"I don't know, and I don't want to know."

"Did Ted carry a gun that night?"

"I think he might have. He kept his right hand in his coat pocket a lot. Now isn't it about time you tell me what this is all about?"

Valdez nodded his head. "I'm not sure that I owe you an explanation, but I'll give it to you anyway. I'm investigating a murder, and I'm trying to figure out whether or not Ted had anything to do with it. He's not a nice guy, Dee. Nice guys don't do drug deals with the Polish Mafia. Nice guys don't deal coke."

"And nice guys don't use escort services?"

"I didn't say that. But nice guys wouldn't drag an escort into the middle of a drug deal, would they? He made you a witness to the deal, and put you in danger by doing so. It didn't take much for me to find you; I'm sure that your Polish friends could, too."

Dee's face went white. "You're just full of happy thoughts, aren't you. So what the hell am I supposed to do about it?"

"Maybe we can help each other. I'd like to know how Ted's wife found out about you. Any chance you could find out for me without telling Ted about this discussion?"

"And why would I do that?"

Valdez shrugged. "Because it might be information that could help keep you safe, and it might help answer my questions about Ted's involvement in a murder. Also, it would be a shame if the cops got a tip about your real profession. Or, about your complicity in a drug deal."

"Nice guys don't use blackmail."

"I'm running out of time and options. In this game, not only don't nice guys finish first, they don't seem to finish at all. I intend to at least finish." He wrote a phone number on a cocktail napkin. "See what you can do, and then call this number in two days. Now, would you like some dessert?"

She put the napkin in her purse. She wasn't hungry anymore, and she wasn't having fun. Her stomach felt like the oysters had come alive again.

Valdez ordered dessert, a Death-by-Chocolate. "Look out there," he said. "It's hard to believe that the lake will freeze over in January. If it gets cold fast enough, and the wind stays down, it might be smooth enough for ice boating. You ever see them ice boating out here?"

She shook her head.

"Maybe only three or four days a year the conditions are right to do it. They can go up to sixty miles an hour or so. A friend of mine races, and a few years ago his boat went through a weak spot in the ice. They pulled him out and laid him on the ice, and his clothes froze right to the ice."

"That's crazy. And did he . . ."

"He's fine. Still races."

Valdez' dessert arrived, and Dee Best declined to sample it and excused herself to go to the rest room. Valdez ate leisurely, but the woman had not returned by the time he finished. The waiter brought the check and Valdez paid with a credit card. Still no Dee. Valdez left the restaurant, stinging from the Edgewater tab but at the same time relieved that Best hadn't bothered to present him with hers. He gave his ticket to the valet, and in a minute he was behind the wheel and on his way up the drive and onto the street.

As Phil's pickup passed Dee Best's Honda Civic parallel-parked along the street, she jotted down the truck's license plate number on a cocktail napkin and noted the bumper sticker – "Chocolate Shoppe-aholic."

Phil's appointment with Lars was at two-thirty. When he arrived at the second floor office he walked into a waiting room full of cops.

"Phil Bardo?"

"Yes?"

"We'd like you to come with us."

Mary sat in the leather easy chair and Sam on the cot. Phil leaned back in the wooden desk chair. "First of all," he said, "I met with Essinger's escort today."

"Bravo," Mary said. "And what did you learn?"

"She confirmed he's not seeing her anymore due to his wife finding out, but she doesn't know how that happened. George King is apparently not involved. She said the other guys on the deal are Polish Mafia."

"Oh goody! Professionals. What do we do now?"

"Steer clear of the drug side of this. I pressured her to find out from Essinger how his wife discovered their arrangement. I really don't know if she'll come through with anything or not. I guess we wait and see." Phil took a deep breath. "Now the big news. I've just been at the City-County building. I was invited to a little chat by our friends in blue."

"What now?" Sam asked.

"You remember that fuss over at the condo site this morning? Well, they found a body over there, embedded in a fresh concrete pillar. It turned out to be Lars Jackson."

"Oh, my God . . ." Sam whispered.

"He was unconscious due to some head trauma when he was thrown into the form and concrete dumped on top of him. Whether he ever regained consciousness or not, they don't know. They say he died of asphyxiation."

"That's horrible!. How'd they find him?"

"A core sample. Use your imagination."

"Shit. And they think that you-" Mary began.

"No, I don't think so. Not anymore, anyway. They fixed the approximate time of death from his body condition and the stage of cure of the concrete. We were at Tom and Nancy's for the Packer game when it all went down. They've already called them for statements. And they want one from each of you, too, so call them after we're done here."

"Statements as to your whereabouts?" Sam asked.

"Yes. And yours. And probably about any last contacts you had with Lars. I talked to Jackson last on Sunday morning. I left a message for him Saturday night. I expect that they'll check phone records to verify those calls. And, each of you met with him in his office Friday afternoon. We were all together all day Saturday, and I was with Mary all Saturday night and Sunday. Sam, I couldn't reach you Sunday at all."

"I told you, I was in Kenosha visiting my mom."

"I expect they'll want a statement from her, too."

Sam nodded.

"You two should each get a lawyer. No doubt the subject of this marriage will come into play."

"Oh, man, the case . . ." Mary clenched her eyes shut and jammed her fingers into her hair.

"Yes," Phil said. "I need a new lawyer. Jackson's brothers will file a request for delay on the trial date due to change in counsel. That shouldn't be a problem, and it will give us some extra time. But I don't think I want to stay with the Jacksons under the circumstances."

"Why do they think it's connected to your case?" Sam asked. "What about his other cases?"

"He was only working mine."

Mary leaned forward. "Were there any clues, evidence, anything?"

"It looks like Barbara left him recently, so he was apparently alone at home Sunday when it happened. They're looking for her. They found a few blood streaks on the floor in his office. Papers were messed up. And, his computer is missing."

"Phil," Sam asked, "just what did you tell Jackson?"

"I left a message Saturday about the marriage, and on Sunday I made an appointment with him for Monday to talk about our theories on the case, the data we've found, and the dates of the real estate transactions."

"You said you wanted to stir something up," Mary said. "Looks like you did."

"Hell, my telling him this stuff wouldn't cause his murder. Who else would have known but him and me?"

"Unless *he* told somebody . . ." Sam offered.

They sat in silence for a few moments.

"I'd sure like to see his phone records from Sunday," Mary said.

"Me, too," Phil replied, "but I don't know how we'd ever get them."

"But why kill Jackson?" Sam looked anxiously at Phil, then Mary. "If you're doing the investigating, why wouldn't they kill you? Or both of you?"

"Because then the only guy around to take the fall for the murders would be the real murderer," Phil said. "I think we all need to be very, very careful. This could be far from over."

Phil dropped Mary and Sam at the City-County building for their initial statements and went back to his apartment to collect a few more pieces of clothing. They'd call him on his cell phone when they were finished.

He gathered a few Chocolate Shoppe polo shirts and some other articles that he had forgotten and put them into an athletic bag and set it near the door. The mail he had picked from his mailbox was nothing but junk and he threw it away. He poured a taste of Ardbeg into a tumbler, added a little water, then sat in his chair in the living room. The apartment was quiet, no people and no animals. No pictures of strangers. No books that he hadn't read. His apartment was all him, his interests for the last fifteen years, with no compromises. The only other people in his apartment were those he invited with the press of a button on the CD player; they were there only when he wanted, and they met whatever mood he was in. Their names were Hawkins, Coltrane, and Mingus, and they left when he had had enough. It suited him, he thought, it's who he was. Or was it? He took a sip from his glass. Maybe it's just who he'd let himself become. Inertia.

How about those nights at Dave's house on Wilson Street, his anticipation each night of going there and finding Sam waiting for him? She with her bandage and unsteadiness, her vulnerabilities confessed before the firelight. It pushed aside the taken-for-granted part of their relationship, and made him really see her again. He loved her honesty, her compassion, her maturity. She was old-soul, well up the reincarnation ladder, as she would say. How he felt when he

311

cooked for her, worrying that it wouldn't be good, and his relief when she was satisfied. Not wanting to leave her in the morning, leaving anyway, and counting hours until he was there again, and she was there and it was warm and good. The day she left he felt the life go out of the house on Wilson Street. It didn't come back until a week later when they met and she cooked and she, sultry-musky and predatory, stirred things in him that maybe he had known but hadn't fully acknowledged. Since then he'd felt different, and the air was cleaner, crisper, and stung his sinuses, and he didn't think he could do without her.

He took another drink. Then again, it had been two nights now, trespassing on Mary's territory, and it seemed less like trespassing each day. An arrangement she'd entered willingly, sharing her space and her things and her body, reserving nothing. She didn't share a dream but gave hers up for what? How to trust her, after her deceptions? What was real? He knew that the risk was part of her appeal for him. But she was also smart, impulsive, and a damned lot of fun to be around. Phil smiled, thinking of her at Tom and Nancy's, screaming and leaping to her feet with fists raised at a touchdown, collapsing to the floor at a fumble. He looked forward to working in the office when she was there, and he worried about her when she wasn't. If any of that were real, could it last beyond a moment?

He finished the drink and put the glass on the end table. He looked around the living room, and it suddenly looked different. It was the same, he knew, but it would never look or feel the same. It was simply not who he was any more, there were too many things missing. Women change men, he decided, intentionally or not. While with Mary he felt the ache of guilt over Sam; when with Sam, he felt a guilty ache over Mary. Alone the guilt was less, but being with either woman and guilt was much better than drinking alone in an empty apartment.

His cell phone rang.

"Can you come get me?"

"Sure. Sam's done, too?"

"Yeah, but she left."

"I'll be there in fifteen minutes."

He put his empty glass in the sink, turned off the lights, then picked up his bag and left.

Phil pulled his pickup over next to the sidewalk at the no parking zone, and Mary climbed into the cab.

"Can I drive?" she asked. "It'll help me release some tension."

They exchanged places without leaving the cab, Phil sliding under and Mary crawling over him. As she drove she told Phil about her statement and the questions the officers had asked. It was all straightforward, nothing that a lawyer would have advised her not to say. She and Sam were seen separately and they had not had a chance to compare their experiences afterward. Sam's interview had taken longer, much longer. Phil watched her as Mary bounced up and down on the seat due to the truck's stiff suspension, bounced on Sam's bloodstains. She drove well and managed the minimal power steering without complaint.

"You said you had some theories on the Scotch," she said. "Care to share?"

"Sure." Phil closed his eyes. "Two theories. They're related; either one or both could be valid. Or neither, I have absolutely no proof or any clues that lead me to these ideas. They're visions, really, of what could have happened."

"All right, stop making excuses. Let's hear 'em." She turned onto University Avenue heading west.

"Theory one. Murderer had previously checked out Dave's office, found your research, found the gun and the Ardbeg in the drawer. He-"

"Or she-"

"Or she comes to the office the night of the murder. Takes the gun to use it for the murder, has a belt or two from the Ardbeg bottle and goes to commit the murder. Comes back to the office and puts the gun back in the desk. He *or she* realizes that someone might notice that the Scotch level was down and goes out to buy a bottle. Ardbeg was too expensive – he *or she* buys a cheaper Scotch instead and comes back and pours it into the Ardbeg bottle. Then, gathers up your research and leaves."

"Okay, that's possible. What's number two?" They made the light and accelerated onto Campus Drive.

"Similar deal, except that the murderer has his drinks after the murder. Or maybe both before and after."

"Hmmm."

"What."

"Just a couple thoughts."

"Well?"

"First of all, Dave had taken to leaving the Ardbeg bottle on his desk, not in the drawer. I saw it every day. It was nearly full the day of the murder."

"So?"

"There's no way one person could drink all that Scotch. And most, if not all, of the Ardbeg had to be drunk."

"Why do you think that?"

"Because if it were only short a shot or two, the killer probably wouldn't have bothered filling it. And if they had just topped it off you would never have been able to detect any distinct brand – it would have mixed and been overpowered by the Ardbeg." She made the turn south onto Odana Road.

"Good points."

"There's more. So what's the likelihood that some murderer takes a drink and likes it well enough that he drains the bottle himself?" She laughed. "And then he manages to walk to the liquor store and back again without falling down drunk in the gutter? I don't think so."

"Ah, I see what you're saying. He's got friends."

She nodded. "That's the way it looks to me. I'm seein' a post-murder round on the house, followed by a cover-up."

"In Dave's own office, his own damned Scotch, with his own damned gun." He envisioned faceless people standing around the roll-top, passing the bottle or glass, toasting their success. "I think that our list of Scotch buyers may have just become more important."

They approached a small grocery store on the west side of the road.

"You have a grill?"

"Yeah, a gas one."

"Pull in here."

Mary turned into the small parking lot and waited in the cab while Phil ran into the store. He returned shortly with a grocery bag.

"Whatcha got?"

Phil closed his door. "Steak. Cabernet. Baguette. Caesar salad."

"What, no dessert as a reward for my brilliant contributions?"

"Oh, I think I'll be giving you a dessert, all right."

"I do love the way you talk."

They decided on their plan for the next day over the medium-rare New York strips. Phil would drop in on the Attorney General, and in the meantime Mary would try to find out what she could about the names from Dominick's receipts. They killed the last of the wine between them, and cleaned up the kitchen. Then they walked Hoover around the block and upon returning Mary went to get ready for bed.

She shed her clothes in the bedroom and put on a white robe, then walked the short hall to the bathroom. After she finished she opened the medicine cabinet and took out a plastic case. Inside was a card with rows of blister-packed pills. She pushed on one of the blisters and popped the pill out through the foil on the back. Staring at herself in the mirror, she held the pill at the edge her open lips. She felt warmth rising into her face. Then she watched herself drop the pill and the plastic case into the wastebasket. She opened the door, turned off the light and walked to the living room.

Phil was on his cell phone, his back to her. She heard him as he talked softly, pausing and laughing. "Xiamorha," she heard him say. Mary froze, then turned and went back to the bathroom. There, she fished the pill and the plastic case out of the wastebasket. She put the pill on her tongue and washed it down with a glass of water, and put the case back into the medicine cabinet.

"I'm going to bed," Mary called. She took off her robe in the bedroom and lay under the sheets.

CHAPTER TWENTY-FOUR

Phil's cell phone rang, and he fished it from his inside jacket pocket as he walked toward the Capitol Square. "Hello?"

"Valdez?"

"Yes, Dee. I was hoping I'd hear from you. What've you got?"

"I called Ted and asked him if he'd changed his mind, if he'd like to see me again. He said no, at first, anyway. I said okay, but I'd at least like to know how your wife found out. He said she hired a PI to follow him. She's got pictures of us."

"Did he say where the shots were taken? What they showed?"

"No, he wouldn't say. Boy, was he steamed! He told me never to call again, and then it got weird. He calmed down real quick, and he said he'd changed his mind. He asked me to meet him, someplace where nobody could spy on us. I told him no."

"That was smart. What happened next?"

"He got mad and I hung up. I'm scared, Valdez! I'm done. Done with you, done with Ted, done with this place. When I hang up I'm moving on to a new name, a new city."

"While you're at it why don't you try a new profession."

"I might. You still owe me, by the way. I'll send you a bill. I'll send it to the Chocolate Shoppe, in care of Phil Bardo."

"Hey, how'd you-"

"I have my sources, too. Bye, Valdez. See you around the hacienda."

"Wait! Damn!" Phil said as the call dropped.

It took little time for Mary to find the addresses of Dominick's Scotch buyers using the Internet. She wrote the names, addresses, phone numbers and email addresses on a piece of paper. Then she loaded her mapping program and typed the addresses into it and displayed the locations on a map. Two were downtown, one was on campus, and two were further afield; one south off of Park Street, and the other near the West Towne Mall. Three apartments, a dorm room and one house.

She knew Phil had gone to see the Attorney General and was going to stop by the Chocolate Shoppe, so in her view it was time for some freelancing. Phil would never approve of her going out alone, and he'd just be in the way if he insisted on going along. She wrote a note for him saying that she was checking out the addresses, and left a list. The UW letter jacket, the tank top, the blue jeans, the tennis shoes, the Bucky Badger stocking cap and scarf that she wore were a deliberate choice of wardrobe. She tucked the papers and map into her pocket, put on her gloves and left the offices of Discreet Detectives. On the way to the first downtown address Mary stopped at a small corner convenience store, where she bought the grocer's entire visible stock of large candy bars.

The first address turned out to be the ground floor unit of a three-story flat, about two blocks from the technical college. It was an old building made of red brick, and the saggy balconies of the second and third units held bicycles and old furniture. The porch of the first floor unit was neat, and contained only some dead potted annuals in large concrete planters. She climbed the front steps and rang the bell. An elderly woman appeared at the door.

"Yes?"

"Hello, ma'am, I'm selling candy bars as a fund raiser for my sorority. Say, you look familiar. Are you Mrs. TaberHaiger, the science teacher from Madison East High?"

"No, I'm Marjorie Kramer."

The woman bought two candy bars. Around the corner Mary took out her list and next to Marjorie Kramer's name wrote '80's, home at ten a.m., not likely candidate.' She hiked over to Langdon Street and headed west toward campus. The second address was on the fourth floor of an apartment building. The lobby door was open but the stairwells were locked and the elevator was secured by a card key. She went to the water cooler and got her hand wet, then deposited enough of the drops on her eyes so that they smudged her eye-shadow and ran down her cheeks. Then she sat on the floor next to the elevator doors and slumped her shoulders and rocked silently back and forth.

Ten minutes later, a man came through the lobby and paused when he saw her.

"Excuse me, is there something wrong?"

Mary looked up slowly, sniffling. "I lost my elevator card key," she said in a tiny voice, "an' my roommate's on campus all day, an' I can't get up to my floor, an' I need to get my term paper."

"C'mon. What floor do you need?"

"Four."

The man used his card key to summon the elevator and when it arrived he held the door for Mary, then pressed "4" and stepped back into the lobby.

"There. That should do it, huh."

"Thank you!"

Mary got off on the fourth floor and wiped her face clean with a tissue from her pocket. She found the apartment, then walked a couple of doors down and started knocking. Nobody home at the first one. A girl came to the door in pajamas at the second, annoyed with Mary for waking her. She definitely did not want to buy a candy bar. Mary listened at the door of the target apartment and then knocked. Nobody home. She reached into her inside pocket for her lock picks, and after a few seconds she was in.

She knew from the name on the list that it was a man's apartment; a student's, most likely, and it lived down to her expectations. It was a sty, smelling of beer, and from the looks of the place it hadn't been cleaned in months. Every container that could hold alcohol was dirty and either in the sink or on the counter waiting its turn. It was easy to find the bottle of Scotch that she was looking for – the kitchen table had twenty different bottles of liquor on it. The Scotch had been opened but the level was down only a couple of shots' worth. She checked the overflowing wastebasket to see if there might be an empty Scotch bottle in it, but found none. There were a few framed photos of people hanging on the wall, and Mary took a small camera from her pocket and snapped some shots of them. She did a cursory look in the two bedrooms; they were both in the same condition, clothes on the floor and beds unmade. She pulled open a few dresser drawers in each bedroom and rifled through them, then she left. Outside on the street she noted the Scotch brand she had found and its approximate fill level on her list.

Her next stop was a dorm room in the old Lakeshore quadrangle. She hopped a campus bus and got off at the corner of Babcock and Observatory. The wind came off of Lake Mendota strong and cold, leapt the flat-topped crew house where the racing shells were kept and rushed up the street. The cold air stung her face and made her eyes water. She ducked her head and wrapped her scarf around her face as she burrowed into the wind. At Tripp Hall she entered the courtyard and headed for a door to the stairwell. The door was unlocked, and she made her way to the second floor and located the room she was seeking. At the door she held her breath and listened, and she heard the rhythmic squeaky-squeaky-squeaky of old bedsprings. At eleven-thirty in the morning! She smiled and decided that it was not a good time for her to visit.

She caught a campus bus back to the corner of Park and University where she transferred to a Park Street South bus. At Ridgewood she pulled the bell-cord, and got off. A block off of Park was a square two-story concrete block building, an eight-unit. Mary walked down the street past it. There were six cars in the parking lot. She walked to the next street, turned and walked a block, turned again and came back to the building from the other side. She went into the building vestibule and climbed the stairs to the second floor. There was loud music coming from the apartment, so she went back down the stairs.

Phil climbed the wide marble staircase in the Capitol Building. He had a bag in his hand containing a quart of pistachio ice cream and a plastic spoon. It had been searched at the guard's station downstairs, and it was all he could do to keep the guard from bisecting the container with his knife. At the end of the hall were two ten-foot wooden doors; a brass plate on one door read 'Attorney General, State of Wisconsin.' He eased the door open and went inside.

"I'd like to see Mr. Kleinstern, please."

The receptionist looked up at Phil over her half-glasses. "Do you have an appointment?"

"No, he told me to just stop by."

"Everyone needs an appointment."

"You don't understand."

"Oh, but I do. He's booked up. Good day, sir."

"Wait, wait just a minute. I do have an appointment."

She picked up the handset of her telephone console, finger poised over the 'Security' button. "Oh? When?"

"Today. Right now."

"My appointment book doesn't show anything."

"Then I guess he isn't booked up now, is he?"

She pushed the "Security" button on the console.

"Let's try this again," Phil said. "I have a delivery here for Mr. Kleinstern." He set the bag on the counter in front of the receptionist. "He's expecting it. It is his favorite ice cream. If you don't call him right now and tell him it's here, it will melt all over everything and his order will be ruined. You don't want to come between a man and his ice cream, do you?"

"Hal? Never mind." She disconnected the call, then looked in the bag and punched a different button on the desk console. She said something he couldn't hear into the receiver.

"Name?" she asked.

"Phil Bardo, from the Chocolate Shoppe."

She relayed the information, then hung up. "Through there," she said, pointing to another pair of doors.

As Phil approached the doors he heard a buzz and a click, and he pulled one door open and walked through.

Kleinstern was there, seated behind a massive desk. Behind him on either side were a State of Wisconsin flag and an American flag.

"She's brutal," Phil remarked as they shook hands. "I thought I was going to have to wrestle her to get in here."

"Yeah, she's a monster," Kleinstern laughed, "and you would have lost. She's at advanced levels of two or three different martial arts. I forget which ones." He eyed the bag. "You have something for me?"

"I do." Phil passed the bag to him.

"Excellent," he said, looking inside. "Thanks." He opened the door of his credenza to expose a small refrigerator/freezer, and slid the bag inside. "Have a seat. What can I do for you?"

Mary was locked in concentration on her computer screen, and the Lyle Lovett CD playing through her computer speakers masked the sounds of the man approaching. He had gotten within an arm's length of her when she suddenly realized he was there, and she jumped from her chair and spun to face him.

"Jesus Christ!" she blurted, "what the hell are you doing here?"

"I'm sorry to startle you. I certainly didn't expect to see you here, either." Dr. Ted Essinger stood with his hands in his coat pockets and a slight smile on his face. "The door was open, and nobody answered when I knocked."

Was the door open? Mary couldn't remember. Usually she was careful to lock it when she was there alone. Maybe today she forgot. Maybe. She cast her eyes around her computer table – some pencils, an architect's rule, the keyboard and a mouse. A desk lamp. Not much to use for self-defense if she needed it. She felt her heart racing. "So, you're here. What do you want?"

"Miss, you'll get more business if you aren't quite so rude to the customers."

"We aren't accepting new business. The owner died."

"I'm aware of that, but I thought the new owner-"

"He's not here right now."

"A pity. I wanted to meet him. I had two things I wished to discuss with him." He continued to stare at Mary. "Now there are three."

"I'm his office manager. Tell me what you want and I'll give him the message."

"I didn't know he had an office manager. You weren't here when I came the last time." Essinger rocked on his heels for a moment, then turned his attention to some of the book stacks nearby and read the titles on the spines. "Interesting collection, by the way. I suppose I could give you a message. The first item was a missing persons job. A friend of mine has disappeared and I thought perhaps your firm could find her for me."

"The police do missing persons, you know."

"They do foul-play disappearances. This one isn't like that. Shouldn't you take some notes?"

"I've got a good memory. What's the second thing?"

Essinger withdrew his hands from his pockets and picked up a book and paged through it. "I had hired the late owner of this business to do some work for me. After a few days he terminated the relationship. I merely want to know what he discovered during those initial days. Perhaps you know?"

"I haven't a clue."

"Oh, that's disappointing. I would think that an office manager would be aware of the progress of cases. You aren't a very good office manager, are you?" He looked sharply at her. "Would it be possible for me to review whatever files he may have left behind?"

"There are no files with 'Essinger' on them. I know that for a fact."

He put a smile back on his face and set the book on the

stack. "I see. When might the new owner be in?"

"I don't know for sure. Later today. What was the third thing?"

He dropped the smile as quickly as it had come. "I want to know what you were doing in my classroom."

"I told you, I was checking it out for next semester."

"Miss, I may have been born yesterday but certainly not last night. I believe that you are not being truthful with me about this."

"Believe whatever you want."

"Shall we try again?"

"I don't think so."

Essinger shrugged his shoulders and his smile magically reappeared. "Very well, Miss–what was your name?" Mary remained silent. "All right, then. Please have the new owner call me. I'm sure you can find the number." He turned and left, and Mary turned off the CD and listened to his progress as he closed the waiting room door, then opened and closed the outer door. She peered out the window and saw him reach the sidewalk, then she ran to the outer office door and locked it.

"Let me tell you, that was creepy," she shuddered.

Phil exhaled and realized that he had held his breath for most of her story. "Thank God he didn't try anything. You've got to make sure you keep that door locked."

"I'm pretty sure it was. I can't swear to it, though."

"Very interesting. And of course we can't believe that he was truthful in anything he said. He knows that Dee is gone; he's apparently looking for her. I can think of only a couple reasons for that. She was smart to leave."

"Why would he come here to find her?"

"Well, he could sincerely want our help to find her and didn't want to seek another detective agency."

"Uh-huh. Sure."

"More likely, he found out somehow that I've been in touch with her."

"Maybe she told him about her meeting with you."

"I can't believe she'd do that; I don't know what good that would do her."

"Or maybe he's already found her and killed her, and is just trying to lay a false trail to throw off suspicion."

"I wish you hadn't thought of that."

"And what about the file?"

Phil shook his head. "Again we don't know what he's really thinking, but it sure looks like he either suspects Dave of having seen something or knows absolutely that he did. And thanks to that classroom episode and then finding you here, now he thinks we know something, too, either about Dee or the drugs or both. He may even know that the call you made to his office came from here."

"So, are you gonna call him?"

"I don't know. Not yet, anyway."

"This has been a busy day. I've got something else to tell you." Mary described the details of her morning excursions to the Scotch buyers' residences.

"Just what the hell did you think you were doing?"

"My job, Phil, I was doing my job. What did you expect to do with those names and addresses? I thought you wanted to see if they had that cheap Scotch lying around."

"I do, but breaking and entering and going alone? Bad idea! We should go to the cops and they can get a search warrant and do it."

"That's crap. You'd be surprised how many unofficial searches go on. You do the unofficial search first to see if it is worth it, then get a warrant and go in officially."

"I can't believe the cops work that way."

"Maybe *they* don't, but I wasn't a cop."

"At the very least I should have gone with you."

"Alone is the only way to do it. You can't go. Can you imagine what that would do to your case if you got caught?"

"And what would happen to my case if you, *my wife*, got caught?" Phil slammed his hand on the desk and stood up. "That's it! Forget about the Scotch, you're not doing any more of that."

"Fuck you!"

"What?"

"You heard me. You can't tell me what to do!"

Phil stood before her, red-faced. He glared at her as she sat in the leather easy chair with her knees pulled up to her chest. She met his glare unblinking. He sat down again in the wooden swivel chair, fuming.

"You know it's the only way, Phil. Now get off my ass about it."

"It's too dangerous. Two people have been killed. I don't want you to be number three."

"I was trained to do this stuff. I'd like to think I know what I'm doing. This is the business we're in, so if you don't like it, get out. Besides, if we're lucky we can wrap this all up."

"How do you figure?"

"What if I find more than Scotch? What if I find Scotch and, let's say, a box of .38 caliber shells with two missing?"

Phil was silent.

"Only two shots were fired," Mary explained. "You can't buy just two shells, you have to buy a box. Dave never had any ammo for that gun. Somebody else did."

He stayed silent, but now he was embarrassed as well as angry. He hadn't thought of that.

"Look," she said, "I'm sorry that you were worried about me. No, actually, I'm glad. But it really is something that needs to be done and I'm the only one who can do it. You know it, too. Now how long are you planning to sulk about it?"

"Another half-hour. When are you going to do it again?"

"It's best that you don't know. I shouldn't have told you about what I've done so far. Here, have a candy bar. You owe me two bucks. Now, are you going to tell me about your visit to the Attorney General?"

"No, actually I can't. He only spoke to me on the condition that I don't share the conversation with anyone. Period."

"Oh, c'mon. I don't like you holding out on me."

"I know the feeling, believe me." Phil studied her for a

moment. "I can tell you that he was familiar with the case."

Phil decided to stay downtown and check in at the store again. Mary said that was fine, that she had some things she had to get done around the house anyway, so she caught a bus westbound.

Sam was still at the store when Phil got there, and they shifted the remaining ice cream inventory from one of the small walk-in freezers to the other. Business was down – the cold weather cut into the ice cream sales in a big way, and though the coffee and hot chocolate and baked goods sales were up, they didn't make up the difference. This happened every year and Phil usually compensated by adjusting inventories and shutting the store for the two slowest weeks in December. This was a mixed blessing for the staff, as they had time off for the holidays but they were cash-short just when they needed it the most.

"We should start talking about the Christmas party," Sam said.

"Let's discuss that over dinner," Phil suggested. He called Mary and told her that he wouldn't be home until late, then he and Sam left the store to the evening staff. There were snowflakes in the air as they hurried down State Street to Paul's Club. They chose a deeply padded corner booth right across from the tree that stood in the dining room; a dead tree that had been exactly there for over 40 years and held little white Christmas lights year-round.

They had mussels in garlic and white wine for an appetizer. The black shells gleamed, the steam and the garlic made a fragrant cloud in the booth. The party would be held at the store as usual, they decided, but this year they'd try a random gift drawing with right-of-exchange. Ella's Deli would cater the food, and Phil would buy drinks from Dominick at State Street Liquors. The last of the shells were emptied as they finished their first glasses of wine.

"Now that we've got the important stuff out of the way," Sam said, "tell me what's new today on your case."

"Not a whole lot. Lars' funeral is the day after tomorrow. As far as I know the cops have nothing to go on, other than it happened Sunday afternoon. Who was on at the store Sunday afternoon? Maybe they saw something."

"Judy, Lisa, and Nick," Sam replied. "I asked them. There was nothing out of the ordinary. What else?"

"I'm looking for a new lawyer. The Jacksons have filed for postponement, and the judge will review that on Friday."

"There's more, isn't there?"

"A few things, but I'd rather not tell you. I don't want you to have to lie about them if they come up in court."

"Okay, but can you tell me if they're good or bad?"

"A little of both."

Their main courses came and they ordered more wine. Phil asked about Sam's mom and Gato, and Sam asked about Mary.

"She's fine," Phil said between bites of stuffed sole. "Maybe a bit of a cold coming on."

"No, I mean how is she? You know."

"Oh. I'm not sure I'm comfortable talking about that."

Sam picked at her plate. "I'm sure I'm not. I'm not comfortable at all."

"Then why do you ask?"

"I'm stuck somewhere between jealousy and curiosity. This arrangement is even harder than I thought it would be. I think about it all the time. I-" She couldn't finish.

Phil put his fork down. "Look. I think you and I share something; something intangible and intimate. I carry you with me every day."

Sam looked down into her lap. "I still have to know."

"I won't lie to you. She's good."

"Better than me?"

"No. How could anyone be better than you, that night?" Phil slid next to her in the booth, and put his arm around her. "Someday soon we'll all be able to start over."

Mary got home and walked Hoover around the block,

then went to the bedroom to get ready. She put on her black jeans, black running shoes, and a black tank top. In the bottom drawer of her dresser was a black Kevlar vest, and she strapped it on and pulled the cinches tight, then put on her letter jacket. In the bottom of the drawer under the vest was a nine millimeter Glock; she threw the holster back into the drawer, checked the clip and double-checked the safety, then slipped the gun into her jacket pocket. Lock picks, flashlight, camera, all in place. She buttoned her jacket and pulled a stocking cap over her loose hair, put on gloves and went out to the car.

She parked her ancient Corolla three blocks from the apartment on Ridgeway and walked back to the bus shelter. From there she could see the apartment. The lights were on and she heard the music. There was loud talking and laughing – a party, or at least a group of guys priming themselves for a night out. She sat in the bus shelter and watched and waved off the bus drivers as they came and stopped for her. It was getting cold even though the shelter blocked the wind. She hated being cold; she felt her skin grow stiff and tight, and she rubbed her hands and legs together. The shelter smelled of urine and cigarette butts. She closed her eyes.

The music stopped, and she opened her eyes and watched as the apartment went dark. She got up and stood outside the shelter and listened, and she heard young men talking, muffled, and then it grew louder as they left the building vestibule. They walked to the parking lot and doors slammed and engines fired, then a car and a van left the parking lot. When they had been gone five minutes she crossed the street and walked into the apartment building.

The vestibule was quiet and warmer than the bus shelter. She climbed the stairs and stood outside the apartment door. No sounds, no voices, no music. No light from under the door. She stood for five more minutes, listening. Then she took the lock picks from her inside jacket pocket and unlocked the door, stepped inside and closed the door behind her. A few passes with the flashlight revealed that it was a two-bedroom apartment. She stepped carefully to each, listened, and hearing nothing, shined the light onto the beds. No one. A few pictures stood on the dressers; she took photos of them with her camera. Back in the living room she examined some plastic cups on the coffee table. She knelt to sniff them. Definitely alcohol of some type. She rose and passed her light over the walls and a bookshelf, and bottles on the middle shelf.

Mary didn't hear them coming, and one hit her from behind, low around the knees, and the other high at the shoulder blades. She was thrown face down to the carpet and her cheek exploded in pain as it hit the floor. One had her legs wrapped up and she couldn't move them, and the other sat on her back. She struggled to reach her gun with her right hand. It was trapped under her in her jacket pocket, and as she tried to free it she felt hands on her neck. They felt for and found her carotid arteries and pressed. She began to feel thickheaded, fuzzy, and as the sparkles appeared before her eyes she heard herself, far away, croak "Don't . . . please . . ." and she felt warm and the sparkles disappeared.

She woke and everything was still black. A blindfold was tied tight over her eyes. Her cheek throbbed, and her mouth was open and stuffed with something; a cloth. She jerked, panicked, and couldn't get enough breath. She lay on her side on the floor, wheezing through her nose, arms tied behind her and legs bound from the knees down.

"She's awake."

A chair moved, then she heard footsteps. "Good evening, Mrs. Bardo. Nice of you to drop in."

"What do we do now?" asked a second voice.

"Shut up and let me think."

The voice sounded a bit familiar but she couldn't place it. Mary labeled him The Thinker.

"I think we-"

"I said shut up!" Footsteps came close to her head, then she heard the thinking man's voice close to her ear. "Did you really think we wouldn't see you out there? We're not as dumb as you thought, huh? And you're supposed to be good at this.

Phil sending a girl to do a man's job – shame on him!"

"Hey, look at this! A Glock!" The other guy was going through her jacket. She realized she wasn't wearing it any more, nor was she wearing her Kevlar vest. His voice was also a little familiar; she dubbed him Other Guy.

"Nice," The Thinker responded. "And the vest, too. She brought all kinds of nice presents for us." His hands roamed Mary's chest, and she jerked as he suddenly pulled her tank top down to bare her. "Take a look at these."

"C'mon, you're making it worse. What's the plan?"

The Thinker felt her, gently, then squeezed her hard and pulled her shirt up again. "You're just a slut, a cock-teaser. It's gonna be fun to have what Phil's been having."

"Stop," Other Guy said. "I'm telling ya, you're making it worse!"

The Thinker stood up. "Look, genius, it's not like we can let her go. We hafta keep her around for a while, for insurance, then-"

"No, not another-"

"Shut up. Nobody's gonna find her. And in the meantime it would be a waste not to have a little fun with her. I will, anyway; I know you're not into the ladies. But you know what they say – rape's a crime of violence, not of love, so you should be able to join in."

"You make me sick."

"Yeah, yeah." The Thinker paced. "We need a place to keep her."

"Not here. My roommate's coming back."

"Right. Not at my place either. Ah, I know. CG. It's closed up. You have something we can put her in for the trip?"

"Let me look." Footsteps retreated, then she heard sounds of rustling from a back corner of the apartment, and then the footsteps returned. "How about this big duffel bag?"

"Perfect."

The Thinker rolled Mary to her stomach, then he bent her legs at the knees and bound her ankles to her wrists. Then they worked her, knees first, into the duffel. "Hang on," he said, as

331

her head was about to go into the bag.

She heard footsteps again, fading, some metallic rattling, then footsteps returned. She felt a cold, sharp piece of metal placed against her neck. "What do you suppose Phil might recognize," The Thinker asked her. "An ear?" He grabbed a big handful of her hair. She took a deep breath and held it, and she wondered if she'd pass out from the pain. He put the blade next to her scalp, sliced, and the handful of hair came away. "No, ears are too messy." He pushed her head down into the duffel and secured the end.

"Gimme a pen, a piece of paper, and an envelope."

CHAPTER TWENTY-FIVE

There were two good things about her situation, Mary decided. Number one, she wasn't dead and it sounded like they were going to keep her alive for a while. Number two was that it was fairly warm inside the duffel bag. That was the end of the good things. Her movement was limited by the way they had her trussed, and she was rewarded for the struggles she attempted by punches and kicks delivered to her through the bag. The men had carried her out of the apartment building and put her into some sort of truck. She wasn't in the trunk of a car, she decided, because she could hear them in conversation and she heard doors shut rather than a trunk lid. Maybe there was a third good thing; Other Guy seemed reluctant to participate in another murder. She'd have to work that angle when the opportunity presented.

What would Phil be doing? She didn't know the time but she assumed it was still night, as they wouldn't risk moving her in broad daylight. Phil might be getting up; hell, he might be sitting up waiting for her. Ah, a fourth good thing was that she had left the addresses on her dresser; Phil would find them and that would give him a start on tracking her down.

The truck came to a stop. She heard two doors open and shut, then two doors open immediately next to her. Then she was lifted and set down, and the ground was cold. The doors shut again, and then the men lifted her and began to walk. She had soaked the ball of cloth in her mouth with her saliva, and she had been able to maneuver her tongue and push the cloth away from the back of her throat so she no longer felt in immediate danger of choking. The men labored with her and did not speak, their breathing loud and their gait slowed as if they were climbing a hill. They set her down again, and the ground was cold and damp through the bag, and she could smell earth and the must of dead leaves. A metallic sound came next, then a creaking like that of a gate. They lifted her and set her down again, partly supported and partly suspended on a hard object – concrete? – and one of them moved past her. She heard an "okay" from somewhere below her, and one of the men swung her leg-end off of its support. Then he grabbed the head end of the bag and lifted, and she was suspended, swinging and banging into a hard object, a wall. Someone grabbed her at the knees, and then she was lowered in jerks until her knees contacted the ground again. Then the head-end of the bag was lowered to the ground. Metallic footsteps came near, paused and a creaking, then more metallic footsteps; a metal ladder. Then came the sound of footsteps on the ground next to her.

"So far, so good."

"Can we rest a minute?" Other Guy asked.

"Sure."

After a few minutes their breathing quieted. "All right, let's go," The Thinker said.

"Do we have to carry her? How about we take turns dragging her?"

"Yeah. Probably easier in here anyway."

One of the men grabbed the head-end of the bag and began to pull. The ground was hard and uneven, and the hard edges and bumps and pits bruised and scraped her through the duffel. She tried to count footsteps; a count multiplied by an average stride would give her some idea of how far they took her. A pothole appeared and she landed on the edge with her ribcage and the pain made her cry out, muffled through her gag.

"Shut up!" The Thinker said and she braced herself for the kick that came. She lost count of the footsteps. The men changed dragging-duty several times. It grew warmer and wetter, and the bottom of the bag became sodden. The smells and sounds were familiar; she knew them – the steam tunnels. They made a few turns, and there were uphill and downhill stretches. Then she heard the sound of a door and the ground became smooth, and then soon there was the sound of another door opening and whoever was dragging her dropped the head-end of the bag. One of the men fumbled with the fastener and then the bag opened. Someone lifted the foot-end of the bag and tugged, and she slipped out onto the floor.

She felt hands at her back, and then the binding that held her ankles to her wrists was severed and she extended her legs with a moan of relief.

"Over there," The Thinker said. "Tie her wrists to that pipe." One man grabbed her by the arms and the other by the legs and they carried her a couple feet and sat her up, then bound her wrist restraints to a pipe that ran cold along her spine. Then someone cut the bindings from her legs.

"Welcome to your new apartment, Mrs. Bardo," The Thinker said. He untied the gag and pulled the ball of cloth from her mouth. "You're in the basement utility room of beautiful Carson Gulley Commons on campus. Been closed since last year. Nobody will hear you in here, so scream if you want. Knock yourself out."

"What next?" Other Guy asked.

"Bring her some food and water a couple times a day. And a bucket. Whatever you do, don't let her have her arms and legs free at the same time. Bring some duct tape – that's good for changing her around."

"Oh, so this is all on me now?"

"I gotta work today, and tomorrow. I'm off Friday so I'll do her then. Yeah, I sure will."

"Can we go now?"

"Yeah. I gotta make a delivery."

They left the room and the door closed and Mary heard the sound of a lock. She was alone.

Phil had not been surprised when he returned to the house and found Mary gone. The surprise had come when he woke at two o'clock and realized that she wasn't back yet, and then worry came on him when he got up at four-thirty to get ready to go in to the store and found she still wasn't home. He left a note for her to call him, walked Hoover, then collected the papers with the Scotch buyers' addresses on them from her dresser and went downtown.

He had the ovens heating by the time Sam arrived.

"G'morning. You got some mail," she said, and handed him an envelope. She shed her coat and put on an apron.

"Where was this?"

"On the floor. Somebody must have shoved it under the front door."

"It wasn't there when I came in." He wiped his hands on a towel and looked at the envelope. No stamp, and it was hand-addressed to Phil Bardo with no return address. It was lumpy. He tore off the end and spilled the contents onto the stainless steel prep table. It was a large handful of hair, followed by a folded piece of paper. They both stared.

"She didn't come home last night," Phil said. He picked up the hair, felt it between his fingers, and lifted it to his nose. He inhaled, nodded, and put the hair down on the table. Then he picked up the paper and unfolded it. It was a note, handwritten in black ink.

"It says 'No cops! Plead guilty now, or she dies!'"

"This is awful!" Sam said. "What are we going to do?"

"I need a quart of pistachio. To go."

Mary leaned back against the pipe. She couldn't work her hands free. She found that she could press her back against the pipe and work her way to a standing position, but once there, there was nothing she could use to escape the pipe or cut the ties on her wrists. She sat down again. The blindfold was annoying. She turned her head and leaned back, pressing the knot of the blindfold against the pipe and tried to lever it up and off. It wouldn't budge; the pipe was too smooth to get a grip on the cloth. One toe pressed against the heel of her other foot and her shoe came off. Then the other, and she was barefoot. She raised a leg and tried to hook it behind her head. If she could just get a foot behind her head, maybe she could lift the blindfold. She used to be able to bend that way, and still could, but she needed her hands to pull the leg there. No good. She put her leg down again and rested. Time to try something else. If she could somehow get her hands in front of her . . . This wasn't going to be pleasant. She hadn't done a dislocate like this since high school. It wasn't a real dislocation, it just looked like it. When she was young she could clasp her hands behind her and with strategic bending of her elbows and a little pressure and wiggling, rotate one arm over her head and then the other, and wind up with her hands in front of her without breaking her grasp. That was her initial claim to fame with the young boys. She pressed and bent, and but the pain was too great. She couldn't do it; the wrist bindings and the pole didn't allow her enough flexibility. She pulled her knees to her chest and rested again. Then she laughed. "Duh," she said aloud. She put her forehead to her knees and jammed her kneecaps into her eye-sockets and pushed her head down. Almost. The blindfold was still too tight. Then she crossed one leg at the ankle over the other knee and bent her head to the knee. A scoot of the foot toward her hip and she had her cheek resting on her big toe. She hooked the toe under the edge of the blindfold and straightened her leg, and the blindfold flew off. The room was dark.

When Phil arrived at the Attorney General's office the receptionist waved him in. Kleinstern was just taking off his coat when Phil came through the door.

"Phil! I didn't expect to see you again quite so soon. Or so early!" He took the quart and put it in the freezer in his credenza.

"There's been a development. They've got Mary. Last night." He laid the plastic bag with the envelope in it on Kleinstern's desk, then showed him the note. "And there's a big hunk of her hair in the envelope."

Kleinstern studied the note and the envelope. "You

realize, of course, that even if she's still alive now, there's no chance that they'll release her alive. Every day that passes makes it less likely that we'll find her in time."

"Yes."

"We'll have to act faster than we wanted. We're just not ready. We may blow this case and still not find her. Do you have any clue as to where she might be?"

"No, but I have a list of the places where she may have been when she was taken." He handed a list of names and addresses to Kleinstern. "She also had a strange visit from Essinger yesterday afternoon at the office."

"Well, now that we've got a kidnapping situation the FBI will have to take this more seriously. I'll call Chicago. In the meantime I'll get my team on it."

"What about the local cops?"

Kleinstern shook his head. "Not unless you've got one that you know is absolutely, positively clean. One that can help without doing it officially."

"I think I might. And I have a few other people that could help out, too."

"Okay. If you have some pictures of her, send people to the *neighbors* of these addresses and ask them if anybody has seen her." Kleinstern sat and tapped at his desk blotter with a pencil.

"What about Essinger?"

"We'll put a tail on him right away." Kleinstern picked up the phone, dialed, had a brief conversation, then hung up. "That should do it. They'll be on him within the hour. So, go prod Essinger."

"Okay, and then?"

"We need to move up the party and expand the guest list. It may not work, and it might make things worse for her."

Phil shook his head. "Seems to me that she's useful to them alive under two circumstances: one, if I haven't yet complied with their demands, and two, if they need her as a bargaining chip to escape. If either circumstance goes away, we're in trouble. Gary, we've just got to try it."

"Yeah. Let's work on the guest list, and see how quickly you can get a room."

Phil charged out of the elevator on the sixth floor of Van Hise Hall and blew past the department secretary without breaking stride. Essinger's office door was open and Phil was in and had the door closed and locked before the secretary could make a sound. Essinger was seated at his desk, and he looked up at Phil's arrival.

"Where is she?" Phil demanded.

"Where is who?"

"You know damned well who I'm talking about!"

"I'm afraid I don't even know who you are, let alone who and what you are talking about."

"I'm Phil Bardo, owner of Discreet Detectives."

"Oh! Your office manager must have given you my message. She is not very good in customer relations; I am sure that you could find someone more personable. You must be interested in the missing person job."

"No kidding! Now where is she?"

"That is precisely why I came to see you. I would like you to find her for me."

"That's cute, Essinger!" Phil planted both hands palms-down on Essinger's desktop. "I swear, if you or any of your pals hurt her . . ."

Essinger let a strange little smile break across his face. "Mr. Bardo, I believe we are talking at cross-purposes. I want you to find a friend of mine. She has disappeared. I believe you may know her: Ms. Deirdre Best?"

"I'd be happy to help you *not* find Best. She's not the issue. My 'office manager' as you put it, is my wife, and she's being held for a ransom. But of course *you* wouldn't know anything about *that*. Oh, look," Phil grabbed a pen out of the holder, "a black pen. The ransom note was written in black pen!"

"My dear sir, I am hardly the only person in this city who uses black pens. And I know nothing of the disappearance of that disagreeable woman from your office."

Phil cleared Essinger's desktop with a sweep of his arm, sending papers, pen-sets and mementos to the floor. "I'm not playing, Essinger. I want her back, safe, right now!"

"Then perhaps you should pay the ransom."

"First my uncle, then my lawyer, now my wife. You'll regret this, you sonofabitch!" Phil spun on his heel and yanked open the office door, marched to the elevator and left the floor. He had the elevator to himself on the way down, and he smiled all the way from the fifth floor to the ground floor.

Essinger stood up and stepped around the mess on the floor. "Sandy," he said as he passed by the department secretary, "my guest had a bit of a tantrum. Please straighten up in there for me. I have to go out for a while."

"Have you called her parents?"

"No, Sam, I don't have their number. She hasn't told them anything. They don't know about the marriage, and they may not even know that she quit the FBI."

"Don't you think they should be told?"

"Sure. 'Hi, I'm your daughter's new husband, under indictment for the murder of my uncle. We got married after knowing each other three weeks. And by the way, she's been kidnapped and is being held by someone who is threatening to kill her.'"

Sam was silent.

"I'm sorry," Phil said, "I don't mean to be nasty to you. I'm just . . ."

"Yeah, me, too." She put her hand on Phil's shoulder. "Anything else we can do?"

"I need some help with some field work."

"Let me round up some crew." Sam returned to the office after a few minutes with Lauren, Aaron, and Ellen.

Phil looked at their faces and said, "I've got a little job for you, some real detective work. Are you interested?" They all nodded. "Okay, here's the deal. My wife is missing. I've got some addresses where she may have been right before her disappearance. I need you to go to these places, or rather, *to the addresses right next door,* and show her picture around and ask if they've seen her or noticed anything unusual going on last night." Phil passed out the addresses and pictures of Mary in her Halloween outfit. The three studied the addresses and swapped them back and forth.

"Questions? No? Okay, go." They left. "Sam, who's left to mind the store?"

"Me," Sam said, "until I can reach Lisa or one of the others."

"When the cops come in, I really need to talk to Dale. Tell him he's got an emergency phone call and send him back here."

"Right!" She turned and hurried down the hall.

Phil reached for the phone book. The first on his list was the Overture Center. "Hello? Yes, I need to book a room for a private party. Maybe fifty or sixty. Drinks and hors-d'oeuvres. As soon as possible."

Before long there was a knock at the office door.

"What's this about an emergency phone call?"

"Dale, come on in. There's no phone call, but there is an emergency."

It wasn't easy to find a suitable room on short notice. The Overture Center, Monona Terrace, and the west side hotel convention halls were all booked solid for the next month. He walked State Street over the lunch hour with gyros in hand, and as he passed the Orpheum Theater he noticed the sign saying 'Closed until Monday for Repairs.' When he got back to the Chocolate Shoppe he called. The film projection system was down, and the manager was thrilled with the prospect of offsetting lost revenue with a private party. Friday night would be ideal.

Phil arranged for food and drinks to be catered. He next turned his attention to writing the text for the invitations, based on the notes he took in his meeting with Kleinstern.

Mary heard the sound of the door lock being turned, and then the door opened and the single overhead light bulb snapped on. She blinked.

"Oh shit, why'd you have to go and do that?" Other Guy set down the bucket and the grocery bag and picked up the blindfold.

"You're gonna kill me anyway, so what's the difference if I see who you are."

He shrugged. "You've got a point." He threw the blindfold into the corner.

"You look a little familiar. I can't quite . . . hey, now I know!"

"Shut up. I'm not in the mood for conversation." The man busied himself emptying the grocery bag. He opened a can of mini-ravioli and knelt next to Mary with a plastic fork. "I gotta feed ya. Open up." He stabbed a piece of pasta with the fork and shoved it into her mouth. She was hungry, even for this, and she ate as fast as he could deliver. They emptied the can. He unscrewed the top of a bottle of water and held it for her, and as she drank rivulets of water ran from the corners of her mouth down and dripped from her jaw onto her shirt.

"'Nuf," she said, pulling her lips from the bottle and the rest of the contents splashed onto her chest. "You know you're gonna get caught. It would go a lot better for you if you let me go. You don't want to go down for a third murder."

He put the empty bottle and can into the grocery bag. "I didn't kill them."

"Sure."

"I didn't. Do you have to go to the bathroom?"

"Yeah."

He looked at the bucket and at Mary, then shook his head. "Forget this bucket shit. There's a bathroom just around the corner." He studied her face. "Behave yourself and I'll take you there. But if you mess with me I'll beat you so bad your own ma won't recognize you. Got it?" She nodded.

The man took a roll of duct tape from the grocery bag. He put her ankles together and taped them. Then he put the blindfold back over her eyes. He untied her wrists from the pipe. "Gimme your right hand." He pulled her right hand to her knee and secured it there with the duct tape. "Let's go." He grabbed her by the arms and pulled her to her feet, and helped her hop to the door, out and around a corner and down a short hall and through another door into the bathroom. He backed her up to the toilet until she felt it with the backs of her legs. "Okay. Do your thing, I'll wait." She got her jeans unbuttoned and unzipped with her left hand but they were tight and she couldn't take them down.

"A little help?"

He helped her peel them down and she sat, and he helped her find the tissue. When she was done he helped her to her feet and pulled her underwear and jeans back into position. Then they reversed course and hopped back to the utility room.

"You helped him, didn't you," Mary said.

The man sat her down on the floor and bound her wrists to the pipe again.

"If you helped him plan it or helped him in any way to do it, the law won't treat you any differently than if you pulled the trigger yourself."

"You talk too much." He took the blindfold off and dropped it on the floor.

"And now you're into kidnapping."

"Shut up, I know what you're trying to do, and it won't work."

"Your friend. He's gonna come back and rape me. I suppose they can't get you for that, unless you help him do it or you do it yourself. Wait, maybe there's an aiding and abetting on that too."

"I thought I told you to shut up!"

"And then when he does kill me, well then, that's the third murder you'll be charged with."

Other Guy searched the floor and found the cloth gag.

"I don't think you really want to see that happen," Mary said. "The rape or the murder. Let me go and I'll-"

He forced the gag into her mouth and tied the cloth behind her head.

"You don't get it," he said. His eyes glistened. "I'm sorry but this is the way it's gotta be." He left the room and closed and locked the door, leaving the light on.

Phil completed his work on the computer and printed a copy. He proofread the document, then handed it to Sam.

"What do you think?"

She read:

"**MYSTERY SOLVED!** *You and your guest are invited to join members of the media at the event of the decade! Please join us at the* **Orpheum Theater** *on State Street, at* **eight p.m., November Sixteenth**. *Enjoy champagne, an open bar, and bountiful hors-d'oeuvres. The highlight of the evening will be the* **NAMING OF THE PERSON WHO SHOT DAVID HELMS** *and how it was done. Please join us! Jacket and tie requested. Your Host, Phil Bardo.*"

She looked at him. "You know who the killer is?"

"Yes. Absolutely."

"Who?"

"I can't tell you now, it would spoil the surprise."

"And what about Mary?"

"This may be our only chance to find her alive."

Sam shook her head. "I don't get it."

"You will. And I'll need your help – a lot of it." He gathered some papers from the desk. "We'll need enough copies of the invitation for everyone on this list, guests and media. And we need to hand-deliver these invitations today. I want our entire staff there Friday night; I'll need them to act as ushers and servers. We're providing desserts – ice cream and cookies – so I'll need them all in here on Friday during the day to do all the extra baking and prep. Can you arrange all this?"

"Sure!"

"I've got a lot of planning to do over the next two days,

so I won't be around much. Oh, Lars' funeral is tomorrow at ten a.m. – would you go with me?"

Sam nodded. "Phil, I sure hope you know what you're doing."

"Me, too." He watched Sam leave, papers in hand. He felt bad lying to her like that but they could afford no slipups. He had no idea who the murderer was; he could only hope that they'd all know by the end of Friday evening.

"I found her car," Dale said. "It's about three blocks from one of those addresses, the one on Ridgeway."

"Great! Anything unusual?"

"No. It's locked, and it hasn't been bothered."

"How about the apartment?"

"Nothing going on there at the moment. Phil, I can't hang around and wait. I really need to get back to my beat before somebody notices I'm gone."

"Yes, I know. Thanks, Dale." Phil pressed the switchhook, then dialed.

"Gary? Phil. We found her car. The Ridgeway apartment. Can you put someone on it? Thanks."

"Thanks for coming over," Phil said. "I can't watch TV, there's too many murders. I keep thinking about her, and I get these visions of her, dead in a ditch, drowned in the lake, hacked-"

"Please stop," Sam said through a bite of spring roll. "I know what you mean, and I don't need you to make it any worse. It makes me all cold inside."

They sat next to each other with their backs against the couch, on the floor in Mary's living room. Boxes of carryout Chinese food littered the coffee table and Sam fed bits of fried wonton to Hoover.

"We need to change the picture," she said. "Visualize her, alive. Tied up somewhere. Escaping. Giving her kidnappers all kinds of hell."

"Police bursting in and freeing her at the last moment,"

Phil offered. That more positive imagery did help. "I wish I hadn't gotten involved with this detective crap."

"Oh, no, you don't mean that!"

"Maybe I do."

Sam straightened up. "Maybe you don't see it, but I do. This 'detective crap' has given you new energy, a spark. You're alive again. And so many good things have happened to you, and to me, over the past few weeks."

"You can say that, after all-"

"Yes. And we'll get through these bad times, and it will be good again." She leaned against Phil and put her hand on his knee. "It can't get much worse."

Hoover got up and walked to the front door. He threw up on the braided rug.

CHAPTER TWENTY-SIX

The service at Memorial Park was brief. It was a closed casket service; there wasn't much the funeral director could do with Lars after the effects of the drill, the weight of the concrete, and the demolition of the column. The remaining Jackson brothers were there with their wives and children, and there were another two dozen friends and relations present. Beth Talbot was there. Phil and Sam sat in the back, he in a black pinstripe suit and she in a black dress that buttoned up the front. The widow Barbara Jackson attended with her son.

"This reminds me," Phil whispered to Sam, "we've still got to do Dave's wake. It won't be anything like this."

"Shhh," she whispered back.

The service went through the usual words from the funeral director and the minister, the eulogy delivered by one of the brothers, and comments solicited from other attendees. After the service one of the Jackson brothers approached.

"Phil, after you're out of your mess I'd like you to find his murderer."

"Sorry, I'm not licensed to do that business."

He dismissed Phil's protest. "That's a minor detail. C'mon, Phil. I'll be your first paying client, and I pay well."

"We'll see." They shook hands. Barbara Jackson approached as the brother left.

"Barbara, I'm so sorry," Phil said.

Her eyes were red and she clutched a handkerchief in one hand and an envelope in the other. She handed the envelope to Phil. "This was in our safety deposit box. It's addressed to you."

"Do you know what it is?" The envelope had 'To Phil Bardo' written on the front in Lars' handwriting.

She shook her head. "No, and I don't want to know." She squeezed his arm and walked away.

"'*Curiouser'-*" Phil began.

"'*And curiouser,*'" Sam finished. "Are you gonna open it?"

They walked out of the chapel into the front circle. The sun was obscured behind the gray clouds, the normal condition for Wisconsin winter setting in. It was cold and they stood in clouds of their exhaled breath as Phil tore off the end of the envelope.

"Hurry up," Sam said, and bounced up and down. "I'm freezing!"

Phil pulled a few sheets of paper from the envelope and started to read out loud. "Dear Phil: If you're reading this it means that I-" Phil stopped. He read on silently.

"What? C'mon!"

"Oh . . . my . . . God . . ." Phil folded the letter and tucked it back into the envelope. "We've got to go."

"What? Tell me! Hey!" Sam trotted after Phil, wobbly in her high heels, toward the parking lot.

"So what's this all about?" James Bradley asked.

"The 'mystery solved' invitation?"

"That's it."

"Sounds like free eats and drinks and a good laugh."

"So you're going?"

"Yeah, I gotta go," Taylor growled. "He invited my competition – all the other outlets. A frickin' press circus. I gotta go. So do you."

"What on earth for?"

"Publicity, son. Free access to the media. You're in a campaign – take advantage of it."

"But he's going to try to make a fool of me, to destroy the case!"

"Who gives a shit about the case? You've gotta take whatever he dishes and spin it your way. Be indignant and refute it, or be magnanimous and acknowledge it. You'll get good coverage either way, I'll see to that!"

"I don't like it."

"Hell, I didn't say I liked it. But you'd better be there, Bradley! Understand?"

"Shit!"

"Do you understand?"

"Yeah, sure. I'll be there."

"So, is there like a ransom for me or something?"

"Nope."

"Really? I must be worth something!"

"Just your husband pleading guilty."

"Has he done it?"

"What do you think?"

"I guess not."

Other Guy was feeding Mary the last bites from the can when they heard sounds of footsteps. The door swung open and The Thinker entered the room.

"Well, hello," Mary said. "It's you. Long time no see."

He stared at her, then at Other Guy. "What the fuck is she doing without the blindfold?"

"She got it off the first day. So what?"

"Yeah, I guess. Did you get one of these?" He waved one of Phil's invitations in Other Guy's face.

"Yeah."

The Thinker held the invitation in front of Mary's eyes. "What the hell is he up to?"

She read it. "I have no idea."

"Oh, come on now. I think you know."

She glared at him. "I don't know. I've been a little out of the loop lately."

The Thinker swung and cracked her across the face with an open hand. "Maybe that will jog your memory. Now what is he trying to pull?"

"Are you deaf? I told you, I don't know."

Crack! Another open hand. "Still don't know?"

"Tell you what. I'll go and ask, and I'll come right back and tell you."

Crack!

"Please, sir, I want some more."

"God," The Thinker said, "what a mouth on this woman! I don't know how he stands it." He pulled back his arm for another swing.

Other Guy stepped in between them. "She doesn't fuckin' know! Now lay off!"

"Excuse me?"

"She said she doesn't know! Don't swing on her again!"

"What the hell's gotten into you?" They glared at each other.

"I'm tired of this whole thing. I'm tired of you, and I don't want to go to jail."

The Thinker laughed. "Too late, bud. You got me into it, now we're both neck-deep."

They both sat down on the floor. "You gonna go?" the other man asked.

"I don't know. He couldn't possibly know it was me. Could he?" The Thinker scratched his head. "Hell, I wouldn't want to be sitting there when he calls my name." He looked over at Mary. "Hey, bitch! Do you think he knows who killed the old man?"

Mary winced, her lips thickening from the blows. "If he says he knows, he knows."

"I can't believe it. But still . . ." He looked at the other man. "You go tomorrow night. If it's me, give me a signal. Send me a text."

Other Guy nodded. "Sure."

"And you've gotta take care of her again tomorrow. I can't. I hafta work after all."

Phil spent the rest of the afternoon and the first part of the evening with Gary Kleinstern at his Capitol office. They went over Jackson's letter and worked on their plans for the following evening's performance. Kleinstern kept his assistant busy with a barrage of coordination phone calls and directives. The pistachio was gone by the time they finished their work.

Sam had worked the afternoon at the Chocolate Shoppe, frustrated that Phil wouldn't share the contents of the letter. She could tell it held something of significance; she couldn't get Phil's attention on the ride back downtown. It had to be important and it looked like it was something good; he sounded excited when he called Kleinstern from the truck. All he'd say was that it helped, that it confirmed what he and Mary had suspected and more. And then later while she was doing the close, she got a call from Phil. He asked her to meet him at Mary's house to go over the game plan.

She got there before Phil and waited in her car until he arrived. "Gyros and fries from The Parthenon," he announced, and held up a large brown paper bag. They went inside and ate at the kitchen table with grease and yogurt-cucumber sauce running out of the pita bread and down their forearms. The refrigerator was low on beer and they shared a bottle between them. Then, after cleanup, they walked Hoover around the block and then settled down on the couch in the living room. Phil went over in detail the things he wanted Sam and the Chocolate Shoppe staff to do the following evening.

"That's clear," she said. "But what about you and Kleinstern?"

"I'm the entertainment."

"Meaning?"

"I present our case."

"And then what?"

"You'll have to wait and see."

"Don't you think you can trust me by now?"

"Sam, it's not that at all."

"It sure looks that way to me."

"Even as good as you are, if you knew everything that was going to happen you could unintentionally tip someone off in advance. A word, a gesture, a glance. An attitude. And you're going to be right up front, the first person everyone sees."

"I can do it!"

"You probably can. But are you willing to bet Mary's life on it?"

She hesitated. "No, I guess not."

"There, that's better." Phil put his arm over Sam's shoulders and squeezed. She half-turned and pressed up against him.

"You can be mighty persuasive, Phil Bardo. Why don't you distract me some more."

"Sam, I-"

"Xiamorha."

"Xiamorha, I've missed being with you like this." He stroked her hair.

"Good. Keep going."

"I've felt so guilty, with her, since last Saturday."

"I don't want to hear about that. Do you want to-"

"I can't. Not while she's out there."

"But what about me?"

"Sorry. Besides, I'm married."

"Don't say that. It isn't real."

"I know, but-"

"Here." She took his hand and moved it over her. "*This* is real."

"Yes, it is. But I just can't."

"There, do that some more. Oh! There. I need this; we both need this. I can't tell you how much."

"No, Sam!"

"She'd do the same thing if our roles were reversed. You know that!"

"I suppose, but tomorrow-"

"'*Let us eat and drink, for tomorrow we shall die.*'"

"You sure have changed your philosophy."

"I've had to."

Phil untangled himself and stood up. "No, Sam, it's just not right! I don't want to do this; not this way. I love you, but you and I are going to have to wait this out."

"I . . . I thought maybe when you invited me here . . . Sorry, I get it. I have to go now."

CHAPTER TWENTY-SEVEN

Phil didn't slept well Thursday night. He was up several times, then finally he took Hoover for a walk around the block. The night was clear and cold; the clouds had blown over and the stars seemed uncommonly bright.

He rehearsed in his head, referring occasionally to the outline that he and Kleinstern had prepared. The plans were laid and now it was a matter of execution. The meeting was to be Phil's show and he had to handle it right, pace it correctly, and be ready to change direction at a moment's notice. The behind-the-scenes action was in Gary's hands and Sam would be hostess and facilitator between them.

He made fried eggs at the stove and the dog sat like a lawn ornament at his feet. He never wagged his stump when Phil came through the door; he saved that for Mary. Maybe she'd be home tonight, and the dog would be happy and the silence that pressed on the house would be broken. He tried to eat the eggs but lost interest. "Want some eggs?" The dog looked at him. He set the plate on the floor. "Do me a favor, don't barf these up."

Kleinsmith had said his men had followed Essinger since Phil jumpstarted his movement with the office visit, but nothing had come of it. Who else could have known of Mary's connection to Phil and to the case? There had been no further communication from the kidnappers, and Gary thought it might be a good sign. But if their plan failed tonight, then . . . Phil couldn't help thinking about it. She'd bluff and she'd fight, but he knew she'd be cold and scared. He felt her alive and afraid and waiting.

Head bowed and hands folded, Phil sat at the kitchen table. "I know you haven't heard from me in a long time. I won't try to make any deals with you or promise things I can't deliver. Please help me bring her home alive. It isn't so much to ask. Please!"

Sam had the place jumping when Phil arrived. She had a full turnout of staff to help with the day's regular activities as well as all the special baking and preparation for the evening. Judy managed the storefront while Sam drove the kitchen. Lisa, Gretchen, and Ellen took care of counter help and tables while Lauren, Aaron, Amanda, and Nick baked and cleaned and washed and baked again. Sam fired up the second walk-in ice cream freezer to hold all the confections to go to the evening's meeting.

"We going to make it?" Phil asked.

"Sure," Sam replied, "if you stop inviting more people to the meeting."

"We're done. No more added to the guest list." Phil and Gary had added quite a few the previous afternoon under the assumption that a broader sweep was better – it meant more sorting later, but it gave them a better chance for success.

Sam was grim-faced, and she wrung her hands in her apron. "Are you really ready? Are you sure this is a good idea?"

"I've got to study a bit more, but I'm pretty much ready. As far as this being a good idea – we'll see. What about you, are you comfortable with what you're going to do?"

She nodded. "What do you want me to wear? 'Course, I don't have a lot of choices in the formal line. The black thing I wore yesterday or-"

"I want you to stand out. The red one again. You could wear that every day and I wouldn't tire of it."

"What if this doesn't work, Phil? What do we do then? Do we have a backup plan?"

"It will work. It has to work."

"Tonight's the night. Your husband's party." Other Guy

shoved the last spoonful of fruit cocktail into Mary's mouth and dropped the can and spoon into the grocery bag.

"It's not too late. You can buy yourself a lot of slack if you-"

"Don't bother. Just shut up."

"At least tell me: your partner did Helms through the tunnels, right?"

"Yeah. Actually I got him into the tunnel and he did it."

"Why?"

"Contract hit for a friend of mine."

"And Jackson?"

"He did him, too. Another contract; Jackson was going to blab. I taught him about locks, then he let himself in the front door and clocked Jackson with a vase."

"What about the concrete?"

"His idea, but I helped. With some others."

"He wasn't dead when you dumped him in there, you know."

"Get off it."

"It's true. Coroner said he died of asphyxiation. Let's see; that would make you a murderer."

He stood up. "I don't know if I'm coming back. I'm sorry it worked out this way for you. If you had just kept your nose out of it . . ." He walked out and locked the door behind him.

Kleinstern said, "We had our guy on him. He left the apartment and went downtown, spent a couple hours in the key shop."

The key shop! That name; Phil hadn't made the connection before. "The kid works there!"

"Then he went onto campus and we lost him."

"What about his apartment?"

"We just received the search warrant. We'll be in there within the hour."

"How about the others?"

"Don't worry, we'll have the other warrants in time. If you want to worry about something, worry about what we do if we don't find her."

"Yeah, I'm way ahead of you on that one. Thanks, Gary, I'll see you shortly." Phil hung up.

A manila envelope came in the mail to the Chocolate Shoppe, addressed to Juan Valdez. Phil took it into the back office to open it. He sat on the desk chair, took a deep breath, then tore off the end of the envelope and shook the contents onto the desk; an invoice, a return envelope, a folded piece of paper and another, chubbier envelope. The invoice was for one-and-a-half hours of "services rendered" at $150 per hour, total $225. No tax. Visa and MasterCard accepted, but not American Express. The return envelope bore a simple post office box number in Madison for an address. He set those aside and picked up the folded piece of paper – it was a brief handwritten note:

"Dear Mr. Valdez,

I've relocated, and business prospects are promising. Could use an ice cream shop here. Thought you'd enjoy the enclosed photos; I know Mrs. E. did. Don't worry, I still have the negatives. Drop me an email sometime. juanitavaldez@email.temptrophies.com

Love & kisses, D.B."

Phil set that aside and opened the final envelope. From it he took a wad of photos, green monochromatic infrared shots of a couple leaving a restaurant, of some men and a woman and some parked cars . . . One of the shots showed a man coupled with the woman, with Ted Essinger's face clearly visible. It was autographed "To Juan, Good luck! I'll always be Dee Best."

Phil smiled as he put all the items back into the manila envelope. Now he knew: Dave had sent the photos to Dee, for her own protection! She had played Phil, at the Edgewater and on the phone. She was the one who had sent the evidence to Essinger's wife when she wanted to distance herself from Ted and his deals! Smart, but not smart enough to consider that she could have caused Dave's death by it. It would be fun to run into her again, someday.

It was time to make the run back to the house, walk the dog, put on the tux, and review the notes one last time.

A crowd had gathered on the sidewalk in front of the Orpheum Theater. The marquee had been changed to read "*Murder In Madtown, starring Phil Bardo. Private Party, by Invitation Only.*" There was a mobile TV transmission van on the sidewalk, antenna whip extended. Phil, Sam, and Gary were just inside the locked front doors in the interior lobby, and they could hear the rumble of the crowd's conversation. The bartenders were set up and waiting behind two rolling bar carts on either side of the lobby.

Phil checked his watch. "Fifteen minutes yet, and we've got a good group out there already. Sam?"

"We're ready," she said. "We brought the food over an hour ago and the caterer is all set up. Most of our staff is back and ready. I've got the lists of the invitees. We'll open only one door so nobody gets in or out without going past me. I'll check them off."

"Cell phone?"

She opened her red sequined purse. "Check."

"And you'll call me-"

"When we know something."

"Gary?"

"We're good. Thirty troopers in position throughout the city, warrants in-hand. A dozen more here, out of sight until the fun starts. We've got five FBI guys here from Chicago. And, I've got Judge Corcoran and Judge Foody in the projection booth to observe and to write any other warrants if the need arises. We'll also turn on the video cameras from there."

"What about the press?"

"Stationary cameras are set up in the side balconies. They'll have rovers on the floor. First row of seats is reserved for the reporters. Oh, and we did the search of that apartment. She wasn't there, but we found a woman's letter jacket. Lock picks in the inside pocket."

"That's her's! We're on the right track Thank God for Dominick; he found that address after my guy missed it. No Phantom costume? Nothing else?"

"No."

"All right. I guess we should get started."

Kleinstern moved off into the wings and Sam took up a spot at the front door with a clipboard and a pen. Phil noticed a janitor looking at him from the restroom entrance, and he went over to see him.

"Dale. How do you like doing undercover so far?"

He shrugged. "It's easy, except for the fake beard. It itches. And the hair coloring job took me over an hour."

"Hopefully there won't be any need for real janitorial stuff."

"Don't worry, if there is I'll ignore it. I've got your back a hundred percent."

"Then it's time."

Phil straightened his tux and pressed some buttons on the wall. The lobby lights came on full, and Sam stood at the front door directly under a spotlight with red sequins blazing. Two large men in tuxes, probably troopers, flanked her. She looked like a singer or a movie star; someone not quite real, on stage. This was an acting job, after all. Somewhere the theater manager turned on the PA system and a Sinatra song filled the space. Phil came over, kissed Sam on the forehead to avoid disturbing her red lipstick, and unlocked the door.

The guest list, not including the press, wound up being nearly a hundred and fifty people. With the press, the Chocolate Shoppe Staff, the caterer's staff, and the law enforcement personnel the total exceeded two hundred. Phil watched from the lobby as they filed in, pair by pair, each pausing for Sam to check her list. They wouldn't have to worry about enforcing the dress code tonight; all the men wore their suits, and all the women their formal and cocktail party dresses. The Jackson brothers came with their wives, and Barbara

Jackson came with them. A clutch of college students tried to gatecrash, and were escorted out the door again by Sam's tuxedoed bookends. Ruppert Taylor led his wife and an entourage through the door. Sam greeted him and reminded him of their meeting at the Charity Ball. "Oh, I'm so glad to see you again, Mr. Taylor," she smiled and gushed, thrusting her chest at him. And, she thought, she'd love to take the pen and shove it right– "Hello, may I have your name, please?"

"Smith. John Smith."

"All right, Mr. Smith John Smith. Gotcha. Thank you for coming and I hope you have a pleasant evening. Next?"

The original list of Ardbeg buyers, the second list of Scotch buyers, and the alumni group that comprised the homecoming committee were all on the guest list. Phil had also invited some of his friends; as long as he was hosting a party, one that might be his last, he figured he might just as well get his money's worth. They helped dilute the crowd so that it would be a little less obvious what was going on. Tom and Nancy, Colin McDermott, Dominick, and Antoine were there. Phil had told them that this would be a night they wouldn't want to miss. They filed in intermixed with a group that included Beth Talbot and Moose Mikleski and his wife. Then Terry arrived from the Car Care Center. And, there were a number of people from various City offices.

Judy began dispatching Chocolate Shoppe staffers and the caterer's personnel with appetizer trays from a back room. There was an ice cream bar set up in a third rolling bar cart, and that was tended by Lauren and Ellen. They were all dressed in rental bartender attire of tux pants, open collared white shirts and black patterned vests.

The crowd quickly spilled from the lobby into the main theater, drawn by the appetizer trays circulating there. The press, carrying notepads and microphones, mingled with the guests. There was a group of them around James Bradley, and a cameraman held a floodlight high with one hand and aimed it down into the knot of people, video camera on his shoulder.

"What are you doing here tonight, Mr. Bradley? Isn't this

likely to be an attempt to try the case in the court of public opinion, to poison jury selection?"

"Well, I'm here because I was invited, Kurt. I don't know what Mr. Bardo is trying to do, but I'm interested in the truth. If he can show us something new, it's in the interest of justice that I listen to him, right? Wouldn't you want your DA or your Attorney General to listen to you?"

"Mr. Bradley, is your opponent, the incumbent, Gary Kleinstern here tonight?"

"I haven't seen him, Bill, and I really don't keep track of where he is. Ask that woman at the front door. I'd think he should be here, unless he isn't all that interested in justice." Bradley flashed a big smile.

"Sorry, I can't comment on the guest list," Sam said to the reporters. She covered her clipboard as they peered over her shoulder. "Fellas?" The two bouncers closed in on the reporters, who scattered back into the main auditorium. The line was nearing an end; there were only a dozen more outside. She checked her watch. They had allowed a half-hour for the check-in and another half-hour of cocktails and talk before the show. Just a couple minutes more and she'd lock the front door and meet Kleinstern in the projection booth.

"Your name, sir?"

Phil looked out at the crowd from the wings of the stage, pleased with the venue. The Orpheum had been in constant renovation for the past ten years, as financing permitted. The guilded scrollwork on the main and side balconies had been repainted, the enormous main stage curtains had been replaced with fabric that was custom-made, a match to the originals that had hung in tatters there for sixty years. The ceiling was once again a work of art; the acoustical tile that had been hung sometime in the sixties had been removed, and the painted plaster underneath it cleaned of cigarette smoke and mildew until the original colors reappeared. The warped and rotted boards of the stage had been replaced and painted. Finally, the last of the wide arc of seats had been taken out, recovered, and re-installed.

Some people had begun to take seats but most stood in the aisles, talking and cornering the servers carrying appetizer trays. A man wheeled a podium out from one side of the stage and parked it dead-center. He plugged a microphone cord into a jack sunk in the floor of the stage. The house lights flashed twice. It was almost show time.

"Got it?"

"Gimme a couple more minutes." Sam worked quickly, finding the no-shows on her master alphabetical list and highlighting them on the categorized subset lists. Kleinstern looked over her shoulder.

"Looking good," he said. "Got most of them right here. We'll start with the ones who aren't here. What about the rest?"

"Which ones?"

"The help."

"You need them too?"

"Everybody."

"I'll be right back." Sam left the projection room and took off her shoes, then she ran down the stairs and down the lobby and around the corner, then down the hallway flanking the theater, past the theater doors, then through the double doors at the end of the hall and into the prep room. She beckoned to Judy. "Make a staff list, ours and the caterer's. Who came and who didn't. Bring it up to me right away in the projection booth!" She turned and ran back, through the doors and down the hall and across the lobby and up the stairs again.

"It'll be here in a minute," she said to Kleinstern.

He was on his cell phone with her lists in one hand. "4629 Amber Trail, go. 12852 North Gallway, go."

Phil walked to the podium at the center of the stage and laid his outline and notes on the slanted surface. He turned on the little reading light, then moved the switch on the microphone. He took a few long, deep breaths, then gave a salute. A spotlight came on, focused on him, and the house lights dimmed.

"Ladies and gentlemen? Please take your seats. We'll take a break for more food and drinks later, I promise." Lisa appeared at Phil's side, bearing a water pitcher and a glass. She set them on the podium and he poured a glass and drank as the last of the crowd came in and sat down. The conversation noise diminished.

"My friends," Phil said, "thank you for coming to my party. As you know, this might be my last one, so I wanted to make it good. I hope you've enjoyed the drinks and the food. And, I hope that you'll find what we do over the next hour or two to be entertaining, interesting, and perhaps even life-altering."

The curtain behind him parted, revealing the huge movie screen. A light cut on from the projection booth and a slide of Dave Helms appeared to Phil's left, covering half of the screen.

"Tonight's story begins with a man, a story not about his life but rather about his death. This is David Helms, my uncle, murdered about a month ago. And we're going to tell you about other stories that came from this." A picture of Lars Jackson flashed onto the screen. "Lars Jackson, found murdered this past Sunday." Then Mary's picture came to the screen. "This is my wife, Mary, missing for the last four days. We're going to solve these cases tonight, and we're going to name names." A picture of the Carillon came to the screen. "This is where it all started."

The Thinker moved through the apartment turning out lights. He pulled a navy-blue stocking cap onto his head and slipped his arms into a leather bomber jacket, then wrapped a scarf around his neck. Under the lone kitchen light he picked the Glock from the counter and pulled out the clip and inspected it. Full. He reinserted the clip and slapped it into position, then pulled and released the slide to chamber a round. Then he set the safety on and tucked the weapon behind his belt in the small of his back and pulled the jacket over it. His cell phone went into his left jacket pocket. He picked up a ski jacket and tucked it under his arm. With gloves in his hand he turned off the kitchen light and went out into the hall, locking his apartment door behind him.

"Move in, all doors." Kleinstern dispatched his troopers from a back room into the halls to wait at every door to the main theater and every exit to the building.

A knock came at the projection room door. Sam answered it and Judy came in. "Here's your list," she whispered. "What the hell is going on, anyway?"

"I can't explain right now. Just get the staff into the main theater."

Judy nodded and backed out of the room.

Sam brought the list to the splicing table, under the light.

"Whatcha got?" Kleinstern asked.

"Only one employee missing."

"You know the address?"

"321 Beech, apartment 2E."

Kleinstern dialed his cell phone. "Mike. Get someone to 321 Beech, apartment 2E." He turned to Judge Corcoran. "One more search warrant, please, for 321 Beech."

"You've seen where it took place, now you'll see how it was done." A slide with a wire-frame diagram of the Carillon appeared on the screen. "We knew that Daman couldn't have done the murder. He was right here on the second level, and couldn't have made it down the stairs quickly enough to shoot Helms and hide the gun. The timing just doesn't work; we ran our own timed tests down the stairs, and we had time-series photos taken from outside the Carillon during the murder.

"So how was it done? There wasn't anybody else in the tower, and no one could get in. One of the great legends of the UW is the system of underground steam tunnels. How many of you have heard of them? Raise your hands. Nearly everybody. Now how many have actually seen them? Aha, I thought so. They really do exist, and the killer knew about them. This is how it worked. The killer knew that Dave was going to be in the Carillon that night, so he entered the steam tunnels and found his way to the Carillon. He waited beneath the Carillon, and at the right moment shot Dave through a heat grate embedded in the floor. Gunpowder residue was found on the grate, proving the method. As you can see," a slide showing the bullet vectors appeared on the screen, "the angles work. These lines represent the angles of the bullet paths through Dave's body. The killer took his shots from the floor grate and walked away through the tunnels while the only other man present in the locked tower, Dan Daman, got framed for the murder. Fortunately for Dan, we figured this out and he is now a free man with all charges dropped. It kinda backfired on me a bit, though; we sent in the evidence to clear Dan, but it made it look like I knew way too much, and that's when I got arrested for the murder."

The Thinker drove to the corner of Park and Regent and left the van at the curb in front of a closed restaurant. No one driving Park Street paid any attention to him as he walked up Park, crossed the railroad tracks, then up to and across University Avenue. A left along the sidewalk past Chadbourne Hall, then he cut north past Lathrop Hall and walked uphill toward South Hall. There was a lot of activity at that hour, students leaving in packs for film society screenings and others heading downtown. He had to wait for several minutes outside South Hall before the sidewalks were clear, then he disappeared behind the bushes.

When Mitzi Essinger answered the knock at her door she was greeted by four armed and body-armored troopers, one large slobbery bloodhound and an overweight beagle.

"Ma'am, we've got a search warrant for your house, garage, and property," announced the man in front. He handed her a folded piece of paper, then pushed past her into the house followed by the rest of the team.

"Ted!" Mitzi Essinger yelled from the foyer. "Get down here! Ted!"

The troopers split into two teams, each with a dog. The bloodhound handler gave the dog a sniff of a piece of cloth from a plastic bag, then followed as the dog meandered through the house. The beagle and his team headed for the garage first, and the handler pointed to direct the dog to inspect specific locations. As they neared the 450SL the dog grew excited, tail raised and quivering. The trunk was particularly interesting to him, and a trooper popped the release from the front seat. The trunk was empty, but the dog wasn't fooled. After inspecting the trunk from the inside he sat down – he had found what he was looking for there – traces of cocaine. Later upon similar inspection of the house the dog would find the two gallon-size plastic bags of the drug behind books in the study.

Ted Essinger had heard his wife call him, but he hadn't gone down. He expected her call; he had been standing by the upstairs bedroom window when the police cruisers pulled into his driveway. He watched the men and the dogs approach the front door, and at that point he went into the master bathroom and locked the door behind him. This had to be the end of it, there, on his terms. He couldn't imagine the trial, the shame before his peers in the academic community. the individual lawsuits from the parents of the students he'd hooked . . . and then jail. The State would put him away for a long time for the quantity of stuff they'd find downstairs, but he wouldn't have to serve the whole sentence. He knew he'd be dead within the first year; the Poles wouldn't tolerate loose ends, and they were well connected on the inside. He heard feet pounding up the stairs as he lifted the toilet tank cover and retrieved a plastic bag taped to the inside of the tank. He took a small vial from the bag and poured its contents into a glass and added water. The water turned cloudy and he swirled the glass. He touched his glass to the one held by the fellow in the mirror before him, then he drank. That done, he set the glass in the sink and sat down on the floor to wait.

"Well," Gary said as he ended the call, "there's one down. Essinger's dead, committed suicide during the search. They found a lot of coke but absolutely no traces of Mary."

Sam looked up at Kleinstern. "How about explaining this to me?"

"Round One was the search of the homes of the suspects who didn't show up here. In Round Two we search the homes of the highest suspects who did show up. The City offices are Round Three."

"Suspects. Uh-oh. You mean you really don't know yet, do you? You don't know who the murderer is?"

"Nope, not yet."

"So you're-"

"Smoking them out. We hope that the murderer and the kidnapper are the same person. Jackson's letter pretty clearly links the real estate scam to the murder, and it sure looks like Mary's disappearance is, too. We started with the assumption that the actual murderer wouldn't dare show up here."

Sam stabbed her finger at her staff list. "It just can't be this guy."

Kleinstern shook his head. "Sam, we'd even be searching your place if you hadn't made it tonight. Still might. The people who would show up here are the ones who are associated with the real estate scam but aren't worried about being named as the murderer. They don't know that we're going to tie in the scam tonight, too. By the end of the night we'll have a whole lot of people arrested."

"But were they all involved?"

"Probably not, at least not all knowingly. It'll take weeks to sort it out, and we'll see a lot come out of the woodwork as people turn on each other. The focus will then get a lot clearer on the ringleaders and the case against the people on the periphery will fade."

"So what's next?" Sam asked as she looked out through the projection window at the stage.

"We play for time. We haven't heard from all the search parties yet. The ones who have reported in so far have found nothing and I've sent them out to start Round Two."

"This is a big gamble."

"Oh, yeah. We gotta find something soon if this is going to work."

Phil continued with his presentation. "Somebody didn't like what Dave Helms was finding during an investigation. Somebody placed Dave Helms in that Carillon that night. Somebody hired a killer and arranged for him to be waiting. Somebody supplied Dave Helms' own gun for the crime, and somebody put it back in his desk afterward. Then somebody drank his single-malt Scotch in celebration, and then replaced it with a different brand in an attempt to cover up his presence. And, at that time, somebody stole the research that Dave and Mary had been accumulating on the investigation.

"Somebody didn't like the fact that I was reopening the same line of investigation and got a couple thugs to beat me and a friend of mine with baseball bats after the Charity Ball to scare me off. Somebody thought that Lars Jackson was going to spill the real story and killed him to keep him quiet. And somebody, in a last desperate attempt to hide the truth, is holding Mary hostage and is trying to blackmail me into confessing to the murder of Dave Helms.

"Most of those 'somebodies' are in this room tonight."

Gene sat in the crowd, angry with John. John had refused to sit with him that night. Too many of his fancy friends around, Gene realized, which showed where he rated. And after all he'd done for the bastard! He fingered his cell phone. Nothing damning so far.

Phil turned some pages of notes. "This is where it starts to get a little complicated." A map of the Madison isthmus popped onto the screen. It had yellow dots on it. "I believe the Bible says that the love of money is the root of all evil. Well, I don't know about *all* evil, but money certainly played a role in tonight's story.

"It all started a number of years ago, perhaps through a chance meeting over drinks, or maybe through an initial business deal. But what it led to was a string of sophisticated real estate deals fueled by insider information that resulted in a number of people making a whole lot of money. My uncle stumbled across these deals, and that's what got him killed." A series of slides ran in progression on the screen. "Here are ten years of commercial real estate deals in the isthmus area. The dots represent locations of sales involving a certain investor. Please notice where these are: the Monona Terrace and Marina projects."

Damn, Bradley thought, where'd he get all this stuff? We've got his computer and all his backup disks. He couldn't have recreated it. Must have had extra backup disks. Or . . . he sent the files to somebody other than me. Kleinstern? No, not likely. Maybe that FBI jerk in Chicago. That means if he's got it now . . . Bradley looked around. They're here. They're here somewhere. They're back on the case. He tried to catch Taylor's eye but Taylor stared at the screen, unflinching.

Mary was sore all over. She could roll and lay on her side to sleep, arms still bound behind her to the pipe. But sitting on the concrete floor was getting to be unbearable. She heard someone working the lock on the door, then the door opened.

The Thinker came in and said nothing and threw the ski jacket on the floor, then the scarf and his cap. Mary watched as he balled up the jacket and lay down, using the jacket as a pillow.

"Well? What happens next?"

"What's your rush?" he replied, eyes closed. "We wait, and then we'll see."

"We can prove a pattern of favorable treatment in the distribution of advance information about City development plans to this certain investor. Through a series of deals, property was seized by the City, appraised low, sold low to this investor, then re-appraised high and bought back by the City at jacked-up prices. All the gains? Well, you can imagine where some of that went, can't you? And this investor just happened to buy additional properties in and near the neighborhoods where City development was going to take place; those buys were done just *before* the City announced its plans. After the announcements, the land prices went up and the investor sold his properties at a substantial markup. Somebody's making a lot of money on these deals, aren't they."

Taylor squirmed in his seat. That shmuck Jackson must have had letters just like he said he had, Taylor fumed . They got his laptop and the letter he was working on Sunday, but . . . he had some somewhere else. Shit. Thought he was bluffing. Too many people involved in the deals, that was the problem. Too many places for leaks. Won't make that mistake next time. And this woman disappearing – where the hell did that come from? Somebody freelancing, goddamnit!

He looked around the auditorium. Guards at the doors, and his own goddamned reporters there. Nowhere to go. Shit.

"As I said before, my uncle came across this scam and was putting the information together in conjunction with the FBI. Somebody got wind of this and decided to eliminate the problem. Some money changed hands, and someone was hired to do the deed. Then it was just a matter of finding the right circumstance to set up the murder and find a fall-guy.

"They had to make their move, and Homecoming provided an opportunity. Some of the people involved are important figures in the community and part of the Alumni Association. Now how to get Dave Helms into it? The Alumni Homecoming Committee, of course. They're active in the Homecoming planning and familiar with the campus. They helped plan the festivities and hire the acts, and when the magic trick called for a witness, they hired Dave. The Carillon magic trick was the perfect setting, providing a confined location with a sure-thing fall-guy.

"They first knew that I was looking into this case probably at the Homecoming Charity Ball. I was foolish enough to go around asking questions, and somebody got worried enough to call in some goons that night to scare me off.

"How do we know all this? Well, we actually figured it all out from data collected, from understanding and deducing relationships and the business deals. Modern detective work. But we had a number of our suspicions confirmed after the death of Lars Jackson. Lars was involved, unwittingly at first, then later for self-preservation. He was kind enough to leave behind a statement for us that validated our theories and named a lot of names. That statement will be made public in the trials to come."

Would have been real nice if he had fingered the murderer too, Phil thought. Then it hit him: Lars had laid out the lead scam participants, but they were only the ones he knew from the deals. Lars could only guess who might be in on the murder plot, but he really didn't know. The big shots wouldn't get their own hands dirty; they'd get somebody else to do it. Besides, some of 'em would never have made it through the tunnel themselves; too fat and too old, except maybe for Smith. Whoever it was, whoever led him on the Halloween chase, had to be somebody pretty young and fit. And by the size and strength, probably male. Quite likely someone who hadn't even been invited to the meeting that night. Shit, this was bad; he felt himself get light-headed for a moment, then he pressed on.

"Now, here's the map of all the players." A large structure chart with boxes and lines on it appeared on the screen. Phil took a laser pointer and began to outline areas on the map. "I know you can't read this very well, so I'll help you. This group over here is the set of companies that bought the real estate. Mostly shell corporations with one common ingredient: Mr. John Smith, known to most of you as the owner of the Importante, an import shop on State Street." Phil moved the pointer. "All the real estate deals involving Mr. Smith were handled by two individuals; Beth Talbot, the realtor, and Lars Jackson as the attorney. Now, let's look at the City's side of the deals. The Mayor, of course, runs the city administration with the help of the City Council, which is chaired by Mr. Ruppert Taylor. Mr. Taylor works closely with the Regional Planning Commission and is in the position to know and influence City development projects long before they are made visible to the public eye. The Property Appraiser's Office reports to the Mayor, but also works with the City Council. Mr. Taylor was a big supporter of the Mayor in the last election. Half of the City employees owe their jobs to Ruppert Taylor. Do I need to spell it out? We've got sweetheart real-estate deals engineered and carried out with inside information and special treatment from high officials in City government. An examination of prices and appraisals drives this conclusion, and I'm sure there'll be an audit done on all these deals over the next several weeks."

Beth Talbot rose from her seat and marched up the aisle to the back of the theater. She clutched her purse under one arm and had her overcoat slung over the other as she confronted Trooper Martinez.

"Excuse me," she said and tried to push past Martinez.

"Sorry, ma'am, nobody leaves." He blocked the door.

"I have an appointment! I have a client I'm meeting in ten minutes!"

"I'm sorry. Please return to your seat."

"Get out of the way, you can't keep me here! I had nothing to do with this!" She pushed against Martinez, dropped her coat, and tried to slide past him.

"Ma'am-" Martinez grabbed her by the arms.

"Let go! I just did real estate deals with them. I didn't know anything about the rest of it!" She twisted and jerked to get free, and kneed Martinez in the thigh.

Martinez let go with one hand and thumbed the microphone pinned to his shoulder. "Backup, door three!" He resumed his grip and pushed Talbot against the wall. Another trooper appeared, and together they pulled her wrists behind her and secured them with a nylon wire tie. The second trooper pulled her through the doors, and Martinez returned to his position.

"But there's more. Here's the Alumni side. Mr. Taylor is a UW alum and very active in the Alumni Association, the Homecoming Committee, and so forth. As was Lars Jackson. The Homecoming Committee selected Dave Helms for the magic trick on the recommendation of the Alumni Association."

"Uh-huh. Yeah. Got it." Kleinstern closed his phone and turned to Sam. "Call him."

Sam dialed her cell phone, then handed it to Kleinstern. She watched through the projection window.

"Finally, somebody hired the murderer. Lars provided a clue there. He said - oops, please excuse me for a moment." Phil turned off the podium microphone and reached into his pocket for his cell phone.

"Yes?"

"We searched an apartment," Kleinstern said. "Didn't find Mary, didn't find the guy. But we did find something else."

"What?"

"Box of .38 shells, two missing. Some Halloween masks and two baseball bats. And a Phantom outfit with a piece torn out. He's our guy: Aaron Ford. We'll run background on him right away."

Phil was dumbfounded. Aaron! He hadn't missed that last address after all; he'd left it out deliberately! He was one of a handful of people who knew of Mary's existence and her ties to Phil and the case . . . and his interest, no, make that obsession with the detective work, was to keep tabs on Phil's progress! He pictured Aaron standing before him, hands stained with black ink. Probably a pen taken from Dave's office, maybe just like the one used for the note.

"Phil?"

"Yeah, I'm just . . . I mean, I never expected . . . God, I should have seen it . . ."

"Phil, we've got to spring it now. I'm coming down."

"Now I'd like to turn the microphone over to someone who's been instrumental in this case. Mr. Gary Kleinstern, Attorney General of the State of Wisconsin." Kleinstern walked onto the stage and joined Phil at the podium.

"Thanks, Phil. Let me just say, folks, that it has been Phil's detective work that cracked this case. Now let's get on with what you've all been waiting for. For the past several hours we've been executing search warrants. We just completed a search of a suspect's apartment. In that apartment we found a box of .38 caliber shells, the kind used in Dave Helms' own gun. There are two missing, the exact number of shots fired in his murder. At this moment a warrant is being issued for the arrest of Aaron Ford in the murder of Dave Helms. Now, just who is Aaron Ford?"

Gene took his cell phone from his pocket. He keyed a brief text message and pressed "send."

The cell phone rang and Aaron took it from his jacket pocket. A simple text message – "run" – was all it said. He cursed under his breath and got to his feet, then put on his jacket and cap.

"Your goddamned husband figured it out," he said. "He's gonna regret it. There won't be a day that he's alive that he won't think about it and regret it." He took the gag from the floor and forced it into Mary's mouth and tied it behind her head. Then he took his scarf and wrapped it around her mouth and neck. He put her shoes on her feet and tied them. He cut the binding that held her wrists to the pipe, leaving her wrists tied behind her, and jerked her to her feet. He wrapped the ski jacket around her and zipped it up the front.

"We're gonna take a walk." Aaron pulled the Glock and brandished it under Mary's nose. "I've got this, so don't try

373

anything. If you do, I swear I'll end it right there." He laughed. "I've got just the thing to preserve your 'love' for each other. Move it!" He shoved her to the door.

He guided her down the hall through the Pine Room and then through a door and up stone steps into the cold night air. They were in Tripp Circle, then he pushed her ahead of him as they skirted Tripp Hall and turned east along the dark Lakeshore path toward downtown.

"Aaron Ford is one of Phil's employees. Now Aaron couldn't be here tonight. He's busy, holding Mary Bardo hostage. But Aaron didn't work alone, and his partner is here in the audience. We searched his apartment this afternoon and found Mary's jacket. Her car was parked nearby. Now I'd like to introduce Aaron's partner in crime, Gene Foster. Gene?"

The house lights went up, bright. Kleinstern held his hand at his eyebrow to shade his eyes as he searched the audience. Phil pointed. A spotlight swung around and panned the audience, and came to rest on Gene.

"There you are, Gene," Kleinstern continued. "Stand up, please." Troopers moved down the two aisles and stopped on either side of the row where Gene remained seated. "Gene's a little shy, I guess. He's about to be arrested for two murders and a kidnapping. Maybe a third murder, unless he's willing to tell us where Mary is."

"I didn't kill anybody!" Gene shouted from his seat.

"C'mon, Gene, at the very least you're an accessory to the first two. Gene's an apprentice locksmith, which came in real handy for getting into the steam tunnels, Dave Helms' detective office, and Lars Jackson's house. And now there's the kidnapping, which if that turns into murder will certainly put Gene away for the rest of his life. You can cut yourself some slack, Gene, by telling us where she is." The troopers edged into the row from either end. "You're running out of time."

Gene looked for John Smith and when he made eye contact, John stared and then slowly turned and looked away. "Basement utility room, Carson Gulley," Gene said flatly. The troopers grabbed Gene's arms from both sides and lifted him to a standing position, then handcuffed him.

Kleinstern looked at Phil. "Go on, I can finish up here." Phil ran offstage.

"Now, folks, there's more to come! Please stay in your seats. I have several lists of names here to read. If I read your name I'd appreciate it if you'd get up and walk to the back of the theater where there will be a trooper waiting for you. It will be a lot easier that way for all of us. The following persons are wanted for racketeering, embezzlement, and misuse of City funds and property . . ."

Phil, Dale, and the troopers ran down the stone steps and found the door to the Pine Room at Carson Gulley unlocked. The troopers led with guns drawn and flashlights on, through the lounge and down the hall. They kicked open every door along the way and checked each room. Finally – the utility room. Empty. They examined the grocery bags, empty cans and water bottles. Duct tape littered the floor.

"This was it," one of the troopers said.

"Look at this." Another trooper shined his light on the floor next to a pipe, near a wall. "Scratches, made by a small stone. No, maybe just fingernail scraped on the concrete." It read in crude block letters 'AARON.' "She must have been tied to the pipe, right here."

Aaron had a fist-full of ski jacket in his left hand and the butt-end of the Glock in his right, the muzzle stuck into his jacket pocket. He propelled Mary down the Lakeshore path. The moon was full but little light made it through the trees to the uneven ground. Some laughing and talking, coming closer – students were on the way back from State Street or Memorial Union, along the path. Mary tried to jerk free and call out through the gag, and Aaron stopped and spun her around and held her, pressing his mouth to hers through the scarf. She wriggled but could not break free. The group of students passed with a sidelong glance and some laughed, perceiving a

375

couple in a passionate and energetic embrace.

"Now that was stupid," Aaron whispered when they were gone, and he put the barrel of the gun under Mary's chin. "I should shoot you right now. But I've got something much better in mind." He clutched her jacket again and shoved her down the trail.

The path dipped low near the water, and they stumbled on some exposed tree roots. Mary swung her knee around and caught Aaron full in the groin. He went down on his knees with a groan and released his grip, and she sprinted ahead. They were near the end of the path. She forced her legs to pump harder, faster, and her lungs ached as she tried to suck air past the gag. Now she could see the lights of the library and of the Union. She prayed to find someone else on the path, anyone, but she had the path to herself. As she neared the boathouse in front of the Limnology building she heard footsteps closing behind her, and then suddenly she was face-down in the dirt and gravel, taken down by a tackle from behind.

"You fuckin' bitch!" Aaron hissed, and he delivered several kidney-punches as she lay on the ground. She moaned with each blow, and dirt collected in the sweat and tears on her face. When he finished he pulled her to her feet, but she was doubled over in pain and her legs collapsed. He picked her up and threw her over his shoulder and carried her past the Limnology building and Helen C. White Library and up onto Park Street.

"She's drunk," he said, laughing, to passers-by on the sidewalk. He carried her to the corner of Langdon and Park and rested for a minute at a bench. Then he shouldered her again and marched down Langdon, then crossed the street and the Library Mall and turned up State Street.

"Gary, we're too late! They're gone."
"Damn it! We'll launch an APB with the City cops. Maybe we'll get lucky. Come on back, Phil. We'll be at this a while."

Aaron whistled as he walked. People looked and cleared a path for him on the sidewalk, some laughed and others shook their heads. Mary, his shoulder in her stomach, couldn't draw a full breath and her head spun. She heard him say "Drunk, passed out" and she saw upside-down blue legs with a black stripe down the side. Even the cops bought the drunk story.

Then they stopped and she heard key noises, and then a door opened. Aaron began his turn too soon and hit her head on the doorframe, then he closed and locked the door. She saw a tile floor in the stray light from the street, some table pedestals, and to the other side – a display case. A hallway – she'd seen it before. The Chocolate Shoppe. They turned and entered the kitchen and Aaron set her down on the floor.

"Man! Thought we'd never get here," he said. He turned on the kitchen light and looked around, then removed his gloves. "Yeah, this will be perfect." He kneeled down and removed Mary's scarf and the gag, and then unzipped the ski jacket.

"Aaron, you don't need to make it any worse for yourself. Give it up now," Mary choked.

"I don't think so. Given what I've done, one more won't make much difference. And I want to teach Phil a lesson that he won't forget. Giving me such shit work. Clearing tables. Checking receipts. He thinks I'm the village idiot." He searched in a drawer and came out with a knife and a roll of packing tape. "And then he doesn't follow simple instructions. 'Plead guilty' I told him, but no, he couldn't do that. Figured I was bluffing; well, guess what. And then there's you." He pulled a sturdy metal chair to the floor near Mary. "I could do the detective stuff, but no, you had to do it." He tucked the knife blade up under her shirt and slit it, then cut the neckband and the hem and the shoulders. A quick tug and it came away in his hand. "You lay the guy and all of a sudden he thinks you're Sherlock Holmes. And then you tease everybody, like they have any kind of a chance with you. You're a whore, that's all." He put the point of the knife at her throat with one hand, and unsnapped her jeans with the other. Then he set the knife aside and used both hands to strip her of her jeans, underwear, and shoes.

"So, that's all the imagination you have, you're gonna rape me now?"

"Nah, I don't have time for that. A shame, really." He looked her over, then ran his hands over her bare skin. "You're a nice piece of ass. I hate to waste it, but I gotta get going. Naked you'll go quicker, and it'll make it worse for Phil when he finds you in a few months." He bent over and lifted her by the arms, then sat her on the metal chair. Then he used the packing tape to bind her ankles to the chair legs, and she kicked at him and he punched her in the stomach until she quieted, then he finished binding her ankles. He pulled her arms over the back of the chair and secured them there with more tape. "Aren't you gonna holler or scream or something?"

"I figured it wouldn't do any good."

"You're right. It wouldn't."

Aaron walked to the door of the second walk-in freezer, the one that had been used to hold the food for the night's party. He opened the door and turned on the light. "Empty, but not for long. And it's a pleasant-", he checked the thermometer, "thirty-two degrees. Seems a bit warm." He moved the thermostat. "Minus-fifteen seems better for preservation." He propped the door open and then grabbed the chair by the back and dragged it and Mary into the freezer. He edged past her, and stood in the open door. "Phil will find you in Spring when it's time to build up inventory again. What a surprise that will be."

"Please, Aaron, don't! I'm sorry if I . . . Is there something else, I'll do anything, I'll help you get away, just please, please don't do this!"

"Hmm. Nope, can't think of anything you can do. Bye." He slammed the freezer door. Then he put the knife and the packing tape back in the drawer. Mary's clothes went into a plastic bag, which he stuffed beneath some other garbage in the bottom of a trash can. He turned off the kitchen light and crossed the hall to the office where he began a search of the desk for the petty cash box.

"Mr. Bradley! Mr. Bradley! Can you comment on the proceedings tonight?"

Bradley was surrounded by reporters and cameramen, painted by the white light of the video cameras. He took a handkerchief from his jacket pocket and patted his forehead with it. He licked his lips and flashed a large smile.

"This was most extraordinary," he began, "and I have to extend my congratulations to Mr. Bardo and Mr. Kleinstern for discovering the incredible scourge that has infected our city. As always, the District Attorney's Office has been and will be in full cooperation with the Attorney General's office as this incredible case moves forward."

"Sir! What was your role in this investigation?"

"As you know, our role is to bring charges and prosecute people for crimes committed. We have done so based on the evidence submitted."

"But the evidence really didn't show either Daman or Bardo as murderers. Why did you charge them?"

Bradley smiled. "You know, sometimes you have to bait a trap. We played our part. If the real murderer thought we were still looking for him he would have been long gone. But with someone already charged with his crime, he gets relaxed and sloppy."

"Are you saying you were in on this from the beginning?"

"In a manner of speaking. Now, ladies and gentlemen, I have to get to work. This has been a great night for truth and justice, and the taxpayers and voters have a right to be proud tonight of their elected officials at the county and state levels. I have no further comment. Thank you very much!"

Sam crossed the street and pulled her coat tight around her. The red dress hung out below the coat hem, and she dodged wet potholes with her red high heels. There was nothing left for her to do at the Orpheum, and it would be hours before Kleinstern completed all the arrests. She had told him that she was going to chill out for a bit at the Chocolate Shoppe and wait for a phone call with news. Once inside she stripped off her coat and then she noticed a light down the hall, coming from the office.

"Phil!" she called, and trotted down the hall and turned the corner into the office. What greeted her was the muzzle of a Glock held inches from her eyes by Aaron.

"Shit, Sam. Why'd you have to come in here now?" Aaron grabbed her by the throat and held the gun to her temple. "I've just about got your problem solved for you, and now you're messing it all up. I really didn't want you hurt, but now I've got no choice." He pushed her backward into the hall and then into the kitchen.

She struggled and twisted, grabbed his wrist with both hands and tried to free his hand from her throat. He squeezed her throat harder and shook her, and her breath came in wheezes. "Now cut that out," he said, "you're making me late." He pushed her to the freezer door. "This will really be an extra surprise for Phil. Now open the door. Do it!" Sam reached for the handle and pulled open the freezer door. Aaron pushed her backward into the freezer and shut the door. Then he poked around in a drawer and found an ice pick and slid it into the hole in the door handle intended for a lock. He went back to the office and searched for a few more minutes, then gave up on the cash box. He turned out the light and left through the front door, locking it behind him.

The troopers spread out in the Lakeshore area, looking for traces of Aaron and Mary or for people who might have seen them. Phil and Dale took the sidewalk back through campus in the direction of State Street. They stopped and questioned students along the way, but no one had seen anyone matching Mary's description. Phil called Sam's cell phone to tell her that Aaron had escaped with Mary but Sam didn't answer.

"They could have gone back into the steam tunnels," Phil said.

"Doubt it," Dale said. "The door to the Pine Room was unlocked. They probably went out that way in a hurry, put her into a car and drove off."

"Don't you guys have any tracking dogs?"

"Yes, but you've kept the City police out of this, remember? It'll take hours to get them here."

They walked on in silence over Bascom Hill and down the green to Park Street. The Capitol Building was lit-up in holiday colors at the far end of State Street, reds and greens and whites played on the dome. They turned a few heads, the guy in the tux and the janitor, walking together down State Street without the benefit of overcoats.

There wasn't much room in the freezer, and as Aaron closed the door Sam fell backward, gasping for breath, and landed on Mary's lap. She jumped up and turned around to see.

"Mary! God, are you okay?" She crouched in front of the naked seated figure and touched her face, gray setting in from the cold. "Mary, it's Sam, can you hear me? Mary!" She held Mary's cheek in one hand and lightly slapped the other.

"Sss . . . ss . . . S . . . am," Mary's eyelids fluttered. "Cccold . . . ssso . . . ccold . . ."

Sam jumped up and felt for the emergency release trigger on the inside door handle. She tripped it and laid her shoulder into the door, but it didn't move. She tried again, pounding the door with her shoulder. No luck – he'd defeated the release with a lock from the outside, she reasoned. She looked around the freezer. Metal shelves, bolted to the metal floor and metal ceiling. Nothing on them; they had moved all the remaining stock to the other freezer. A single bare light bulb was set in the ceiling, surrounded by a heavy metal cage.

"Hhhelpppp . . . ccccoldd . . ."

"Yeah, I'm trying. Somebody will come and find us soon." Sam reached to untie Mary, but stopped. Her skin was sticking to the chair; it would be worse if Sam had to lay her on the metal floor, and she certainly couldn't stand in her condition, so Sam left her bound to the chair. The light bulb. If

DAVE HEISE and STEVE HEAPS

she could break the bulb and short the circuit . . . was the compressor on the same circuit? She didn't know. She removed her shoe and stood on the chair between Mary's legs and pushed the heel through the metal cage. Two inches too short. She put her shoe on again and got down.

The icy air came in through a vent in the wall near the ceiling and left through another vent on the opposite wall. If she could only block it, Sam thought, the temp in the freezer would climb, the thermostat would call for more cold, and the compressor would run harder . . . and maybe it would freeze up and shut the system down.

"Mary, Mary, are you still with me?" No response. Sam held Mary's face in her hands and rubbed. "Mary, c'mon, don't go to sleep. Stay with me, we'll get out of this."

"Uhhhhh . . ."

Sam looked at the vent again, and then around the room. There was nothing that she could use to block the vent, except . . . She reached back and unhooked her dress and unzipped it, and let it fall to the floor. She picked it up and wadded it into a ball and climbed the shelving to the vent. There she jammed the dress into the vent, filling all the holes in the grate with the red fabric. Still not packed tight enough. She pulled her bra over her head with one hand and wedged that into the vent as well, then she climbed down.

"Mary!"

"Uhh . . . cccco . . ."

"Mary, please don't take this the wrong way. You need some body heat." Sam sat on Mary's lap, facing her, and pressed her body tight against Mary's. With one arm she held Mary's head in the crook of her neck so she could speak directly into her ear and warm her face against her neck. Mary's shivers shook them both. Sam rocked against her.

"I'mmm . . . sssoo . . ."

"Think of something warm, c'mon Mary, a warm place. Feel the sweat, the heat? The humidity must be near a hundred percent . . ."

"C . . . ccc . . ."

382

"I used to live in Tahiti. Now that was a warm place. Have you ever been there? It can get really hot during the day. It usually cooled off some at night, but we didn't have air conditioning in our house, and sometimes the trade winds didn't come, and it would be hot at night too . . . Ssstill awake? Good, just listen to me. We'd sleep naked at night to try to stay cccooler, but it didn't work and we were hot, so hot. And my mama would get up and use a big palm leaf to fan us."

"Mm . . . a . . ."

"Andd . . . you cccould feel the ssweat rrrunning dddown."

"Mmmomm . . . wwhere's dddadd . . ."

"He's cccoming, hhoney, he's cccoming . . . I pppromise."

The sidewalks held the usual Friday night crowd in spite of the cold. The restaurants were closing up but the barhopping was just getting into full stride. Phil scanned the figures and the faces, first on his own side of the street and then on the other. A figure on the other side paused and melted into a doorway. Phil stopped and grabbed Dale by the arm.

"Other side. Doorway to the Frisky Feline." They waited. The figure slowly emerged, then pulled back again.

"Let's check it out," Dale said. They started to cross the street. The figure came out and moved with the crowd toward campus. Dale and Phil broke into a trot on an angle to intercept and the figure started to run, dodging people on the sidewalk. There was no street traffic so Dale and Phil sprinted down the center of State Street. The figure crossed Lake Street and headed for Park Street and Bascom Hill.

"Tunnel entrance, South Hall, back side!" Phil gasped. "You flank left!" The cold air felt like a steel rasp in Phil's windpipe as he ran. The figure crossed Park and started up the sidewalk of Bascom Hill. Dale broke left and ran behind Music Hall. The figure stopped and turned and a moment later Phil heard a pop, a whistle and a crack as a slug slapped into the sidewalk at his feet. Phil took cover behind a retaining wall and

383

the figure resumed his sprint up the hill. Phil came out and charged up the sidewalk behind him.

"Aaron!" Phil yelled, but the figure kept going. It turned the corner around South Hall and disappeared. When Phil reached the corner he moved from the sidewalk to the face of the building, then edged his way around the corner pressed tight to the stone walls behind the bushes. He heard a metallic rattling – the lock on the grate. Phil left the wall and took four long strides and a flying leap and landed on top of the figure crouched on the access grate. Aaron let out a yelp of pain and then they were rolling, tumbling off of the concrete housing to the ground.

Phil groped for a grip on the slippery leather jacket, and found an arm. Where's the gun? Aaron used his free arm to reach, digging for Phil's face, trying for an eye. Phil punched at Aaron's head and made good contact. An elbow caught Phil in the side of the face and he lost his grip, then they rolled again and Phil's nose was in the dirt, then another roll and his face was smashed into the bushes. Aaron was on top of him, with one arm wrapped around Phil's throat and something hard pressed against the base of his skull.

"Yeah, Phil, it's me," Aaron said. "And do you know what I've got right here?" He poked the gun against Phil's head.

"I could guess."

"You'd be right. Now you've been way too much trouble for me lately. It's gonna stop right here."

"Where is she?"

"Who, that little slut of a wife? Gee, I dunno."

"I've gotta know."

"Ha. Like it's gonna do you any good. Well I suppose since I'm gonna kill you anyway, and you ruined my surprise. You were real close, Phil. They're on ice at the Chocolate Shoppe. Gotta be dead by now. Maybe if you hadn't chased me you could have saved them. You think?"

"What do you mean, 'them?'"

"Them? Oh, didn't I tell you? I got 'em both. Your wife

and your girlfriend. That's what you get for being so greedy."

"You goddamned bastard!"

"Say goodbye, Phil."

"Freeze! Police! Hands in the air!" Dale commanded.

Aaron released his grip on Phil's neck and slowly raised both of his arms over his head.

"Stand up!"

Aaron slowly rose to his feet and turned to face Dale's voice.

"A janitor? A goddamned janitor?" Aaron laughed and lowered his arms and drew a bead on Dale with the Glock. Then - pop-pop, and Aaron fell backward and collapsed.

Phil got to his hands and knees and felt in his pockets for his cell phone. "Gotta call 911!"

Dale put his small service revolver back into his ankle holster, reached Aaron and felt for a pulse. "No rush for this guy."

"Not for him. For Mary and Sam; they're at the Chocolate Shoppe. Shit, it must be on the ground here somewhere. Shit!" He swept both hands over the ground in wide arcs.

"I'm calling it in right now!" Dale said. "You get down there!"

Phil took off, running down the hill. He was sore, he was dirty, his lungs and every muscle ached. He didn't hear the car horns as he crossed Park Street through the traffic, and he didn't see the people on the sidewalks turn their heads to watch him as he ran down the middle of State Street. He heard his breath, rasping, and the pounding of blood in his ears and his heart in his chest, and his shoes slapping on the pavement. He didn't hear the sirens of the police and the ambulance units, as they had only to come a couple blocks from the Orpheum where they had been stationed. His brain was numb, and all he could think was "Please-God-please-God-please-God" in rhythm with his footsteps. He arrived, finally, to see an ambulance pulling away. The lights were on in the back, and through the rear window he could see emergency personnel bent over and working.

He came to a stop outside the store and coughed, doubled over, and spit phlegm into the gutter. He felt a hand on his back as he fought for breath.

"We got the call in time," Kleinstern said. "They're alive, but it'll be touch-and-go for a while. Hypothermia."

"Both?"

"Yes. But Mary wouldn't have made it at all if it hadn't been for Sam."

CHAPTER TWENTY-EIGHT

A sign hung on the door to the Irish Pub, 'Closed for Private Party, the Wake of Dave Helms. Informal attire required.' Muffled music leaked to the sidewalk and turned loud and clear with the occasional opening of the door. Paul Desmond and Dave Brubek mixed with loud conversation and laughing, and passers-by looked in through the door and windows at the celebrants packed shoulder to shoulder in the pub. There was a photo of Dave Helms blown up to poster size, hanging over the bar with a spotlight on it.

Phil set the Ardbeg bottle on the table in front of Colin McDermott and sat down. McDermott picked up the bottle and held it to the light, turned it, and watched the powder inside tumble upon itself.

"Aye, sometimes the man consumes the bottle and sometimes the bottle consumes the man. I've never before witnessed it this way. It is good and fitting; Dave wears it well." He set the bottle down on the table. "And for you, Phil, this has been quite the experience. Saint-Exupery said, '*Life has a meaning only if one barters it day by day for something other than itself.*' You have bartered, have you now found meaning?"

Phil thought for a moment. "You know, I thought I was living before. I never really thought about my vacations – the element of danger, how everything comes to sharper focus, how different the air tastes and feels on those trips. These past weeks I've found that here, too. '*The aim of life is to live, and to live means to be aware, joyously, drunkenly, serenely, divinely aware.*' Henry Miller said that. Some very good people, and some very bad, have reminded me that I can be fully engaged for more than a week or two a year. Life's too short not to live it fully every day."

"Dave would have agreed. And he would have approved of this, tonight, and of what you have done the past few weeks. Well done, Phil."

Phil smiled and stood and grabbed the bottle by the neck. "Thanks for everything, Col. We've got to continue our rounds."

"And now you've got your bond money back?"

"Yeah, picked it up this afternoon," Tom said. "I guess you weren't such a bad risk after all. Nancy was worried you'd skip – ow!" Nancy had punched Tom hard on the shoulder.

"Jerk! I was not!" she said, laughing. "Phil, we're so thankful it all worked out. Can you come out to the house for the game on Sunday?"

"Thanks," Phil said, "I don't know yet what my plans are. I've been thinking I might get away for a week or two. I'll let you know. And thanks again – if you hadn't put up the bond we'd never have solved this and I'd be on my way to trial. If there's ever anything I can do for you, all you need to do is ask."

"Just bring Mary by again. Ow!" Tom grimaced after another shoulder punch. "Shit, that hurts! Phil, some practical advice: don't ever annoy a farmer's wife."

"I'll remember that," Phil said, and picked up the bottle.

"And by the way, you can bring back my kayak any time."

"Uh, I've been meaning to talk to you about that . . ."

Phil wedged his way between Antoine and Dominick, standing at the bar. They each had a glass in front of them about a third full with golden liquid. Phil set his bottle on the bar and signaled the bartender for a third glass with a similar pool of Scotch.

"Uh-oh," Phil said, "this is going to inflate the bar tab!"

"Don't worry, he doesn't have anything older than

MURDER IN MADTOWN

twelve-year," Dominick replied. "I'm working on him. I can sell him some good stuff."

"The lady, your taste-testing companion, where is she tonight?" asked Antoine.

"Sam and Mary will be along soon; they were released from the hospital two days ago. They were very lucky. If the medics hadn't gotten to them when they did . . . well, a few more minutes and we'd have had two more wakes to attend. The hospital spent a couple days thawing them out and treating the frostbite."

"A toast!" Antoine proclaimed, "To good health, good friends, and good taste. And especially to healthy friends with good taste!" The three touched glasses and sipped.

"It's the peat," Antoine said, "you can really taste the peat. It is too much."

Dominick shook his head. "No, it's the charcoal. They didn't change barrels soon enough."

"Peat."

"Charcoal."

"You're both wrong," Phil said. "It's the glass. It smells and tastes of dishwasher detergent. It should have been hand-washed, or better yet, only rinsed and dried."

Antoine and Dominick looked at each other and shrugged.

"It is the peat, definitely."

"No, no, it's the charcoal . . ."

Phil sat down at a table occupied by Gary Kleinstern and a petite blonde woman. He set the bottle with Dave's ashes next to his glass of Scotch. "The guest of honor," Phil said, nodding to the bottle.

"Phil, I'd like you to meet my wife, Desiree," Kleinstern said.

"I'm pleased to meet you," Phil said, shaking her hand.

"Oh, and I'm so glad to meet you," she said, "Gary has told me so much about you!"

"Texas," Phil said, "you're from Texas, right? How'd a

Texan wind up here in the frozen tundra?"

"Shoot, that's what I'd like to know," she laughed. "Ought to have my head examined."

"How's the roundup going?"

"Fine," Gary said. "It's amazing how quickly people get in line to turn each other in. Stuff that we only implied and hinted at during the presentation because we didn't really know or have proof turns out to be true and more. And people just handed us the evidence! There's probably a dozen more indicted from inside city government. It'll take a year to get all this to trial. I love this job!"

"And does this satisfy the FBI?"

"Believe it or not they're still pursuing an independent case. They contacted me about the real estate scam long before Dave's murder. Their major concern, other than the racketeering was that they didn't know whether it might lead into local law enforcement – that's why we handled everything away from any City government bodies. They still don't know for sure, so they're continuing to investigate. Personally, I think the cops will come out fine."

"Did Smith say anything?"

"No, he's still not talking. But Gene says that Smith asked him to find someone for the contract on your uncle. Gene knew Aaron from some class at the UW, and he put him in touch with Smith. Smith and maybe Taylor called the shots for Jackson's murder as well, but we're having some trouble finding evidence on Taylor; he's a slick one. We're hoping that phone records will help. In the meantime he'll be busy with the racketeering charges on the real estate deals."

"I heard you picked up Moose Mikleski."

"Yeah, but we let him go again, no charges. Looks like he got favorable treatment on building contracts with the City, but we haven't found anything to suggest that he paid kickbacks. Yet."

"And Beth Talbot?"

Kleinsmith laughed. "Racketeering for sure, but she had nothing to do with the murders as far as we can tell. And we can't charge her for banging Taylor the way she has for the last few years."

"Gary!"

"Oops, sorry, Desi. That was a bit indelicate."

"Did you find anything on Bradley?" Phil asked.

"No." Kleinstern shook his head. "Wish I could, for obvious reasons. But other than his taking credit for being part of the investigation, we just haven't found anything. I know there's something there, tied through Taylor, but I can't prove it. Can't nail him for being dumb in charging Daman, or for charging you."

"Well, if there's anything I can do to help you with your campaign against him, just let me know."

"Just keep lots of pistachio around. I'll be needing it."

Phil didn't see them come in, but he heard the cheers from the patrons near the door and he knew that Sam and Mary had arrived. Over the heads of the well-wishers he saw a glove fly, then another, and a stocking cap followed by a scarf, and applause following each. He shook his head and smiled. That would have to be Mary, he thought, and meanwhile Sam would be tucking her articles into her coat pockets and handing her coat to the bartender. Mary would be in sweatshirt and jeans and running shoes, and Sam would wear a neatly pressed blouse and wool slacks or maybe even a dress. He'd catch up with them later.

Lars Jackson's older brother Nils was there with the youngest brother Leif, both partners in the Jackson law firm. Phil spoke with them, standing under the TV suspended from the wall in the back corner of the bar.

"He had little choice," Phil said, "he was really swept along by the current. I'm just glad that he left that letter. It helped fill the gaps in our investigation."

Nils shook his head. "He betrayed both you and your uncle," he said, "and that's unforgivable for an attorney, unforgivable for a family friend. But I thank you for bringing his killer to justice. If there's anything we can do . . ."

"I do have some ongoing legal items with my uncle's estate, for one, and I have a couple things I want to do with the Chocolate Shoppe and Discreet Detectives. I'd like you fellas to help me with them."

"You're sure you want us to do it?"

Phil nodded.

"Okay, but only on the condition that you let us do it pro bono. That can't begin to make up for all the trouble Lars caused, but maybe it's a start."

"I can't beat that deal," Phil said. "I accept." They all shook on it, had a drink on it, and talked through Phil's plans.

Phil pushed his way into a knot of cops. They all stood, longneck bottles in hand and passed the Ardbeg bottle containing Dave's ashes around, clinking the necks of their bottles against the Scotch bottle.

"I'm back," Dale said. "The internal affairs investigation came up justified, so I'm back on active patrol. Thank God, that desk stuff is like an eight-hour prostate exam every day!" The other cops laughed and one of them pulled a rubber glove from his belt kit and pulled it on with a snap, and wiggled his fingers. "C'mon, Dale, time to go to work!" They all roared again and slapped Dale on the back.

"Tell you what, Dale," Phil said, "I'm sure glad you were there but what the hell took you so long to get to South Hall? I thought I was dead for sure."

"It's kinda embarrassing." Dale looked around the circle at his fellow cops. "At first I had the wrong goddamned building . . ."

The employees of the Chocolate Shoppe occupied a long table pushed close to the side wall of the room. The table was littered with assorted bar-foods and pitchers and glasses, and was sticky with beer spills.

"Can I see some I.D.'s here?" Phil asked as he joined them. "You guys all look underage to me."

Without a word each went to purse or wallet and pulled out an I.D. and waved it in the air..

Phil examined each one, fake in very case, and returned it to its owner. "Good, everything looks in order to me," he announced with a wink. "Thank you all for coming, and for carrying so much extra load at the store during all this. It has certainly been a strange month for me, and I'm sure it has been for you, too. I'm still in shock about Aaron. I'm hoping that maybe now things can get back to normal."

"I think it would be easier to just redefine what 'normal' is," retorted Judy, and the group cheered and applauded.

Phil felt a pinch on his right butt-cheek as he heard "Hey, good-lookin', I like the new threads!" Sam appeared to his right, and everyone at the table greeted her. Phil gave her a hug.

"I did do a little shopping," Phil said. He was in his usual jeans, but he had worn a black silk t-shirt and a black cashmere sport coat for the occasion. "Sam, I had you figured all wrong!"

"What? Oh, this! I hope you're not disappointed," she laughed. She was dressed in jeans, tennis shoes, and a sweatshirt.

"Not at all, you look great! Nice, cute and comfortable."

"Mary and I decided to do a little role reversal. Did you catch my striptease when we came in?"

"That was you?"

"You betcha. Who's got a beer for me?" Her eyes sparkled as Phil poured a beer into a clean glass and steered her to a small standing-height table nearby.

"Sam, I need to talk to you for a minute. You okay?"

"Never better!"

"Staying warm?"

"I'm fine. What's up, Phil?"

"I wanted to take a moment to thank you for everything. Words are so inadequate. There are so many things to unravel, to get back to a starting point . . . I . . . hell, Sam, is there anything I can do to repay you, to thank you? Is there anything you want?"

"I could use a new red dress; the last one didn't survive the freezer vent. C'mon, Phil, you know no thanks are necessary."

"I . . . Sam, I have to tell you that I've decided to take on a partner in the Chocolate Shoppe."

"Oh." Sam's eyes fell to the table and her shoulders slumped forward. She played with the beer glass.

"I need a bit of a break. I thought I'd take some time off, maybe spend more time with the detective business, and we need someone with the commitment and experience to help. It'll be a fifty-fifty split."

She said nothing.

"Sam, it's for the best. You'll agree when you hear who it is. Sam? It's you, you're the partner! I'm offering you fifty percent of the business."

"Wha?" Sam looked up, eyes wide and mouth open.

"Just say yes. You won't have to put in any cash; just sign the papers and you'll have fifty percent of the assets, liabilities, the profits or losses. It's your chance to be a business owner. It's what you always wanted, isn't it? Please say yes."

Sam came around the table and wrapped her arms around Phil's waist and squeezed so hard and so long he had trouble breathing.

"Can I take this as a 'yes'?"

She nodded, head against his chest, and as he stroked her hair and cheek he felt her tears. "It's okay," he said, "go on and tell the staff we're under new management." She gradually eased her grip, and after wiping her eyes with the backs of her hands she smiled and turned and walked back to the long table against the wall.

Phil watched her. The noise of the bar blended to a homogenous background hum. Her back was to him as she addressed the table and he couldn't hear her, but he saw the faces of his employees - *their* employees - brighten and then they were standing and applauding and surrounding her with hugs and handshakes and kisses. Phil felt his own eyes filling.

"Hey, Boss, got a minute?" Mary's voice broke his concentration, and he turned to face her. She stood there, one hand on the bar table, in knee-high boots and a long button-up denim skirt. Her white blouse was pressed, the top two buttons were unbuttoned, and she had a large silk scarf tied as a quasi-belt around her waist. She wore her hair down, swept back on one side and anchored with a barrette. "Take a good look, I don't do this very often."

"Oh," Phil said softly, "you clean up pretty well."

"Thanks. Sam helped me with my makeup; I never paid much attention to learning that stuff as I was growing up. She lent me this red lipstick. The best part is it tastes like strawberry." Mary nodded toward Sam and the crowd around her. "She's a special person. She saved my life in that damned freezer, or that's what they tell me, anyway."

"That's right, she did."

"I was pretty well out of it and I don't remember a whole lot. I hope you gave her something nice."

"I did, at least I think so. I made her a partner in the Chocolate Shoppe."

"Well, that's good. It's a good start, anyway. I've got some good news and bad news for you. I filed today."

"Filed?"

"Filed. For divorce."

"Oh, uh, thanks." Phil looked down at the table, feeling strangely embarrassed.

"Hey, c'mon, that's your good news! Your bad news is that it will take six to nine months to become final. Don't worry, there won't be any alimony or asset division involved."

"I wasn't worried. Not about that, anyway."

"You know, if I didn't know you better I'd swear you were sad to hear this. I thought you'd be dancing on the table. You knew this was coming. I promised you both before we got into it that I'd do it."

"Yes, I know."

"Phil, I see this as going back to neutral corners, leveling the playing field, whatever. I owe that much to Sam," she laughed. "After it's final, all's fair. Wait and see what happens then!"

"I'll move out of your place tomorrow. I've decided to move into Dave's house on Wilson Street and let my apartment go."

"Makes sense. But you don't have to rush."

"Thank you, for everything. You know, you're quite a special person."

"Damn right, and don't you forget it."

"So, what do you want to do now that the case is over?"

Mary shrugged and leaned on the table with her elbows. "Job hunt, I guess. They decided not to charge me for breaking and entering those apartments, so I don't have a record to worry about on job applications. I don't know if the police would take me, but I might try. Or maybe Kleinstern's team. Gee, I should go ask Sam for a job; maybe she needs a scooper. I hear she's short an employee right now."

"What about the detective business?"

"I thought you were going to close it."

Phil smiled. "I think I'd miss it. Thought I might try for my PI license, and keep the business going."

"No shit?"

"No shit. And I could use someone like you . . ."

"Use *someone*? Hell, you need *me*, and you know it."

"'Bardo and Haiger, Detectives.' Sounds pretty good."

"'Haiger and Bardo' would sound better, but what the hell."

"'*Of all the gin joints in all the towns in all the world, she walks into mine.*' Partners?" Phil stuck out his hand.

"Partners. '*Louis, I think this is the beginning of a beautiful friendship.*'" She took his hand and shook it. Then she went to the bar and had a brief conversation with the bartender, and as she walked back to Phil the music changed to Bob Marley's 'Is Dis Love.' She grabbed Phil's hand and pulled. "C'mon and dance with me."

Phil shook his head. "No, I really hate Reggae."

"That's 'cause you've never danced it with *me*. I won't take no for an answer! Just come on and do what I do, and you'll be fine."

She tugged and wouldn't give up, so Phil followed her to a clear patch of floor. Mary raised her arms over her head and started walking in place, moving her hips and swaying from side to side to the music. Phil followed her lead, and she gradually moved closer and closer until they danced a fraction of an inch apart without touching. Soon they were surrounded by others, swaying in rhythm. Mary stopped for a moment and trotted away, then returned with Sam in tow and the three of them moved, together, close, and they forgot that there was anyone else in the room.

ABOUT THE AUTHORS

Dave (David Ross) Heise is an information/communication technologies consultant, living with his wife, Mary, in Tampa, Florida.

Steve (Steven James) Heaps is the owner/manager of the Chocolate Shoppe Ice Cream Company on State Street in Madison, Wisconsin.

Life-long friends and mystery aficionados, they embarked on a writing project together to see if they could do it.

For other titles and information, please visit:
www.madtownmysteries.com

Made in the USA
San Bernardino, CA
19 October 2013